HERE TO STAY

HERE TO STAY

A FIGHT FOR TOLERANCE

PHILLIP H. LEONARD

TATE PUBLISHING
AND ENTERPRISES, LLC

Published by Tate Publishing & Enterprises, LLC
127 E. Trade Center Terrace | Mustang, Oklahoma 73064 USA
1.888.361.9473 | www.tatepublishing.com

Tate Publishing is committed to excellence in the publishing industry. The company reflects the philosophy established by the founders, based on Psalm 68:11,
"The Lord gave the word and great was the company of those who published it."

Published in the United States of America

ISBN: 978-1-63418-013-9
1. Fiction / Historical
2. Fiction / Native American & Aboriginal
14.11.28

CHAPTER 1

THE CHICKASAW TRIBE was never conquered in war, but they succumbed to the white man's ways by intermarriage and the love for trade goods and whiskey. The mixed-bloods, those men born from white men who married into the tribe, gained control of the governing body by the 1830s and, after observing the treatment of the Cherokees on the Trail of Tears, sold their lands in Mississippi and the five thousand tribal members, took their one thousand slaves and moved to Indian Territory, which is now Oklahoma.

Since the Chickasaws were close relatives to the Choctaws, the U.S. government put them all together in the southern half of Indian Territory. There were three times as many Choctaws so that the Chickasaws had very little say in the joint government set up in Indian Territory. In 1855, the Chickasaws separated and received the south-central part of Oklahoma, and both tribes held title to the so-called "Leased Lands" in southwest Indian Territory, which was controlled by the raiding Plains Indian tribes of Comanches, Kiowas, and Kiowa-Apaches. At the end of the Civil War, most of the bands of the Plains' tribes had not been defeated and corralled into reservations, so they were still keeping people out of their hunting grounds west of the 98th meridian that cut down the middle of Indian Territory.

As to the Civil War, the Chickasaw mixed-bloods that ran the tribe considered themselves Southern businessmen and declared war on the U.S. government and joined the South. The Chickasaws were the last nation to surrender to the U.S. at the end of the war, and in retribution, the federal government took the southwest part of Indian Territory from them and ordered the Chickasaw and other tribes who supported the South to make their ex-slaves members of their tribes. All tribes eventually complied with the integration order except the Chickasaw tribe, who refused to make their freedmen tribal members.

Some slaves of the Chickasaws ran off and fought for the North. Although Mondo Hobbs was never a slave, he was the product of a full-blood Chickasaw and the female slave he owned. Mondo had no rights in the Chickasaw tribe since legal status came down through the mother and not the father. Mondo went north to fight for the United States but found very little acceptance as an equal from the Yankees. After the war, Mondo Hobbs returned with a goal to raise horses in the unsettled area located between the Chickasaw nation and the land controlled by the Plains Indians. Mondo's father helped him build his small fortress. Mondo and his horses were protected with the help of a Comanche peace leader named Ten Bears, but Mondo's luck was about to run out when the first winter storm hit in November of 1867.

An ice storm raged outside, but Mondo Hobbs felt the danger of a human presence, a sixth-sense he attributed to his half-Indian, half-African roots. His horse cried out for him beside the cabin, and Mondo sprang out of bed. He immediately suspected that the howling wind had lured the famous Comanche horse thief known as "Storm" to steal his Kentucky thoroughbreds.

Mondo grabbed his rifle and threw open the cabin door just in time to see lightning illuminate. All twelve of his stock horses charged out of the corral and through the swinging stockade gate. He didn't see anyone, but someone had unlocked the gate, and he'd heard very few ever saw the great warrior who stole during dangerous weather.

Throwing on his buffalo coat, he raced outside to his horse, Tree Top, tied to his cabin. Mondo spoke reassuringly as he threw on a horse blanket and took off bareback against the icy gale, hidden in darkness except for flashes of lightening that revealed the hoof prints of his stampeding horses. The Little Beaver Creek's natural fortress that surrounded his cabin had proven to be no match against Storm. For the last year, several Plains Indians had come after his horses, but only Storm had succeeded. Mondo had dropped his guard because of the bad weather.

The cold wind and ice raked Mondo's face raw and weighed down his buffalo robe like he was carrying stones, but he plowed ahead in anger and desperation. Mondo and his father, Bear Chaser, had spent a year building his rock cabin and stockade, where no one including his father expected him to last a month. Mondo had planned to stay forever on the land he loved about fifty miles north of Texas, far away from all the permanent settlements in Indian Territory. No horse trader dared stay in the area dominated by Indians whose main occupation was stealing horses. His survival meant recovering his thoroughbreds and teaching a lesson to Storm and the rest of the unconquered Indian tribes so they would quickly learn the risk of retribution. He gently urged Tree Top on, trying to keep up a trot without slipping on the ice as he thought back on his life and why he had settled in such a dangerous place.

Even though the other boys in the Chickasaw tribe had long taunted him for his curly black hair, he remembered feeling relatively happy until his doting mother died of the fever when he was twelve. At a very young age, Mondo had learned his Indian father had once owned his mother as an African slave, and that the Chickasaw school allowed half-whites to attend classes, but not a half-Negro. His father had freed his mother from slavery when Mondo was born and Mondo's parents had married.

Mondo grew up with his protective parents and animals as his friends. Since he wasn't allowed to attend school, his father took him into the unsettled plains where they spent time with Ten Bears, the Comanche peace leader who realized early on that survival of his band would require treaties with the whites.

Mondo's father was a proud Chickasaw, and he did not agree with the numerous part-white rulers of the Chickasaw Nation who wanted Indian culture abolished. Although the Comanches and Chickasaws didn't get along over control of the plains being divided by the white world, Bear Chaser and Ten Bears became close friends, united as Indians against the whites and the part-white Chickasaw leaders who wanted the old ways forgotten.

During his time with Ten Bears, Mondo learned the Comanche language and discovered Little Beaver Creek, a stream that circled around a little rocky hill and formed a natural corral.

When Mondo returned as a teenager to his father's settlement in the Chickasaw Nation, he was struck anew at the superior attitude he encountered from those in his tribe with lighter skin and straight black hair. Mondo's serious face reflected both his Indian and African blood, with full lips, a large flat nose, a square jaw and high angular cheekbones. He always held his curly head high and never let on to the rest of the tribe the pain that twisted like a blade in his gut when he was teased and left alone. Mondo never forgot that when he was eight, he'd been overpowered by several older boys who'd tied him up and left him in the woods where he'd starved and suffered until his father found him. After that, Mondo learned to hide like a spirit and fight like a warrior, and he was never overpowered again.

As he grew up, Mondo and his father camped out and hunted and caught and sold wild horses to pay for their supplies. He was sixteen when the Civil War broke out, and despite his father's warnings, Mondo left to fight for the North to help free the people who represented one-half of his blood. The Chickasaw Nation, led by mixed bloods more white than Indian, joined the

South and declared war on the US government. The leaders and moneymakers of the Chickasaw Nation owned many slaves, so the decision to act like "Southern gentlemen" and help whip the Yankees seemed like an easy one.

But the war didn't bring Mondo any more acceptance from the white Yankee officers, who seemed like they couldn't decide where he belonged. In Kansas, the US Army placed him in an Indian unit, but, upon protest, later transferred him to a Negro fighting company. He grew big and strong and fought with bravery and intelligence during the battles, and all men, no matter their color or background, wanted to be around him. Yet in the battle of Honey Springs, Mondo ended up fighting with a white unit who treated him as their leader, until the fighting stopped and the white soldiers acted as if they didn't know him. It was then Mondo decided he couldn't live around people and expect fair treatment, and he began dreaming of Little Beaver Creek's natural fortress where he could live alone and raise horses.

No settlements existed in the desolate Little Beaver Creek area because of raiding Indians, primarily the Comanches and Kiowas. Ten Bears' Comanche band had been forced out of Texas and lived in and around the Wichita Mountains, near the area where Mondo wanted to settle. Mondo felt that his mentor, Ten Bears, the Comanche peace leader, might help keep him and his horses safe from raiding tribes.

When he wasn't fighting battles, Mondo dreamed of the taller horses he'd seen that came from Kentucky, grazing inside the natural corral made by the circling creek, and building a cabin tucked into the little rocky hill, away once and for all from all the hate and prejudice. Sadly, it seemed women were out of the question for him as, first of all, who would have him? And second, what woman would want to live out there? He tried not to think about it, burying the familiar pain that churned in his gut with the thought of his Kentucky horses.

When the war ended in 1865, Mondo took his muster-out pay and headed by word-of-mouth to Arkansas to buy a fine

Kentucky stallion from an ex-Confederate officer who needed the money to feed his children. As he rode his horse through northern Arkansas, he viewed the rampant devastation and poverty all across this Southern state, simultaneously experiencing residual horror and numbness from the atrocities of his battles, compassion for the hungry families left fatherless, and elation for the victory and new-found freedom of the Negro. On the journey, his head kept filling up with images from battle, the broken bodies and shattered limbs, the screaming dying and the silent dead, and it seemed best to try to forget the violence he had participated in and the darkness of men's souls at war. Because of his nature, it also had been very difficult to see so many dead and wounded horses in pain, and he had been quick to help put them out of their misery when he could. Deep down, he found the sacrifice of thousands of horses in the name of war deeply disturbing.

Because of his size, Mondo named his new horse Tree Top, and the two became fast and inseparable friends. Mondo stayed on, picking up construction jobs to rebuild war-torn Arkansas, and acquiring twelve more long-legged mounts by racing Tree Top. Tree Top never lost a race, and as they ran with the wind to victory, the air streaming across his face and the stallion's hooves heavily pounding the ground, Mondo recovered some of his early boyhood joy, confidence, and enthusiasm. After all, he was only twenty-two, and his whole life was ahead of him. With his new stock of horses, he thought he could make it a good one.

But after a year, Mondo couldn't wait to leave Arkansas and get away from the hate-filled eyes triggered by the loss of the war and the presence of Yankee troops. The losing South hated all Yankees, especially an ex-soldier with Negro blood who had fought for the North, and Mondo wore his Yankee coat as if daring anyone to challenge him. They did, repeatedly. People shot at him from the woods, bullied him to fight, and treated him with such great loathing, like the lowest of the low, that he finally gathered his horses and left for his home in the plains and the unwavering love of his father.

Mondo knew to expect the same lowly treatment from the Chickasaws who fought for the South. Even though the Yankee army never entered the Chickasaw Nation during the war, the Indians were devastated by the loss of their assets that went to support the Confederate effort. Mondo rode Tree Top through his childhood home, driving his stock through a Chickasaw Nation who was envious of his new-found wealth, and who hated the three-inch Afro and the Yankee coat billowing behind him as he left them in a cloud of dust.

His father had warned Mondo against living so close to the raiding Indians of the plains, but by the time Mondo got home, he was determined to get away from all people and not be afraid of anything, especially after surviving the Civil War. But Mondo had brought the fine-looking tall horses into an area where horse stealing was considered an honorable profession. Despite his doubts, his father had helped Mondo build his fortress, which had kept his horses from being taken by top-notch horse thieves until now. There was no question in Mondo's mind that he had to do whatever it took to get his prize horses back. He rode west deeper into Comanche-Kiowa country with no fear at all, his strength of spirit united with his horse who had never lost a race, and whom he loved with all his heart.

When he was younger, Mondo would have listened to the advice from his father, but he felt he had returned from the war a real man. He had grown confident in his physical strength and ability to think quickly and intelligently in the heat of battle. He wore the wiry coils of his hair high like a crown of thick, matted buffalo hair, and he never wore a hat, as if to dare someone to call him a name because of his mixed blood. Mondo was no fool. He knew he traveled among people like a moving target of hate, and a part of him wanted them to attack so he could show them all that nothing could bring him down.

A sudden gust of icy wind brought Mondo out of his thoughts and back to the problem of finding his horses. He noticed the gust seemed to signal the end of the worst of it, and Mondo picked up speed, patting Tree Top on the neck with encouragement. The wind kept blustering violently, but the storm was turning into more rain than sleet, and they made better time. About an hour before sunrise, Mondo came up upon East Cache Creek, and the outline of the small Wichita Mountains that sprung up from the flat plains like huge gopher mounds that didn't belong. He could see the horse tracks cutting across East Cache Creek and continuing west along Medicine Creek. As Mondo moved along the creek bank, a long flash of lightning suddenly revealed a human form on the top of a high cliff that the Indians called Medicine Bluff, a place for spiritual gatherings.

Mondo figured the person had to be the horse-thief warrior since nobody else would be crazy enough to stand on a high cliff during a lightning storm. Or at the least, the person on top of the bluff must have seen his horses pass below along the creek. Mondo circled around the hill and started up the back side toward the top where the figure still stood with arms raised toward the sky. He saw no horses in the area as he slowly approached the praying Indian.

The rain and north wind blowing over the top of the bluff kept Mondo from getting a good look at him, but he looked short and stocky like a Comanche and wore the leggings of that tribe. *This had to be Storm*, Mondo thought as he crept up on the still, praying figure. The noise of the storm kept Mondo's approach from being heard by the Indian who seemed to be in some kind of trance as the rain and sleet poured over him. But just as he was nearly upon him, the Indian statue came alive and whipped around with a rifle pointed at Mondo's chest.

"Who are you that interrupts a warrior's prayers?" asked the Indian in Comanche.

Mondo fingered the trigger of his rifle by his side and glared down at the shorter Indian. "I am the man looking for his stolen horses. I'm sorry I disturbed you, but you must have seen them since their tracks follow the creek right below where you pray."

"Your horses are now my horses. They are hidden in a corral nearby," the warrior said.

Mondo's eye narrowed in concentration—it was Storm.

"The peace-loving Comanches that camp around here said that your horses could not be stolen," Storm said. "I come from the band that stays in the area the whites call the Texas Panhandle. I can take anyone's horses, and I've got your tall horses now."

"I will get my horses back," Mondo replied with conviction.

"Not tonight, unless you want to die." The Comanche never changed his mask-like expression.

Mondo could feel the confidence of the man, issuing forth like rays of light. The Comanche was taller than most men of his tribe but still at least six inches shorter than Mondo. His barrel chest stuck out like an Indian known for big medicine. His face was all Indian, and his dark eyes seemed to glow in the dark like an animal. He wore buckskin pants and knee-high moccasins, but nothing except war paint protected his chest from the bitter cold. As big as Mondo was, he still felt the great strength of this shorter but broader Comanche as he existed in great confidence caused by his God.

Mondo shrugged. "My life is more precious at this moment than my horses. But there will be other moments."

The Comanche shook his head. "You are not Comanche. Pride and honor would make a Comanche attack so to not lose face by losing his horses."

"I am not a Comanche, but Ten Bears is my friend. I know Comanches. They let me hunt on their hunting grounds and let me live where I live without burning me out. Some have tried to take my horses, but all have failed. You better kill me now or I will follow my horses until I get them back."

A slight smile appeared on the Comanche's face. "You talk brave with a rifle pointed at your chest. I like your courage. You will be a challenge. You shall live, and you may try to take my horses back that used to belong to you."

Mondo felt the strong medicine of the Comanche who stood straight and strong in the cold wind and sleet. Mondo backed away slowly. The Comanche watched without fear even though Mondo still carried his rifle. Mondo knew better than to attack the Comanche, who seemed to rise above the storm as if there was no rain, lightning, or thunder. The Comanche warrior had not even bothered disarming Mondo, so great was the Comanche's confidence. Mondo would pick another day to take back his horses. This Comanche's medicine was too strong for right now.

Mondo backtracked and set up a night camp to wait out the storm. The longer Mondo waited, the harder the Comanche would be to track. But another day would bring another time.

Sometimes an Indian possessed super-power and knowledge as if the Great Spirit blessed him. Mondo had experienced such big medicine. It was as if supreme confidence from a spiritual force took over one's thoughts and actions. The blessed one seemed to enter into a trance-like zone, overcoming any thoughts of a mistake or failure. Mondo had seen other Indians reach this level of absolute belief in their power. Unstoppable and knowing all, a warrior with big medicine could accomplish unbelievable feats.

The Comanche who took his horses was acting with all senses heightened by the Great Spirit. The time was not right to challenge this Indian in his spiritual zone. But big medicine did not last forever. In the spirit world, there were ups and downs. Experienced with a discipline beyond his years, Mondo kept his anger and desperation in check. He knew to wait for a day that was clear, a better time when the medicine was more balanced.

CHAPTER 2

THE SUN CAME up the next day and Mondo mounted Tree Top and raced off toward Medicine Bluff. He found no tracks or sign of his horses, but the Comanche said his band lived in the Texas Panhandle, so Mondo moved out west at a fast pace. The Comanche was driving twelve animals, which would slow him down. With a little luck and some good medicine, Mondo could catch up to his horses.

As Mondo rode west, he thought about coming back to the Chickasaw Nation after the Civil War. He recalled moving his horses across the Chickasaw Nation in south central Indian Territory in the early part of 1867. At that time, Mondo still wore his Yankee blue coat through an area that had fought for the South. The Chickasaws had lost nearly everything for choosing to side with the losing Confederates. The once-well-off Chickasaw people had been slave owners and cattle ranchers, but all was gone now, and the Chickasaws were bitter losers. Mondo's Yankee coat was a red flag for trouble. He had no rights in this nation even though he was half-Chickasaw.

As Mondo entered the Cross Timbers, a thick forest of small trees that was almost impassible, Mondo had his first encounter with the Chickasaw Lighthorse Police. Mondo remembered it well. At first he heard a couple of rifle shots that stopped him in his path. Mondo then turned his horse away from the sound and tried to move out without being noticed. At the edge of a post oak patch of woods, a young Negro man ran out, carrying a small child. Mondo stopped. The Negro froze, stared at Mondo, noticed his African hair, and eased toward him. The light-brown-skinned man was tall and thin with bright intelligent eyes, and he was holding a little girl who looked to be about four years old. The man glanced nervously toward the woods and then back at Mondo.

"Sir, will you help me and my little girl? Three Chickasaw Lighthorse law-men are trying to run us back to Texas."

Mondo could hear horses crashing through the thick trees, the sound growing nearer. "Why are they after you?"

"The Chickasaws want to keep the ex-slaves of Texas out of their land."

"Are you an ex-slave from Texas?"

"Yes and no. I just came across the Red River from Texas, but during the war me and my daughter were sold away from my wife by a Chickasaw to a man in Texas. My name is Hudson Greer. I'm trying to get to my wife who, I understand, is living in Wildhorse Creek."

"Where is Wildhorse Creek?" asked Mondo.

"It's a new Negro town where Wildhorse Creek runs into the Washita River. I got word that my wife, this little girl's mother, lives there now."

Three riders broke out of the trees, pulled up and stared at Greer and then paused as they looked Mondo over carefully. Mondo sat very still and calmly looked back at them. The three were obviously Indians, but were dressed like white cowboys, and each carried a pistol in his holster. Mondo wished he had discarded the blue Yankee coat, but it was too late now.

Finally, the older middle-aged man moved his horse a few steps closer to Mondo and looked him in the eyes. "Thanks for catching this trespasser. You look familiar. Who are you?"

The man who spoke was a mixed blood of average height and build, but with a stern confident appearance like he was used to giving orders and having them obeyed.

Mondo did not change the expression on his face. "My name is Mondo Hobbs, son of Bear Chaser Hobbs, and I'm on my way to see my dad. Do you know how he survived the war?"

The man nodded his head as if he remembered Mondo and then spoke. "He didn't join the South, so he survived pretty well. Most Chickasaws lost everything fighting for or supplying the Confederate army. I wouldn't wear that Yankee coat around here. You're liable to get back shot and those tall horses stolen. I'm surprised you have gotten this far."

"I haven't received any friendly greetings, but nobody has tried to take me on so far. And, that's probably because they know better," spoke Mondo in a soft, steady voice laced with a warning of much power.

The Lighthorse policeman smiled. "If I remember right, you're an ex-slave yourself, just like this Negro from Texas who is trying to slip into our country. Wasn't your mother Bear Chaser's slave?"

"No. My dad freed my mother before I was born, and they lived together as man and wife, common law. Why is that any of your business?"

The Indian leader's face turned into a mean smile. "My name is Hurbert Dixon. I'm captain of the Chickasaw Lighthorse Police of Pickens County, Chickasaw Nation. I've got orders to keep ex-slaves from moving into our country and to remove all ex-slaves that weren't Chickasaw slaves at the end of the war and to remove any person with Negro blood that causes trouble. This ex-slave standing by you with this little black girl is a Texas ex-slave. Those freedmen from across the Red River are coming here and causing big problems. I've been told by a good source that those Texans are chasing all the bad ex-slaves over here. We are carrying out our official duty by taking this one and the girl back to Texas. Are you going to try to interfere with the law and the three of us?"

Hudson Greer, the black ex-slave holding his little girl, stepped forward. "I am a Chickasaw ex-slave. My master took me and my daughter into Texas when the war started. I left my wife here. That is why my wife stays in Wildhorse Creek now. I have a right to be here, and I am not causing any trouble."

"That is a lie," growled Dixon. "All of you Negroes are causing trouble, wandering around like free people, stealing food, not working, just hanging around drinking homemade whiskey, fighting, and trying to rape Chickasaw women. And you all would rather lie, even if the truth helped you out. You're going back to Texas."

Mondo moved his horse between the Lighthorse Police captain and Hudson Greer and waited for Hurbert Dixon to make the next move as a stiff silence grew longer.

Finally, Captain Dixon spoke. "I'm warning you, Hobbs. Get out of my way. There's three of us against only one of you. This Greer fellow won't fight. He's a runner, and he ain't got no weapon."

Mondo paused, smiled, and then spoke softly. "You're being right unfriendly. I'm trying to move far away from people like you, but I'm not there yet. I have had enough of you ex-slave owner people who don't know they lost the war. Why don't you take your two little helpers and move on down the road. Me and this here ex-slave are going on about our business without you getting into our way. Do you understand?"

Captain Dixon puffed up and stretched tall in his saddle. He looked up at Mondo and glared. "You don't understand. A lot of ex-slaves from Texas and Louisiana are hiding over here because the Yankees are saying we have to make our freedmen citizens of the Chickasaw Nation. Every man, woman, and child who has an ounce of Negro blood is claiming to be a Chickasaw ex-slave that got his or her freedom after the end of the Civil War. Our records are not good. Owners were killed during the war. Some left and never came back. We don't know for sure just who was and who wasn't a Chickasaw ex-slave. We've got to keep these lying Negroes out of our country. Some say there are more ex-slaves in the Chickasaw Nation than sure enough Chickasaw Indians. You understand why I have to kick this fellow out. Stay out of it. Since you claim to be Bear Chaser Hobbs son, I'll let you stay, but not this Negro and his girl child."

"I'm not staying around people like you. I'm moving on west where you are not brave enough to live, but this ex-slave is going to take his girl to her mama. Talking is done! If you and your henchmen are going to do something about it, go for your pistols. I'm ready to die, are you? I'll kill you before anybody gets a shot off in my direction."

Dixon turned red and then looked at the new Henry rifle that hung on Mondo's saddle and the new six-shooter in the well-oiled slick holster, and Dixon thought of his own death. Mondo was really big with buckskin trousers, knee-high leather boots, and that damn Yankee coat. He wore no hat as if he was real proud of the three-inch-high coiled black hair that clearly made him a Negro. What Dixon saw and felt coming from this calm but fixed gaze of Mondo made Dixon think that the odds of his death were high, and Captain Dixon was not ready to die. The tall, black Thoroughbred that this half-breed Negro sat on was at least a third bigger than the Chickasaw horses. The big man looked down on the three Chickasaws like they were children. And this Mondo spoke without a trace of fear in his voice. Captain Dixon had learned during the war that this trait made a man very dangerous. One more Texas ex-slave was not worth dying for.

Captain Dixon relaxed, but before he could speak, Hudson Greer eased between the two men and looked up at Mondo. "Don't draw on these Chickasaws. The word got back to me that my people are having trouble at Wildhorse Creek. Let's move on before we make things worse."

Mondo glanced down at Greer and then over to the Lighthorse captain. "Are you going to let this man and his baby go on to his people, or am I going to have to kill you right here and now?"

Captain Dixon nodded his head in agreement without hesitation. "He can go on for now. You don't pay no attention to the law, do you? You're threatening an officer in charge and protecting an illegal fugitive. You better not stop long at your father's place. You keep on riding west into Comanche country. That's where you belong. They have no civilized law, which means no one has police protection. If you live very long after entering Comanche-Kiowa country, I better not see you back in the Chickasaw Nation."

Mondo smiled, "Like I said, I'm not living here. I'm heading toward Little Beaver Valley that is right on the edge between Chickasaw and Comanche land. I don't want to live around anybody."

"Go ahead. Nobody wants you here. Your old man was like that. He spent more time horse trading with the Comanches and hunting with Ten Bears, that old Comanche chief. You belong with those thieving raiders that would rather kill and capture civilized people than do an honest day's work. You'll fit in real well. You remind me of someone who gets up each day trying to figure out how he can break some law. Go on! Run with those savages. You don't belong in the Chickasaw Nation. We are too civilized."

"I don't want to see you again, Captain Dixon, and if I do, you better come with your pistol drawn and firing away because I won't ride away without shooting next time."

"You'll be on foot real quick like if you try to settle in Little Beaver Valley. Ten Bears can't make good citizens out of those natural-born horse thieves. If the young Comanche warriors don't get your horses, the Kiowas will. You'd better go back up north. Those Yankees might let you dig their ditches, or they might let you do the fighting for them. There's some Negro soldiers that the Yankees sent out to Fort Arbuckle on the Washita River, right here in our Chickasaw Nation. Isn't that a laugh? Did you stop in there and talk Yankee war stories when you passed by the fort back yonder?"

Mondo put his hand on his pistol. "It's time for you to leave. Here's hoping my life is not bothered by your presence in the future. Go now or draw your pistol. I'm tired of hearing your mouth flap, so move on or plan to rest in peace where you now sit."

Sneering and snorting and showing as much false bravery as he could without getting shot by Mondo, Captain Dixon jerked his horse around and led the other two Lighthorse police back into the thick post oak forest.

Without a word, Mondo turned his horse away from Greer, but Greer caught hold of Mondo's bridle. "Hold up a second. I want to thank you and find out who you really are. We could sure use someone like you to keep those policemen off our backs."

Mondo shook his head "no." "You heard me tell that sorry-ass Dixon where I was going. I've been trying to get back to Little Beaver Valley since I left six years ago. I'm tired of being around people like Dixon. There's always trouble like this here today. I'm riding alone, enjoying the day, and thinking about seeing my dad and getting my horses to my valley and I run into you and then comes the law and trouble. I just about had a shoot out with three Lighthorse policemen. No. I don't want to go with you to this Negro settlement you call Wildhorse Creek. I belong in my valley alone."

"But they are your people. They need you. You got fighting know-how. You stood up to Captain Dixon. That has to be taught to people who did nothing but take orders all their life. We're short of people who can toe the line."

"That's a long, hard, and dangerous lesson to learn. I'm not the one to teach you. I don't know who my people are. I don't have any people. When you got my mix, nobody really claims you. If I went to Wildhorse Creek with you, the majority would want me gone because I'm half-Chickasaw."

"No. That's not right," said Hudson Greer. "We are all in this together. We've got to get along with the Indians. Our battle is not with the Chickasaws. It's the whites who want to keep both of us down."

"You heard the captain. He wants to be white and act like whites, so his kind won't ever treat a man with a drop of Negro blood as an equal. I'm tired of being looked down on, so I am going to live away from anyone that lives with their nose in the air, thinking they are better than someone with black blood."

"You're going to live a lonely life, Mr. Hobbs," answered Hudson Greer.

"I can live with that. I've been to Kansas and Arkansas during the war, and before the war, I rode with Dad in Indian Territory and over into Texas. I've been around so-called "civilized tribes" and the Plains Indians that the whites call the "wild tribes." Let me tell you something. If I want to live like a real man and not take any crap off those that think they are better than anyone else, I'll live better among the Kiowas and Comanches than I will among the Indians who call themselves civilized."

"I hear tell those Comanches will kill you for your horses, rape your wife, and kidnap your children. How can you feel better living among those savages?"

"At least you know who your enemies are and what they want. I found that it's those who act friendly you got to watch. I fought beside some white boys during the war who treated me like an equal during the battle. But when the fighting was over, they hardly acknowledged they knew me. I plan to live alone. If you leave me alone, I'll do the same for you. We've talked too long, Mr. Greer. Words float away with the wind. They don't mean much. It's what you do that counts. I'm fixing to be away from people, and you're fixing to join up in an all-Negro community. We'll see who lasts the longest in this new world of the free Negro."

Mondo shook himself out of his thoughts of the past and looked at the trail west as he followed after his horses. He hadn't seen Hudson Greer for almost a year now and probably wouldn't see him again. As Mondo pushed his horse after his stolen herd, he wondered if the Wildhorse Creek all-Negro town still existed. It had been all work for the last year as Mondo and his father built his rock house and the fort around it. If his father had been at Mondo's during the storm, maybe he would have stopped the crazy Comanche warrior from stealing all his horses. But his father had gone back to his place along Cow Creek ten miles southeast from Mondo's.

Mondo had been hoping to catch up with his stolen horses within an hour, but the Comanche thief knew how to move a small herd. It was the middle of the afternoon before Mondo spotted his horses being herded at least five miles ahead on the flat treeless prairie. In his anger, Mondo wanted to charge ahead and attack the Comanche at once, but the strange warrior possessed strong medicine, so Mondo circled carefully and waited to ambush the Comanche from a small rocky hill that popped up from the level plains.

CHAPTER 3

S AVANAH WAS HALF-ASLEEP when the black giant crashed through the trees and onto the road. The horses panicked, and the driver had to hold the reins of the carriage with both hands to prevent a runaway. The black giant froze as the bodyguard, who rode on the back of the carriage, leaped down and started for his pistol. A machete came off the giant's shoulder and swished through the air and decapitated the guard before the pistol was fired. Blood splashed across Savanah's face, and she screamed as she covered her eyes to avoid the sight of the head flying across the carriage and onto the side of the road. The horses reared up and lifted the driver off his seat. As soon as the horses came down on their feet, the driver reached for his gun, and the machete cut through the air again and took off his arm. The cry of shock and pain that came from the driver was cut off when a large fist drove his nose bone into his brain. The ease and quickness of the killings paralyzed Savanah. Even the horses settled down as a quietness engulfed the scene as if nothing had happened. As the smell of fresh blood drifted through the air, Savanah was too frightened to continue her scream. It was like both horses and the beautiful light-skinned lady were in shock, frozen by the action of a Negro that stood about six feet six inches with 260 pounds of all muscle.

The dark-black man took a step forward and looked into the fearful light-green eyes of the beautiful Savanah and gently reached out and touched her face with his huge bloody hand. "I don't kill white women," he softly spoke.

Savanah opened her mouth to speak, but nothing came out. She was still too afraid to utter a sound. She did not know how to answer. A friendly smile appeared on the giant's face, and she relaxed enough to speak. "I'm not all white," Savanah said, and the big man actually laughed, so Savanah continued, "These two guards have kept me a slave even though the Yankee government says I'm free."

"I don't kill part black girls either." The huge Negro extended his clean hand and helped her down from the carriage, removed a handkerchief from his pocket, and gently wiped the blood off her face. The girl looked to be about twenty years old, and she was the prettiest girl he had ever seen. She seemed to relax even more at the giant's gentle treatment.

"Who are you?" she asked.

"The white men call me Girt Taylor. My real African name is Maboola. I'm on the run from South Texas, and I am trying to get out of this here place before they lynch me from a tree."

Savanah looked at the two dead men and then looked back at Maboola, who appeared to show no guilt for the brutal murders. "I suppose these are not the first white men that you have killed."

Maboola's face showed mean again. "No, they are not. The first one was the owner who put these on my back." Maboola turned, lifted his cotton shirt, and exposed old scars on new scars that made his back look like raw meat stacked so that hills and valleys streaked across the twisted muscles and torn skin.

Savanah fought to keep from throwing up her lunch once again.

Maboola's angry hatred slipped away from his dark face for a second as he saw Savanah's light face pale. Maboola had a sudden desire to help this beautiful woman. "Sorry. Why did these dead men guard you? Who wanted to keep you a slave?"

Savanah took a deep breath and looked up at Maboola with anger in her face. "My ex-owner thinks of me as his wife and won't give me freedom. Haven't you heard of Purify Jones?"

"No. Like I said, I'm not from around here, but it looks like the guy that owns this fancy rig and can pay two white men to keep track of you, didn't lose all his money during the war."

"Oh no. Old Purify found a way to sell cotton through Mexico. He got richer, and he didn't fight. The little bastard hires people like these two to do his dirty work and all his fighting."

"Are you saying you want to run away? If he treats you like his wife, doesn't he keep you in those fine clothes and feed you pretty well?"

The light-skinned girl blushed. "I don't want to be his wife anymore. Do you understand?"

Maboola stared into her eyes, and she dropped her gaze toward the ground. "Lady, you don't want to run with me. I'll not mistreat you, but there's a lot of white men wanting me dead. I think they've even got the Yankee soldiers looking for me. To be with me won't be like a walk down plantation row."

"I feel like I'm free for the first time in my life. My name is Savanah, but not Savanah Jones. I'm tired of doing everything that Purify Jones asks me to do. I've been ready to run for two years. Where are you going?"

"North. I've been told that you cross a river called Red River and you're in Indian Territory. I don't know how the Indians treat ex-slaves, but I do know that I'll be hung if I stay around here. If you are going to run with me, shouldn't we pick up some of your things before we go?"

"No. I just bought some new clothes in Gainesville. I don't want anything that no good bastard saw me wear. You've got to understand that Purify Jones is very rich and he's got a lot of men working for him, men that learned to kill during the war and don't want to stop killing now that it's over. So, you are buying a lot more trouble than you have now if you take me with you. I'll try not to slow you down if you will let me go with you."

Maboola knew that to take this girl with him would only decrease his chances of making it out of Texas alive, but she looked at him with eyes so desperate that he knew he could not say 'no' to this young lady who had been mistreated by a white man with so much power.

Maboola patted the two horses. "Are these saddle horses?"

"Oh, yes," she answered, and Maboola started to unhook the horses from the carriage.

"Do you know how far it is to Indian Territory?", asked Maboola.

"Around seventy miles. We're about ten miles northeast of Fort Worth. If we ride straight north, we will stay in the Cross Timbers. It's easy to be hidden in that thick brush."

Maboola smiled for the first time. "Well, lady, you're free. I don't know how long you'll stay free, but I'll tell you this, some more white men will die if they try to take you back."

With that said, they mounted the carriage horses and rode north toward Indian Territory. Savanah carried her carpet bag full of new clothes, and Maboola had picked up the two pistols belonging to the dead men and put them into his belt and grabbed a sawed-off 12-gauge shotgun that had been attached to the carriage. After they had ridden a while, Maboola looked over at Savanah.

"Where were you born?", he asked.

"The servants of Mr. Jones say I was born in New Orleans to a high yellow prostitute. Mr. Jones bought me for a thousand dollars at an auction. He wanted to raise me to be his second wife. He once was a preacher who married a rich lady. The old cook in Mr. Jones's house told me about his first wife. She prayed a lot and died under strange circumstances. Mr. Jones bought me to train me to be white and pass as a white woman. This is the first time that I ever have been away from Mr. Jones or his guards. If he wasn't watching me, those two men you killed were keeping an eye on everything I did and said."

"Did he treat you like you were a real white wife?", asked Maboola.

"I know how to act like a white plantation woman for all occasions. He had a white woman come up from New Orleans to teach me how to be a Southern belle. I also was taught to read and write."

"You didn't have a hard life. You weren't beaten. Why would you want to leave?"

"Purify Jones is an evil man with lots of power and money. I had no life of my own. He was using my body by the time I was thirteen. As long as I never questioned him about anything, everything was all right. I learned at an early age that if I didn't do what he asked immediately, I was locked up in a bare room and not given food or water. I've seen him kill a slave for not answering him quick enough."

"Will he kill you if he catches you?"

"I don't know. He likes to escort me around big cities as his wife. He will have to kill me because I'm not going back."

"Where will you end up? You could pass for white easily. You're lighter than a lot of white women. You don't really have any Negro signs. Your hair is straight. Your nose and lips are small. Why don't you go North and just be a white woman?"

"I just wanted away from him. So, you better know that Purify Jones will come after me. He hates to lose any of his possessions. We better separate when we get out of Texas. You really stand out. Where do you think you're going?"

"Up north and then work on a boat back to Africa. My father was a big chief of my tribe back in Africa. I have a lot of family deep in the jungle. I'm not even very big for my people. Or at least I don't think I would stand out too much. I know they are much larger than most people here."

"How did they catch you? If your tribe was so big and tough, it looks like those slave traders would not mess with your people."

"I was traveling with my mother away from our territory. I was captured when I was ten years old and slipped into this country after a law was passed against bringing in new slaves. I grew up outside of Houston on a rice plantation. I ran away first when I was sixteen. I was caught, beaten, and kept chained, but I got away again. This time, I barely lived after the foreman gave me fifty licks. They didn't tell us we were free until months after the war ended. I went back into the swamp and lived a while. When I came out, I was full grown and strong. I killed the white man who beat me and headed north. Then I found you."

"How old are you now and just how big are you? I've never seen a man your size."

"I'm twenty-seven years old, and I've never seen anybody, white or black, close to my size, but I've never gone far from the rice fields. It's kind of hard for me to hide. That's why I mostly travel at night unless there's a lot of thick woods, like what we are going through now."

"It's slow, but at least it is hidden," Savanah answered. "I've heard white men say that Jones's plantation was about seventy-five miles south of the Red River. Do you think the Indians will let us enter their territory?"

"I don't know the answer to that. I just keep moving north to get out of Texas and try not to hurt anyone unless they get in my way. I have nothing against Indians. They have never beaten me, but you must know that I'm not going to be caught alive. If Mr. Jones and a bunch of men come after you, I'll try to kill them. So, it would probably be better for us to separate when we get across the Red River. You just need to go into the nearest town and catch a ride north. You act white except you look down at the ground like an ex-slave when you talk to me. Any white man would help a beautiful white lady just for the possibility of having his way with her. You would have plenty of men who would want to help you get North."

"I'm not sure I want to live like those whites. I don't know how to act around you or any Negroes. What I have seen doesn't speak well of white people. They go to church and claim to live by the 'Golden Rule', but they just live by that rule one hour each Sunday."

"What's the Golden Rule?"

"Do unto others as you would have others do unto you."

"You're right. I've never seen or heard of a white person who goes by that rule. You'll have to decide pretty quick whether to act white or black. If anyone sees us together, I will have to be your servant. I don't know anything about Indians. I don't know if they hate Negroes like whites. But, first, we've got to get out of Texas and then you have to decide whether you are safer being black or being white."

CHAPTER 4

T HE STORM HAD passed long ago. The sun had dried the grassland, and the skies were clear. Mondo felt the change, and his confidence grew as the unsuspecting Comanche pushed Mondo's horses near the rock cropping. Mondo looked at the Comanche and knew the Spirit was no longer favoring the horse thief. The Comanche rode with a different posture. No longer did he sit high with the air of the "Great Spirit." No longer did the Comanche warrior move as if he was protected by a hidden shield of magic. His Indian God had gone with the storm. The Great Spirit had switched sides, and Mondo felt his strength and confidence grow. Mondo's Great Spirit removed any fear or doubt.

Mondo let out a war cry and charged. The Comanche jerked his horse around and charged toward Mondo. Both fired wild shots with their rifles. The speed and size of Mondo's horse was too much as the animals crashed into each other and both lost their rifles. The Comanche's horse went down, and Mondo dove onto the horse thief. The impact stunned the warrior, and Mondo's size pinned the Comanche to the ground. The fight was over before it really got started. Mondo's right arm circled the Comanche's neck and held him in a headlock that cut off the Comanche's breathing. The more the Comanche struggled, the tighter Mondo clamped. The more air the Comanche fought for, the more pressure Mondo put on his windpipe. With his oxygen cut off, the Comanche passed out.

Mondo tied up the Comanche and gathered his horses that appeared to be in fine shape. When Mondo returned, the

Comanche was awake and looking without fear at Mondo. Mondo sat down across from the Comanche and spoke in the Comanche's language that Mondo had picked up while hunting with Ten Bears.

"Why did you ride so far to steal my horses? Didn't you know I was a friend of Ten Bears?"

"I've only heard three men who were not Comanches speak our tongue. Did the old peace warrior teach you?"

"Yes. I've hunted many times with Ten Bears and my father. I've spent much time with the peaceful Comanches who now live near the small mountains called the Wichita."

"Those are the Comanches who no longer fight the Texans. We have very little respect for those bands who were forced from their hunting grounds. I am from the Comanches who live near the Great Canyon. Some call my people the Antelope band. No one has ever made us move."

"I've heard of your great band. All fear the power and strength of the Antelopes. Again, I ask why did you want my horses?"

"For two reasons. There are no horses like your tall, fine, long-legged beauties, and they are very special. Word reached our band a year ago that such horses lived east of the Wichita. Also, we heard that several of the non-fighting, peaceful warriors tried to steal your horses and you turned them away each time. I cannot sit on my hands and listen to stories about how a part-Chickasaw and one who is part of the black tribes from across the water, kept his horses from the peace-loving Comanches who no longer live like the warriors of our fathers. I had to show you what a real Comanche warrior could do. My Spirit told me to go to you. I thought the Great Spirit wanted me to steal your horses. Maybe not, since you seem to have stopped me."

Mondo nodded. "You picked a strange time, but a smart time to take my horses. No one expects anyone but a fool to steal horses during a big storm. Do you always raid when the weather is so bad?"

"Yes. I am called Storm. My name is my medicine."

Mondo was surprised that this warrior would reveal so much about his relationship with his Great Spirit. A Comanche religion was personal. His direction in life and even his name was connected with his beliefs or medicine, which were not discussed except with medicine priests or close family members. Mondo did not ask any more about his spiritual belief. Each Comanche was named for some event experienced in his spirit quest. Mondo knew all about this famous and unusual warrior.

"Ten Bears has spoken of you. I remember you now from his stories. You only hunt or raid during a storm. You always go alone. You are talked about by all Comanches. The Great Spirit protects you when no other warrior will leave his tepee because of the lightning. It is an honor to meet you and more of an honor to get your horses that were once my horses."

Storm smiled. "My power slips away in the sunshine. What are you going to do with these tall horses?"

Mondo's anger faded with the calm, honest discussion concerning the business of stealing horses. Mondo smiled back and answered, "Build my herd and trade them. I'm going to see what comes out if I bred them to the smaller Indian horses. Maybe I can make a breed that is better for this area."

Storm nodded his head in agreement. "I would do the same. Would you trade me a couple of your tall horses since it looks like I can't steal them from you?"

Mondo laughed and thought for a second and then looked Storm in the eyes. "I'll tell you what I'll do. My dad and I, with the help of Ten Bears, have convinced the peaceful Comanches to leave my horses alone. But, we have never dealt with or even talked to anyone from the Antelope band in the Texas Panhandle. I'll trade you two horses of your choice, except my "Tree Top" that I ride mostly, if you will take me to your band as your guest and help me try to talk them out of trying to steal my horses."

Storm frowned. "I really don't know you. Are you Indian or are you a member of the tribe with dark skin and curly hair that they say come from across the big water in a land some refer to as Africa?"

"My mother was a slave that was part-white. My father is all Chickasaw. So, I guess that I am more American-Indian than anything."

"The Chickasaw were pushed off their lands by the whites. Are they cowards who can't keep their homes?"

"I asked my father the same question. He said when the whites first came, they were not so strong or so many. They brought sickness that had never been known by the Chickasaws, and many Chickasaws died without a fight. But most of all, the white traders brought guns, whiskey, trinkets, and iron pots and iron weapons. All were given to the tribe to weaken the tribe. Guns and cannons increased the number of killings whether at war with other tribes or in a battle with whites. The Chickasaws never lost a war with any tribe or country. But, many of our great warriors soon needed and wanted the whiskey. The women wanted the white man's trinkets and iron and other trade goods. The US government gave us these things with a promise to pay for them later and took much of our land to pay back the debt. The whiskey took the fight out of many of our warriors. We were defeated by things, not by men. We were forced to sell our old hunting grounds and move here next to the Indians of the flat plains."

Storm looked concerned. "Traded your soul and pride for whiskey, guns, and iron pots. I can see that happening. Most whites are cowards. They have to trick you or talk you out of your land, like they did the peaceful Comanches. They don't fight with bravery. They ride like pregnant squaws. They can't travel without water. Only a few rangers from Texas are worth the respect of a warrior. The whites who build wooden houses and stay in one place are not warriors, and they die easily. They are not worth killing if you are a powerful warrior. A Texas Ranger's scalp is valuable, but the rest of the whites can't stand up against a Comanche warrior."

Mondo nodded in agreement. "They don't fight you until you're weak from sickness or whiskey. They never run out of people. They don't wait for good medicine. They fight any time. They keep coming and don't stop until you do what they say or your whole tribe dies."

"Why do they have to have all the land? No one can farm where our band stays. It's too dry. Maybe that is why they have left us alone. I cannot understand why whites have defeated so many tribes back east. I thought at first the Indians in the far east were only weak warriors that lived off the soil and could not fight. I've met some good Indian warriors that came from tribes back east that the whites defeated long ago. It doesn't make good thinking that these pale, skinny, ugly white people can have so much war power."

"My grandfather said he didn't know whether more whites came across the great waters or more were born here. They breed like rabbits. Some of their women have fifteen to twenty babies. Twice as many as most Indian women. You can't stop their growing numbers. They keep coming. Kill one and ten will take his place. Like I said, they don't wait for good medicine to fight. They fight all the time. An Indian will not go out to do battle unless the Great Spirit gives him good signs. The white warriors go where and when the leader says. It doesn't matter what the Great Spirit says to whites because their Great Spirits don't talk to them about war."

"What do they believe? What does the Great Spirit tell white people?"

"Their Great Spirit says all must believe in their God. They have the only real God and the Indian Great Spirit doesn't exist. So, the whites take our land and try to force us to obey their Great Spirit so we will be able to go to their happy hunting grounds after they kill us. It is hard to understand."

"I've heard the Spaniards did the same thing to the tribes in the southwest. They killed many warriors so the rest of the tribe would be saved and go to their great place in the sky after they die. I guess you need to be white for this to make sense. Do you think the whites use their act of saving Indians as an excuse to take our land?"

"I think most of the smarter whites know it is an excuse to get the other whites to push us off our grounds. The white leaders call it saving or taming the wild savage. My father says their religion calls for them to treat all people like they want to be treated, but they still kill to make Indians Christians. Greed for more land that they don't own is not wrong in their religion."

"It's a strange belief. The Great Spirit owns all things, and we are here to use them. It's real hard to figure out what makes a white man think. The Americans seem different from the Texans. The Texans are evil and refuse to share the earth with anyone. But Texans are not bad warriors, while Americans are weak. We saw a few whites going through our country to Santa Fe. They were soft, and a lot died of thirst. They can't live on our dry land. They bring evil, killing diseases, and we try to stay away from them. We don't want to be around whites. We want only to trade with the Mexican half-Indians."

"It's best to stay away from all whites," answered Mondo. "I have found little comfort from being around these people. I spent a lot of time among the whites during the Civil War, and I didn't like their idea that I was beneath them because of my Indian blood, and worse to them, was my African blood."

"I hear tell that many whites died during that long war. We were hoping they would kill each other off. No more whites, and we'd get along fine back here."

"I think a half million died. That's more than stars in the sky. Like I said, for every one that dies, ten takes his place. Back east, they live in big cities. There are more towns than there are Comanches. They will come, and you will lose your land."

"The whites don't want our land. They ride through it. There's no water. They can't farm."

"They take the best land for planting and then they take the rest for grazing. Their cattle will replace the buffalo."

"Is that what happened to the Chickasaws?"

"Yes. We held out for many years. The whites didn't control us. White sickness and whiskey weakened us. Don't let the white marry your women. We took the ones that married our squaws into our tribe. Their children, the mixed bloods, took over, and now the Chickasaws are controlled by part-Indians, who are really more white than Indian. The leaders of our tribe owned slaves and behaved like whites. Money is everything to them. They don't care about the old ways."

"How do you fit in? Are you a Chickasaw Indian or are you like the buffalo soldiers who were once slaves?"

"I don't belong to any tribe. I'm on my own. The Chickasaws say that because my mother was a slave. I never was a slave, so I am not a Chickasaw freedman. They say I have no rights in their tribe. I am more like a Comanche than a Chickasaw."

"Good. I'll take you to my band for two of your horses. You will be my guest and will be welcomed and no harm will come to you."

Mondo untied Tree Top, and they started west toward the Antelope band winter camp. Mondo wanted to make friends with one of the toughest bands of all Comanches. If he could make friends with them, his chances were greater that he could live near the Comanches and keep his horses.

Mondo knew he could trust Storm who lived by the honor of a great Comanche warrior. Storm's word of peace could be trusted until he said otherwise. This was no white man. Storm obviously respected Mondo's reputation as a warrior who was brave enough to live by the Comanches and still keep all his wonderful horses. Even though the Chickasaws and the Comanches were not friendly tribes, they did not hate each other like the Tonkawas and Comanches. A Comanche warrior stood on his own two feet as an individual, which meant more than the tribe as a whole. That was the Comanche way. The Great Spirit ruled a Comanche's choices, not a governing body within the tribe. The other Comanches honored those choices. Mondo knew that when Storm made Mondo his honored guest, the rest of the Antelope band would treat him as a friend, at least while he was in their winter camp.

CHAPTER 5

A BOUT THE TIME Mondo and Storm were discussing the history of their tribes, Maria Rodriquez, who hadn't been called by that name in three years, dug for poison herbs to kill Eagle Eyes, her second husband. The medicine woman Rising Moon watched her closely as Maria, now called Skywalker by her Kiowa captors, dug for the roots and herbs that healed the wounded and sick of the Kiowa band camped west of Wichita Mountains along the North Fork of the Red River only about sixty miles west of Mondo's compound.

After Skywalker's first forced husband got killed by a fall off a horse, she was taken in as a wife by the deceased's brother named Eagle Eyes, as was the Kiowa custom. Her first husband feared her and had let her alone because he knew that since Skywalker was good with medicine, that made her good with poisons. Eagle Eyes, her first husband's brother, was not gentle and demanded total obedience from Skywalker, which she wouldn't give any man. Eagle Eyes had struck her for the last time. She found the necessary poisonous herbs and dug them up without Rising Moon, the number one medicine woman of the Kiowa band, noticing what Skywalker was doing.

Skywalker respected the medicine woman and had worked with her and learned much from her. Skywalker knew that if she wasn't good with healing, she would have been killed by the Kiowas a long time ago. How she had survived three years, she didn't really know or understand. She could still remember the time when she lived a good rich life as an aristocrat in Mexico.

Her family was Spanish, and she was a debutante from a family that owned one of the largest ranches in Northern Mexico. She was the third child and first daughter of Antonio Rodriquez, the fourth-generation landlord of four hundred thousand acres that ran north up to the Rio Grande, and prior to the Texas War of Independence, had included another two hundred thousand acres on the north side of the Rio Grande in Texas.

Early in her childhood, she realized that she lived a charmed life and that many people were there to serve her. She was spoiled by her father, mother, and brothers, as well as the many servants and ranch hands that worked for her father. Maria, now called Skywalker by the Kiowas, realized early how much power she had with her name. She could get by with almost anything. She lived a free and independent life. She ignored the rules of most rich females raised in the Spanish-Mexican aristocracy. She loved the outdoors and raced horses. Her father indulged her every whim.

She was finally forced to go to school in Mexico City where she received an education and learned to speak English. Her father hoped that in time, he would get back from Texas his lost property north of the Rio Grande. He wanted his daughter, the wild, free, and a fearless horse lady, to be there with him when he re-crossed the Rio Grande and won back his ranch from the evil Texans that had stripped him of his property.

As Maria Rodriquez grew up, she was afraid of nothing because she always had several ranch hands riding with her and protecting her. She grew tall at five feet six inches with white skin, big brown eyes and curly dark hair. Even though she would sometimes lose her bodyguards with her fast horses, she always knew that they were around and would protect her. One day, her free and independent life changed completely. Maria had ridden off and left her bodyguards and was riding through the countryside when all of a sudden, at least ten Kiowas and Comanches took up the chase to capture her. The Kiowas and Comanches laughed and enjoyed her spirit as she raced from them. They passed her off like a relay team and chased her across the ranch until her horse finally gave out and stumbled dead.

As they rode back toward the headquarters of the ranch, she could see the smoke and the fire, and when she got near enough to view the scene, she could see hundreds of Kiowas and Comanches that had finally organized a big-enough raiding party to take on the Rodriquez ranch. For a hundred years, these tribes had not been able to penetrate Rodriquez's hacienda and steal his many horses. Now they had destroyed the ranch.

In 1864, the Antelope band in the Texas Panhandle, along with several other bands, had decided to organize a huge raiding party and go after the Rodriquez hacienda. Seventy Comanches and thirty Kiowas had swarmed across the Rio Grande and attacked.

Her captors made Maria look at her father's headquarters as it burned. She could see bodies all over the place. Tears began to stream down her cheeks as she recognized her father, her mother, and her three brothers all laid out in a row, massacred and ravaged by the Kiowas and Comanches.

Her capture and total destruction of the ranch was over in less than an hour, and the Indians were going back with horses, cattle, and many bolts of material and supplies and other items they had carried off from the ranch. It had been a very successful raid.

The Kiowas and Comanches knew that a rich, politically connected man like Antonio Rodriquez would bring lots of Mexican soldiers down upon them, so they rode hard and fast toward the Rio Grande. It was night when they crossed the Rio Grande, and they never stopped. They just kept riding north until she was so sore she couldn't stay on the back of the Indian horse. They tied her legs underneath her mount so that if she went to sleep and rolled off, she would be trampled to death. They pushed on, and she learned that she could live a long time on a horse. The Indian captives rode forever without showing any hurt at all. They would ride their horses to death, stop, cut them up, cook them, eat them, and then take off with a new mount.

After two days, the Kiowas and Comanches rolled dice to see who would get Maria Rodriquez, and the Kiowa called Crow Feather won. Crow Feather walked over, grabbed her by the hair, dragged her into the bushes, and raped her. That was her wedding night. At first, Maria Rodriquez was too frightened to say or do anything but duck her head and hope not to be seen. She tried to hide in the group of other Mexican captives. When she was won by Crow Feather, she no longer could hide. He forced himself on her all the way back to Indian Territory, and when they joined the main Kiowa band near the North Fork of the Red River, she had been bruised, strangled, raped, and Maria Rodriguez knew that she would be dead in less than a month if she didn't find a way to maintain some of her pride while living as a captive among the Kiowas.

From that day on, she carried herself tall with her eyes looking up in the sky. She tried to act as if she was not afraid. The Kiowa women laughed at her and struck her and tried to bring her down to her slave status. Maria Rodriquez would not appear to submit to her husband's will. She did what she was told, but she did it in a manner that almost appeared like it was her own idea. She had much anger and hatred for the Kiowas, but she was smart and practical enough to stay alive. However, she knew that if she didn't keep some feeling of worth, she would slip away into death. She was amazed at the number of Mexican captives that she saw in this band and in other Comanche and Kiowa bands. Most of the Mexican captives had been peasants, and their life was not much different back in Mexico than it was with the Indian tribes. Therefore, a lot of them liked and accepted their new roles and became strong Kiowa and Comanche citizens. Maria Rodriquez's life had been much different, and she had gone from the top to the bottom. She had been a wealthy, spoiled aristocrat; and now she was supposed to be a Kiowa savage, obedient to her husband and work all day for his benefit and the benefit of the band.

Maria Rodriquez began to be called Skywalker because she moved around with her nose in the air, and her eyes always pointed upward like she was above all others. No expression was ever on her face. She never smiled, she never laughed, she never cried, and she never got angry. She had a calm, sad, and determined expression on her face at all times. She obeyed her husband and other Kiowa men, but she never seemed to move quickly enough for them or move with the proper respect. She was struck several times and would never let out a sound.

Skywalker knew that the only woman in the band who was respected by all Kiowas was the old medicine woman, Rising Moon. She walked around in the band as free and independent as any great Kiowa warrior. She did what she wanted to do without any interference from anyone. She was provided food by all the men in the tribe, and she was obeyed by all the women. She was the healer, and all that were wounded or sick were tended to by Rising Moon. She was also a fortune teller who would predict the future. Many warriors sought her advice before going on a raid.

Skywalker followed her around, studied her, and asked for her advice and help. Rising Moon ignored her at first but then recognized the intelligence of Skywalker. The medicine woman had been looking for someone to train to take her place. Even though Skywalker was not a Kiowa and even though Skywalker obviously was not an obedient Kiowa woman, Rising Moon knew that the woman that took her place would have to be smart, independent, tough, and would have to have much confidence to deal with the inflated egos of the Kiowa warriors. Therefore the number one medicine woman began training Skywalker in the art of healing and taking care of the sick.

Crow Feather, her first husband, didn't like his wife's training at all, but nobody stood up to Rising Moon. Therefore he endured the absence of his Kiowa wife. Since Crow Feather was a good warrior, he had two other wives. Soon he didn't miss Skywalker at all, but he received a lot of teasing from the other Kiowa warriors about how this Mexican captive had totally divorced herself from his bed and, instead of becoming an obedient wife, had become someone that was gaining more power and respectability than Crow Feather himself.

Crow Feather had finally had enough, and when Skywalker went out by herself looking for medicine plants, he went after her. Crow Feather charged her, and his horse drove her to the ground. He pointed his lance near her heart and yelled at her.

"You've made a fool of me. I lost face and respect from all the Kiowa warriors in my band. My friends laugh at me. They say that I can't control you and that my wife has moved above me. That I am cheated since I receive nothing back from you. I want you to stay in my teepee and do as I say. You can still work with Rising Moon, but you are to come back to my teepee and act like my wife and do what I say or you'll die."

He poked her with the lance, and blood saturated her left shoulder above her breast. Skywalker got up and stepped forward. She rubbed some strong sage into the nose of his horse. His mount snorted, sneezed, bucked, and jumped up in the air and twisted before landing on top of Crow Feather, breaking his neck. Luck was with Skywalker.

Skywalker immediately tried to mount the Indian pony and ride south, but in the jump and fall, the pony had broken his leg. The horse couldn't get up and continued to lie on her dead husband.

Skywalker hurried away and circled the encampment and came in from the other side. It was three or four hours later that her first husband was found dead under his horse. It was a bad accident and one that did not occur often with a good Kiowa rider. There was suspicion that something had been done to the horse because of the ground-up leaves that had been found in the horse's nose. Some of the Kiowa thought Skywalker had killed her first husband. Instead of making her life more miserable, her life improved. There was a certain amount of fear and suspicion surrounding the death of her first husband. The Kiowas were superstitious people who believed in mysteries and ghosts and who knew that the Great Spirit singled out and selected certain people to bestow power upon. Since this Mexican woman had been captured, she had behaved in a non-fearful way and had secured the protection of Rising Moon. The warriors of this band began to fear Skywalker, and most of them didn't want her around. It was only when they got hurt or sick that they were thankful Skywalker was there because she became a better healer than her teacher. Skywalker had received first aid training in Mexico City as Maria Rodriguez, and she combined what she had learned in Mexico City with the teaching of Rising Moon and became someone who could save lives, heal the sick, and repair the wounded.

Now Skywalker had a problem with her second husband. She began to plan how she was going to kill Eagle Eyes, brother of the deceased Crow Feather. Like his brother, he had been teased without mercy by the other Kiowa warriors because Skywalker had lived independently of her husband. Eagle Eyes had to feed her without receiving any benefits from his wife. She didn't even speak to her second husband, and he was laughed at by the whole tribe. Therefore, like his brother, he decided to beat Skywalker to submission. Even though she was respected, she was never liked by anyone in the band except maybe Rising Moon. The women hated her because she had total freedom and walked around like she was better than any other Kiowa woman. The men feared her because, again, she didn't act like a squaw; she acted like a Spanish aristocrat with the knowledge to kill. Even thought the Kiowas did not know anything about Spanish aristocrats, they knew when a woman acted way above her place. The men knew when a woman carried herself with the pride of a great warrior. It was not done, and it was not good for their way of life. Finally, Eagle Eyes decided he would beat her into submission, but his fear of her spiritual power was too great. When she looked at him, Eagle Eyes knew she could tell what he was thinking, and all of a sudden, she would smile an evil smile and nod yes, like

"You're next." Skywalker would hold up the poison herbs and look at whatever he was eating and smile again.

Eagle Eyes began to fear the food he ate. The only time he would eat was when he was a two-day ride away from Skywalker and had killed a buffalo or a deer and finally got to feed himself. He would never eat when Skywalker was around, and he eventually got where he could not even drink for fear that she would poison the water. He knew her intent was to kill him, and he knew that she could get it done. If it wasn't for Rising Moon, Eagle Eyes would have just attacked her and chopped her up right there in front of everyone. Even then, he wondered if lightning would strike him or a tornado would carry him off right as he was attacking her because of her great spiritual power. Skywalker must get her big medicine from the Great Spirit in the sky. She seemed to be looking up and talking to the Indian god all the time. She walked around with her nose in the air and even moved her lips as if she was conversing with the Great Spirit.

The warriors would have let her escape and probably would not have followed her at all if it wasn't for the fear that she had the power and intelligence to round up their enemies and destroy the whole band. The Kiowas thought that this woman could talk to the gods and the gods would talk to all their enemies and unite them against the Kiowa band.

The warriors of the one hundred Kiowas in their band finally gathered and voted to trade her. They were afraid to kill her, and they were afraid to let her escape, but they could not stand to have Skywalker in their band any longer. She was too dangerous.

The warriors began looking around to find someone to trade her to, someone who would take her away, keep her happy, and might keep this spirit woman from wiping out their whole band.

CHAPTER 6

MONDO AND STORM herded the horses west and crossed into the Texas Panhandle before they stopped for lunch. After the horses had been secured in a rope coral, the two men made a fire and started chewing on beef jerky when Storm raised up his hand for silence and both dropped to the ground as a distant sound of pounding hoof-beats cut through the approaching darkness.

As twenty Indians screaming war cries charged toward their campsite, Mondo dove for his rifle and raised up to fire at the oncoming Indians. Storm pushed the rifle toward the ground. "Stop! Those are my people." Storm rose up and signaled the riders. All but one pulled up. A young warrior raced up to Mondo and stopped so suddenly that the horse slid up close to Mondo and about knocked him down. The others circled, letting out bloodcurdling yells.

Mondo knew to stand straight and calm and show no fear. Storm held his hands up, showing a sign of peace. The Indians stopped and stared hard at Mondo. Silence loomed until all the dust had settled. A handsome older Indian inched his horse forward and looked over at Storm.

"Who is this one that comes before us? Is he your captive, or does he have you captured? And who owns those tall, skinny horses?"

Storm smiled. "Once those horses were mine. Now they are this man's again, except two which he has promised me. I was his captive. But now he is my guest."

The leader looked confused. "This must be a long story. I can't wait to hear how all of this came about. Who is this man? Does he speak Comanche?"

"He speaks our tongue pretty well. He's the one that our eastern peace-seeking brothers call 'the man with tall horses that can't be stolen.' I stole them all, but he took them back. He's mostly Chickasaw Indian, but his curly hair shows he is part-African like the buffalo soldiers at Fort Arbuckle. Mondo, this is Bull Bear. He has much power and respect from all the Antelope people."

Mondo stepped forward and raised his hand toward Bull Bear. "I've heard of the great warrior called Bull Bear. I'm pleased to be in your country. I would like to visit the Antelopes that have never been defeated or moved by the whites. I would welcome your invitation as Storm's guest."

Bull Bear looked Mondo over carefully and then spoke. "You I have heard of. Bring your tall horses, and if you are Storm's guest, you will be welcomed by the Antelope band. Let's ride to our winter home now. I smell a snowstorm coming."

Without further discussion, Mondo and Storm mounted up, rounded up their own horses, and were gone within minutes; and sure enough, a snowstorm blew in from the north.

As they rode west, Mondo noticed that the Indian who had almost run Mondo down kept glaring with hate at him. Mondo finally edged up even with Storm and motioned toward the mean-looking warrior.

"Does he always look that way, or should I watch out for that one?"

Storm shook his head in the affirmative and smiled before he spoke. "That's Chickasaw Killer."

"You mean that's his name because that's what he does?"

"That's his name, and that's what he does. His father was killed by Chickasaws. He tries to make up for his loss by killing as many Chickasaws as he can."

"I guess I better steer clear of him. Am I safe as your guest?"

"I think so. He's just killed two or three that I can remember for sure. His lifetime goal of vengeance is to kill as many Chickasaws as he can before he dies. I think he'll probably honor you as my guest."

"Is that why he hasn't tried to kill me yet?"

"Sure, you're my guest, and he would be shunned by the tribe if he attacked you. Also, your curly black hair confuses him. He won't try to kill you as long as you are in our camp. If, however, you decide to leave, you would want to watch your back. I think he's still trying to decide if you're more African or more Chickasaw."

"That's just great," said Mondo "I'll have to stay in your camp forever to keep from fighting that mad Comanche who loves to kill Chickasaws. Is there any way I can make peace with him?"

"Oh no. His medicine says he must kill Chickasaws. If he denies what his god or Great Spirit has told him, then he's going to miss out going to the happy hunting grounds. If he decides that you are a real Chickasaw, he'll try to kill you after you leave. He's got to. That's his religion."

Mondo smiled. "That's a great religion. That's my life everywhere. No matter where I go, someone is after my ass because of my blood at birth whether it's Indian or Negro. That's why I like to live by myself and away from crazy people."

"You'll be safe at our camp at the Palo Duro Canyon. Chickasaw Killer would be ashamed to try anything while you are my guest."

"Maybe he would rather kill Chickasaws than be given the silent treatment of no talk by your little band."

"Oh no. A Comanche would rather die than have the whole tribe ignore him like he didn't exist. That's the worst punishment for a Comanche."

"Don't you have police or someone who punishes those who break the rules or disobey your laws?"

"No. Problems between families are settled by giving horses to whoever has been wronged. There is really no crime or laws.

You do what you want without hurting the other tribe members. Comanches don't steal from each other. That would cause banishment from the band. Sometimes when a warrior beats his wife too severely and damages her for no reason, her family will demand payment in horses, and if they don't get payment, then the brother of the damaged wife can beat the wrongdoer. A lot of family problems are settled in that way. We don't have any judges or police that make decisions, like I heard white people do. It's all worked out in the band, and it's been working for a hundred and fifty years."

"You have no laws, no police, no judges or chiefs, and no one is punished unless they hurt someone bad that is not approved by the tribe, and then the punishment of hurting someone wrongfully is that nobody speaks to the attacker? Is that what you are trying to tell me?"

"Yes," said Storm. "And it works. Have you ever seen two Comanches fight each other or ever heard of anything stolen by a Comanche from a Comanche?"

"No," answered Mondo. "Everybody seems real peaceful unless they go on the warpath. Never knew of a Comanche accusing another Comanche of stealing from him."

"Well, it does happen sometimes, but it's always settled, and like I said, they won't bother you while you're camped with me. By his own medicine, which sets out his rules of life, Chickasaw Killer can go after you when you leave this band, but not before."

They rode west, and more snow started falling before they reached the Great Canyon. They were going across flat country, and Mondo couldn't figure where this canyon might be located. After three hours, they came to a sudden drop-off that came out of nowhere. Mondo could barely make out a huge hidden hole that fell away and snaked deep into the flat plains, forming a beautiful valley. Mondo couldn't see the extent of the canyon in the snowstorm, but he knew he was entering a large freak of nature.

The Comanche Indians started down the steep canyon wall on a narrow path that caused their horses to slip and slide in the snow. It seemed like an eternity before they slid to the bottom of the canyon. They rode around the bend and stopped. Mondo could see almost three hundred teepees spread out on both sides of a blue running stream of water that wasn't larger than ten feet across.

They rode up to the village, and the people ran out to greet the returning warriors.

Mondo tensed as the crowd of Indians pushed in on the returning riders. However, the Comanches seemed more interested in his horses than in Mondo. The bigger Kentucky-bred horses that Mondo had brought into the canyon were a source of close inspection by almost all of the Indians. Mondo was glad that he had brought his horses.

It was approaching dark and Mondo was trying to find a place where he could set up a lean-to and build a fire to stay warm during the night when Storm invited him into his wigwam. Mondo entered the teepee and was welcomed by three Comanche Indian women and four young children. They all seemed happy to see Mondo and totally devoted to Storm. The teepee was about ten feet across and about fifteen feet high with a buffalo rug that hooked up inside of the teepee so that there was no wind that reached inside the Indian's home. The cold north wind had died in the canyon, and Mondo realized that this was a perfect place for the Plains Indians to winter.

Storm stepped forward and motioned in the direction of the three women that were all staring at Mondo.

"These are my three wives. Talking Bird is wife number one and the other two are Gray Deer and Sunflower."

Mondo nodded but already was feeling closed in and crowded by the women and children in the tent.

"You are my guest, and you will sleep in my home," said Storm.

Mondo looked astonished at this request. There was no room, and he could tell the way the three wives were looking at Storm that there was going to be some activity in the tent that night. He was embarrassed even thinking about what would happen and certainly did not want to stay in this teepee.

"No," said Mondo. "I don't want to be in the way, and besides, I think you will be busy. Are you going to take care of all three?" whispered Mondo.

"Oh no. I just take wife number one first. That's best. You can have the choice of the other two."

When Mondo finally realized what was being offered, his eyes popped open, and he took a step back. "Oh no, I couldn't do that. I'm going to go find my own place to bed down."

"That would insult me. You are my guest, and you are entitled to my hospitality. This includes my permission to use one or both of my other two wives. That's the custom."

Mondo was embarrassed. He had no experience with women. They confused him, and again, his blood mixture kept him from thinking that a woman wanted to have anything to do with him.

Before Storm could object any more, Mondo apologized and said he didn't feel well and didn't want to stay here since he was sick. Storm looked at him strangely, and even though Storm didn't accept the explanation, he could tell that Mondo was not comfortable staying the night in the Comanche's teepee. Storm wasn't going to make his guest stay. The Comanche was not really insulted and accepted whatever caused Mondo to turn down his offer. Mondo excused himself and went out and built a lean-to and a fire and rolled up in his bedroll and went to sleep.

The fire got low, and Mondo woke up at the crack of dawn, and four inches of snow covered the huge valley in the Palo Duro Canyon. Tree Top, his favorite mount, was tied close to his lean-to. Mondo mounted up and rode off to check on his other horses.

As he rounded a bend in the canyon floor, he came upon a huge herd of horses. Mondo estimated there must be two thousand horses down in the Palo Duro Canyon. Indians were already out scraping the snow away so the horses could eat the grass on the valley floor.

Mondo could easily pick out his horses since they all were at least a foot taller than the shorter Indian horses. He wondered which two Storm would keep. Mondo slowly rode through the herd and checked the condition of his Thoroughbreds and then started toward Storm's teepee.

As he rode through the valley, he noticed that there were tee-pees with different markings that seemed to be clustered together. Very few Indians stared at him. He picked up some Kiowa and some Cheyenne markings, and he knew that there were at least two other tribes gathered in the canyon for the winter. Then he saw Chickasaw Killer, who continued to glare at Mondo as if he were the devil himself. Mondo ignored him and approached Storm sitting before the fire in front of his teepee as his three wives hurried around, preparing the morning meal.

"Did you get cold last night?" asked Storm.

Mondo nodded an affirmative as he dismounted.

"I was plenty warm," said Storm with a slight smile on his face. "You should have stayed in my teepee. You would have been warm and relaxed."

Mondo avoided the statement and changed the subject. "How many tribes are down here? By counting the teepees, I estimate there are at least six hundred Indians in this gathering."

"Sit down and we'll have some breakfast. There are about four hundred Comanches, around one hundred Kiowas, thirty or forty Cheyenne, and two Arapahos. All the Plains Indians know this is a good place to winter. We have no problems with each other, especially when it is so cold. Everyone stays in the teepees except to hunt a little when there is a break in the weather and to make sure that the horses are taken care of."

The two younger wives of Storm were short and kind of stocky but had a real sparkle in their dark eyes. They both giggled when they brought Mondo something to eat. Mondo looked away and tried not to guess why they were laughing.

"How long have all these different tribes been gathering in this canyon?" asked Mondo.

"I'm not sure about that. The Comanches came here about a hundred fifty years ago and ran the Apache's out. I think as the stories go, the Kiowas came down from the north eighty or ninety years ago, and we made peace with the Kiowas and they have been partners with us for at least seventy or eighty years. We had a lot of bloody battles with the Cheyenne, but around 1840, so many warriors died from each tribe that we got together and made a lasting peace. The white man keeps pushing the Cheyennes farther south into our area, and they have been coming to this canyon only the last few years. The Arapahos are to the Cheyennes as the Kiowas are to the Comanches. They are a little smaller tribe that have been close friends for a long time. Those other tribes come and go, but the Antelope band of Comanches have always stayed in this area, but we raid south as far as Mexico. We also go against Utes up in Colorado territory, and back east, we fight the Pawnee and the Osage and some of those defeated tribes from the east like the Chickasaws who have been pushed up against our hunting area. This has always been the Antelope's home."

Mondo nodded. "The whites have pushed all the tribes east of the Mississippi toward Indian Territory. Washington has made enemies out of tribes that never knew each other. Even though the Cherokee were given land northeast of here, the Osage didn't like their coming to Indian Territory, and there were a lot of bloody battles between those tribes."

Storm nodded in agreement. "I've been told that the Americans keep stacking tribe upon tribe so that we'll soon kill each other off."

"Sounds white to me," answered Mondo and bit into some Comanche bread.

Storm's children played in the snow and came up to talk with the two men during the meal. Mondo observed that the children seemed to have total freedom without any interference from the adults. No one yelled at the young ones, and they were treated with respect. This was a lot different from what Mondo had observed in his childhood. He wondered what cheap whiskey would do to this untouched band when the bootleggers reached Palo Duro Canyon.

After breakfast, Mondo and Storm checked their horses and made sure they had plenty to eat and then rode up to the top of the canyon and viewed the beautiful flat white snow-covered plain that seemed to stretch west to the end of the earth. The wind was cold, and they didn't stay very long before they returned to the canyon floor.

Mondo decided to wait until the weather cleared before he started back, and he enjoyed the next few days with Storm and his family, but he still slept in his lean-to, away from the main body of teepees. When the weather broke and the sun came out and melted away most of the snow, Mondo didn't leave because he found he liked the company and wanted to observe these Indians that the whites hadn't tainted. He had heard from his father about how the Chickasaws lived before the white man intruded into their territory, and he was trying to compare that with the way these untouched Comanches lived in their canyon. There had been very little contact with the white man by the Antelope band, and he was trying to see the differences, if any, of what he had heard about the Chickasaws before they were forced to Indian Territory and how these Comanches lived. He especially observed how the Comanches treated their children. He never once saw a Comanche spank a child, nor did he ever hear a Comanche yell at a child. All the Comanches were very gentle with their children.

When he got a chance, he brought this up with Storm.

"I've heard a lot of tales about the Comanches and the torturing that they do to their enemies and how they treat captured white women and children, and it doesn't seem to make sense to me because I have never seen anybody be so gentle with their children."

Storm looked at him quizzically and shook his head in doubt. "I never thought about it. Most Comanches don't torture, but there is nothing against it. If a warrior likes to hurt for no reason, he is usually shunned by all in the band. I know of two warriors that can't even find a place to stay with any band. Those two Comanches love torture, and they have to move from band to band because nobody wants to live near them. They keep their teepee way out away from the others, like your lean-to," smiled Storm. "Nobody wants those warriors around. Soon they disappeared from all bands and now live by themselves. Every warrior can do as he pleases, but if he goes too far, nobody speaks to him."

"That's hard to understand, but I guess it works. One thing that you don't have yet in this band is a lot of whiskey. Wait till the whiskey comes. You'll need a lot of rules and a lot of police then," said Mondo.

"I know there have been bootleggers selling whiskey to some of our peaceful brothers that are over by the Wichita Mountains. The ones who were run off from Texas. They are having lots of trouble. The old ways seem to go when the whiskey comes," said Storm. "We are trying to keep whiskey away from the Antelopes. The Mexican traders provide whiskey, but it's usually gone in two or three days. There's just not a lot around."

"It's still hard for me to understand how a band can be gentle with children and as a warrior smash a captive baby's head against a tree," said Mondo.

"Oh, you've heard about Baby Killer. He lives alone or with a couple of other mad dogs. Nobody wants that vicious snake around. After he killed a couple of babies on that raid, none of the warriors would allow Baby Killer to go with them. Baby Killer and a couple of other skunks, one I think they call Loco Killer, wander around by themselves, and nobody speaks to them."

"What about the Tonkawas?" asked Mondo. "I have heard that you torture Tonkawas, and Tonkawas eat the Comanches."

"Tonkawas are a different story. Everything goes with a Tonkawa. I don't know how it started, but we've been doing awful things to each other for a hundred years. You don't have to punish a Comanche child if you tell the children the Tonkawas will eat them if they misbehave."

Mondo said, "When you deal with the Tonkawa, it sounds like you don't need whiskey to be cruel and brutal. A lot of men get drunk and then get mean. My father told me that warriors lived on pride and then their life was ruined and changed by the coming of the white man. The defeated warriors lived in the bottle to try to feel that warrior pride again."

"I can understand that. Comanches are raised to go out and commit brave deeds in warfare or steal many horses and to come back and stand in front of their people and tell of their great deeds. Those warriors that do the most and tell about it the best are considered the most successful and respected of all warriors. If they had become farmers like you say, then they'll have nothing to be proud of. Their life would be over. I've tried whiskey, and it sure makes you feel powerful and brave. But it makes you sick the next day. It's bad medicine that gives a man false pride and makes him think it is good medicine. And most all of the best-known Comanche warriors give most of their stolen goods to those Comanches that need it. To steal from others and give what you steal away to the poor makes a man a very respected Comanche."

Mondo was trying to compare what he learned with the way that he was told how the Chickasaw lived a hundred years ago. There were a lot of similarities but differences too. He thought maybe farming made the difference since the Chickasaws had farmed as well as fought before the white man came. The Chickasaw man had something that he could rely on to feel good about himself besides stealing horses and counting coup or touching a live enemy. Mondo and Storm became close friends as they openly discussed the difference between a Comanche and a Chickasaw.

CHAPTER 7

As Maboola led Savanah through the thick Cross Timbers, she became less afraid of the black giant. He took his time and listened for pursuers. She had stopped worrying and began to feel safe being away from the absolute control of Purify Jones who ruled her every action.

Jones had hired unmarried Southern ladies that were raised on large plantations to teach Savanah how to sit, walk, talk, dress, eat, and wave a fan. Strict rules and strict habits were constantly forced onto the little girl with green eyes and a slight-tan skin color. Now she was moving through thick short trees in order to keep hidden from white Texans. They chewed on some jerky when the sun set and kept going through the night. Her fancy dress got ripped apart. She was riding in her long white undergarments by the time they reached the Red River in the early morning. She got into her bag of newly purchased clothes and dressed in a casual house dress.

The river was up, and they rode east, looking for a safe crossing. The red water was moving fast and the stream was at least two hundred yards wide. When they rounded a bend, they saw that the river narrowed to about ninety yards up ahead, but waiting on the Texas side were three white cowboy riders that looked to be trying to decide whether it was too dangerous to cross or wait until the river went down.

As Maboola and Savanah rode toward the three men, Maboola cocked his 12-gauge shotgun and whispered to Savanah. "Are you going to be white or black? You'd better act like you are a rich white lady and let me be your servant. Those three men look pretty tough."

At first, Savanah looked afraid, but sat up tall on her horse and tried to act rich and white as if she was in charge. She called out to the three cowboys. "Are you going to try it? And how far downstream is there a ferry crossing?"

The three men looked her over very slowly and then eyed the black giant with the shotgun in his hands. She obviously looked tempting, but the big Negro looked like he could hurt all three real quick and real bad. The middle man answered, "I think we can get across. You'd have to ride at least eighty miles east to get on Colbert's Ferry. It's either here or lose a day or two. You're not trying to go into Indian country all by yourself, except for that big servant, are you, ma'am?"

Savanah smiled, relaxed, and then answered. "Sure am. Don't they allow non-Indians to go into Indian Territory?"

"Sure. But begging your pardon, ma'am, that country over there is real wild. There's a lot of no-good ex-slaves living up and down this river that are doing nothing but looking for trouble, and on inland there's outlaws and Indians all over the place. They'll steal everything you've got if you let them. And, ma'am, they might do worse things to you, begging your pardon for mentioning such. Now, your boy here is real big, and he's got a big shotgun, but these black outlaws travel in gangs, large gangs. It's not safe. Why do you want to go where a bunch of no-good Indians and escaped slaves live anyway?"

"My husband has made a deal with some of the Indians. He has cattle. He wrote me to come and meet him and to bring Maboola here to keep me safe. My husband has a big spread of grassland and there's a lot of cowhands working for him. If I get to him, I'll be safe, and so far, I've been safe with my servant here."

"What's your husband's name? Maybe I've heard of him. Where's his place?"

"Oh, his place is south of Fort Worth, and we're heading for his leased grazing land near Fort Arbuckle on the Washita River. His name is Sam Jones. Ever heard of him?"

"No. But I'm new around here. Me and my brothers were heading to the Chisholm Trail looking for work. I've heard some men are going to drive longhorns up into Kansas where a new railroad has been built in a town called Abilene. A Joseph McCoy sent some fliers down to Texas telling us to bring 'um on and he'd get them sold for good money and get them headed back east on the railroad."

"I'll tell my husband about that if he doesn't already know. Why don't you all try going across? If you make it, we may give it a shot."

The cowboy smiled and tipped his hat. "It will be my pleasure ma'am. Anything for a fine-looking lady like yourself. I guess you know you will be safe if we leave you alone with this big ape. He doesn't look or act very friendly. How long has he been with your family?"

Savanah smiled. "Oh, my servant Maboola has been with us from the very beginning. He would not harm me or let anyone harm me. I'll be fine. Can we help you get started?"

"No, ma'am. We were fixin' to dive off about the time you rode up. Good luck, and I hope you have a safe trip."

With that, the three men jumped their horses off in the river and hung on as the ponies started to swim across the red rushing water.

Maboola watched as the current moved the struggling animals east going downstream with the swift muddy water. "Can you swim?" Maboola asked Savanah.

"No. Swimming wasn't something a Southern lady was supposed to be taught. Now I can ride sidesaddle with the best of them, but I'm going to have both legs locked around my horse when we hit the water."

"I'm a lot of weight on my ride. I'm going to float along, holding on to the horse's mane. I will have a free hand to help you. We could camp out a couple of days and let the river go down, or we could ride downstream and get to Colbert's Ferry. It's your call."

Savanah was staring off into the swirling river as a shot rang out and a bullet whizzed over their heads. Five riders were coming down the hill fast. Without a word, Maboola and Savanah jumped their horses into the cold water. Up ahead, they could see the three cowboys struggling out on the north bank of the river. A shot splashed up water to their right, and both of them hunkered down into the water so that only their heads stood out. Halfway across, the horses got into a swirl that spun them around and floated them downstream. Maboola about jerked his horse's head off before he turned the animal back toward the north bank. Maboola grabbed hold of Savanah's reins and pulled her with him. Bullets splashed around them. Maboola looked back and saw that the five Texans firing their rifles had not entered the river. They floated east at least two hundred yards farther down than where the three cowboys had come out of the river. By the time Maboola and Savanah finally reached the other side, they were cold, wet, and exhausted. As their horses stumbled up the north bank, the three cowboys were waiting with their pistols drawn. The five Texans on the south bank had stopped firing but were not crossing the river.

The talkative cowboy spoke as he glared at the two. "Who were those shooters and why are they after you?"

Savanah answered. "I don't know. They might think we are someone else. Or they may be trying to rob us. They started shooting at us before they were close enough to see who we were. Maybe they realized that I am not the one they are after and that is why they stopped shooting."

Before the three cowboys could answer, a voice came from behind them. "No, ma'am. Those five shooters stopped because they saw us coming up to check on the noise." The three cowboys turned and faced fifteen armed black men standing in a semicircle about three yards apart, each holding an old pistol, rifle, or shotgun. The men were dressed in old, torn cotton rags and were shirtless, but all were armed and all had a hard, no-nonsense look on their faces.

"We over on this side of the river watch them white boys trying to come across, and those white boys know it. They stopped shooting because we came up over the hill. We're used to checking on who crosses over the Red. We don't like them to come across shooting and trying to recapture ex-slaves. If I was you, three cowboys, I'd put those guns back in the holster and go on back across the river to Texas."

The three cowboys turned and glared at the tattered Negroes, but said nothing and re-holstered their pistols. "We were just heading through. We are not stopping. We heard there was work for cattle herders along the Chisholm Trail. We don't want no trouble."

The spokesman eyed the cowboys and nodded that he believed them. "Fine. You ride on north and cut back west about five or ten miles and you'll hit the cow trail. There's a bunch of herds heading to Kansas. You are in our country now. We don't mind cowboys going through, but there's still a bunch of bounty hunters chasing down ex-slaves. Those ex-rebs think they still own or want to lynch Negroes. Ex-rebel Negro hunters like the bunch across the river want to put the hurt on us. We don't like them to get near our campsite on this side of the river. If you are real cattle herders, we don't have a problem with you."

The leader looked around at the other black men, and no one objected. "Get on your horses and ride on out of here."

The three cowboys mounted up and rode off, and the blacks looked at Maboola. "We could sure use a big, scary, cold black man like you on our side and you got extra guns too. What's your story?"

Maboola spoke. "They are after me. I dealt with the man who scarred my back. They don't like what I did to him. Thanks for helping us. We're moving on north."

"That's fine. But this pretty white woman's got to be protected. The country north of here through Chickasaw land is rough going. Lots of outlaws, both black, white, and Indian. Are you her boy?"

"I'm nobody's boy, and she's part-Negro, and I am helping her get away from a rich white man who still wants to own her. So I'm with her."

"You're big, but you'll have your hands full. I'd stay away from any town. Just keep moving out of sight. There's an all-black town just been started at Wildhorse Creek near the Washita River. They'll treat you right. The Negro settlement is near Fort Arbuckle. Wild Indians control things to the west of here. A man, one even as big as you, traveling alone with a pretty woman is in big danger. You might take her over to Tishomingo City and then join us. We sure could use your help on our side of the river. You are one big, scary man."

"He's not my servant," said Savanah. "I'm not all white, just mostly white, but as you know, that doesn't count with white folks. I'd like to rest and see where and how you all live if you don't mind. I've never been around black folks much and never around free black folks."

"Sure. You're welcome to visit our hidden village. We live along the Red River in the thickest undergrowth. When the war started, a bunch of Chickasaws who weren't going to fight for either side came down here and hid out with their slaves. We learned to hide and survive along the riverbank. When word reached us that the war was over, most of us just refused to go with our ex-masters and stayed right here. Our little community has really grown with ex-slaves from Texas and Louisiana running away from bad memories and joining up with us. Come on. We'll show you around, fill your bellies, and try to talk both of you into staying with us 'river rats,' as the white men call us."

Maboola and Savanah followed the Red River blacks west until they came to a high cliff area on the north side of the river that was surrounded by heavy thick cross-timber post oak trees.

A path had been cut out so that the group rode to the top where a small village of dugouts, lean-tos, and tents were hidden from view by the trees. From there, the river blacks could see for miles east and west along the bank of the Red River.

"I'm called Catfish," spoke the black leader as the party dismounted around a central area and the ex-slaves gathered around to view the two newcomers. Most were dressed in ragged, torn cotton pants and shirts like the ones supplied to slaves who worked the cotton fields.

"Sit down," advised Catfish. "We don't have much, but we'll share what we have with our kind. Our main meal usually is catfish. There's plenty of big old flathead living in holes along the river. We've learned to noodle them or catch them with our bare hands."

Maboola looked over at three big catfish hanging up to be cleaned. They were all about four to five feet long and must have weighed over a hundred pounds each. He looked at the hands of the men and laughed. "Are you telling me that you people caught these fish bare-handed? I would have thought that there would be some hands missing if you lived by reaching down and pulling those big fish up without a hook or line."

"We learned to noodle this fish during the war. There wasn't much else to eat. So we've kept it up after our ex-owners left out."

"Did you run them off? And how did you get hold of those guns?"

"They had us doing the hunting to add to the fish we caught. When we decided to keep the guns, they left in a hurry. I don't know why. We were just going to kill one of those owners who kind of liked to beat his slaves. Anyway, we stayed and they left."

"Are you going to try to stay here forever and live hidden away up on this high ridge?" asked Savanah.

"Probably so. The whites don't come back here. They aren't welcome. Most whites don't know where we stay cause we roam the river and watch out for who is crossing over. We think it's safer back in the boondocks here than running around in small groups. Safety in numbers, so to speak."

"Have you fired on white men?"

"We've never killed no whites yet," said Catfish, "but they know we're here and gathered in numbers with guns. Nobody bothers us really. When we leave our hideout here, we travel in groups of at least twelve, and we carry firearms."

"Thanks for helping us out," said Savanah, "but we probably should be moving on. I'd like to visit the Wildhorse Creek settlement. Can you tell us how to get there?"

"Sure. Ride north until you see those rocky hills that the whites call the Arbuckles. Hit the Washita and go north to where Wildhorse Creek runs into the river. That's where another group of blacks are gathered up and trying to make it on their own."

CHAPTER 8

A s the ground dried out on the Palo Duro Canyon floor, horse races began. Mondo was approached by several Comanches trying to trade for his long-legged horses. Mondo held out. The Comanches loved to gamble, and one activity that brought about a lot of bets was racing horses. When it warmed up, the Comanches set up a racetrack along the canyon floor that curved in and out beside the river stream at the bottom of the valley. The Indians wanted to see Mondo's horse run.

All the Indians in the Antelope band and the Kiowa, Cheyenne, and Arapaho visitors came out to see the horse races. Mondo immediately noticed that the track that ran along the stream through Palo Dura Canyon was about a quarter mile long. Mondo had raced Tree Top against Indian horses before and knew that the quicker, smaller Indian horses would start faster, and the best of the shorter horses might beat his horse in a quarter-of-a-mile race. However, Tree Top had never lost in a half-mile race. Therefore when Mondo showed up with Tree Top, he refused to race any of the Indian horses until they had agreed to race up and back, which amounted to a little more than a half a mile.

It took about an hour to negotiate the betting. Mondo put up five of his horses against fifteen Indian horses that Mondo had picked out of the whole herd. Mondo's special, more valuable tall horses enabled him to get three to one odds.

When they finally lined up at the starting point, Mondo noticed that the jockeys for the Indians were young, lightweight

Indian boys that weighed half as much as Mondo. The Indians had picked their best riders, and Mondo knew that he was in for a hard race.

When the gun was fired, all six horses leaped forward, and at once, Mondo was in last place. The five Indian shorter horses got at least ten yards ahead, and Mondo was holding back Tree Top. He knew after the turn at the halfway mark he could catch the smaller mounts, but he was concerned about passing all five horses since the racing path was not but six to eight feet wide along the river stream. If he wasn't careful, Mondo felt like the Indians could block him from passing.

At the turn, Tree Top stumbled and almost went down, and as Mondo regained control, he was at least fifteen yards behind the leading Indian horse. He relaxed the rein and let his horse go. He was halfway through the return quarter mile stretch when he caught the trailing three Indian horses. As he tried to pass, two Comanches paid by Chickasaw Killer moved in unison to block his way.

Mondo waited for his opening and spurred his horse in between the two Indian riders as they rounded a curve and started for the last hundred yards. Tree Top knocked the two smaller horses aside and pushed through. The contact caused Tree Top to stumble again, but the great horse regained his balance and tore after the leading two Indian riders that were at least five yards ahead.

At the fifty-yard mark, Mondo caught both horses, and again, the two tried to prevent him from going around. But Tree Top's size was too much, and Mondo moved to the inside lane along the riverbank and just edged his horse forward, pushing the two horses aside. At the twenty-five-yard mark, Mondo took the lead and charged forward, winning by at least five yards.

The crowd had been yelling for the Comanches. The yelling stopped as Mondo finished the winner. Chickasaw Killer, who had bet and lost his best three horses, charged Mondo and

knocked Mondo off his horse. Chickasaw Killer swung a tomahawk at Mondo, who ducked and flattened the Comanche with a
powerful right uppercut. Mondo was afraid the whole tribe would
attack him, but everyone ignored Chickasaw Killer as he lay
unconscious. Bad behavior was not defended in this Comanche
band. Some argued that Mondo had fouled the Indian's ponies
and held up delivering the horses they lost. Since there were very
few rules in an Indian horse race, Bull Bear, the top warrior in the
group, quietly raised his hand and ended the argument by declar-
ing Mondo the winner. Mondo had increased his herd from ten
Thoroughbreds to twenty-five total horses with the fifteen Indian
horses he'd won.

After the race, an Indian messenger from the eastern band
of Comanches rode in and announced that there had been a
big treaty made by the other bands of Comanches at Medicine
Lodge in Kansas. Bull Bear immediately called a counsel so that
the Antelope band could hear what some of the leaders of the
eastern peace-loving Comanches had agreed to with the white
men. Mondo, the great warrior and horse owner, was invited to
sit in with the others at counsel.

That night, about twenty of the Antelope leaders and a couple Kiowas and Mondo sat in a large circle and passed the pipe
around before Bull Bear opened the discussion.

"Brothers, we are in council tonight to hear some news that
has come from the east. You all know Burning Sun from the eastern band because he has been a guest of ours in the past. Burning
Sun was in the area called by the whites Kansas, near Medicine
Lodge. He has much to tell us. Speak, Burning Sun."

A young Indian, about twenty-five, who was short and stocky
like most Comanches, stood and began to speak.

"There were about five thousand Indians there. The white
men gave many gifts. The Comanches and Cheyenne made up
about eighty percent. However, there were important Kiowas,
Arapahos, and some other Indians, people from the eastern tribes

forced into our area thirty to forty years ago. Ten Bears made a great speech about how the Comanche feels about the intrusion of the white man and our hatred for the vicious Texans. The white Americans seemed to listen as always, but they still made the Plains tribes agree to stay in the country between the Arkansas River and the Red River. The Comanches and Kiowas are supposed to stay on the land between the Washita River and the Red River on this side of the trail used by Jesse Chisholm. The white man is not supposed to come on this land unless they are invited by us. The white man has agreed to provide us food and other necessary things to live on until we all learn to farm, but we are not to raid any whites, even the Texans. This agreement includes most of the land that the Antelope occupy, but the Antelope band is not supposed to go into Texas and into Mexico on raids. No buffalo will be killed by the whites on our allotted property."

There was a long silence after Burning Sun spoke. Finally, Bull Bear spoke. "All know that Ten Bears has no right to speak for the Antelope band. The Antelope band has never gone to any treaty counsel and has never agreed to anything with the white man. We live in our country, and we control who comes into our country. When a warrior sees a vision, he goes and leads other warriors to Texas or to Mexico for horses, prisoners, or scalps. We have been doing this for a hundred years, and we will not stop living our way by some kind of a promise that Ten Bears or any other so-called Comanche leader makes with the Americans."

After Bull Bear finished his speech, there was no disagreement among the Comanches at the counsel meeting. There was not much more to say. The treaty meant nothing to the Antelope band, and they had no intention of living up to any of its terms. As far as the Indians at Palo Duro Canyon were concerned, the treaty at Medicine Lodge did not include them, and they would not change their ways.

After some discussion, one of the Kiowa leaders named Lone Wolf stood up. Lone Wolf looked over at Mondo. "There is much talk, and I've had dreams about this warrior that calls himself

Mondo. He seems to be a great warrior, but he never brags about his deeds. We don't know if he's a great warrior or just lucky. We don't know what he's done, and we don't know who he really is. The Comanche and Kiowa cannot steal his horses, and the Comanche and Kiowa cannot outrace his horse. The Comanche and Kiowa cannot slip up on him, and many times, he has counted coup on our warriors. He touches them, tells them he's a friend of Ten Bears, and sends them away without his horses. He acts like a great spirit. I can't tell from my dreams whether he is good for us or bad for us. Is the Great Spirit trying to tell us that we must mix with his kind? Is the Great Spirit trying to tell us that someone with a lot of Indian blood mixed with African blood is the greatest warrior? Are we going to be protected by this warrior, or are we going to be defeated by this warrior? We know very little about the black people. What does his presence and his actions mean to our tribes?"

There was silence after Lone Wolf spoke. All the Indians at the counsel were staring at Mondo.

The Kiowa were superstitious and believed in magic and dreams more than the Comanches. The Kiowa chief had made a great mystery out of Mondo and Mondo's presence among the Kiowa and Comanche.

Bull Bear turned to Mondo. "Do you want to answer? As our guest, you do not have to. The Kiowa wants to know, will you fight for the Comanche and Kiowa, or will you fight against the Comanche and Kiowa? He also asks what tribe do you belong to? You may answer or you may remain silent."

Mondo rose and looked over the gathered Indians. "I have no tribe. I am African and Chickasaw and, to my sorrow, probably a little white. Both Indian and African men at one time came from various tribes. Some far away and some in this land. I am not fully accepted as an equal by any of these tribes. Therefore I do not belong to a tribe. I come to the Kiowa and the Comanche with a peace offering and a request for friendship. Since I have no tribe, I prefer to live alone. Since I have no place or location that is acceptable to any tribe, I choose to live in between tribes. I am on the border between the Comanche-Kiowa and the Chickasaw tribes. I do not fight against or with the Comanches. I am not for or against the Chickasaw. I chose a side during the great white war and saw many deaths. I chose a side and really wasn't accepted by the side I chose. It is said five hundred thousand men died in the Civil War over the slavery of the African tribe. I want to live in peace with all tribes and independent from all tribes. I will not attack you or steal your horses, and I expect the same from you," Mondo sat down.

The Kiowa chief Lone Wolf shook his head as if he hadn't received a satisfactory answer to his questions. "Tell us what you know about the Civil War where whites killed a lot of other whites. Why did they fight and how did they fight? We have not seen too many great warriors with white skin."

Mondo rose again and studied Lone Wolf, a serious man with sad but intelligent eyes.

"The white man is a different type of warrior. They fight by overpowering a tribe with numbers. Always they fight as a group and don't have individual warriors charging into the enemy to touch them and count coup to show bravery, but as a whole, the American whites walk into guns as if the guns were not even loaded or couldn't fire. It's hard to understand it if you're not white. It's like a whole group of soldiers committing group suicide. They walk into weapons in the bright daylight and fall dead as the bullets and cannon balls rip their walking lines apart. Why they do it is a mystery. I think it has to do with losing face with the other soldiers. No man whether brown, red, black, white, or green, wants to show the fear he really feels deep down. Cowards are looked down upon by all males no matter the color of their skin. I think the whites are tired of death and that's why the black soldiers are coming out here to fight your tribes. Whether black or white, the whites will always have more fighters. They grow like a creeping vine and strangle all tribes that stand in their path so they can own and control all land. The Civil War was fought over freedom of Negro slaves so that the slaves could continue to push all Indians off their land."

There was a stunned silence after Mondo sat down. The men gathered at the council seemed to have no questions to ask and the information was too much for them to absorb all at once. Bull Bear rose and called an end to the discussion. The Antelope band and other Indians in the Palo Duro Canyon seemed to avoid Mondo as if they wanted to treat him as a great liar. The Indian holdouts could not or would not accept the defeatist view presented by their guest.

Mondo gathered his horses and said good-bye to Storm and started for his compound, keeping an eye out for Chickasaw Killer, the one who was being shunned by his own band for attacking a guest. Mondo didn't know for sure whether he was a permanent friend or still an enemy of this Antelope band.

CHAPTER 9

MABOOLA AND SAVANAH rode north through areas of thick post oak trees and spots of open grassland. By late afternoon, they spotted five riders that looked part-Indian but were dressed like whites coming toward them. Maboola and Savanah pulled up and waited. Maboola rested the shotgun across his arm and shifted the machete hanging across his shoulder so he could get to it real quick. It was too late to run. Savanah felt fear but showed none of it as she stretched tall in the saddle. The lead man halted, stared at Maboola for a second or two, and then looked over to Savanah.

"Howdy, ma'am. I'm Hurbert Dixon, Chickasaw Lighthorse policeman. May I ask you where you are going?"

Savanah smiled. "Sure. I'm going to meet my husband who is supposed to be camped somewhere around Fort Arbuckle. He's moving some cattle north. Have you seen him?"

Hurbert Dixon answered, "Maybe. What's his name?"

"Sam Jones," she answered.

"No. I've stopped a few herds and collected the Chickasaw grazing fee of ten cents a head, but we've not met a Jones herd. Is he waiting for you and your boy here to catch up with him?"

"Not sure. If the creeks are down, he may move on. I'm just supposed to catch up to him as fast as I can. He might have moved and be out of Chickasaw country by now."

"How many head is he driving north?"

"I don't know how many he ended up with. Some neighbors were throwing in with him."

Hurbert Dixon nodded and then eyed Maboola and looked back at Savanah. "I think you will be safe. I hate to admit it, but since the war, we've got a lot of undesirable people coming into our country. This here boy looks big. He's got two pistols, a shotgun, and a sharp machete, but there are some gangs running loose and wild that might take a real liking to you and your horses."

Maboola gave Dixon a smile that wasn't a smile, but one that said he wasn't afraid of any gangs. Dixon noticed and then looked back at Savanah.

"Don't let that big black stop here and stay," Dixon said, nodding toward Maboola. "We've had all kinds of trouble with ex-slaves coming over from Texas and other places. They think Indian land is free land. We have enough trouble controlling our own freedmen without all these new, strange troublemakers coming across the river. Will he stay with you?"

Savanah glared at Dixon. "He's free. He can come and go as he wishes. Why don't you want him here?"

Dixon frowned at Savanah. "The Federals are trying to say we have to make our freedmen members of our tribe. So every Negro that comes here claims he's a Chickasaw freedman. Our records have gotten messed up during the war. So what we've got now is a bunch of ex-slaves mixing in with our own Negroes and causing a lot of trouble. Our freedmen were a pretty good bunch, but not anymore. They've been listening to all these bad ones that the whites have run off from their own states. He can't stop here and stay. At that Wildhorse Creek settlement, there's whiskey making and gambling and living in the sin of prostitution. It's an evil place. So if he takes a notion to join up with some of those outlaw bands of freedman, let me know. He looks and acts like double trouble. I don't want him around, and after I check on some shooting I heard about on the Red River, I'm going to find your husband and make sure he pays my tribe ten cents a head for driving his cattle across our land."

Maboola tensed and Savanah answered before Maboola could speak or make an aggressive move. "Yes, sir. I understand. We'll be moving on as quick as possible and be out of here real soon like. Come on, Maboola, let's go find my husband. I'm sure he will pay what he owes, if anything."

Savanah spurred her horse and rode off with Maboola trailing behind her. Maboola looked back and gave Hurbert Dixon a look that wasn't friendly. "That's one real bad dude," said Dixon.

Maboola and Savanah camped together when they reached the south end of the small Arbuckle Mountains. Maboola built a fire and cooked a couple of rabbits he'd killed as they rode through the short timbers. Spring was in the air, and a fresh, clean, cool climate made them comfortable and tired from the ride. They ate a warm meal. Maboola seemed more relaxed every mile farther they got from Texas. Savanah began to feel nervous and upset, not over where they were in Indian Territory but where she was going in the future. Savanah had never made a decision on her own and had been trained like a robot to act and think like a white Southern wife. She didn't feel that way. She really didn't know who she was or who she wanted to be. Maboola, who had been trying to get out of Texas for ten years, felt like he'd just succeeded for the first time in his life.

"Are you going north to find work and earn your way back to Africa?" asked Savanah.

"Yes. And what are you going to do? Are you going to try to pass for a real white person?"

"I don't know. I don't know me. I can't tell who I am. I don't feel right playing white. But I have never learned to live around Negroes. I don't feel I'm black. I feel lost without knowing where I should try to go. Do you understand what I'm trying to say?"

"No, not really. I don't like whites or anyone who tries to be white. White is evil and has done nothing but cause me much pain. So I don't know what to think about you. I feel hate when you play the Southern belle, but I feel like I should fight for anyone who is mistreated by whites. You are going to have to decide pretty soon. I'm going to find that Wildhorse Creek place and they may not like white people to come there. They probably have a lot of bitter ex-slaves that are trying to keep away from the white people that harmed them."

A gun went off and dirt kicked up a few feet from Maboola who rolled away from the fire and grabbed his shotgun and fired a blast of buckshot in the direction of the sound.

"Better give up, boy. We've got you surrounded" came a voice from the night air.

Savanah didn't move as if she was paralyzed.

"Get down," hollered Maboola as two more shots rang out, one catching Maboola in the leg as he rolled farther away from the fire.

"You white boys back off and move out or you all are dead," came a shout from the other direction that carried an accent of an ex-slave.

Silence held for a few seconds. "Who are you boys? Don't you be pushing in on us. We're after them two Negroes who broke their work contract with Purify Jones. We're not backing down from some ex-slave's threats coming out of the darkness."

From the north came an answer. "Fire off your guns so these bounty hunters will know we ain't lying and we mean business." At once, it sounded like a full-blown battle as the sound of at least a dozen guns exploded in the darkness and from all directions. After a few minutes, the bounty hunters finally replied. "Wait a minute, boys. Let's don't be doing anything stupid. We don't have to get them two right now. We're leaving. Let us pull out and there's no need to get anyone killed. Mr. Jones will just raise the bounty for those two the longer they are gone. We'll be back with more men, and we'll be keeping an eye open for you black gun-carrying troublemakers."

Maboola could hear movement of men mounting up and riding off. After the bounty hunters had clearly left, a black man came out of the dark and gave Maboola a hand to help him to his feet.

"Are you hit bad?"

"Just a scratch on my leg is all." Maboola looked around as more Negroes came out of the woods and eased up to the fire. "Where in the hell did you people come from?"

"We're a patrol out of Wildhorse Creek. My name is Hudson Greer. We try to keep track of these Texans coming across the river. Those were five bounty hunters trying to take you people back or trying to lynch you two for bad manners or just for fun. We get word of their crossing the Red River by drums from the rats. We try to stop them and send them back to Texas. We've been fired on quite a few times at Wildhorse Creek. We hear about and keep track of these killers and black haters that come across the Red River."

"It's good to meet you, Hudson Greer. You seem to be my kind of man. I was just telling Savanah here that I was going to Wildhorse Creek, but I didn't expect a welcoming party to save us and escort us in."

"We heard about you two just as soon as you crossed the river. These bounty hunters were the ones who fired on you and were stopped by the same Red River boys that signaled us that they were coming after you. These bounty hunters went east and slipped across the river. We've been watching you two and them ex-slave catchers for a couple hours." Hudson looked at Savanah. "What's she going to do?"

Savanah was still shaking from the gunfire and barely able to stand up and face Hudson Greer.

"Right now, I'm going with you if you'll take me."

"It's just not good for whites to stay in our town. There's still some hate and anger against whites."

"I'm not white," she said. "I've got mostly white blood, but that's never counted much for nothing in the white world. I'd like to go to Wildhorse Creek. Just tell everyone I'm a Negro like the rest of them there."

Hudson Greer nodded in agreement. "Let's get going. We are just about an hour ride from town. Some of my men will follow those night riders to make sure they don't cause any more trouble and force them back across the river."

With that, Maboola and Savanah mounted up and rode off with Hudson Greer and his men and headed for the Wildhorse Creek settlement.

CHAPTER 10

As Mondo drove his twenty-five horses back across the Texas Panhandle into western Indian Territory, he feared that the small enclosure that he and his father built along Little Beaver Creek might no longer exist by the time he got back. Mondo had ended up spending about eight weeks with Storm, and it was too long to be away from his fort. His father had gone to his own place to winter, and nobody was there to guard his rock house. The wooden stockade they built around his house might be burned to the ground by young warriors of any of the Plains tribes that roamed through the western half of Indian Territory. Since the Medicine Lodge Treaty in Kansas in late November of 1867, the Cheyenne and Arapaho tribes were ordered onto the land that was occupied by the Comanche, Kiowas, and Kiowa-Apache tribes. Young hotheads of these tribes didn't like to be pushed around, and Mondo's compound was the closest structure standing except for the US Cavalry outpost at Fort Cobb and a small garrison in Anadarko along the Washita River.

All the work Mondo and his dad had put into building his little fort may have been a wasted effort. Mondo thought back to the first time he saw his father after the war.

He had driven his twelve Thoroughbreds up to his father's cabin, which hadn't changed since Mondo left seven years before to fight in the Civil War. His father stepped out of the cabin and smiled. Without a word, the two men put his horse into the corral, and Mondo climbed down and father and son embraced.

Mondo smiled. "You said I wouldn't be back. You told me that the white man's war would kill me off. You were wrong about my death, but you were right that it was a stupid war and it was not a place for an Indian to die."

Bear Chaser, who was a couple inches shorter than Mondo, nodded in agreement. "You look much older and maybe a little wiser. You've grown to be quite the man. Come in and tell me what you have learned in the seven years away from your home."

They sat at the rough but simple table that Mondo remembered,and his father put some coffee on the stove. His father had put on a few pounds but was about the same, five eleven, 210 pounds, the way he'd always looked before Mondo left. His father's lifestyle was simple, and he always lived more Indian than white. *Nothing new and nothing changed* is what Mondo thought. Without showing much emotion, both father and son felt the love they had for each other.

Bear Chaser looked seriously at his young son. "How was the great war?"

"Not as exciting as I thought it would be. In fact, I should have listened to you and stayed home. Killing people is not fun, and it did not make me feel more like a man. The army was slow to move, and all we did was hurry and wait. It was very boring. You were right about the Yankees. They don't like Indians any better than the Southern boys, and they talk about freeing slaves, but they don't treat Negroes as equal by a long shot."

"Were you in any of the battles I've heard about?"

"Pea Ridge in Arkansas was the biggest one. Once again, the powers that be from the Federal forces couldn't decide where I belonged. At first I fought with an Indian company, and toward the end, they moved me to a black outfit. During the battle, the Yankee whites would treat me as an equal because the danger made them color blind. But after the fighting was over, I was a lowlife once again. The last battle I was in was at Honey Springs here in Indian Territory. The black troops did a good job and proved a lot of white people wrong. Black blood does not lessen your ability to kill and fight."

"Well, that's over. You can live and work with me. Those horses you've got make you kind of rich right now. There's a real shortage of good horseflesh since the Confederates took every horse that was able to move. There's plenty of grass out here and you can just live right here in Pickens County, Chickasaw Nation, and make a living breeding and selling those good-looking horses. No one lives near me. The Comanches leave me alone because of Ten Bears."

"How's old Ten Bears? Is he still around? Does he still carry a lot of weight with the tribe? I kind of want to move out a little farther west."

"West! I'm about as far as you can go unless you're right up against those Plains Indians. Ten Bears is all right. I just talked to him about a week ago. He's old but still knows what is going on."

"I hope he can keep those young Comanche bucks off me because I'm going to build on Little Beaver Creek and raise my horses right there. I thank you for the invitation to live with you, but I made up my mind during the war that I'm going to make it on my own, and there's only one place where I want to try to raise horses, and you know where that is. I've always loved that Little Beaver valley that we used to hunt in. Besides, I'm not living where I'm not wanted. I ran into Hurbert Dixon when I was coming in, and he told me no ex-Yankee and nobody with Negro blood was welcome in the Chickasaw Nation. I've had enough of that. I'm not sure whether my dream valley is in Chickasaw or Comanche country, and I don't give a damn. It's where nobody lives and that's where I want to live. I've had enough of people, and I've decided I'm going to stay there until I die."

"That's a pretty bold statement for a young man. Of course, I made bold statements too when I was young. You might die sooner than you want. Ten Bears can't keep those young braves from trying to steal your horses if you insult those warriors by living right under their noses. Stay with me a few years. The US will take the Comanche land soon. The US Cavalry and the US government is a taker of land, and we have lived through it, and we know that very well. Wait awhile. Why go looking for trouble? Trouble to the Plains Indians will come from the Federal cavalry. They will move them to some kind of reservation to keep the peace. No Indian will be allowed to keep their old territory. Only that land that's good for nothing else will be given to the Indians in the final say. Any Chickasaw that was moved from Tennessee to Mississippi and then to Indian Territory knows and feels the truth in being pushed aside to worthless land."

"The Comanches and Kiowas live with the buffalo. You can't farm their dry land. Maybe the US government won't steal their land. Their land is just not wet enough for farming."

"Farming! If buffalo can live on that grass, then those long-horns can do so too. There will be cattle on there because that's what the whites want to do. The US never keeps a promise. You know about treaties. They're a joke. How many treaties did the Chickasaws have and how many were kept by the US government? The white man's greed has no bounds, and their word is not worth a hoot. And the mixed bloods that rule our tribe now only look part-Indian because they're all white. They do and want and want just like the white man. The Comanches are still Indians, but they will be broken. So just give the US Cavalry time to settle the Comanches down and try to make them white. For now, the Comanches are still in the horse-stealing business. If you settle down by them, you will have yours taken. That's the way they make their living. I really think you are a little war crazy to want to settle right up against their hunting grounds. You're young and haven't seen enough blood. You just haven't had enough fight yet to want to back off and settle down and use your head instead of your muscle."

"What do you mean war crazy? I don't want to fight anybody, but I don't want anybody to mess with me, and I want to live in that valley."

"Well, what I've learned in my many years is that to kill or be shot at makes a man change. It takes a while for his natural self to resettle. When you eat, sleep, and ride scared, you have to live in peace before you realize that killing and fighting are not necessary all the time. You've killed men, and men have tried to kill you. Afterwords, being alone and away from humans is natural, but it's not good for you, or it shouldn't be and won't be permanent. Also, living in danger all the time makes a man come to want it or think he needs danger to really be alive. Please stay with me at my place for a while. I'm at least six miles inside Chickasaw land for sure. Where you are going might be outside the 98th meridian, which officially ends the Chickasaw Nation."

"I don't know anything about meridians and territory markings. I know where I want to live. I don't need to prove my courage to anyone. I'm satisfied that I'm not a coward. I don't want to live in the Chickasaw Nation where my black blood makes the government people look down on me and want me gone. I'm not challenging the Comanche or the Kiowas. I'll leave them alone if they will leave me alone, and that goes for everyone."

"Even me?" asked Bear Chaser.

"No. You're welcome any time at my place. Don't you think that Ten Bears will help me keep my horses?"

"He can't control the young Comanches of his own tribe, and the Kiowas won't listen to him. You'll have to build a fort to keep your horses, and you know how much the Comanches hate forts. Those high wooden-fenced army camps popped up in west Texas, and soon the southern bands of Comanches were forced to move to Indian Territory. Are you really going to try to build something like that within their eyesight?'"

"Yes. I've thought it all out. A rock house on the little hill that is surrounded on three sides by Little Beaver Creek. You remember? The hill had enough rock exposed to build a house. There's enough timber along the creek to build a ten-foot wall around the hill. I plan to dig a tunnel under the rock house that comes out on the west bank of the creek. It will be an escape hatch in case anybody gets over the walls of the fort or they try to cut me off from drinking water in a siege."

"That will take you a year to complete even with me helping you."

Mondo smiled. "That's one reason I stopped by here first thing. I can't handle those logs by myself, and there's a lot of work that you could help me with. Some of those rocks take two men to lift. I sure could use your help. How about it?"

Bear Chaser shook his head and then smiled. "You were always too stubborn for your own good. You have no business building on Little Beaver Creek, but I'll contact Ten Bears and see if he can help save your horses and your scalp. I guess I'll give you a hand, and maybe after a few attacks from young warriors, you will be ready to come back and live at my place."

Mondo thought about all the work they had both put in to making his compound, and he was proud of what they had accomplished. He hoped it was still standing. He remembered seeing the valley for the first time and knowing that's where he wanted to live. Together with his father, they completed the construction.

The creek still circled the little rocky hill. Little Beaver Creek came up from the north and touched the edge of the hill at the northeast corner, and then the creek turned back north and made a wide horseshoe-like circle and came right back past the little rock hill on the west side. The valley was about three hundred yards long and a hundred yards wide with the hill surrounded by the creek.

Mondo and his father worked sunup to sundown digging the basement and the tunnel to the creek and then the two room rock house on top of the hill. They kept Mondo's horses close by and didn't see any Indians. At first, Ten Bears kept the warriors from trying to steal Mondo's horses. Mondo grew stronger and darker as he worked in the warm sunshine. The rock house had a ten-by-twelve-foot room and a smaller room for sleeping and a hidden trapdoor on the floor with a ladder dropping to the basement. Four rifle holes, twelve inches by twelve inches, peaked out each side of the stone house.

As Mondo rode back toward his stockade, he recalled the time Ten Bears came to visit his father and himself. It was a hot day in August, 1867 when Mondo and his father looked up and saw Ten Bears riding up to the ten-foot wooden fence surrounding the little hill. The two men stopped working on the large gate on the north end of the fort and walked up to greet Ten Bears.

"Welcome, great warrior with big medicine," said Mondo.

"Good to see you, old friend," said Bear Chaser. Mondo helped the seventy-two-year-old Comanche leader down from his horse.

Ten Bears took a deep breath and looked at both men for a few seconds and then spoke. "Had to see what my old friends were putting together so no warrior could steal these fine long-legged horses that my young friend Mondo has brought into our country."

"You remember I always said I was going to live here some-day," said Mondo.

The white-haired chief nodded in agreement. "Yes, but who would have thought that you would bring those tall horses to tempt our young warriors? All the warriors want to steal one of these good-looking Thoroughbreds."

"We've had a few sneaking around," answered Bear Chaser. "I'm sure we owe you many thanks since we still have Mondo's horses."

Ten Bears smiled. "I just told the young bucks that these horses were too high to ride under trees, and the short Comanche warriors couldn't jump high enough to get on the back of one."

Ten Bears went over to the big black horse that Mondo had tied up near the rock cabin. "Is this your main ride?"

Mondo nodded his head. "You bet. I've had him two years. He's the best horse I've ever owned."

"Can he move those long legs fast enough to out run a good Comanche horse for a long distance and through trees?" asked Ten Bears.

"He starts a little slower, but he can run a long ways, and if he ever catches one of those short horses, they won't catch him back."

"What do you call this horse?"

"Tree Top," answered Mondo.

"Good name," answered Ten Bears. "That horse is too big to run all day. I would bet that a good Comanche horse could catch him and pass him if they ran for a long time."

"Maybe," said Mondo. "But that hasn't happened yet. No horse has ever caught up to Tree Top once he gets the lead."

"We'll see," said Ten Bears. And he looked at the wooden walls and the rock house. "Are you preparing to do battle with the Comanches and Kiowas like the whites did in Texas? You know that we have not had much love for these forts."

"I know. But I am preparing to stay here and live my life without any more battles. If anyone, white or Indian, comes to move me off, I'll use this fort for protection. There's enough land for the Comanches to allow me to live in peace in this little valley. Come on in and let's sit down and smoke for a lasting peace and friendship. I'm not an enemy to the Comanches, and you know that."

The three men entered the cabin and sat around a crude wooden table. Bear Chaser pulled out a pipe, lit it, and passed it around. Mondo studied the two older men, both all-Indian. Ten Bears was older, and wisdom lines streaked across his face surrounded by white hair. His eyes were still bright with intelligence. Ten Bears was shorter and stockier than Bear Chaser. Mondo's father was big for a Chickasaw, about six foot tall and weighed at least 210 pounds. His dark hair was streaked with gray, and his face seemed more square, featuring a broad nose and full lips. The main feature of Bear Chaser's face was the long, deep bear claw scar on his right cheek. Bear Chaser still had a lot of life left in him, but Ten Bears seemed like an old man that had worn down to a peaceful life by too many battles in his youth.

"I know you are not the enemy of the Comanche," said Ten Bears. "But these are dangerous times. The Comanches have been killed by Texas Rangers, and white man's disease has weakened us so that our largest bands have been pushed out of Texas, an area we controlled for over one hundred fifty years. The pride of a great warrior nation has been smashed. The young men are very angry and full of hate. They want to attack any and all who dare move in next to our territory. I can't keep the hotheads from stealing your horses and taking your scalp. You've built a hated fort right in their faces. We are going to a big pow-wow at Medicine Lodge in what the whites call Kansas. The big chief in Washington, D.C. wants to stop the Plains Indians from raiding, and that usually means that they will try to restrict our travel to a certain territory or area. More insult to our young men. Your horses and yourself are no longer safe. You have built a place right up close to one of our favorite campsites in the Wichita Mountains. You can almost see your fort on top of Medicine Bluff. The Comanches remember how they lost Texas. First cabins of white settlers, then Texas Rangers and forts of white soldiers. You need to move back to your father's place on Cow Creek inside the Cross Timbers and farther away from the Wichita Mountains. Your father says he can provide you all the land you want through a lease with him. Go back to the Chickasaw Nation. Stay out of the Comanche and Kiowa land."

Mondo stood up and looked down at Ten Bears. "Because of my Negro blood, I am not allowed to lease land in my own name.

I'm half-Chickasaw, but have no rights in that tribe. I will not move into the Chickasaw Nation and let my father hold my hand like I was still a child. I cannot ride under my father's protection or live on land where I'm not wanted. I'm here to stay. Let the young Comanche warriors come. I'll die before I run away any more."

Bear Chaser stood up and put his arm around Mondo's shoulder and smiled at Ten Bears. "I've raised a stubborn man. You remember when you were twenty-two years old, you were not afraid of anything, were you, Ten Bears? I know you are trying to help us. And we do thank you for all you've done. But right now, my son has to learn the hard way that he can't have everything he wants. There has to be some give-and-take. Remember how it took a few years of hardship before you finally saw the view of anyone else? I'll stay close and watch his back, and maybe we'll survive this stubborn streak of my son. I'm sorry that we can't take your good advice at this time."

Ten Bears rose and gripped Mondo with both arms and then did the same to Bear Chaser. "I'll do my best to keep Mondo from being burned out, but I can't stop the young men from trying to steal these horses. You might let them take a few. The challenge can't be as much if a warrior gets a few. Good luck, and may the medicine god protect you from flying arrows."

With that, Ten Bears left, and the next night, some Comanche warriors tried to steal Mondo's tall horses. Bear Chaser and Mondo ran them off and hurried to complete the gate on the wooden fence. A pecan tree fort, ten feet high and a hundred feet across and seventy-five feet long, was completed.

All that work last fall hadn't kept Storm from stealing his horses, but Mondo had now made friends with the Antelope band and hoped that they would not come after his horses or him again. As Mondo continued west past the Wichita Mountains, he neared his compound and hoped that all the effort he and his dad had put into his fort last year was not lost. In his mind, Mondo could see his wooden wall fence burned down, and he looked to the eastern sky for smoke. He didn't see any. As he neared the valley, he could see a bunch of horses outside the wall, and the gate stood wide open.

A bunch of people were waiting for him. Mondo spurred his horse toward his home.

CHAPTER 11

H UDSON GREER AND party led Maboola and Savanah past Fort Arbuckle and explained that Fort Arbuckle was the home of Negro troops in the Tenth Cavalry. The fort was surrounded by rock and timber walls, and through the front gate, they could see a rock-built headquarters, the stable, and two rows of brick bunkhouses. Maboola and Savanah had just ridden through the short, rocky Arbuckle Mountains and north to more flat-land containing thick timbers with a few spots of bare grass-land. As they dipped down toward Wildhorse Creek, they could clearly see the wooden shacks, lean-tos, and tent-like structures put together around the trees on both sides of the creek.

Negroes came out of the structures to watch Hudson Greer lead Maboola and Savanah to the center of the small community. A lot of the people were dressed in bright colors and wore their kinky hair in knotty little braids bound with lots of strings. Feathers were in their hats, and some had large brass earrings. Savanah had never seen Indian Negroes before and could see that the majority of the town dressed more like Indians than ex-cotton field workers.

In the center of town, there were several wooden cabins that had no written signs on them, but the largest was clearly a general store and a community meeting house. A small crowd gathered as the riders pulled up. Most were staring at Savanah even though this huge, deep-black Maboola caused much attention too. Hudson Greer dismounted and turned to the Negro Indians and ex-cotton field workers of Wildhorse Creek, who were all freedmen trying to survive in their own community.

"These here people are our guests. They are both freedmen from Texas. They will be staying with us for a few days, and I hope that they will stay with us forever. This big man is called Girt by the white folks, but his African name is Maboola. He likes to be called by his African name. He remembers our original homeland in Africa, so it would interest all of you to know everything about where he and our ancestors came from. But Maboola is wanted for killing the white Texan who put the deep scars on his back. If he stays, we must be ready to keep him from those bounty hunters and slave chasers who would lynch him in a second. So get to know him, and we'll have a free general vote on whether he stays on or not in a few days."

"Wait a minute," said Maboola as he dismounted and walked up to Hudson Greer, "I don't want any votes. I'm not staying just to bring trouble down on you all. I plan to move north anyway, and I might as well move out tomorrow."

Hudson smiled. "We'll see. Let's settle in and rest a while. We'll talk about it later." He then helped Savanah from her horse. "This here girl is called Savanah and was listed on the white slave roles as Savanah Jones before the Civil War. She was raised like a white woman and taught everything a white woman was taught, so she can read and write English. She knows no Chickasaw. A rich white man named Purify Jones has already sent some Texas gunmen to fetch her back. She may cause more trouble in our little town than Maboola himself. Again, we must get to know her and vote on whether she becomes part of our town."

"I would like to live here," said Savanah. "I want to be part of this place and get to know you all. I've never been around many ex-slaves. I don't want to bring bad outlaws down on you, but I'd like to see how you all live. I'll move on if I bring danger to this town."

With that, the group of ex-slaves living at Wildhorse Creek came forward and welcomed the newcomers. Dave Stevenson, a freedman from the Colbert plantation, welcomed Maboola and then Savanah and invited the both of them into his little log cabin for refreshments. Dave, Hudson Greer, and Maboola sat down at the table while Dave's wife showed Savanah the small garden each family had near their living area.

Dave looked at Maboola. "So, you're on the run, are you? You're not the only one. We have a whole plantation of ex-slaves from South Carolina that when the Yankee troops freed them, they took all they could from their master and headed toward Indian Territory. We have a little dispute going on with most of them. They are the ones who run the drinking and gambling joints on the "wild side" west of here up the creek. They encourage whites to come to their bars and prostitution houses, and they are making money. We would just rather live alone and keep watch out for the black haters who come sneaking around and causing trouble. We've got this place guarded, and we've got twenty-three pistols and rifles in our part of town, but the South Carolina blacks, controlled by a fellow by the name of Tan Bishop, have a lot more guns and ammunition than we do. They make money off sin living and buy better weapons."

"What do the Chickasaw Lighthorse Police say about your little community?" asked Maboola.

"Well, old Hubert Dixon rides in here once a month and tells us we have to leave, but we kind of gather around him and give him hard looks, and he moves on without getting off his horse. He tells us that the US government is going to move us out pretty soon and settle us out of Chickasaw country. According to Mr. Dixon, the three hundred thousand dollars the US government promised the Chickasaws and Choctaws, if they would make their freedmen members of their tribe, will be used to buy us land and move us on that new land away from here. Dixon says they will never make us members of the Chickasaw tribe.

So we just sit here and wonder whether we will get to stay here and whether the US Army will come and make us move. Most of us were raised in the Chickasaw Nation, and most of us have a lot of Indian ways. We don't want to leave the country we know. We want to stay here. A lot of us speak Chickasaw better than we speak English. We dress and farm like Indians and not white folks. We like this land. For the last thirty years, we've learned to live and farm here. We're not going. We are here to stay and if we have to, we'll fight to stay."

Hudson Greer nodded in agreement. "We're all for this. We've set up a town committee, and we vote on most all things. We are learning to live free and make our own way. Most of the Chickasaw freedmen who used to belong to full bloods, lived pretty much free even before the war. The Chickasaws who didn't have any white blood treated slaves like people. It is the mixed breeds who want to live and act like white plantation owners who want most of us out of here and who look down on us like we are savages. Even though whites look down on mixed-blood Chickasaws, no matter how much white they have, the Chickasaw half-breeds still do the same to anyone with black blood. It's hard to understand. But we are going to build a town here and show them that we can survive as a group and live like a civilized community. We are here to stay. That's how all of us voted in the church side of our community. Tan Bishop and his gang really don't care about making a town. They just want to make money off the weakness of all men."

Dave Stevenson spoke. "We need for Savanah to stay. She can read and write. We hardly have anyone who can do that. She can teach our children. We can't protect our rights and try to make agreements to stay unless we can read what they are trying to do to us. Failure to understand writing took the Chickasaws' way of life away and put the mixed bloods in charge. The full bloods as well as all Chickasaw freedmen are still being kicked around by the rich half-whites."

Maboola finally entered the conversation. "There were no whites or white blood in my father's tribe in Africa. We lived free and were our own boss. I was stolen as a child and brought here. I want to go back where the pure-blood blacks rule."

"You could tell us all about Africa," said Hudson Greer. "There's nobody here that's ever been there except you. There's all kind of stories passed down, but the whites tell us that we came from ignorant, uncivilized heathens that didn't even believe in Jesus. So most of us feel less of a person because we were taught that we are savages and beneath the civilized whites."

Maboola grunted in disapproval. "Yeah. Those poor second- and third-generation slaves don't know anything about being a person. They've been brought up being made to act subhuman. So they don't think they deserve to be free. I could never talk any other slave to try to break out and run for freedom with me. They were too afraid. They did not believe that they could live in the outside world. Their world was limited to one plantation, one master, and they had no belief in themselves. I never could understand why they didn't believe that freedom was good. They were so beat down that they couldn't or wouldn't think on their own. A lot had no thoughts. Most had no mind. The majority of slaves lived like animals because they were taught they were animals. That's going to be hard to change but it looks like you're getting a start right here in Wildhorse Creek. I hope you succeed, but it will take a while."

"That's why you must stay and help. Even before the Civil War, the Negroes that were free were looked down on by the Southern whites as free animals. You were a child in Africa where your dad ruled. You've been on top, and you've got to try to help us climb up there in our minds," said Hudson Greer.

"You don't want me here," said Maboola. "If the Texans let me get away with killing that white man who beat me, there's going to be a lot of ex-slave owners who beat slaves, who won't get any sleep. I've been told that among the whites, if another white man says something bad about his sister, that as a Southern gentleman, he would challenge that man to a duel and try to kill him. Now, think a minute. If you were willing to kill for a few words, wouldn't you certainly kill any man who kidnapped you and forced you to do his labor and chained you up and beat you with a whip? If those Southern people ever think of Negroes as human beings, with intelligence and pride and feelings, then the Southern whites could only think that all the free slaves will try to kill all the ex-slave owners because that's what a Southern plantation owner certainly would do if anybody had treated him like he treated his slaves. If ex-slaves start acting white, that will spread like a wildfire. The whites have to keep us in their minds as nonhuman, as animals, or they will certainly fear that we will try to rise up and kill them all. And another thing, if the so-called good Christians who believe in the Golden Rule admit that we were human, they are going to feel like they may go to hell for their sins against us when they die. Fear and guilt will rule the South for a long time. The South will have to stay drunk to keep from thinking about their past sins toward black people."

"You've done a lot of thinking on this," said Dave Stevenson. "I'm for spending more time thinking about now and what we're going to do to stay alive and grow and become educated. We can't change the feelings of the white people or the Chickasaw Indians, but we can stick together, work our farms, and try to make life better for each generation. Payback won't work for us. We don't have the numbers. There's not enough of us to fight the majority now or anytime in the future. We've got to learn to live together with the white man and the red man and grow with education. Equality will surely come with time."

Maboola nodded in agreement. "Well, right now, I'll stay a while and see how things go and see what Savanah decides. She doesn't really know what she wants to do. I think she should go with me up North and pass as white. She'd catch her a white husband real quick like with all her beauty. I'll help you protect this place for right now, and we'll see how bad Purify Jones and the Negro haters want to catch me and return Savanah to her place in Purify Jones's bed. It sounds like to me that you have enough trouble from within with the likes of Tan Bishop and his gang and the Chickasaw Lighthorse Police without me and Savanah bringing these Texas KKK people paid by Purify Jones down on your heads also." With that said, Maboola and Savanah agreed to stay at Wildhorse Creek for a while.

Chapter 12

As Mondo rode into the sight of his fort, on return from the Antelope band, his heart sank. The gate was open, and he could see many horses and men standing around inside the walls. Mondo turned his horses loose to graze in his valley. As he approached the gate and looked inside his stockade, he saw an argument going on between two men. He recognized his father and Hurbert Dixon, the Chickasaw policeman who had confronted him over a year ago when he first rode into Pickens County and came upon the ex-slave from Texas. His father was nose to nose with Dixon as about twelve Chickasaw Lighthorse Police stood around and watched the loud argument.

As soon as Mondo rode in, the talking stopped, and all turned to stare at him. Hurbert Dixon stepped forward, drew his pistol, and aimed it at Mondo.

"There you are. I knew you'd be out stealing more horses with those Comanches. You got a bunch of new horses since I seen you last. Those Comanche savages just killed Mr. Overton at Spanish Fort. Governor Harris has sent me to tell the commanders at Fort Arbuckle and over at Fort Cobb that if they don't stop the Comanches, by God, we Chickasaws will."

Mondo calmly dismounted and walked over to Hurbert Dixon. "So what's that got to do with me?" he asked. "I won those horses fair and square."

"If you weren't on the Comanches' side, they wouldn't let you keep this fort. And if you are with them, you are either helping them steal and kill, or you approve of it. I'll bet you stole those new horses with the Comanches," said Dixon.

"I don't steal. I won these horses racing when I was with the Antelope band of Comanches in the Texas Panhandle. What does that have to do with my stockade here? Why are you trespassing?" asked Mondo.

"I went to Fort Cobb and talked to Colonel Levinworth. Without a survey, we don't know whether this place is on Chickasaw land or on Comanche land, but either way, you have no legal right to build here. Colonel Levinworth heard that you were out in the Texas Panhandle riding with the Antelope band. Those are the wildest, meanest, and most hateful band of Comanches that ever lived. If you can return alive from being with them, then you have become a Comanche. Colonel Levinworth told me I had permission to burn this place down."

Bear Chaser stepped forward and looked at Mondo for a second and then turned to Hurbert Dixon. "I've told Mr. Dixon that you and I have entered into a partnership. That this is Chickasaw land and that I'm going to file a lease for you at Tishomingo City. He knows I'm full-blood Chickasaw, and I can lease to anyone unused land anywhere in the Chickasaw Nation. Now, until they have a survey, nobody knows whether this is Chickasaw or Comanche land. But if I put this property down in my name and I make a deal with Mondo to live here, then it's legal, and you can't do anything about it,Mr. Dixon."

Dixon answered, "When are you going to file the papers?" Before Bear Chaser answered, Dixon turned to Mondo, "Do you have a deal with your father? When did you two become a so-called partnership?"

"Were you fixing to burn my place down?" asked Mondo.

Bear Chaser stepped up. "That's right, son. He was going to burn the walls of this stockade and then have his Lighthorse Police tear down and scatter the rocks of your home."

Mondo looked at Dixon. "My father and I have a deal. We are in this together. I am going to raise horses and live here. We'll be heading for Tishomingo City real soon to finish signing and filing the necessary papers."

Hurbert Dixon frowned. "I'm going to check with Governor Harris. This fort is also a problem with the Texans that are driving their cattle herds to Kansas. These herders claim that Indians, both Chickasaw, Comanches, and all kinds of others, are stampeding their herds and taking their cattle. We're charging a dime a head for grazing rights as they cross our nation. The Texans say they have bought protection, and this fort is in their way."

"Yeah," said Mondo. "I saw a few of those herds last year. I don't bother those Texans, and they certainly don't bother me. To hell with them! The trail runs about two to three miles east of my place. I'm no problem to them."

"There's going to be a lot more herds in '68. As soon as spring hits, there's going to be cattle by the thousands rolling right near your fort. And those owners don't like a fort right on their trail that belongs to an Indian Negro. They are having big trouble from both the Indians and their freedmen down there in Texas. Some of the cattlemen have told Governor Harris they are not going to pay a dime a head to come through unprotected land. They claim this is the home base for raiding and stealing cattle. I'm going to recommend to Governor Harris that we destroy your fort. Also, you're too friendly with these Comanches and those foreign ex-slaves at Wildhorse Creek."

"I can choose my friends as I please, and I don't steal cattle. Did you find any cattle around here? I raise horses, and good horses, and that's all I do. I'm not with the Comanches. And I'm not with the Chickasaws. And I'm not with the freedmen. I'm here alone, and I expect to be left alone. Now just as soon as the weather breaks, my father and I are going to Tish City and get this settled. He has a right to this land because no one can prove it's not Chickasaw land. When we get it registered, I won't take any more crap from you or your Lighthorse Police. I strongly suggest you leave my home right now, and you're not welcome back."

Hurbert Dixon looked around and then turned his eyes to Mondo and then to his father. "I'm going this time. But if I find out you have been raiding with the Comanches or if Governor Harris tells me that this fort has to go for the protection of the cattlemen on their way to Abilene, Kansas, then I'll burn you out. You've been nothing but trouble ever since you rode through here. You should have stayed up with the Yankees and lived with the people you fought for. You can only stay alive in Comanche country by joining those savage raiders. I think you are helping them. I don't know where you belong, but it's damn sure not here whether it's Chickasaw country or Comanche country. Your days are numbered."

At that, Hurbert Dixon ordered his men to mount up, and they rode from Mondo's compound. As soon as they were out of sight, Mondo and his dad went into the cabin and sat down. "Why is Dixon in such an uproar?" Mondo asked.

"The last two months, the Comanches have been stealing horses and raiding all over the Chickasaw Nation. I heard that Dixon and the Lighthorse Police were going to Fort Arbuckle and then over to Fort Cobb to complain. Also, the rumor was you were raiding with the Comanches, so I came back to your place to try to help you keep them out."

"I've been out in the Texas Panhandle with the Antelope band. Who told Dixon that I was visiting that band?"

"I don't know, but word travels fast when there's Indian raids. Ten Bears was upset with his young warriors. He says that the Comanches are not staying on the reservation like Ten Bears promised at the Medicine Lodge Treaty. Dixon is right about the raids by the young Comanche warriors."

"Where did you meet up with Dixon?"

"I was here waiting for you. Dixon was going to burn your place down. Since the Comanches had not destroyed it and you were gone, Dixon figured you were riding with the Comanches. He heard those rumors about you being in the Texas Panhandle.

When I saw you coming with all those horses, I knew this place was going to go up in smoke. You rode in looking like a good Comanche horse thief."

"Well, I'm not a thief, and you know it. Do you think Dixon will come back and try to burn me out?"

Bear Chaser nodded. "I'm sure of it. He doesn't like ex-Yankee soldiers and where you live. Let's get this one thing settled first. Ride with me to Tishomingo City, and I'll register this stockade under my name. Then if this land is on Chickasaw land, you'll have a legal argument to stay here. The Chickasaws can't run you off even if you have some kind of deal with the Comanches. Let's lock up your horses in the stockade and leave them some feed and head off for Tish City. We'll be back in three days. Do this one thing, and I'll feel a lot better about you living out here on Little Beaver Creek."

Mondo agreed, and they set off for Tishomingo City.

CHAPTER 13

MONDO AND HIS father rode in silence toward Tishomingo City. Bear Chaser said nothing, and Mondo hated to ask for help whether it was from his dad or the Chickasaw Nation. About ten miles West of Fort Arbuckle on the Arbuckle Trail, a dark black giant rode out into the middle of the trail and stopped them.

Mondo looked at the biggest, blackest man he had ever seen. Even though the man sat on a normal-sized horse, his feet almost touched the ground. The man carried a double-barrel shotgun in his hands, had a pistol in his belt, and a machete hanging from his shoulder. The man had to be at least six and a half feet tall, and his black eyes glared with hatred.

Mondo, who hadn't been afraid for a long time thought to himself, *that's the scariest man I've seen in my life*. There was a long stalemate with both the riders staring at each other waiting for someone to make a move. Mondo was about to go for his pistol when a voice came from behind the trees. "Hold it, Maboola! I know this man. He saved me and my daughter when we first came here about a year ago."

Mondo glanced to his left as the ex-slave named Hudson Greer rode out of the brush. Mondo remembered the encounter with Greer when he was first going to his valley.

Mondo looked back at the man called Maboola and then asked Greer, "Who is this big man, and why is he blocking my path?"

"Maboola's an ex-slave from Texas. He's staying with us at Wildhorse Creek. There's a bunch of Texas bounty hunters coming after the girl who came with Maboola and escaped from a rich plantation owner in Texas who wants her back real bad, if you know what I mean."

"Does this guy talk English? He looks like he just got off the boat. There's sure no white blood dirtying his soul," said Mondo.

"Oh yeah, he can talk English," said Greer. "He just doesn't talk much until he gets to know you. He hasn't been at Wildhorse Creek long, and his life has been real tough. He is helping us guard our little town."

"Tell him I've got African blood, and my dad, Bear Chaser, here, he doesn't go for those part-white Chickasaw's being against ex-slaves. I know my dad thinks a man should be born free and stay free all his life."

"In that case, we'll let you both pass unless you want to join us. We're waiting for a bunch of bounty hunters. We got a message from our friends on the Red River that there's about eight or ten bounty hunters who have been sent to take back Savanah, the woman who rode in with Maboola. We've got people all around here ready to move if anybody sees those killers. We had word they were coming right through here, and that's why Maboola stopped you two."

"Tell him we're not bounty hunters. I'd feel a lot better if he'd lower that shotgun and let us get on our way to Tishomingo City."

Before anybody could answer, a shot rang out and tore the shotgun out of Maboola's hands. Mondo had his pistol in his hand when eight riders dressed like cowboys with pistols drawn, broke from the post oak forest on the south side of the Arbuckle Trail and surrounded the four men. Mondo eased his pistol back into his holster and turned to face the white men.

The first man that caught his attention was the ugliest man he had ever seen. His face was cut in half, right down the center. It looked like somebody had taken a knife and started from his hairline down between his eyes and to his chin and had split his nose in half as well as both his upper and lower lips. A big red scar separated what at one time had been his whole face. You could hardly notice the scar when you looked into the man's eyes. Mondo had never seen more insane hatred glaring from each side of the quarter-inch red scar. The man was glaring at Maboola and was gripping and squeezing his pistol as if he couldn't wait to shoot the big black Negro.

But he wasn't the man that spoke. The big blond-headed Texan with a white Stetson hat, sitting on a large horse smiled an evil smile and spoke, "Now, boys, we didn't come to kill you all. We came for Savanah. Purify Jones wants his house gal back, and he's paid us well to come get her. We know she lives with a bunch of ex-slaves at Wildhorse Creek. You've got about twenty minutes to ride in there and fetch her out or we are going to kill you all and then we are going to raid that place and shoot every darky living on that creek except her."

At the sound of that threat, the ugly man with the scarred face tried to smile, which only widened the cut space on his lips.

Hudson Greer raised his hands and eased his horse up close to the speaker. "I don't know what you men have heard, but there's no Savanah at Wildhorse Creek. I don't think you have any idea of how many ex-slaves are staying there now. We don't want to start trouble and we don't want an army of white men trying to raid our little town, so I'd advise you all to turn around and go on back to Texas."

The leader smiled, but before he could speak, Split Face pushed his horse close to Hudson Greer and yelled, "Boy, who do you think you're talking to? You're already dead for talking to a respectable white man like that. Darkies don't tell whites what to do. Now take us to this Savanah before we kill every worthless soul at Wildhorse Creek."

"Simmer down, Bart," said the white leader. "We want to negotiate this without a whole lot of killing. We're being paid to bring back the Negress named Savanah, and that's all we want right now. If you coloreds want to build you a town back there in the woods and just stay out of the way, that's good by me. But you got to give us Savanah, or we'll go in there and take her. That's the Lord's truth. So, what's next? Are you going to get her for us, or are we killing you first and going in there and get her second?"

Hudson Greer raised his hand and, without a sound, twenty-five armed Negroes eased from the northern woods with guns pointed at the bounty hunters. It was such a surprise that the white men didn't have time to fire a shot. The Texans were shocked into no action. They had never seen a group of so many armed blacks in their life. These men did not look like beaten slaves. There was no fear on their faces. The ex-slaves stepped forward and aimed their guns at the whites as if they had no hesitation in killing them right there on the spot.

Hudson Greer spoke. "Best move on out. Like I say, we don't want white trouble or Indian trouble. But if we see you again around the Wildhorse Creek area, we're going to fire on you. We've got lookouts all over the place, and we'll know when you cross the Red River. We will be waiting for you, and this is not all the men and weapons that we got. There's over five hundred of us back there, and our town is well guarded. Now go back and tell your master to look somewhere else for this Savanah girl or get himself a white piece of ass like he should."

The leader looked around and nodded in agreement, "All right. Boys, we better move out. It looks like they got the numbers and the drop on us. Wait till the KKK hears about armed darkies drawing down on whites. We'll be back with a lot more men, and we will get Savanah, and we will destroy your town. Let's go, men. We've got to go talk to some big-time people."

As he turned and rode, everyone turned with him except the man with the split face. He looked like he was going to have a heart attack. He stuttered and sputtered, and tears came out of his glaring eyes. It was obvious that he wanted to kill every black man standing around there but decided the odds were he'd get killed in the process.

Maboola took his machete off his shoulder. Split Face glared back and then turned his horse and followed the others away. As the Texans disappeared in the post oak forest to the south, Hudson Greer eased up toward Mondo and Bear Chaser. "Looks like you fellows got caught in the middle of what was almost a big white-man killing. We knew these guys were coming. We staked out this place, and Maboola and I were out here for bait. We wanted to stop them before they got close to our town."

Mondo looked around. "You've got a pretty strong-looking bunch of men. But those whites are going to come back. That Savanah must be some kind of gal if her ex-master is going to pay big bucks for her." Mondo looked over at Maboola, and the giant just nodded and then rode off down the road away from the group and turned into the south woods where the whites had gone.

Mondo looked back at Greer. "What's with that man? He talks less than I do."

"He's real nice if you're his friend. You just don't want to be his enemy. I've heard that you built you a fort right down on the Comanche border. The Chickasaws are even saying you sided with the Comanche. Our scouts have seen a bunch of Comanches raiding Chickasaws around here, but they sure haven't touched us. We're trying to make a safe place for our kind up at Wildhorse Creek. The woods are really thick back there, and we know the way in and out. We've trained our people, and we're real careful about who comes and who goes. So far, there has been very few white men come back there looking for trouble. We have only one problem. Tan Bishop operates a bar, a gambling house, and sells girls at the west end of town. He wants the white man's money. Mostly we good citizens keep to ourselves on the east end."

A shot rang out in the forest to the south. Everyone looked in that direction. They waited. Then all of a sudden, Maboola burst through the thick branches and rode out with the leader of the Texans lying across his saddle. The man was bleeding and unconscious. Maboola dismounted.

Hudson Greer stepped forward and glared at Maboola. "What did you do that for? We don't want to bring the whole state of Texas down on us. Is he dead?"

"Not yet," said Maboola and lifted up the man's head by his hair and cut his head off with his machete. As the others watched in shocked silence, Maboola wrapped a rope around the leader's feet, threw the rope over a tree, and lifted the white man's body in the air upside down.

"Cut him down," said Hudson Greer.

Maboola turned to Greer. "I'll kill any man that touches that rope. This white bastard was slipping up on us to back shoot us. The rest went on. This bounty hunter is going to hang in this tree right along this trail to warn every other white man that comes in here not to mess with us and for sure Savanah. It's my upside-down lynching.

I want every white man to see this and feel the fear that their lynching is causing us. Let's see how they take a little of their own medicine."

Maboola surveyed the group, and no one objected.

"You're wrong, Maboola," said Greer. "We're still few in number. This isn't going to help us with the Chickasaws, and this darn sure isn't going to keep our people safe from the KKK in Texas and from coming across over here and doing us harm."

Maboola glared at Greer. "The only way we can live halfway free at Wildhorse Creek is to scare the hell out of anyone coming around here to make trouble for us. The KKK is ruling by fear in Texas, and we're going to do the same right here."

Mondo looked over at his dad and nodded. "We better go." Mondo then looked at Greer and spoke, "I'm leaving. You men just started a war, and I just got out of a war. I don't want anything to do with this. All I want is my land and peace and quiet. If anybody asks, me and my dad were not here and never saw any of this." At that, Mondo and his dad started east in a hurry to Tishomingo City.

CHAPTER 14

WITHOUT A WORD said between father and son, Mondo and Bear Chaser pushed their horses toward Tishomingo City and away from the hanging of the Texas bounty hunter. Both men had grim thoughts about a very black Negro lynching a very white Texan. They had heard stories about the occupation of the Yankee troops in Texas and their takeover of the state government activities. The Texans hated Yankee control. A vengeful US Congress had assumed control over the reconstruction of the South and had intended to punish all those who fought for the Confederacy. Anyone that did not remain loyal to the Union during the Civil War was not allowed to vote. All slaves were put on the voting rolls, and the US Freedmen's Bureau attempted to protect the ex-slaves from hostilities. However, at night, the KKK had appeared and had used violence and fear to keep the ex-slaves from voting and living as free citizens. Hanging without a trial was a white activity.

The black community on the Wildhorse Creek wasn't but about fifty miles north of the Texas state line, and outlaws from Texas had been coming into the Chickasaw Nation for years, stealing horses and raiding without fear since no white US citizen could be caught and tried in the Chickasaw Nation but had to be delivered to the Federal courts in Arkansas. Now the secret society of hooded men, known as the KKK made up of ex-Confederate veterans with killing experience, had a new target. As soon as the word got back to Texas that a citizen of their state had been decapitated and hung by his feet by an all-black community, reward money would be posted, and every broke gunman in Texas would be gathering gangs and coming after anyone in Wildhorse Creek and mainly the highly recognizable *Maboola*. Most Texans felt that Texas law and Texas justice traveled anywhere a Texas citizen went and was mistreated.

In addition, the Texas ranchers were starting to send thousands of cattle through the Chickasaw Nation to Abilene, Kansas, and anything or anyone who stood in the way of the large herds of cattle would be dealt with by the tough ex-Confederate cowboys from Texas. Cattle were about the only way a broke Texan with initiative could make some money.

Mondo worried about all the explosive problems that would come from the hanging of the Texan as he rode across the Pennington Creek Bridge into Tishomingo City. It had been several years since Mondo had been there. A new three-story wooden capital building had been built on the hill north of Pennington Creek, and several shops and stores had opened along the main street that ran east and west paralleling the creek. Without wasting any time, Mondo and Bear Chaser entered the Chickasaw capital building and went to the land lease office on the first floor. A young man named Jason Colbert rose from behind the desk and greeted them.

"Hello, Bear Chaser," said Colbert. He looked over at Mondo. "I guess this is your son I've heard so much about. Fought for the wrong side, but the side that won."

Bear Chaser nodded a quick hello and got down to business. "I've come to file on some land way out west in Pickens County near Comanche and Kiowa country. My son has built on the property, and I've agreed to lease it to him."

"That's fine. A lot of Chickasaws are leasing property and making deals with white men and even Chickasaw ex-slaves to operate it. In fact, Mort Johnson up around Paul's store, has two or three ex-slaves raising cattle on property that he has signed up for his use. Now, where is this land that you want your son to operate?"

Bear Chaser nodded to a map on the wall. "It's on Little Beaver Creek, right on the west edge of Pickens County."

Colbert got up from his chair and looked at the map and shook his head. "I'm not sure that's in the Chickasaw Nation. The federal government took all property west of the 98th meridian from us after the war for picking the wrong side to fight for. The government has just started to survey all our nation and probably won't get to that area for three or four years. However, I'll put it in your name and we'll just see where it falls after the survey. You're doing the right thing. It's the only way a person with Negro blood can work the land."

Mondo spoke for the first time. "And why is that? I'm half-Chickasaw!"

Colbert sat back down and looked at Mondo. "In the treaty we had to sign last year with the US government, Washington, D.C., gave us two years to make all the Chickasaw ex-slaves Chickasaw citizens, and the government would pay the Choctaws and Chickasaws $300,000. If in two years we don't make them Chickasaw citizens, the US government will take that money and find a reservation or some land for all the Choctaw and Chickasaw freedmen. Most Chickasaws want the US government to settle our ex-slaves someplace else. We can't make them members of the tribe."

"I was not a slave, and I was born free as Bear Chaser's son. I'm just as much Chickasaw as black, and I've got more Indian blood than some of the Chickasaw leaders. The treaty with the US doesn't concern me."

"Well, some of the Chickasaws, mostly mixed-bloods like me, think like Southerners and are against a person who has black blood becoming tribal members. But the majority of the tribe realized that it's a numbers problem. As you know, there were a lot of Chickasaws who owned slaves. We don't know the exact number. However, nobody can enroll as a Chickasaw freedman unless they are registered by the Chickasaw who owned that slave. We already have over three thousand Negroes trying to claim they are Chickasaw freedmen. There has been a lot of ex-slaves come in from Texas and Louisiana, and they're all wanting us to take care of them. If we took their word for it, there would probably be more Chickasaw freedmen than Chickasaws. There's just five thousand Chickasaw. If all ex-slaves living here became members of our tribe, the Chickasaws would be a minority in their own nation. Now how would you like that?" he asked, looking over at Bear Chaser.

"We were making contracts with the Chickasaw slaves and living side by side with them before the Civil War. Most Chickasaws, especially the full-bloods, got along with them pretty well. I have met some pretty rough characters that have come into our nation since the end of the war, but there's more bad white men than bad black men. My son is half-Chickasaw, and he shouldn't be punished just because he's got a little Negro blood. He's not part of the problem. He was free before the war and half-Chickasaw, and he should have as much rights as any Chickasaw."

Colbert spoke. "I understand what you're saying, and I agree with you. But we haven't got good records at all on most Negroes. As soon as we make an exception in Mondo's case, every freedman in our nation would claim he was part-Chickasaw. We'd spend all our time going to court trying to determine without any records who had Chickasaw blood. All these ex-slaves would have to do is get three or four witnesses to lie for them, and we would have hell in a US Yankee court disputing their claims. Once we give in to people with Negro blood that are living in our nation, we will lose control, and the Chickasaw tribe will be no more. We don't mistreat slaves. Never have. Some of my best friends are Negroes. They were part of my family. I loved the nanny that raised me. It's just politics. We have to maintain control of our own tribe. After all, the Chickasaw Nation is a government of Indians."

Bear Chaser knew it was pointless to argue. "All we want right now is a piece of paper that shows that through me, Mondo has a right to stay on his place. I would appreciate it if you'd get started on the paperwork."

Colbert told them to come back in an hour and he would have everything ready to be signed. Mondo and Bear Chaser walked out of the courthouse and looked over at a group of people standing in the center of Main Street. There seemed to be much excitement, and Mondo and Bear Chaser walked toward the people standing around a man yelling at another man.

As they got nearer, they both froze in their tracks. The ugly man with the red scar down the center of his face was yelling at Hurbert Dixon, the captain of the Pickens County Lighthorse police.

"They shot him in the back, cut off his head, and strung him up by his feet. They didn't even have the decency to hang him proper like. They lynched him like he was worse than a damned darky! King Harper went back to get an ex-slave that broke her contract with her master. When we looked for King, there he was, hanging by his feet from a tree, bleeding from the neck of his headless corpse. We cut him down. It was the one they call Maboola, a big coal-black ex-slave that kidnapped Miss Savanah. He's the main one we're after. Now if you don't do something about it, by God I'll go back to Texas and bring in a hundred man posse with guns blazing, and we'll kill all the darkies as well as all the Indians helping them."

Hurbert Dixon held up his arms to calm the man called Bart, but known as Split Face, and the six other armed Texans standing around him.

"We'll investigate. And if there's evidence, we'll take this Maboola to Little Rock, and he'll be tried and hung. You Texas bounty hunters don't have any right to come into the Chickasaw Nation and try to enforce your version of the law. We'll look into this matter. But I suggest you men ride on back to Texas and let us handle this problem."

One of the Texans noticed Mondo and Bear Chaser. "There's two of them now. They were with them."

Split Face drew his gun and started to turn toward Mondo and Bear Chaser. Before Split Face completed his turn, Mondo had his pistol aimed at the Texan. Nobody fired, and the crowd eased back so that Mondo and Bear Chaser were facing the seven Texans. All had pistols cocked and ready to fire.

"Hold it!" yelled Dixon and drew his gun, and when the Chickasaws looked over and recognized Bear Chaser, most of the Chickasaws in the crowd who had weapons drew their guns and aimed toward the Texans.

The Texans looked around and saw they were out-numbered, and the red from the scar spread all over Split Face's complexion as he tensed, aching to shoot Mondo.

Dixon spoke, "Take it easy and nobody is going to get hurt. I know these men, and they do not live at Wildhorse Creek. If you've got evidence they were in on the killing, I'll arrest them and we'll try Bear Chaser here and take Mondo to Arkansas."

"They don't deserve a trial," said Split Face. "All of us saw them with that colored hangmen. We can kill them now or we can kill them later, but those bastards are going to die. No darky or any-body with him is going to get away with lynching a white man."

"These two weren't there," said a tall, thin, blond-haired cow-boy that eased up from the crowd. "Mondo and Bear Chaser were with me all day looking at horses. I'm Mick O'Ryan from Texas, and all these town-folks know me. I've been in and out of the Chickasaw Nation for years, buying and selling horses."

Mondo and Bear Chaser recognized Mick O'Ryan. Mondo hadn't seen Mick in years, and the kid had certainly grown. He was at least six feet tall, very thin, blue-eyed, and a handsome, cocky-looking cowboy. Before the war, Mick's father had sold horses in the Chickasaw Nation, and he had a good reputa-tion as an honest trader. Bear Chaser had done a lot of business with Mick's father. Mick and Mondo had spent time together when they were youngsters. Mick was about two years younger than Mondo.

"That's a damn lie," snapped Split Face. "I don't know why you are a yellow-bellied turncoat to decent white people, but you don't want to get mixed up in this. These two are as good as dead, and if you're not careful, you will go down with them, young man. You haven't seen enough of life yet to die so young."

Mick smiled. "I just think you're making a mistake, Mr. Split Face."

With his face turning deep red, the scarred Texan yelled at Mick. "My name's not Split Face. My name is Bart Bradford. The last man that called me Split Face ain't around no more. You sure are begging to die. You just don't have much sense."

Mick's smile broadened. "I'm so sorry, Mr. Split Face. I didn't know you were touchy about that big red scar that runs right down the middle of your face. But I agree with the law here in Tish City. You have no business in the Chickasaw Nation if you come to do harm. My dad and I were trading in this country before the Civil War, and these are honest, hard-working people. I've been listening to your hollering. If some big plantation owner back in Texas has a claim on one of his house Negroes, I think he better get over it. The South lost the war. The sooner those big-shots South of the Red admit they lost, the sooner everyone will be able to get back to the business of living."

Split Face took a step forward to Mick. "Don't you be telling me what for." He looked at Dixon. "If you don't arrest these two, there's going to be a lot of killing right here and now."

The cock of rifles and pistols startled Split Face as the Chickasaws readied their weapons on the Texans.

Hurbert Dixon spoke. "If there's any killing, I know of seven Texans that are going to die for damn sure. I'm giving you ten minutes to mount up and get out of Tish City, or Texas blood is going to run through these streets like it was the little Red River."

The red-faced Texan grumbled and mumbled and breathed hard in and out for a few seconds, spewing mucous and spit. Then he jerked around and started for his horse, and the other six Texans followed. As soon as the seven Texans crossed the Pennington Creek Bridge heading south toward the Red River, the crowd put away their weapons.

Dixon looked over at Mondo. "From the first day that you rode into the Chickasaw Nation, you've been nothing but trouble. Every time I see you, there's a shooting about to happen. I'm also tired of those uppity Texans coming over here and acting like they run our nation. I suggest that you and your father get on back to that fort of yours and stay there. I don't want to know about no white hanging. If your father's got the legal papers, I won't bother you, but you stay away from here. Besides, the Comanches or Kiowas will finally do you in. You can't trust those renegades. I don't feel good about you. Deep down I know someday, if you don't stay out of my way, I'm going to have to shoot you."

Mondo started toward Dixon, and Mick stepped in front of him and gave a big smile and stuck out his hand. "Good God, Mondo, you've grown up to be quite a man. I doubt if I could whip your ass anymore."

The big smile stopped Mondo, and he took Mick's hand and shook it. "You never could whip my ass. You were always a skinny Irish runt. You're just a little taller now, that's all."

Mondo leaned over and whispered in Mick's ear. "And you always were a good liar. Thanks for the help. I owe you one."

Bear Chaser walked up and patted Mick on the back. "Good to see you again. How's your dad?"

Mick frowned and shook his head. "He never came back from the war. He made me promise not to join the Confederacy, but he said he had to fight for Texas, even though he didn't believe that it was a good fight. As you know, I stayed on the Texas frontier and in the Chickasaw Nation, taking care of the horses. Dad never came back."

Mondo said, "I'm sorry to hear that. The war cost the lives of a lot of good men. I'm in the horse business now. I've got a small herd of about twenty-five over near Comanche-Kiowa country. What are you doing now?"

"I'm trying to build up my own herd. I've got about thirty corralled outside of town. I've been buying mostly Indian horses and selling them to the Texas outfits herding cattle to Abilene, Texas. It's been good to me so far."

Dixon walked up. "Just soon as your business is complete, I want you out of town," he said to Mondo.

"Don't worry. I've stayed here a lot longer than I want. I don't hang around where I'm not wanted. But no one runs me off. In the future, always be sure that I'm ready to leave before you tell me to go."

Bear Chaser took Mondo and Mick by the arm and turned them away from Dixon.

"Let's go check Mick's horses. Why don't you ride back with us and see Mondo's spread?" asked Bear Chaser.

Before Mondo could object, Mick shook his head in the affirmative. "I might do that. It's been a long time since I've seen you two. Besides, my horses need some fresh grass, and I've heard that where you live, ain't nobody but wild Indians raising horses. How in the hell do you keep from being scalped by the Comanches or the Kiowas?"

"Oh, I get a little protection from Ten Bears. And I know a few good warriors that I get along with. So far, I've been able to keep my horses, but it hasn't been easy. It's too dangerous for you to stay long, but why don't you ride back with us and I'll show you my setup?"

Mick agreed to visit Mondo, and the three of them gathered Mick's horses and started toward Mondo's compound. They swung north toward Paul's store on the Washita River to avoid the Wildhorse Creek settlement near the Arbuckle Road. They followed Rush Creek west toward Mondo's fort.

Mick was a talker. The ride back toward Mondo's fort was full of conversation. Mick was one of those people that just couldn't stand silence. He was either talking about something or asking questions about everything. Silence made him nervous. They weren't far out of Tishomingo City before Mick started talking about the Texas bounty hunters.

"Do you know about that Split Face?" asked Mick.

Mondo answered, "Never heard of him. What's his story?"

"He's been notorious for quite a few years. He used to be a famous runaway-slave catcher before the end of the Civil War. One day toward the end of the war, he bit off more than he could chew."

"Is that how he got that ugly scar?" asked Mondo.

"That's what I hear. The story goes that he got a hold of one slave that attacked him and even after Split Face put three bullets in the runaway, the slave was able to bury a hatchet right down the middle of his face. It wasn't deep enough to kill him, but it sure was deep enough to mark him for life. Before that, catching slaves was a business for Split Face. After that, instead of a slave catcher, he became a slave killer."

Mondo nodded and asked, "Who is this Savanah they keep talking about? I gather she belonged to some white plantation owner in Texas and ran off and now belongs to that mean-look-ing black man they call Maboola. We ran into him on our way to Tish City."

"I've heard Maboola's mean enough to keep her," said Mick. "The story goes that she used to belong to that Purify Jones who owns a big plantation in North Texas. He used her for his own pleasure and didn't let her go after the war. She ran off with Maboola and made it to Wildhorse Creek. Purify Jones hired that King Harper to go get her back, and King Harper hired Split Face. Stringing up that King Harper was a mistake. Wildhorse Creek is too close to Texas, and in Texas, there's a lot of men who won't allow any colored person to live that stands up to a white man."

Mondo shook his head. "I never could figure why those white people hate so much. I understand why Split Face has a lot of hate, but what did the black people ever do to the rest of them

Texans to make them hate people with color? Is it because we're a different color, or is it really because they're afraid the ex-slaves will seek revenge or won't work the low-paying jobs?"

Mick answered, "When I was growing up, I spent a lot of time with you and your father and I met a lot of good black people. I never did understand color hate myself. I studied on it when I was back in Texas and listened to some of those hating men talk. It's kind of like those evil people think they have to have someone below them. They feel if it wasn't for the black people, most of the sorry, dumb whites would be at the bottom of the barrel. Most haters are bad people. They know they're not worth a damn. And they don't feel good about themselves. A man that feels good about himself doesn't need to feel that somebody is beneath him."

Mondo added, "Or they're afraid the ex-slaves will kill their ex-masters. The white owners sure would kill anybody who treated them like they treated their slaves. Whites can get together and kill in a group better than nonwhites."

Bear Chaser spoke. "The Indian tribes could never get together to stop the white man from taking all the land. Each tribe thought their tribe was the best and had all the answers on how to live with the Great Spirit, and each thought they had the best warriors. There were so many different languages they never could sit down and really work out their differences. If they'd spoken the same language, they'd understand how much alike they all were. The Chickasaws and Comanches don't like each other at all. But with Ten Bears, I learned to talk Comanche, and we found out there wasn't a whole lot of difference between us, but Indians have to be able to understand each other to discover their likeness."

Mick nodded and looked over at Bear Chaser and then glanced at Mondo. "Did you know that your dad saved my life?"

Mondo looked up in surprise, "No, I don't know much about what my dad did while I was off fighting the war."

Mick continued. "When my dad went off to war, I kind of wandered around, trying to sell some horses in Texas and Indian Territory. I hooked up with your dad, and when a bunch of Texas enforcers for the Confederacy captured my horses to use in the war, they took me back to Texas to make me join the army. We spent the night just across the Red River, and your dad slipped into our camp, untied me and I got away. Of course, I never did get my horses back, but if it wasn't for your dad, I'd probably died just like my dad."

There was silence for a while, and then Mondo looked over at both of the other men. "Neither one of you fought in the war. Why was that?"

Mick answered first. "My dad made me promise not to go. He said it was a silly war, and only one of us was going to risk our life, and it wasn't going to be his only son. That's what he said, and that's what I did."

Mondo looked over at his father. His father looked back at him. "I kind of hoped those white men would kill each other off. They destroyed the Chickasaw way of life. Of course, those half-breed rich Chickasaws thought they were white and had to join in the battle. I think they just didn't want to lose their slaves. It wasn't my war. The Americans have taken enough from the Chickasaws. I sure wasn't going to give them my life. They both just wanted to use Indians for cannon fodder like always."

They rode in silence for a few minutes as they eased their horses north of the Arbuckle Mountains and headed west toward Mondo's fort. Mondo heard Mick ask Bear Chaser, "Why did you send for me?"

"I heard you were trading with the cattlemen in Texas and doing pretty good. I thought you could help Mondo."

Mondo stopped and looked back at his dad. "You mean you sent for Mick?"

"That's right. How are you going to trade with those white Texas cattlemen with your black blood? The ones that will trade with you will try to cheat you."

Mick spoke up. "I think most of the trail bosses and the owners will trade fair with Mondo even though he's part-Negro, but they are all hard traders, and they will want the best deal. However, there will be a bunch of Texas haters that will think Mondo's curly black hair will be a license to cheat and steal as well as kill."

"That's why I sent for him," said Bear Chaser. "You can raise them and Mick can sell them."

"I'll think about it. All I know is the more people I'm around, the more likely trouble. Mick may not want to partner up."

"Let's look at your place and your stock. I know already that we're getting close to Comanche and Kiowa territory. I'm just going to visit for right now. You live too close to death, Mondo," said Mick.

They rode in silence for a while and then Mick rode up to Bear Chaser. "If I remember right, you got your name because you chased a mother bear down to return her cub that she had lost. Isn't that true?"

Bear Chaser smiled. "Yeah, that's right. But that was a long time ago. When I was a kid, I found a cub that had got lost from his mother. I tried to return the cub, but the mother had another baby, and she kept running from me. For two days, I chased her, and when I finally got near her, she attacked me. That's how I got this scar on my cheek. I stayed up in a tree for another two days before she finally wandered off. The Chickasaws laugh when they think about how I got my name. It wasn't for bear hunting or bear killing, it was for being too kind to bears."

"Well, you've still done a lot for people. You sure took care of me when my dad left. I sure miss my old man."

Bear Chaser nodded. "Did you ever hear anything from him?"

"Not a thing, and I've asked around a lot. I heard he went all the way to Gettysburg with that Texas unit, and a whole lot didn't come back from there. It's been about four or five years, and if he were alive, I'm sure he would have made it back to me or got word at least. The old man was kind of tough on me, but it was good for me. You don't know how much you care about someone until they're gone for good."

War cries echoed through the air. The three turned and saw twelve screaming Kiowas riding down on them at full speed.

CHAPTER 15

THE KIOWAS CHARGED from a thick, matted scrub oak forest, and they were on the three men before anyone had time to react. The herd of horses stampeded. Mick's horse was shot out from under him. Bear Chaser was knocked off his horse with a blow from a Kiowa's lance. Mondo's horse turned and reared, twirling Mondo around so that he couldn't get a good shot at the screaming Indians. By the time Tree Top settled down, Mondo saw the Kiowas moving out with all of Mick's horses. Mondo fired from the hip and took a Kiowa off his horse about thirty yards away. Mondo charged toward the fallen Kiowa, jumped from his mount, lifted the Indian up by the neck, and put a pistol to the Kiowa's head.

The Kiowas pulled up and turned when the Kiowa fell from his mount and all, but the two driving the horses away charged toward Mondo. Seeing that Mondo had a gun at the Kiowa's head, the Indians halted.

The captured Kiowa, wounded in the shoulder, yelled at his friends to attack and kill Mondo. By the time the dust settled, Mick had run over to Mondo's side, and Bear Chaser limped up, bleeding from a wound to his hip. A short, but desperate stand-off occurred.

Bear Chaser saw at once what Mondo was doing. They both knew that a Kiowa would never leave a fallen warrior, and the attackers would do anything to get him back alive. Bear Chaser spoke in Comanche and advised the Kiowas to return the horses and the warrior would be returned. Most Kiowas could under-stand Comanche.

The Kiowa leader answered in Comanche, "We will let you three live if you return Eagle Eyes to us."

Mondo answered back in Comanche. "We are just a few miles from my fort. You send somebody after those horses and bring them to my place and we'll talk about a trade. We won't kill Eagle Eyes unless you attack us again. Do we talk, or does this man die?"

Without hesitation, the Kiowa answered, "You think that we should return the horses of the one we call Buffalo Spirit? We've been trying to get your horses for a long time, and now that we've got some, it would be a great dishonor to give them back."

Mondo smiled. "They're not my horses. Don't you see how short those horses are? Those horses belong to this puny white man. There's not much honor in stealing his horses."

"Who is that white man? Is he a Texan?" asked the Kiowa leader.

Mondo looked over at Mick. "He asked if you are a Texan."

"I'm from Kansas," lied Mick.

Mondo interpreted in Comanche. "Why, he's not even from Texas. He's a mere skinny white from Kansas. Anyone could steal a horse from a weak white kid from Kansas."

The Kiowa leader thought for a minute and then answered, "We will send for the horses and meet you back at your little fort. We'll talk trade. Eagle Eyes has a big family and is well thought of. If you kill him, the whole Kiowa nation will burn you out."

At that, the Kiowas turned and rode off and Mick crawled on behind Mondo. Bear Chaser caught his mount, and the three men headed for Mondo's place with the Kiowa captive tied up and walking behind them.

"See what happened?" said Mondo. "I was with you two and we were talking instead of listening. I was thinking about something other than keeping safe, and for the first time, Indians slipped up and surprised me. When I'm around people, I can't keep myself alert. These Kiowas and Comanches around here have been trying to steal my horses for almost a year, and this is the first time they succeeded."

"They ain't your horses," said Mick. "They're mine. And if you had been alone, they would have killed you, but with the three of us, they knew we would get a bunch of them. A man has to be crazy to ride alone through this country."

Bear Chaser, who was leading the Kiowa with a rope around his neck, finally replied. "Those Kiowas will trade back most of Mick's horses to free this warrior. You haven't lost your horses yet. Mondo was smart to take this captive. Those Kiowas never leave one of their own behind. They've lost too many warriors from disease and bullets to give one up."

By the time they reached the fort, the Kiowas and Mick's horses were already waiting outside the fort. There were several more warriors and a Kiowa girl sitting on a horse off to the side. Her back was straight and her eyes were turned up to the sky.

"Now that's a good-looking girl," said Mick.

Mondo glanced at her and replied, "If you want your horses back, you better keep your mind on trading and off that girl. She's probably here to distract you."

Mick studied the Kiowa girl. "She doesn't look like a Kiowa to me. She looks more like a Mexican captive."

As the three men rode through the gate to the compound, they found all of Mondo's horses safely inside. They bandaged Bear Chaser's flesh wound and started a fire so they could sit around and bargain with the Kiowas.

About twenty Kiowas had gathered outside and waited to come into Mondo's compound. After Mondo tended to his own horses, he walked to the door and signaled them to ride in. The Kiowas brought the girl in with them.

The Kiowas dismounted, but the girl stayed on her horse. They immediately started examining Mondo's horses in the compound and then finally walked over, and three of the Kiowas sat down around the fire while the others stood behind the powwow circle.

Mondo, Bear Chaser, and Mick all sat down cross-legged. And Bear Chaser pulled out a peace pipe, lit it, and passed it around. After each had smoked, the Kiowa spokesman pointed to the Kiowa captive and asked about his wound.

Bear Chaser answered that they had examined his shoulder and he would heal. Since the Kiowas came into Mondo's fort under a flag of truce and a request to trade and bargain for the captive, Mondo and Bear Chaser were not concerned about being overpowered by the Kiowas. Mick didn't understand all the ways of the Plains Indians and was real nervous and didn't like that the Kiowas were inside the fort. However, Mondo and Bear Chaser knew there was great honor among the Plains Indians regarding honoring a white flag or a truce for bargaining. Trading discussions, whether involving horses or captives, were done without incident since it was important to survival for the enemies to have a time when they could sit down and exchange goods and captives without fearing that the other side would attack.

The Kiowa girl remained on her horse and didn't make eye contact with anybody. Mick kept glancing over at her since he thought she was one of the most beautiful girls he'd ever seen.

Bear Chaser did the talking because he talked Comanche better than Mondo. Unknown to the Kiowas, Bear Chaser even understood quite a bit of the Kiowa language.

Mondo looked over at his dad and said, "Tell them this will be an easy trade. If they promise to leave us alone, we'll give them back the warrior and they give us back Mick's horses."

Bear Chaser frowned at his son and whispered. "You're too much in a hurry. We've got to do some small talk with these Kiowas before we get down to business. They would be insulted if we started out with the main topic at the beginning."

Bear Chaser turned to the Kiowa man sitting in the center of the three across from the fire. "You have done a great thing. Only the Kiowas could have taken all of our horses. You surprised us with great speed and were gone before we could do anything. We were lucky to wound one of your warriors."

The Kiowa nodded and replied, "Our scouts saw Mondo bringing more horses, so we decided to try to take them. The Great Spirit has protected Buffalo Spirit's horses in his compound. This must be a sacred place. But we didn't think the Great Spirit would keep us from getting his horses before they entered this holy ground."

"That was smart. You've got it figured right, and you got the horses before they were in Mondo's spiritual valley," replied Bear Chaser.

The Kiowa spokesman nodded. "I am Grey Fox, and with the help of the Great Spirit, I have studied your son and his sacred ground. I have seen with my own eyes that he goes into the fort and suddenly appears at night outside the fort. He has much magic, and we will receive great honor from taking the horses in his care whether they belong to Buffalo Spirit himself or this skinny white man," he nodded toward Mick.

Bear Chaser looked over at the captive. "Do you not value your own warrior, or are you going to throw him away like he was a broken arrow? Do you put the pride of stealing from the man you call Buffalo Spirit over the value of your honored tradition that no Kiowa is left behind? Is he not wanted? Does he have no relatives with honor?"

Grey Fox looked over at the captive and back to Bear Chaser and then at Mondo. "You captured Eagle Eyes, an important warrior. If he was not valued, we would have attacked Buffalo Spirit even though this man you call Mondo may have killed Eagle Eyes."

Bear Chaser spoke. "Then it will be an easy trade. You return the horses and promise to leave us alone, and we will return to you this good warrior that you call Eagle Eyes. His family and all Kiowas will be happy."

The Kiowa spoke and shook his head. "Not so fast. We've got a better trade. We have been watching Buffalo Spirit that you call Mondo for a long time. He's lived alone for almost a year without a woman to comfort and take care of him. Eagle Eyes lost his brother and inherited an extra wife from that brother. We will keep the horses and trade to Mondo Eagle Eye's extra woman. One human for another human. It's a good trade. We want to keep the horses that we took from the famous Buffalo Spirit."

Bear Chaser looked over at Mondo and Mick and spoke in English. "They want to trade that girl for this warrior. They want to keep Mick's horses."

Mondo frowned. "We're having no girl in this fort. Now, if Mick wants to give up his horses, that's up to him, but as soon as he does, then he has to leave with her. I didn't intend for anyone to live here, especially a woman."

Mick looked over at the girl who still stared up in the sky like she wasn't involved in the trade. "Wonder what's wrong with her. She's a real fine-looking gal. She must be diseased for them damn Kiowas to want to get rid of her."

Mondo frowned. "I'm sure there's something wrong with her. She's not staying here!"

Bear Chaser looked back at the Kiowa. "Buffalo Spirit wants no woman. He's a warrior who lives alone. That is part of his big medicine and the word to him from the Great Spirit. You can understand that."

The Kiowa nodded his head in agreement. "I thought it would be something like that. But the skinny white man keeps looking at Skywalker. Since you claim it was this man from Kansas who used to own these horses we took, then he should be willing to trade his horses for this beautiful Mexican captive."

"Does this Mexican captive not want to stay with Eagle Eyes, the one that we captured and the one you said was a popular warrior with a large family that cared for him?"

The Kiowa shook his head no. "She's a good wife to Eagle Eyes. But he's willing to give her up for his freedom and some horses. She will make an excellent wife for that puny white man. She's a Mexican captive we call Skywalker. He looks like he needs being cared for. She's nice and clean, and she cooks and sews well, but most of all, she can heal."

Bear Chaser looked up at the girl, and she continued looking into the sky. Mondo got up, walked over in front of her horse, and stared up at her. Mick followed and they both examined the woman. She finally glanced down and stared at Mondo for a second before her eyes flashed in anger and she looked back up. She was trouble, thought Mondo. Mick smiled real big and thought she was a real looker.

Bear Chaser raised his hand and called for a parlay. He asked for a break so he could talk to Mondo and Mick away from the Kiowas. The Kiowas also gathered and were talking among themselves.

Bear Chaser spoke, "Mick, if you want to give up your horses for that gal, then you can, but you got to remember that she's some captive who will probably want to go home just as soon as she gets free of the Kiowas. And you're not a Kiowa, so you won't own her. You'll have to give her up if she wants to go back to her people, and she looks like she's not too happy being where she is now."

Mick said, "After being with those Kiowas, she ought to be tickled to death to be with me. There's nothing wrong with me, and I get along with girls. It's been a long time since I've been with such a good-looking woman, and I don't mind giving up six horses for that one."

Bear Chaser signaled for them to stop talking, and he started listening to the Kiowas who thought no one could speak their language. They were discussing the trade and how things were going well if they could get rid of this woman who was bad luck. The return of their warrior and some horses would make a good trade for her.

After a few minutes of listening, Bear Chaser whispered to Mondo and Mick. "The Kiowas say she's bad luck. This is her second husband, and the other one died. Besides, she hasn't made any babies, but she can do medicine. I think we can trade for her and get most of Mick's horses back."

Mondo raised his hand and snapped at Bear Chaser, "I've told you she's not coming into this compound. Nobody stole my horses. Nobody slipped up on me except during a storm, and I took care of that problem. The next thing I know, I'm riding back with my father and an old friend and all the horses were taken. When I get around people, trouble happens. I was talking to you and not paying attention. If I hadn't been with you two, I'd have felt those Kiowas coming and avoided this problem. Now you are talking about putting a woman into the mix. It's bad enough when I'm around two men, but this is a woman. One woman can cause more trouble than ten bad men. You can have her, Mick. And you can trade for her with all your damn horses if you're fool enough to do so. But just as soon as you get her, you have to leave. I want that woman out of my sight."

Mick looked at Mondo. "Settle down now. Those are my horses and I can do what I want to with them. And you invited me out here to visit. If I buy this woman, then you should let her stay a while because I'm your friend and she'd be my woman. I won't make her stay here, and I'm not going to stay where I'm not wanted, just like you. We'll be gone, but let me trade for what I want to trade for without you sticking your nose into my business."

Mondo shook his head. "Go ahead. Be a fool. You can just look at that woman and see she's nothing but trouble. You can tell by looking at those Kiowas, they are tickled to death to get rid her. They act like they're afraid of her. Now, if she was worth a damn, they'd want to keep her. I admit she's not bad looking, but her husband has already died, and I wouldn't be surprised if she didn't kill him. Just look at that gal. She's surrounded by all these warriors, all these armed men, and she's sitting on that horse like she's not afraid of anyone, like she's above all this. She looks like she's got those Kiowas captured instead of the other way around. That's bad medicine. The Kiowas are right. She's not even worth a three-legged horse."

Mick laughed at Mondo. "What's your experience anyway? Are you an expert? I bet you've never even been with a woman. You're afraid of her. That's the first person I've ever seen that you were afraid of, Mondo. Man, the Kiowas and Comanches would get a big laugh out of that. You've got all of them thinking you are a great warrior that the Great Spirit protects, and you're afraid of that skinny Mexican girl. Now, you back off and let me do my own trading with my own horses."

Bear Chaser tried to ease between them and looked at Mick. "How many horses do you want me to give up for that woman?"

Mick said, "Start with three, but I'll give them six."

Bear Chaser sat down with the Kiowas and they made a deal so that Mick got the Mexican captive called Skywalker, and he gave up five horses, and the Kiowa captive called Eagle Eyes returned to his tribe. Everyone seemed happy, but no one asked or cared how Skywalker felt about the trade.

CHAPTER 16

T HERE WAS TROUBLE at Wildhorse Creek, not from the
outside, but from within. What kind of town was this place
going to be and who would decide? There was a group of ex-
slaves from South Carolina that controlled the vices and wanted
to further open up the town to more gambling, drinking, and
whoring and invite the whites in to partake and get rich off the
human weakness of all men no matter what color. Tan Bishop
was the leader of the gang wanting a wide-open community
where everything goes.

Hudson Greer and Dave Stevenson wanted to build a family-
type town with a church and a school and a general store, but
not a place ruled by the profits of sin. There were more single
men than couples, and the family group was outnumbered. When
Hudson made a population count, he determined that half of the
residents were Chickasaw freedmen, 25 percent were freedmen
from other tribes in Indian Territory, and only a quarter of the
residents were freedmen who came from other states, Texas being
the most, followed by Louisiana. Both towns had grown closer
together along the creek so that they were almost one community
that didn't agree on anything.

Maboola stayed out of the arguments and in fact stayed out of
the town most of the time as he patrolled the perimeter, watching for white men paid to bring him and Savanah back to Texas.
Savanah was caught up in the relaxed happy energy of the women
who seemed to enjoy the freedom of running their own homes
no matter how small and roughly put together. There was much

singing at night as the whole group of people wanting a family town usually gathered at a clearing above the creek and would sing a mixture of Christian songs and songs that were not so Christian. The singing was loud and lively and seemed to bring all together in a peaceful, free atmosphere.

Tan Bishop and his boys passed out the homemade white lightning on his side of town that led to some wild barroom songs late in the night after most of the good Christian inhabitants had gone to bed. The town seemed evenly divided among the fun lovers who wanted to celebrate freedom forever and the more responsible ex-slaves who wanted to build a respectable community.

The arguments on the future of the community came to a head at a town meeting called by Hudson Greer to form a city government and collect tax money for a school. Tan Bishop handed out free swallows of his corn liquor to get his support for a town without government or taxes.

Hudson Greer rose to speak. "We've celebrated freedom long enough. It's time we showed the white world that we can build a town that will grow into a family place to bring up our children in a safe world. We will not be given anything anymore. We must build together and learn to live free in a proper way. We need to elect a town council who will make laws, have a police force to carry out those laws, and build schools so our children will learn to read and write. If we all are known only for our cheap homemade brew, for our games of chance, and our lively whores, this town will become a play thing for blacks and whites. We must show the whites that we can be responsible and civilized. They think we are stupid savages! We must prove them wrong!"

Some applauded his speech as Hudson Greer sat down. Before Dave Stevenson could rise and call for a vote to establish an elected town council, Tan Bishop jumped up and fired his pistol into the air and silenced the crowd. The large light brown Negro had a big voice.

"When me and my boys left South Carolina over two years ago, we promised ourselves that we were not going to take orders from no man, no more. We were going to have some fun on our own. All our life we've broken our backs for the white man and told what to do. That's over. No man, colored or white, will ever stop our doings. We play hard and long and help others do the same. We're just making up for lost years we lived as a slave. There will be no city law here. We are the law, and if you don't like it, move on or go back being a yes man to the whites. You town darkies are cowards who are going to try to live like the evil bastards who put you in chains. Not us. We live like we want, and nobody tells us what to do. Go back to your shacks and get off this town government crap."

Dave Stevenson jumped up and started to object when Tan's boys drew their pistols and cocked the hammers. A stillness settled over the gathering until the crowd heard a horse riding up. All turned to see Maboola easing his horse toward Tan Bishop. The double-barrel shotgun was pointed at Bishop, and Maboola's machete was lying across his lap.

Savanah stepped out of the crowd and reached up and grabbed Maboola's rein. "This isn't your fight, Maboola. Stay out of it. I know you're for a family town, but Tan's got the most men and the most guns."

Maboola looked down at Savanah. "Tan wants to sell out to whites. He wants to open this place up and take money from the people who kidnapped us. I really don't care what free people do with their lives, but no white man needs to stop here. If Tan wants to sell his corn whiskey to the whites, that's fine by me, but I don't want to have to drink near those bastards. He can move his whiskey and whores farther up the creek."

"You're just one man," said Tan. "A big man, all right, but I've got at least ten guns on you right now. Back off and live to kill some more whites if you want to. What is it to you anyway? Aren't you trying to get back north and to Africa? Give up and live!"

"You're right. I'll die, but I guarantee you one thing. This here double-buck shot-loaded gun will take your head off before your boys get me. Now let Greer start his town and the town will let you do your thing. Stay apart. Both can work together, but no whites are allowed on our side. Colored only in this town, or you die. What's it going to be? Your death or separate towns."

Tan Bishop smiled. "I believe you. I'm not ready to cash in." He looked over at Hudson Greer and then nodded an okay to Dave Stevenson. "Build your town, but go easy on my doings. We might be able to agree on this, but be careful. Don't try to shut me down. You keep near the river, and we'll build up the creek."

With that, Tan Bishop signaled his men to lower their guns, and he left the crowd. That night, a town council was elected, and Hudson Greer was elected mayor. The first Negro community in the Chickasaw Nation was formed with the help of an ex-slave who wanted to go back to Africa.

After the meeting, Maboola walked Savanah back to a small log cabin she had obtained from a couple who wanted some of the fancy clothes she had purchased in Gainesville, Texas, before she was rescued by Maboola. When she thought of her guard's head flying through the air and his blood splattering her face, she shivered and again felt afraid of the black giant who was walking her home.

At the meeting, Maboola's huge powerful frame had again prevented violence by his domineering presence. She had almost accepted Maboola as normal until he challenged Tan Bishop and his men and backed down the powerful men from South Carolina. Maboola had never entered her small cabin, but sometimes if she got up at sunrise, she would see the black giant sleeping near her place.

"Don't you think that Tan Bishop is a dangerous man to push around?" she asked.

"He thinks he's a lot tougher than he really is. He's got everyone buffaloed, even the men that work for him. He wasn't a runner when he was a slave, so he doesn't have the deep-down guts that it takes someone to try to get away from the slave catchers and become free."

"He didn't like you throwing your weight around at the meeting. He had pretty much control of what was going on, and he didn't want any organized, civilized town. He likes every man for himself because he controls a lot of men, and he's making a lot of money off what he sells."

"I don't think he will try to cross me. He's too interested in making money off the whites to bother with the likes of me."

As the words left his mouth, Maboola felt a strong arm encircle his neck from behind and saw a large black man step out in front of him and drive his fist into Maboola's stomach. Maboola hardly felt the blow as the hard muscles that circled his middle tightened, and he spun to his left, carrying the man on his back into the man that had hit him. Maboola's move was done so quick and so easily that the two attackers blasted into each other, knocking the hitter to the ground and staggering the man off Maboola's back.

Savanah screamed, and the attacker, still on his feet, backhanded her to the ground. Before the striker could turn back from the blow he had delivered to Savanah, Maboola took hold of the man's arm with both hands and brought his knee up against the bone and splintered it into half as a roar of pain drowned out Savanah's screams. By the time the other attacker got to his feet, he stopped dead in his tracks and stared at his friend's dangling, exposed arm bone cut in half and barely hanging by skin and broken tendons.

Maboola spoke in a soft calm voice. "Tell Tan he's a coward, and if he's not brave enough to come himself, he'd better learn that he doesn't have enough men to get the job done. Now you two boys run along and be happy that I don't kill black people."

The two wide-eyed men limped off with one holding on to what was left of his arm like it was a precious jewel. Then

Maboola turned to Savanah, who was picking herself up from the ground with a bloody nose.

Maboola helped her to her cabin and entered for the first time. It was one room with a bed and a table and two chairs. She washed her face off with the pitcher of water that sat on the table.

"I'm sorry you got caught in the middle of that little ruckus. I wasn't even mad until that man hit you."

"Again, I owe you for taking up for me, but I don't think they were after me. Will they be back?"

"Maybe. Who cares? Black people don't know how to kill yet. They haven't had enough time to really get the hang of doing someone in. It will come with time. It was easy for me to acquire the joy of killing whites and knowing how to defend myself and take care of those trying to catch me. But I came from a proud African tribe."

"You still scare me. You always have, but at the same time, I sure like having you around. Nobody has bothered me since I watched you cut that man's head off."

"I'll never harm you or let anyone else harm you. That's a promise, and I mean to keep it."

"You've done a lot for me. I've seen you be extremely gentle to baby animals like you could never hurt a thing, and then I see you break a man's arm right in two and act like it didn't bother you at all. It's hard to figure you out."

"I can't figure myself out sometimes. I just know when that white bastard tore the skin off my back, I promised myself I would kill him or be killed and I keep my promises. The rest were killed to stay alive, and I kind of got used to it and liking to do white men in. It's my business, and I'm good at my business," Maboola said, and then smiled like he was a gentle giant who wouldn't hurt a flea.

Savanah stared at him for a while as the silence spread through the small cabin. She felt a stirring in herself and realized that she wanted to hold and kiss this big gentle giant who protected her. "Do you want to stay with me tonight?"

Maboola smiled. "I don't think that's a good idea. We're both trying to find where we fit in and where we want to end up. Besides, you're too white for my blood."

Savanah frowned. "Are you serious? You've never looked at me like most other men. I can tell that they are thinking about going to bed with me. Don't you think I'm pretty enough?"

Maboola smiled again. "You're nice, and I like you a lot. But you're so skinny I think I would break you in two if I ever slept with you. Besides, where I come from in Africa, you hardly got any ass at all."

Savanah put her hands on her hips and glared at Maboola. "Are you trying to tell me that I'm too ugly or too white for you to think about lying with me?" she said pointing to the small, single bed that looked rickety and worn.

"I'd break that little bed by myself even without you," said Maboola.

"You're not answering my question. Do you hate whites so much that any person with an ounce of white blood is your enemy? If so, you're just as bad as those KKK haters. Now get out of here. I could sleep with any man in this town if I wanted to and you say no because you're too carried away with hate to be a real man."

Without a word, Maboola slowly got up from his chair, walked over to Savanah, and gently picked her up into his arms and kissed her long but softly. They went out into the dark and into the woods so they wouldn't break her rickety bed.

CHAPTER 17

The Kiowas took Skywalker from the horse and placed her in front of Mick, gathered up their five new horses, and left the compound, hollering in jubilation as if they had won a great victory. Mondo had this sick feeling that poor Mick had been cheated. He felt the Kiowas wanted to get rid of Skywalker more than they wanted Mick's horses, but all Mick could see was this tall, thin, dark-haired lady that stood looking at Mondo and not Mick. Her dark eyes flashed a warning of something to someone. Scary but certainly beautiful. Mondo's first thought was that even though she had her nose in the air, she saw everything that was going on around her and was aware of who owned the compound.

Mick stepped forward and spoke some Tex-Mex language, which even to Mondo sounded like Spanish baby talk with a Texas drawl. She glanced back at Mick, but the expression on her face never changed. Mondo couldn't decide why she was so angry since she was free from the Kiowas.

"You," said Mick, pointing to her, "belong to me." Mick then pointed at his own chest.

She stepped forward real close to Mick and frowned at him. "I've never belonged to anyone in my life," she said in perfect English.

All three men showed their surprise and looked at each other as if to find an answer without asking her. "You talk," said Mick. "I sure didn't know you spoke American. If I'd known that, I'd have paid more than five horses for you."

Skywalker stepped back and put her hands on her hips and increased her frown. "You paid a lot more than the first man who claimed to own me. Thank God he's dead. Now where's the nearest civilized town or army post? I haven't been home in three years and I'm ready to get out of this god-forsaken country."

"Oh, you're still a long ways from anywhere," said Mick. "Why don't you just settle down and be happy that you no longer belong to the Kiowas. Stay here awhile, and I'll take you back when I get free."

Mondo stepped forward and glared first at Mick and then looked over at the girl. "Now I warned you about that, Mick. She's ready to go home, and I'm ready for her to go home. I'll watch what horses you got left and you just take her on to Fort Worth or over to Fort Arbuckle. The government will get her back to her family."

"No, that's not necessarily right now, Mondo. The Kiowas said she was a Mexican captive, not a Texan. If she's no US citizen, the army won't spend a lot of time trying to find her people way down in Mexico."

"Then you take her back all the way to the Rio Grande," said Mondo. "My place is already too crowded. I agreed to let you stay awhile, but I never wanted to have a woman here. It's going to be hard enough for me to guard this place with you here, but throw in this English-speaking Mexican who hates Indians and probably killed her Kiowa husband. No! This won't work at all."

Skywalker's dark eyes seemed to heat up as she stepped up close to Mondo and glared up into his eyes. "You're no gentlemen, are you? I didn't come here on my own free will, but my family always treated any guest with hospitality. What kind of man are you anyway? Are you afraid of me? All I want is a little time to gather myself and I'll start home, alone, if necessary. I've been around more sorry men than a woman should be burdened with in a lifetime. I've learned to live without much help at all from the opposite sex."

Both Mondo and Mick blushed at the word sex used by a lady in public, and only Bear Chaser, who stood back with kind of a smile on his face, seemed to be enjoying the discussion.

Mondo jabbed his finger toward her face and kind of reared up on his toes so he towered over her about half a foot. "Look here, squaw. Gentlemen don't live long out here in this country. And as far as I can tell, there are no ladies out here either. Whatever you were and wherever you came from makes no difference to anybody. Out here, you live or die based on how smart and tough you are. People just try to stay alive. You're in my house and you're calling me names and you were just purchased by this man here," he pointed to Mick. "You act like you own my place and are the boss of all three of us. No wonder the Kiowas wanted to get rid of you."

Mick reached over and took Mondo's arm and eased him back. Skywalker looked too mad to even answer. "Take it easy, Mondo. Now, I bought this girl, and she's not yours. And it's not your business to run down my trade goods. I'll take care of her, and we'll leave you alone. You weren't willing to give any horses for her, and I was, so she's my problem not yours."

Skywalker looked over at Mick. "You two are worse than the Kiowas. I thought I might be getting close to civilization, but what I've got here is some kid who thinks he's found someone to bed and a half-breed Negro who is afraid to be around women." At that, she spun around and went into Mondo's cabin like the cabin was hers. Bear Chaser was chuckling to himself, and both men turned to him like they'd seen him for the first time.

"What's your problem?" asked Mondo.

Bear Chaser raised his hands, said nothing, and limped off, still favoring his wounded hip, laughing to himself.

Mondo looked back at Mick. "My dad's getting crazy in his old age. But you're old enough to know better. If you trade for horses like you trade for women, then you'll go broke before the year's out. What did you think you were going to get anyway?"

"I just felt sorry for her living with those damn Kiowas. She deserves to be free like anybody else," said Mick.

140

Mondo laughed. "If she weighed two hundred pounds, you'd never looked at her twice. You'd have left her with the Kiowas in a second. I know what was on your mind, and you can't treat her like a whore. The whole Civil War was about owning people, and the South lost. So you can't order her around like a slave and you can't do what you want to do with her because it's obvious she doesn't like you or men for that matter."

"You've got me all wrong, Mondo. If she wants to go home, I'll take her home. But she could earn her keep while she's here. We could use a little woman's touch around this place. I'm not real anxious to eat your cooking. And the Kiowas are right. Aren't you lonely? You've lived out here by yourself for a year now except for some part-time help from your dad. You should be jumping up and down with joy that I had the guts to trade a few measly horses for a fine-looking girl."

Mondo jabbed Mick in the chest again. "Well, she's your problem, and you better get her out of here as soon as possible. And if I were you, I'd find out if she killed her Kiowa husband. There's not a place for her in the cabin. I'm not going to sleep with that crazy woman in the same room. I can damn sure tell that she's a killer!"

"You mean you're going to lock her out? You're worse than the Kiowas, Mondo. They probably treated her like a slave and made her do exactly what they wanted. After one night at your place, she'll be ready to go back to the Kiowas. Now you have to be nicer than that. Let's go in and sit down with her and have a talk to find out more about her. I won't force her to do anything. But I think you are being just downright mean."

They stared at each other for a moment, and then Mondo nodded as they started for the cabin. As they entered, they saw Skywalker busy trying to clean up the place. Dirt and dust were flying everywhere. It looked like an inside-the-house sandstorm. They both started coughing and went back out.

Mick looked over at Mondo. "Man, you sure got a filthy cabin. And you see her? She knows what to do, and you sure need a woman around this messy place."

Mondo turned and hollered, "Skywalker, come out here. We need to talk. Stop scattering that dirt everywhere and let's get a few things straight."

She came to the door as the dust settled and walked out. The two of them stood there, and it was quiet until they heard a noise and looked over to see Bear Chaser pulling up a log to sit on with the same grin on his face. He sat down and crossed his arms as if he expected to be entertained. It grew quiet much to the irritation of Mick and Mondo, who thought the old man had lost his mind.

Mondo stepped forward and addressed Skywalker. "We need to come to some kind of understanding. I've lived alone with my dad coming and going for a year, and all of a sudden, I got a kid from Texas and a Kiowa-Mexican captive moving in on me all at once. Now, this here Mick does not own you. Nobody owns nobody on my place. Mick says he'll take you back home when the trails dry out, and you can stay until then. I expect you to earn your keep just like I expect my father and Mick to earn their keep."

Mick stepped up close to Mondo. "Hold it. I bought this woman, and you're trying to make the rules for her."

Mondo glared over at Mick. "You want to make the rules, then take her out of here. As long as she stays in my place, then I decide what's what."

Mick frowned, stepped back, and then nodded in agreement. Mondo looked back at Skywalker. "Why do they call you Skywalker?"

"The Kiowas say I'm always looking up into the sky, walking around with my nose pointed up, and they're right. Also, I fooled them into thinking I had big medicine. I was more civilized and educated and didn't let them bring me down to their level." Skywalker answered and snapped her head up as if she was looking down on Mondo.

"Did you kill your Kiowa husband?" asked Mondo.

"I didn't have any husbands. I haven't killed any man yet," she said. "But I've thought about it, and I'm thinking about it right now. My father owned a large ranch in northern Mexico. I was captured three years ago. I'm twenty years old and considered used and useless by the Kiowas and probably by my own people now. If I didn't know healing and practiced a little medicine on them, the Kiowas would have gotten rid of me long ago. The first man that claimed to be my husband was killed when his horse fell on him. I was glad he went to his happy hunting grounds. His brother then took me as his wife. He's the one you captured and traded for me."

"How do you speak English if you are a Mexican girl?" asked Mondo.

"My father had money. I was educated. I learned English in Mexico City. The Kiowas told me they killed all of my family. I saw most of them dead, mutilated, and scalped. Do you really wonder why I hate Indians?"

Mondo looked at the fire in her eyes and eased back a step. "We'll get along fine. Since my mother's death, I haven't met a woman that hadn't been anything but trouble. You can go on hating Indians, and I'll go on not trusting women," he said.

Mick eased forward and smiled. "Kiowas think they own all squaws, and Mondo here, he just doesn't trust women. You've never been around a real gentleman from Texas. I'll look after you. You don't have to worry about a thing. We'll all settle in and rest awhile, and then I'll take you wherever you want to go."

"I've never heard of a Texas gentleman. All Texans are killers. I agree with the Kiowas on that," she said and then Skywalker looked over at Mondo, and finally she glanced at Bear Chaser, who still had a funny grin on his face. She shook her head, turned, and marched over to Bear Chaser.

"Whoever tried to bandage your hip didn't know what they were doing. Come on in and I'll boil some water and fix it right."

Skywalker took Bear Chaser by the arm and walked him into the cabin.

Mondo looked over at Mick. "Did we get things straightened out?" he asked.

"Sure. She's going to do a little cleaning, cooking, and healing, and I'm going to get to know her real well."

"In a gentlemanly way, of course," said Mondo. "And where is she going to sleep? We didn't get that settled."

"Well, it's only right that she sleeps in the cabin and all of us sleep out here. That's what a gentleman would do," said Mick.

"I've never considered myself a gentleman, Mick. And I'm sure no Southern gentleman ever considered me one either. It took me ten months and three weeks to build this compound. I've got a warm cabin, and I'm not sleeping outside. Now you bought her, so you go in and settle this right now. Don't you think for a minute that I'm going to sleep out here in the cold in my own place."

Mondo turned and looked back as Mick reentered the cabin and got Skywalker's attention.

"I've just talked to Mondo, and I found you a place to sleep. Why don't you spread your furs over there by the fire so you'll be nice and warm. Bear Chaser and I will sleep outside. But this is Mondo's house, so he's going to sleep over there on the mat he laid out for himself. But if he tries to bother you, just yell, and I'll come in and keep you safe."

Skywalker shook her head in the negative. "I don't need your help," she said and then quickly withdrew from under her dress a dagger with an eight-inch blade and pointed it at Mick. "No man is going to touch me again unless I want him to. If anyone tries, I guarantee you I'll slice him open."

With that, she turned and began to undo the bandages on Bear Chaser's leg. Mick's eyes kind of widened, and he thought to himself, *Mondo may be right. I sure could have made a bad deal on this trade.*

CHAPTER 18

WHEN DARKNESS CAME, everyone went to their assigned places to get some sleep. Mondo ignored Skywalker and climbed into his bedroll. When he looked over, he saw that Skywalker was leaning against the wall, looking at him, and holding the dagger with the eight-inch blade.

He sat up in bed and yelled at her. "How do you expect me to get any sleep with you pointing that big knife just waiting for me to close my eyes? You give me that dagger or go sleep outside. It's not very cold tonight, and besides, the man that bought you is out there waiting for you."

Skywalker shook her head. "I'm not going to sleep out in the cold, and I'm not going to close my eyes with you in here. I've done that before. Just as soon as I nod off, you'll jump me. I'm not going to slip up on you and slit your throat, but if you come toward me, you're going to find my blade."

"You don't trust me, and I damn sure don't trust you. One of us has got to go. And this is my house."

"I'm not going outside. You saw how that Mick looked at me. He thinks that just because he bought me he has the right to use me. Even though you seem to be a mean, hateful man, I don't think you're going to rape me, but I'm not taking any chances."

Mondo sighed and shook his head. *Another standoff in the house I own. Before anybody came except my dad, I never had one argument. Nobody gave me any back-talk, and I was a very happy man. I allow some kid I knew years ago to come stay here, and the next thing I know, there's a dagger-carrying, crazy Kiowa-Mexican gal just waiting for me to shut my eyes so she can cut my balls off.*

Mondo got out of bed and reached over to his holster and drew his gun and pointed it at Skywalker. "I said leave and I mean it. If you don't think I'll shoot you, then just keep sitting right there, pointing that dagger at me and the next thing you know, you'll have a bullet between your eyes."

"Go ahead and shoot me. There's been many times in the last few years that I wished I was dead. I'm not starting over being a slave to any man."

Mondo lowered his gun and glared at her as she looked back, remaining completely still. The standoff lasted a few minutes before Mondo re-holstered his pistol, grabbed his sleeping gear, and stomped out of the cabin. Just as soon as the door shut, he heard the board locking the entrance fall into place.

Mick heard the racket. He sat up from his bedroll and hollered at Mondo. "What did you do to her?"

Mondo spun around and yelled. "Not a thing. It's just that I can't sleep with panther lady sitting eight feet away with an eight-inch dagger and blood in her eyes. You're taking that woman out of here in the morning." Mondo turned back around and stomped off to the far corner of the compound.

Mick got up and eased up to the door and knocked. "Skywalker? Is everything all right? Do you want me to come in and protect you?"

There was no answer, and Mick tried the door, which had been barred shut when she dropped the wooden plank securing the door.

"Did that Mondo bother you? I think you need me inside to make sure that you are safe."

"Go away. I'm safe now that all three of you are locked out of this cabin."

"I'm not sure Mondo's going to like that very much. You know, it is his cabin. I think you better come out and stay here with me and let Mondo back in, or he's going to run us both off in the morning."

"I'll be packed and ready to go. This place is not much safer than staying with the Kiowas. If you won't take me away from here, I'm going to start out on my own."

"It's too dangerous to go alone, and I can't take you tomorrow. We'll talk about it in the morning," said Mick, and he elected to walk away and settle back in his bedroll. The next morning, Mondo was awakened with the smell of bacon frying. The sun was already up, and he realized he'd slept a lot later than usual. He then remembered that he was sleeping outside because of the female called Skywalker. Mondo jumped up and started for the cabin.

When he opened the door, Mondo saw Bear Chaser eating in his long underwear. Mondo stopped at the entrance of the cabin, stared at Bear Chaser, and then looked over at Skywalker. Both glanced back at him. Bear Chaser went back to eating breakfast, and Skywalker went back to stirring a pot that was cooking over the fireplace. Each acted like nothing strange had happened and that Mondo didn't need an explanation. Mondo walked over to his dad and looked down into his face.

"When did you get in here?"

Bear Chaser looked up and replied, "Real early this morning. If you sleep this late every day, you won't get anything done."

"I didn't sleep good last night," said Mondo. "You know I'm usually up before dawn."

"You need to be to run this place. I set some traps last night and caught some rabbits and brought them for Skywalker to cook. She says the kitchen is bare and you have hardly anything to cook with let alone enough chairs and furniture."

"I don't need much. I have everything I want in this cabin, and I don't need anything else. What are you doing in your long underwear? Is she washing for you too?"

All this time, Skywalker kept busy without turning around and acted as if she didn't hear the discussion. Bear Chaser smiled and replied, "She's going to wash my pants later. She was doctoring my hip. The Kiowas were right, she's good with medicine. She's got some herbs I've never heard of, and she fixed my wound good. I don't hurt at all. I can tell you right now that this woman is handy to have around."

"No. We're not going to start that. I didn't build this cabin for any woman and for me to sleep outside."

Bear Chaser interrupted. "She said I could sleep inside and protect her," he smiled. "She doesn't seem to be as threatened by me as you two young bucks. I told her I didn't mind sleeping inside and watching out for her."

"Are you crazy!" Mondo pointed his finger in his father's face, and about that time, the door slammed open, and Mick hurried in. Mick frowned at all three. "When did she let you two in?"

Bear Chaser smiled. "Oh, she let me in right after you talked to her last night so I could protect her from you two young bulls."

Mick looked down at Bear Chaser's long underwear and replied, "Who protected her from you?"

"She can trust me," said Bear Chaser with a slight grin. "I'm almost fifty years old. I'm not dangerous anymore."

Mick looked over at Mondo and shook his head. "I'm beginning to think you're right, Mondo. I made a bad trade. I can't talk to her, but your old man can. She's not worth five horses."

Mondo nodded. "You can say that again. She's certainly not a five-horse woman."

Skywalker spun around and glared at the two men. "What would you two know about the worth of a woman? I can cook, I can sew, and I can doctor. Bear Chaser seems to be the only one here that recognizes my worth. I can do a lot of things for you that have nothing to do with using my body. Sit down and I'll give you some rabbit stew."

Mondo and Mick looked at each other then found a place to sit. She took some stew out of the pot and put it in wooden bowls and placed the bowls down before them with one spoon.

"You'll have to fight over the spoon. Mondo needs a lot of things to make this place livable. He has some venison hanging in the basement, but he doesn't have much else."

Mondo's head snapped up. "You found the trapdoor? Nobody's supposed to know about the basement. Now, you'll probably blab everything so that the Kiowas and Comanches will know how I slip out of my cabin."

"I don't care if I never see another Kiowa or Comanche or any other Indian for that matter. Bear Chaser is the only civilized Indian I've ever met. Now, if I'm going to have to stay here awhile before Mick takes me home, then I'll do my part, but I've got to have some things to work with. Where's the closest store?"

Mondo looked back and started to answer when Mick interrupted him. "Red River Station. It's about the same distance from here as Fort Arbuckle, and Fort Arbuckle doesn't have the supplies they do at the crossing. There's a ferry there that brings the chuck wagons across. Almost all the herds coming from Texas cross the river at Red River Station."

Mondo looked around at all three of them, and they seemed to be waiting for a reply. He thought to himself that he'd better seize command of his own house, or this woman would be ruling from here on out.

"Here's what we're going to do. I'm going to let the horses out and let them have a good run and check them out to see if there's any problems. Bear Chaser, you ought to go and get some more meat and do some hunting 'cause that's what you do better than anybody I know. And you, Mick, are going to ride to Red River Station and bring back what we need. Skywalker, you make a list if you can write and then clean this place up. It still looks dirty."

Mondo kind of reared back and stuck his chest out and glared at Skywalker. For the first time, she smiled and then asked, "I can write, but can Mick read?"

"Mick can read," answered Mondo. Skywalker turned back to the fireplace.

She's sure a strange woman, thought Mondo. *I guess it will be fine for her to stay around a few days just to fix this place up. Then Mick can take her back to Mexico and get her out of my hair.*

Since the Kiowas had killed his main riding horse, Mick really didn't have a good, well-trained mount to ride to Red River Station. Mick asked Mondo if he could use Tree Top. At first, Mondo refused since he didn't let anybody ride his favorite horse. However, Mick finally talked Mondo into allowing him to ride Tree Top, convincing Mondo that he needed to get to Red River Station and back as soon as possible in order to smooth out the living arrangements with Skywalker. Also, Mick reminded Mondo that he didn't have an agreement with the Comanches or the Kiowas that allowed him protection, and being a Texan alone on the trail, he could be attacked by both tribes. The day that Mick rode off on Tree Top, a late winter storm rolled in, and snow covered Mondo's valley.

That night, both Mondo and Bear Chaser came into the cabin to sleep. It was too cold for Mondo to stay outside especially when he had just completed a warm rock house. Skywalker looked at the two men and this time did not pull out her dagger. All she said was that she trusted Bear Chaser, and as long as he was inside, Mondo could stay inside. When she added that, she thought Bear Chaser could take Mondo in a fight. Mondo again went to bed mad at Skywalker. But they all went to sleep without incident in the warm cabin as the wind howled outside.

The next morning, Bear Chaser and Mondo both worked hard to make sure that there was grass available for the horses and added hay that Mondo had stored in his shed near the corral. The next few days, the three of them settled down to a routine that included Skywalker preparing good, warm meals and keeping the rock house clean and cozy with the men taking care of the horses and killing game for the dinner table.

Mondo expected Mick back in three days, but after five days had passed, Mondo began to worry about Tree Top and Mick.

At the end of a week, Mick rode up with a big smile on his face, herding twenty nice-looking cow ponies. He jumped off his horse and approached Mondo. "Here's some more horses for you. You've got a half interest in all twenty of these horses since I won them by racing Tree Top."

"You did what? You were supposed to get supplies and get back here as soon as possible. Are you trying to tell me you raced my horse? Tree Top could have been injured. You don't know him that well."

"Well, I got across the Red River all right, but the storm kicked up a lot of water, and the Red River rose so high and was so swift that the ferry couldn't get across let alone all those cattle. The cattle drives from Texas backed up, and there must have been twenty herds waiting to cross the Red River at the ferry. Well, the weather broke, but the river was still running too fast to attempt a crossing. All the cowboys had to do something to pass the time, and as you know, they love racing horses. Well, I knew you had one of the fastest horses in all Indian Territory, so I just raced them all. And I won all these cow ponies. Since it was your horse, I figure you got a half interest in this bunch and I've got a half interest myself since, of course, I rode the horse."

Mondo examined Tree Top carefully to make sure that there was no damage and then turned around and faced Mick. "This is getting awful mixed up. You originally brought thirty over to my place and traded five for that Mexican girl in there and now you are bringing twenty more and claiming a half interest. That's fair. But when you leave, which ought to be pretty quick now, you're going to take the twenty-five you've got left that you brought in and ten of these new ones along with that girl, Skywalker. I just never figured myself partnering up with anybody. We'll have to divide up these new ones. And even though Skywalker cooks a good meal, she's your purchase, and there's just too many people in my cabin and there's no room for a female."

Mick smiled and then nodded his head in agreement. The men separated the horses and branded *MH* on Mondo's horses and *MO* for Mick O'Ryan on the ones Mick owned. They now had a good-sized herd.

Mick thought he was on a roll. He was proud that he had won the horses, and he could tell Mondo was pleased to add to the herd even though Mondo honestly didn't like that he raced Tree Top. Mick's father had raised Mick to be an optimist. Mick usually didn't spend long worrying about his mistakes or what others thought about him. Living with his father and riding back and forth across the Red River trading horses helped keep him away from civilized life in towns and had taught Mick to deal with people up front and hoped they treated him the same way. Because he had no mother, or really any females around when he was being raised, he learned about life by observing the men that he was around.

Mick had always liked Bear Chaser and always looked up to Mondo. Since Mondo was two years older than Mick, Mondo had always learned things first and did things quicker than Mick. Mick worked hard to live up to Mondo's example and became a good rider, a good shooter, and a good horse trader.

They had little teaching in regard to the opposite sex. Mick's father would go into Fort Worth, Texas, every once in a while to visit the whorehouse, and many times, he took advantage of Indian women by getting sex for the trade of a horse. No matter what anyone said, Mick thought that you got sex by trading horses. Therefore the fact that Skywalker wouldn't have anything to do with him did not seem quite fair. Also, Mick noticed that Skywalker seemed to be looking at Mondo when Mondo was not looking at her, even though Mick was the one that gave five horses for her. Mondo deliberately ignored her. Mick couldn't understand why she would be interested in Mondo except that Mondo owned the place.

Mick had never met a wealthy, educated girl and really didn't understand Skywalker at all. The more he tried to entertain her, the more he tried to impress her and be with her, the more she seemed to ignore him. He was beginning to get angry. Here he was, a young man with many horses, which in the West made him well-off, and he treated Skywalker right. Mick hadn't tried to rape her or make her do anything she didn't want to do, and it still didn't impress her at all. For the first time in his life, Mick was jealous, and for the first time in his life, Mick's hero, Mondo, seemed to stand in his way.

Skywalker noticed the change in the usually happy Mick and really didn't know what to do about it. She could tell by the way Mick stared at her that he thought that she should be his woman, body and soul. However, for the first time in three years, she had a little piece of freedom, and she wasn't about to give it up to any man. Mick was friendly, but he was a Texan, and all the Texans she knew could be as bad as any Kiowa. Skywalker had been raised by her upper-class parents who despised Texans who had taken much of their property that was north of the Rio Grande. In fact, her father and his vaqueros had been in a battle for years with Texas rustlers coming across the Rio Grande. That war had been going on for forty years, and there was no love between the high-class Mexican ranch owners and the Texas cattle barons. They stole from each other and killed each other and had for many years, and as far as Skywalker knew, there would never be peace between the Mexicans and the Texans. Therefore she had one thing in common with the Kiowas. She had been taught to hate Texans. Even though Mick didn't seem to be as mean as she had been raised to think of Texans, he still was a blond-headed Texas cowboy, and she had never met one that was worth his weight in salt.

Even though Skywalker wanted to go back to Mexico, she really didn't know how she would be accepted. She knew her entire family had been wiped out and their land and wealth had probably been passed on to distant cousins. The high-class Mexican society did not accept women who had lived three years with the Kiowas. Her chances of a good marriage were almost nonexistent. She did not feel like she could marry a peasant, and she didn't feel like she was eligible any longer for an upper-class husband. Therefore even though she wanted to go back to Mexico, she was afraid of what waited for her there.

Mondo was a strange, big, nice-looking man who perplexed her. She couldn't pigeonhole the man. The more she observed Mondo, the more she wondered about his relationship with people and especially this skinny white Texan named Mick. Something was wrong with this Mondo, but she couldn't put her finger on it. However, his father seemed responsible, kind, and understanding. He was good-looking. She felt comfortable around him and could talk to him. Every time Mick or Mondo walked into the room, she was on guard. She liked to have Bear Chaser around.

Bear Chaser had lived a sad and lonely life since his wife had died and his son had left. He still went through the motions of staying alive, but he had very little feelings. It wasn't until his son had come back from the war that he again thought that there might be a second chance for him to be happy and live like a man should live. Therefore his whole life revolved around taking care of his son and being a good father instead of living in the past.

Bear Chaser had often daydreamed about Mondo's mom. Spring Blossom was her name, and she lived up to the name. She had long, dark, curly hair with blue eyes and tan skin. He fell in love with her on sight and spent all his money to buy her within a month after they met. Spring Blossom's father had been a full-blood Irishman, and her mother had been a Negro slave. To Spring Blossom, Bear Chaser had been a big, strong, handsome Chickasaw who believed in the old ways. She was happy to live with Bear Chaser, and everything was fine until the mixed-blood Chickasaws took control of the tribe and worked desperately hard to transfer the Chickasaw Indians to white people. It wasn't like they passed laws that forbid a Chickasaw to live like the Chickasaw used to live. It was that they ignored the full-blood Chickasaws and tried to wipe out all the old customs.

The more Bear Chaser saw where the government of the Chickasaw Nation was headed, the more he seemed to move over to the way of the Comanche and Kiowa who hadn't been tainted by the white. That's how he met Ten Bears, and that's how he got the right to hunt and stay with the Comanches and Kiowas. He had become a friend of a Comanche chief whose band had just been pushed out of Texas, and they spent a lot of time together. When he wasn't hunting, he was back in his home about twenty miles east of Comanche country on Cow Creek.

After Spring Blossom died and his son went off to war, Bear Chaser began living alone, hunting alone, and spending more time away from the Chickasaw Nation and more time with Ten Bears and the Comanches. He knew a few Kiowas, Wichitas, and Caddos, and he seemed to drift away from the half-breeds that controlled the Chickasaw government and the Chickasaw Nation and live the old ways, mostly by himself. It wasn't until Mondo came back that he realized what the Great Spirit wanted him to do. He must live for his son. Bear Chaser was happier than he had been for a long time. He was like a guardian angel to his only son. For the first time, there was something more important than the old ways of the Chickasaw or any other thing. Bear Chaser was with Mondo to protect, guide, and make sure that his son stayed alive.

Deep down, all three men enjoyed the company of Skywalker. What man wouldn't? She was beautiful. Mondo wouldn't look at Skywalker because every time he looked at her, there was a surge of lust. Therefore he avoided eye contact with Skywalker, and he seemed to be angry at himself every time he thought how much he really wanted her. There were two things he knew. One, that if he got involved with Skywalker, he would let his guard down even more, and he wouldn't last long out in this country. And two, that he knew Mick had bought her and Mondo felt like she was Mick's responsibility, even though he didn't think that a woman belonged to a man. Mondo still could not get over his desire for this beautiful Mexican woman. He had no experience with the opposite sex, and he didn't know how to approach her even if he decided to.

Mondo was uptight and nervous about three other people living in his rock house. He knew his father was trying to help him, and he appreciated the help, but Mick and the woman were just too much. He liked Mick and wanted to partner up with him because he had to admit, Mick was a good trader and could deal with the Texans coming through with their herds a lot better than Mondo could deal with the white men. Mondo could feel the tension between Mick and Skywalker, and he didn't like it at all. Every time he went into the rock house to sleep, he felt closed in and trapped. There was always noise, people, and he couldn't put himself in the zone of thinking and feeling where he could detect danger.

As the countryside greened and spring came to Mondo's valley, the four people living together settled in to a guarded routine. Mick and Mondo worked the horses, Bear Chaser did the hunting, and Skywalker did the cooking, sewing, cleaning, and doctoring. Each day, the four of them appeared to relax a little more, and the conversation became almost normal, except Mondo didn't talk much. The more the parties got used to each other, the more Mondo feared that disaster was approaching. He couldn't totally relax knowing that people, no matter who they were or how well they got along, always caused him trouble. He was used to taking care of himself and himself alone. These three people living in his house seemed to add responsibility to Mondo that he did not want or need. However, he had to admit that life was sure easier when he had his father, an old friend, and a housekeeper-cook-medicine woman working and living in his compound. About once a week, Mondo would ask Mick when he was going to take Skywalker home. Each time, Mick would make excuses since he was afraid that if he left Mondo's, he would have to take Skywalker to some place or somebody that would take her back to Mexico, or he would be obligated to take her back to Mexico himself. Mondo knew that Mick was stalling for time trying to interest Skywalker into hooking up with Mick and not making the trip back to her home. Skywalker appeared ready to go but seemed to work hard to fit into the routine of making life easier while she took care of everyone living in the compound.

One nice evening in May, the four of them had settled down after a good supper, and Skywalker, who talked mostly with Bear Chaser, asked Bear Chaser if he intended to live with Mondo.

Mondo glanced over at Bear Chaser, who looked back at him. Then Bear Chaser spoke. "I've got a place over by Cow Creek that I'm leasing to a Chickasaw freedman. He farms it and takes care of it. I don't like farming, never have done any farming, and probably never will do any farming. I'd rather raise horses and hunt. Right now, this is the best place for that. Whether I stay here very long or not, it's up to my son."

Mondo nodded affirmatively at his father. "You're a lot of help. I like your company. But there's too many."

"You've got to learn to be around people. Don't you want to settle down and have a family?" asked Bear Chaser.

"Dad, I don't want my child to go through what I did. When I fought with the Yankee whites, I never was treated as a real man no matter what I did. When I went to Arkansas to buy my horses, it was worse. The blood in my veins that I got from mother and not you caused me the most trouble. When I came back here, I didn't want to be around people because people have not treated me right. I feel like I can take care and protect myself if I'm alone. If I've got a bunch of people around that I have to look after, then I don't concentrate on taking care of me, and that causes trouble."

Skywalker looked over at Mondo. "Have you ever thought that you might be the problem? You don't like people because they haven't lived up to your idea as how people should act. Nobody does all the time what the other person wants them to do. I'm sure you were not treated well by a lot of people because of your mixed blood, but you don't need to chase off those that treat you as a man and don't hold it against you that you have Indian and Negro blood. Do you think you make everybody happy around here, walking around with a scowl on your face and suspicion in your eyes? It's one thing to be suspicious and cautious about other people, and it's another thing to make people think you hate them when you don't even know them."

Mondo turned red with anger and stood up. "When are you going to leave? I don't care that you cook, sew, and doctor around here. You've got this know-it-all act, and you think you have been given the smarts to know the answers to everything. Have you ever thought maybe what anger I may have is because you came in here and tried to take over everything and tell everybody what to do and what not to do? No matter what you were at one time, you're now an ex-Kiowa woman with Mexican blood. I was born with black blood, and I have to deal with that, but you were born with rich blood, and you can't leave that alone. It doesn't mean that you're any better than anybody else. You may have had a little education, but you don't have a right to tell everybody what to do."

"Wait a minute," said Mick. "There you go again, Mondo. I mean, she's taken care of us as well as any woman I've ever heard about. I mean, she makes the meals, she sews up the clothes, she's got a garden she's planted out here for vegetables and stuff. If somebody gets hurt, she's like magic. She's a medicine woman. There's lots and lots of men living out in the wild that would pay big bucks to have her whether they got their bed warmed by her or not. Now, if you can't see how important she is to the way we are living around here, by God, Bear Chaser and I can see what she's worth. Isn't that right, Bear Chaser?"

Bear Chaser nodded, then smiled. "She's good for all of us. And she's right about Mondo. Son, you act like a grouchy old man. You're not even twenty-three years old and you gripe and raise cane and go around snorting and huffing and puffing and talking angry to everyone here. Most people would think, without ever looking into your face, that you were the old man around here instead of me. It's about time you took that chip off your shoulder and tried to get along with the world."

Mondo turned on his father. "You're taking their side. You're my father. You should understand. It's probably best for everyone to get out of here."

Skywalker stood up. "What's the matter with you? Any time somebody tries to help you, you act like they're trying to hurt you. Can't you accept kindness? Are you afraid that you will care for someone and they will die like your mother? You've had a lot of experiences, and most of them are bad, but you haven't learned a damn thing about life. If you want to run everybody off, then that's fine with me. Everybody has got some place they can go besides living with a bitter man who cannot receive from or give to anybody else. I'm getting out of here first thing in the morning. Are you going to take me, Mick?"

Mick stood up and raised his hands up in the air. "Now, let's just hold it right now. Let's all settle down, have a seat, and enjoy this fine spring day. I'll take you back to anywhere you want to go, Skywalker, but we ought to wait until the rains stop and the creeks go down. Then we can move out south, and I'll take you to Fort Worth or San Antonio, or wherever you want to go, but let's not leave in a hurry. You can stand Mondo for a few months. I know he's mean. He's always been kind of mean. But he's really a lot nicer than he seems. Even though he never says so, he really likes what you're doing for us around here. Don't you, Mondo?"

Mondo looked over at Mick. "Well, she does some good things. I know that. And I don't mind if you stay a couple more weeks, but I don't want all this talk about what's in people's minds. People just shouldn't talk about things like that. Life is just as it is. You are what you do. And I just don't think we ought to dig into somebody's past and bring up personal things about how they think, why they think, what they do, and why they do it. There's not any good answers. Is that all right with everyone?"

There was silence as all four of them looked at each other, and finally, Skywalker sat back down and looked at Mondo. "I'll stay until the summer on one condition. I'm tired of living in this rock cave and having hardly any furniture and things to eat with. Now, Mondo, I know you and Bear Chaser can make furniture, and, Mick, surely you could help out in some way. We need tables, we need chairs, we need beds, we need to make this place liveable. I'm tired of living like we're stuck in a cave. Will you agree to that, Mondo?"

Mondo looked at her for a while and then said, "I'm not against having furniture. You'd think I was totally uncivilized. Of course, we can make some furniture. I was going to anyway. I don't need you to tell me what I need and what to do. There you go again. I was planning to do that anyway and you're telling me to do it like it was your idea and that I'm following you. We will get the furniture made, but it's my idea and not yours."

Skywalker smiled. "Good. Then I want you to have another idea. I want Mick to go to the store again. We need plates, and we need silverware or spoons or something. If I'm going to stay here another two months, then we're going to make this place seem like a home for people to live in. This is not a dugout, and this is not a Kiowa tent or a Comanche teepee. This is a home, a settlement, and a place where human beings live. Now, do you agree with that?"

Mondo shook his head in agreement. "I was going to do that too. We'll get that done. Now let's all settle down and quit arguing about little things like furniture and utensils. That's silly. Mick can go to a new store opened by a guy named Fitzpatrick over on Cow Creek just about eight miles away."

They all settled down, and then Skywalker looked over at Bear Chaser and asked, "How did Mondo get the name Mondo? What the hell does that mean?"

"It means nothing. His mother and I liked the sound of Mondo. She didn't want for him to have an Indian name. And what was your name before the Kiowas took you?"

"Maria Rodriquez," she answered.

"And how was your life as Maria Rodriquez?" asked Bear Chaser.

"I had a good life. I guess I was a little spoiled. My father had money and power. I didn't listen to him enough. I was educated in the Catholic school in Mexico City, but I preferred the ranch. I didn't have enough sense to be afraid of anything. I used to ride hard and a long ways. I raised horses by myself. My father warned me many times about the Comanches and Kiowas that poured down from the north and stole and killed in our area in northern Mexico. One day, there was probably a hundred Kiowas and Comanches that hit our ranch. Burned it down. I don't know how many of my family members were killed, but I saw most of their butchered bodies. I tried to run, but a Kiowa scout saw me and ran me down. After that, my life changed completely. I was no longer a spoiled child. I was a slave. Many times I thought about killing myself, and I know the Kiowas thought about killing me. I just refused to let them take over and control my life completely. No matter what I had to do, I acted like I still possessed some self-worth and some control of myself."

Bear Chaser asked her if she had any children.

"I got pregnant a couple of times, but I knew how to stop that. I learned a little about healing at college, and while I was with the Kiowas, I learned a lot more from a Kiowa medicine woman. The Kiowa medicine woman taught me more than reading books. I figured they wouldn't kill me if I could fix them up."

"It looks like to me they wouldn't want to trade you off if you were a good doctor," said Mick.

"My first so-called Indian husband died when his horse fell so his brother took me as his wife. That new one liked to beat me. I kept away from him. The Kiowas are real superstitious. They never did like my attitude, and they would have killed me a long time ago if I hadn't learned medicine. But the brother of my husband who had the responsibility of taking care of me, and was my second husband, just didn't want to take a chance of dying too. When you captured him, the family and the whole Kiowa tribe found a way to get rid of me. If you had traded a little better, Mick, you wouldn't have had to give up five horses. I think they would have given you five horses just to take me off their hands."

At that, Mondo laughed and looked over at Mick. "And you think you're such a great horse trader. You better keep trading with those dumb Texans and stay away from Indians. You think you've got a 'five-horse woman', and what you've really got is a minus-'five-horse woman.' By taking her, you lost five horses."

Mick blushed and looked over to Skywalker. "I think she's worth many horses. I'd given them my whole herd." Mick smiled real big.

Skywalker frowned. "Do you think I like to be compared to merchandise in a store? You just remember that you don't own me. And if you don't take me out of here within the next sixty days, then I'm going to leave by myself."

That ended the conversation. The three men looked at each other, and even Mondo realized how comfortable Skywalker had made their lives. But even knowing that, Mondo knew that it was time for him to go back to living alone in the place he built where nobody else would live.

Chapter 19

THE LITTLE MAN in his big plantation was very upset. Savanah was still gone. The ignorant trash that he had to pay to bring her back had failed. He missed her more than he ever thought he would. Not only the beauty of her naked body was missed, but her quiet agreement with everything he said was needed to make him feel good. Purify Jones had built a perfect life with money and all that wealth could provide and a perfect wife, bought and raised to meet all his needs. Then a big black African native with no brains at all but a lot of brawn took her and escaped across to the backward country of wild savages, a place in America where civilized citizens sent worthless inhabitants to make room for the white rulers that were necessary to make this a great country. And with all his power and money, Purify Jones could not gain back what he wanted the most.

As he sat on his front porch and surveyed his plantation, Purify Jones grew red with anger as he thought of the incompetent white people he had to rely on to bring Savanah back. The ugly, hate-filled Split Face was so ingrained with hate he couldn't think in a logical manner. However, Purify Jones realized that he and the other Southern leaders had to rely on the poor white trash who were all a little crazy to keep the war going and keep the South from being overrun by the conceited Yankees and the freed darkies trying to interfere with the peaceful life of a Southern gentleman. Purify Jones knew he should lead the expedition into Indian Territory to find and free Savanah from the awful clutches of the evil giant and the savages across the

Red River. A good man had to do it himself sometimes to get the job done right. But he refused to lower himself to the common riffraff of the sick that loved to gang up on and hurt people. Most of the hooded night riders got a sexual gratification from the pain of the helpless, whether white or black skinned. He would not be caught in the company of such low life. So he had to rely on the cowards like Split Face, who let his hate do his thinking for him and who would cut and run if the numbers turned against him. Purify Jones smiled because he had the perfect plan to get the job done and get to Wildhorse Creek and slip up and attack the gathering of darkies and kill Maboola and free his woman, Savanah. Purify Jones knew it took a smart man to make a competent organization out of the KKK people who lived with hate. So Purify Jones carefully explained the attack to Split Face and gave him plenty of money to buy the longhorns and hire the ex-rebel killers to go along as cowboys and accomplish what Purify Jones wanted to do about the two people that stayed on his mind all the time: Maboola and Savanah.

As Split Face eased the cattle across the Red River at Spanish Fort, he again went over the plan in his mind and counted the five hundred longhorns he had bought instead of a thousand long-horns Purify Jones gave him the money to purchase. More money for his own pocket, thought Split Face, and less cattle to worry about when they slipped up on the Wildhorse Creek settlement.

Split Face still stung from the ass eating he got from Purify Jones for the last failed attack on the Negroes who lived along Wildhorse Creek. The little rich man thought he was better than anyone else just because he figured out a way to beat the cotton blockade during the war and make a lot of money.

Jones had told Split Face to hire twenty-five haters of darkies who had killed before and let them play the part of trail drivers and take a thousand head of longhorns east of the Chisholm Trail and drive the herd to where Wildhorse Creek went into the Washita River. If Split Face did it right, and they looked and acted like cowboys, then the river rats would not identify them as potential enemies coming across the Red River and notify with their drums the people of Wildhorse Creek. And the Wildhorse Creek scouts would not know who the attackers were as they drove the cattle right up to the village and hit them with a surprise attack. Other Texas herds were being driven north by this more eastern route, and no one would suspect a thing. The size of the herds varied, but the average number of cattle was about 2,000 to 2,500 head, and the number of cowboys pushing the herd ran about fifteen. That's why Jones gave Split Face money to at least buy a thousand head so that no one would get suspicious. Jones told Split Face to make sure he killed Maboola and brought Savanah back unharmed, and the thousand head of cattle would be sold and divided among those cowboys that came back to Texas with Savanah.

Split Face wore a handkerchief over his face like he was trying to keep the dust out of his nose so that nobody would recognize the man with the ugly scar down the middle of his face. Split Face and the twenty-five killers herded the cattle east after they crossed the Red River and moved around the Arbuckle Mountains to the Washita River and moved the herd slowly toward the Wildhorse Creek settlement. Everything was going just as Purify Jones had planned, and nobody had noticed the real makeup of the crew as they approached Wildhorse Creek.

Up ahead, Savanah was teaching the children to read and write, and everything was peaceful on the church side of the community. Purify Jones and Split Face had never been to the Wildhorse Creek village and did not know that it had a church side and a wild side. The wild side was farther back from the Washita River and nearer Fort Arbuckle while the church side was right down in the area where Wildhorse Creek met the Washita River.

The church side consisted of a general store, which was a meeting place and school, a livery stable, and shacks and tents and lean-tos where families lived. The wild side had one large two-story building, which was a bar on the first floor and a sleeping area used primarily as a whorehouse on the second floor. The wild side also had a livery stable where horses were kept when the customers came in to buy the booze or gamble or participate in the pleasures of the flesh. There was a small bootlegger's cabin not connected to the bar and a two-room cabin for gambling. All of this was run, controlled, and owned by Tan Bishop, the leader of the South Carolina ex-slaves.

It was Maboola who first saw the Texas longhorn herd moving toward the wild side part of town one early morning and immediately noticed that the trail drivers seemed to be ignoring the herd and moving up toward the front of the cattle drive. Maboola thought they were sure bad cowboys as they let the cattle drift off to the left and right and didn't keep them in a good formation. Then he counted the number of cowboys and he realized there were a lot more men than necessary for such a small herd. When the trail drivers pulled up and started loading rifles and checking their pistols, Maboola knew at once that this was not another Texas herd passing around the village but a planned sneak attack.

Maboola rode hard toward wild side, and as he entered the main area, he fired off his shotgun and yelled to get ready for an attack. Tan Bishop and his men woke up and poured out of the bars and shacks, most in their ragged long johns. The attackers, a mile from the creek, heard the shotgun blast and charged toward the buildings. Maboola did not slow down but circled the village and headed back to the church side to get Greer and help.

Tan Bishop and fifteen of his bouncers saw the twenty-five Texans riding directly toward them into their area, and the blacks ran into the two-story bar and whorehouse. The Texans surrounded the building, but the Texans had to seek cover as the men in the whorehouse opened up on them so that the Texans ran for the livery stable and hid around behind the bootleggers shack. Some ran into the gambling shack and killed the two blacks inside. The attackers then opened up a treacherous fire on the two-story building.

Within about five minutes, everybody had cover and was firing shots into the wooden structures trying to kill each other. Split Face knew they had to charge or try to burn out the people in the two-story bar, but Split Face did not know that there was another community with more people in it than in the wild side.

As Split Face hollered to charge the bar, shots rang out from behind them as twenty-five men, some on horses and some on foot, all carrying weapons, fired on the back side of the attackers who were trapped between the gunfire from both sides.

Split Face thought it was the Lighthorse Police and ordered his men to take off. He realized they were outnumbered, and the KKK never fought when they were outnumbered. That was not his plan or their way of doing harm. Therefore within ten minutes after the Texas attackers had come into the wild side of Wildhorse Creek, they had remounted and started fleeing without losing a man. Split Face was not about to get anybody killed by these lowlife darkies.

Both sides of the town met in the middle of the street as they fired at the retreating attackers.

"Mount up! Let's get those sons-of-bitches before they cross the Red River," hollered Maboola.

Tan Bishop looked over at Hudson Greer and shook his head no. "Hey, they're gone. They're not coming back for a while. We don't want to be caught running down a bunch of white men through Indian Territory. That will just bring more white men across the Red River."

Hudson Greer nodded in agreement. "He's right. They're gone. They slipped up on us and we ran them off. That ought to keep them out. They probably know now that they can't come into this place and kill black people at will without losing a lot of their own. That will keep those cowards away."

Maboola reared up and glared the two men. "You don't understand a damn thing. These haters are going to come and keep coming until we kill as many of them as they've killed of us. They are the majority, and they know that they have got more guns and more people that will come after us. Therefore they can't stand to let us defy them in any way, shape, or form. We just ran twenty-five Texans out of our town, and you think they will let us forget that? We've got to kill them so bad and so many times that they will never, never try to come back against us again. That means we've got to ride after them and we've got to let only one go back, not twenty-five, but let one go back and let him crawl back all bloody and tell them, 'By God, don't go over there again or they will kill you.' I guarantee you, there's a number. I don't know what that number is. Whether it's a hundred Texans or a thousand Texans, but there's a number of white haters we have to kill. When we reach that number, then they won't bother us anymore. That's the way they think. That's the way they live, and that's the only way that we can protect ourselves and not be mistreated until the day we die."

"You're crazy," said Tan Bishop as he turned and directed his men to clean up around the place and get back to business.

Hudson Greer shook his head no again. "Maboola, slow down. We don't even have the animals, enough fast horses, to run them back, and you think the Lighthorse Police won't help them out if we cornered a bunch of whites in their country and tried to kill them? The Chickasaw Lighthorse Police don't let us bother anybody that comes after us. If we start chasing Texans back across the Chickasaw Nation, the police are going to stop us because they are afraid of what the Texans will do to them. I'm not for it, and that's it. My people aren't going to go chasing after that scum, the KKK."

"They only understand one thing, and that's force. I'm going. The rest of you damn cowards can stay." Maboola grabbed his horse, jumped on it, and took off after the retreating Texans.

There were many an Indian, many a black, and even some whites that witnessed that day something they would never forget. Split Face led twenty-four men as fast as he could south, toward the Red River. They rode their horses like they were afraid that they were going to be killed. But unknown to the retreating men, only one big black giant on a horse that was too small for him was chasing after them. They never looked back. They just kept going, and so did Maboola. People in the area observed twenty-five white men riding as hard as they could, looking back every once in a while to see if the devil was after them. And then here came a big black devil whose legs almost touched the ground, chasing twenty-five rough-looking Texans.

Split Face thought the whole Chickasaw Nation was after him, and he never slowed down. However, one of the Texan's horse went lame, and he slowed down and had to stop. None of the Texans stopped to help him. So naturally, Maboola caught the attacker, shot the attacker, cut the attacker's head off, and hung him up in a tree by his feet.

Maboola didn't stop chasing them till they got to the Red River and the river rats slowed him up and talked him out of crossing the river to chase down the white killers who had disappeared into Texas.

The white attacker that had no head and hung in a tree by his feet was never cut down. Soon, the flesh had disappeared, and all that was hanging was a corpse without a head. The skeleton hung near a main trail, but no one dared remove it. Many people rode out just to observe the skeleton with no head hanging by his feet. After the story of Maboola's ride and of the KKK's retreat and run back into Texas, people began to call Maboola the Black Death. He became almost like a god among the ex-slaves in Indian Territory and a devil to people with white blood.

CHAPTER 20

THE WEATHER WARMED in late spring. The men slept outside, and Skywalker took care of their needs like a mother hen. Mondo himself began to think against his better judgment that it really wasn't all that bad to have Skywalker and his father and Mick living with him. Furniture was made, and his home became comfortable.

The herd of horses that Mondo and Mick took care of grew to eighty with the addition of several colts that spring. They did not keep the horses inside the fort itself because there was enough grass in the valley created by the horseshoe-like circling creek to graze them within the boundary of the tree line along Little Beaver Creek.

One morning in the middle of May 1868, as they were sitting around enjoying their coffee, Mondo felt a sudden anxiety that spread through him like the old warnings he received when he lived alone. At once, he jumped up, ran out of the cabin, and threw open the gate to the compound. The horses were no longer in the valley. He yelled at his dad and Mick to mount up, and the three of them saddled their main riding horses kept in the corral.

Mondo and Bear Chaser immediately picked up the tracks of the stolen horses. It appeared that about seven or eight riders on shoed horses had eased the herd across the creek at a low place and had pushed them east toward the cattle trail to Abilene, Kansas. The tracks didn't seem to be over four to six hours old, and the three men took off after the stolen horses.

About two miles east of Little Beaver Creek, they ran into the main chuck wagon path along Jessie Chisholm's trade route, identified by the deep scars that the iron wheels made in the prairie. All around for at least a hundred yards, on each side of the wagon wheel cuts thousands of hoof prints from longhorn cattle, flooded the prairie, and made it almost impossible to determine whether the stolen horses had been driven north or south along the cattle trail. It took them about an hour to carefully examine the area before Bear Chaser picked up a chipped hoof track that belonged to one of the horses that the rustlers rode. The stolen horses were being driven south, down the Chisholm Trail, and the three followed the tracks with Mondo and Mick on one side and Bear Chaser on the other, looking to see where the rustlers might have driven the horses off the cattle trail.

They rode south at a quick pace for seven miles until they ran into the Arbuckle Road going east. Again, Bear Chaser found the chipped footprint of the rustler's horse, and they determined that the stolen horses had been driven east along the Arbuckle Road. Within two miles, they entered the heavy Cross Timbers where the US Army had cut through the thick twisting-vine area sixteen years before in order to make the short, thick post oak woods passable by a wagon. Because of the narrow trail, the stolen horses had to slow down, and it wasn't long until the three men came upon tracks not over a half-hour-old.

As the three rode over the top of a hill and looked down, they saw their horses grazing in a clearing at the bottom of the hill. There was no one around, and they immediately pulled up and realized that they had ridden into an ambush even before the first shots were fired. Rifle fire erupted all around them, and all three of them dove from their horses and hit the ground. As the shots continued to pepper them, they crawled on their bellies to a slight gulch, an old buffalo wallow, and slipped into the shallow hole to try to hide from the hail of bullets. It was the perfect trap, and all three of them knew they were lucky to still be alive. The rustlers had surrounded them and caught them in an open area. The outlaws themselves had good coverage behind the trees around the clearing. The bullets came at them so fast that they didn't even have time to rise up and fire back. All three of them tasted red dirt as they kept close to the ground. They just hoped that they didn't get shot before they had a chance to shoot back. Mondo knew that they wouldn't get a good shot unless the outlaws abandoned the trees and came forward to kill them off. All three knew death was near.

Someone hollered, and the shooting stopped. A voice came from the dense trees. "Don't waste your bullets. Just take your time and let's move closer and pick them off one at a time. If they rise up, they're dead. Make sure you got a good shot before you fire."

Mondo raised his head to look over the small indentation, and immediately, a bullet kicked dust and dirt into his face and he went back down against the ground. The shots began to ring out more slowly but more accurately. Each a little closer. It was just a matter of time.

Mondo whispered. "We've got to get out of here. Eventually, they are going to hit us. Let's charge the area where that voice came from. Maybe we can get the leader."

"Jesus, Mondo, there must be six or eight rifles aimed at us. We've got twenty to thirty yards of open space. I think we should wait them out. At some point, they're going to have to come a little closer to kill us off in this gully," said Mick.

About that time, there was a loud terrifying scream in the south portion of the thick woods and then a shotgun blast and then complete silence.

"What was that?" hollered the same voice within the trees. "None of us are using shotguns. Harry, was that you that yelled?"

To the west, someone else yelled, "Holy Mother of God," and then a scream of terror that suddenly went quiet.

"What's going on over there?" shouted the leader's voice. "We must have someone coming in from the south. We need help over here!" shouted the same voice. "Some of you, men, swing around and come over to the south side. We-" Before the sentence could be finished, a shotgun blast boomed, and the voice was quiet.

"Hey, boss, what's happened?" came a voice north of the three men.

"Boss, are you still there?" There was nothing but silence. "Let's get out of here!" shouted another voice to the east, and Mondo rose up, and so did the other two. They could hear men running through the woods to the north of them and west of them. Mondo rose up to fire at one of the outlaws that was heading back west. Before he pulled the trigger, a big black man stepped out from behind a tree and cut the outlaw's head off with a machete.

"Jesus," said Mick. "Did you see that?" Behind them, they heard men crashing through the short trees on their horses as they raced through the woods and left the stolen herd.

Mondo, Bear Chaser, and Mick slowly got up from the gully and started walking toward the dead outlaw with no head. The black giant just stood and waited for them. There was no expression on his dark face.

Mondo walked up to him and then looked down at the decapitated outlaw and then looked back at the giant. "You're Maboola, aren't you? You saved our lives. Are you alone?"

"No," Said Maboola. "Savanah's with me."

Mondo asked, "She's the woman who came to Indian Territory with you, isn't she? What are you doing so far west of the Wildhorse Creek settlement?"

"Jones has sent so many bounty hunters and killers after me that I left Wildhorse Creek with Savanah. That rich Texan who wants Savanah back put a three-hundred-dollar reward on my head and five hundred to the man who brings Savanah back alive. There's so many hungry gun fighters pouring across the Red River after us that the Wildhorse Creek is always under fire. It's too dangerous for the people there. Savanah and I slipped out, and we're not going back."

About that time a beautiful, light-skinned tan girl rode out of the bushes leading a large black stallion. All three of the men were stunned to silence at the beauty of the girl. She looked up once and then cut her eyes downward. Her eyes were green and her hair a straight brown. She was tall and thin but large in the right places. Mondo saw the perfection of this woman and turned to Maboola. "Why did you risk her life helping us?"

"I didn't look at it like I was helping you. I just saw some white outlaws that were scattered out and alone and ready for killing. I didn't even know who they were shooting at. I just try to kill as many whites as I can when I get the chance."

Mick stood there, began to smile, and said, "I hope you don't mean all whites. I was born white, but I live with Mondo and he's a Negro, you know."

Maboola looked over at Mick and said nothing. Bear Chaser stepped up and extended his hand. "Thanks, Maboola. We'd all be dead now if it weren't for you."

Maboola looked down at Bear Chaser's hand and then looked back into his eyes. He hesitated a second, and then the two shook hands.

"Where are you two heading?" asked Bear Chaser.

"I don't know. Probably go north and try to get out of this country and as far away from Texas as we can."

Bear Chaser nodded and then replied, "Why don't you help us gather up these horses and start them back toward Mondo's. His place is about ten miles from here. The least we could do is give you a feed. We've now got a darn good cook back at Mondo's fort."

Maboola looked over at Mondo and waited for him to extend an invitation.

"Sure," said Mondo. "You can rest up there before you start north."

Mick stepped forward and stuck his hand out to Maboola. "Will you make one exception to killing whites? I'd feel a lot better if I didn't have to watch my back all the time that you're around."

Maboola didn't extend his hand to Mick. "I'll let you know before I decide to kill you. I learned a long time ago not to turn my back on any white man. They all stick together when the chips are down. When danger comes, people seem to side with their own kind. So for the moment, I'll just hold off killing you."

Mick turned a little pale and backed away.

Maboola turned to Savanah and said, "Savanah, why don't you get down and let Mondo have your mount. We can go round up their own saddle horses, and then all five of us can drive the herd back to Mondo's."

Savanah, who hadn't said a word to anyone, eased off her mount and shyly glanced up at Maboola without looking at the other three men. Again, they all marveled at her good looks before Maboola interrupted their thoughts. "Come on. Let's go find your riding horses and get on with it. I don't like to stay in one spot very long. There's too many white outlaws and sorry-ass Texans hanging around that want my head. Let's get moving."

With that, Mondo jumped on Savanah's horse, and Maboola mounted up, and the two rode off to recover the horses the three men were riding when they were ambushed. They found three more dead outlaws and buried the four rustlers in a shallow grave. It wasn't long before all five people were on horses and driving the herd back. They didn't stay on the Arbuckle Road but cut across the countryside as soon as they cleared the Cross Timbers and headed northwest toward Mondo's.

CHAPTER 21

D USK HAD SETTLED in by the time the five riders had returned with the once-stolen horses and coaxed them across the creek into Mondo's valley. Skywalker had seen that there were two extra riders and had gone back into the cabin and prepared more food. As the riders approached the compound, Maboola stopped and looked over the small fort and then rode around the outside of the walls before he entered the compound. Mondo watched as Maboola dismounted and looked inside of the fort, climbed up on the walls, checked the top of the stone cabin, and then finally walked up to the three men and Savanah, all who had been watching his movements.

Mondo spoke first. "Does it suit you?"

Maboola shook his head no. "I'm not staying in here tonight. Savanah and I will sleep back in the trees along the creek. I make it a habit of not getting trapped inside anything. This is a pretty strong little fort, but it wouldn't take a lot of bounty hunters to pin us down and starve us out."

Mondo smiled and said, "Come on in and look around. I'll show you a little trapdoor that has been very helpful to me in the past."

The four of them walked into the house and stared at Skywalker who was setting the table.

Mick stepped forward, "This is Skywalker. I traded five horses for her, but I don't own her. She owns herself. She's a good cook and she knows medicine and besides, she hasn't killed anybody with that eight-inch dagger she carries under her dress."

Mick, Mondo, and Bear Chaser laughed like it was a big joke. Skywalker frowned. Maboola didn't smile but continued to stare at Skywalker. Savanah continued to stare at the floor.

Finally, Maboola asked, "Is she an Indian?"

"No," said Mick. "She's a Mexican girl that was captured by the Kiowas and lived with them for about three years."

Skywalker glared back at Maboola and asked, "And who the hell are you?"

Maboola actually grinned for the first time and said, "I'm the meanest African that was ever carried across the sea in chains and forced to work the fields before I fought my way to freedom."

Skywalker nodded. "Not much fun being a slave, is it? So how long have you been free, and did you help get the horses back?"

Maboola nodded in the affirmative, but before he could answer, Mick interrupted. "I'm hungry. Let's all sit down and get a bite to eat. We can hash out all this history after we've filled our bellies."

"There's not enough room around this little table Mondo made," said Skywalker. "I'll just set the food there, and everybody can grab something to eat and sit around where they can find a spot."

They all started for a plate, except Savanah who stood back and waited.

Maboola looked back and spoke, "Come on, Savanah. When are you going to learn that you don't have to wait on nobody? When you're not acting like you're white, you act like you're still a slave."

After they had all filled their plates, they sat on the floor or on the four newly built chairs. It was pretty quiet as everyone attacked their meal. When they had finished eating, they stacked the plates and eased outside where a beautiful sunset was making for a cool and pleasant late spring evening. They all grabbed a spot to sit, and Mick and Bear Chaser rolled a cigarette and began to smoke.

Mick finally looked over at Maboola and asked, "How long have you been in America, Maboola?"

Maboola looked at Mick and didn't answer right away. "I was brought over here in 1850 as a boy, about seventeen years ago, after it was illegal to bring slaves into America. That didn't stop a bunch of pirates from making money. I was sold to a planter in South Texas. I was twenty years old when the Civil War started, and by then I was much bigger than anyone on the plantation. I ran off for the last time right before the war ended. The man who beat me I killed and then hid in the swamps until the KKK found me, and I took off. When I got to North Texas, I saw Savanah, and I took her on with me to Indian Territory. That doubled the price on my head. We ended up at Wildhorse Creek, but by staying there, we were making it real dangerous for the rest of the black people that lived there."

Mondo looked over at Savanah and back to Maboola. "Did you steal her or did she want to go with you?"

Maboola frowned. "Of course she wanted to go with me. She was tired of servicing that old fart that forced himself on her."

Mondo glanced back to Savanah, and when she didn't raise her eyes to meet his, he looked back at Maboola. "Does she talk for herself, or do you make all the words for her?"

Maboola said, "She talks after she finds out that the people she meets won't hurt her. She's never done much on her own, and she's not sure enough about herself to say anything right now. She knows how to act white but doesn't know how to live nonwhite."

Mondo again looked back at Savanah. "Is that true? Are you where you want to be?"

Savanah finally raised her head, and those light green eyes had a questionable look in them. She then glanced over at Maboola as if to ask him for permission to speak or to let him speak for her. Instead, Maboola stared back at her, and everyone waited. Savanah blushed and dropped her eyes to the floor again.

Skywalker got up and walked over to Savanah and put her arm around her shoulder. "Don't worry, honey. You can talk or not talk, just whatever you want to do. None of these overgrown boys have much manners. They're not as tough as they think they are. You'll get used to them. I didn't know what to say either when I was first captured by the Kiowas. Tell Mondo it's none of his damn business how you feel."

Mondo spoke. "I just wanted to know whether she wanted to be with Maboola. He would scare most people into silence. Maboola does all the talking for her." Skywalker spun around and faced Mondo. "Just let it go. Can't you see you are embarrassing this girl?"

"You always forget that this is my house. I have a right to know about the people staying here. You're not the boss around here."

"I think it's going to rain," said Bear Chaser. Everyone stopped and stared at Bear Chaser as if he had lost his mind. Bear Chaser looked up at the sky and continued. "Yes, sir, I smell a few clouds rolling in. We might ought to put a rider out tonight to control the horses. I think there's going to be a lot of thunder and some lightning."

There was a long silence as everybody wondered whether to discuss the weather or continue talking about Savanah. As Bear Chaser continued to look at the clouds, the silence grew.

Finally, Savanah lifted her eyes and looked over at Mondo. "I was ready to go when I left. I'm trying to get used to living on the run. A whole bunch of real mean white men are chasing me. I feel safe with Maboola."

Mondo thought about the white men with the missing heads and could understand why she felt safe with Maboola. He nodded and then looked over at his dad. "Well, I don't think it's going to rain at all."

Instead of ending the discussion, Mick had to speak up. He looked over at Savanah and said, "I don't think that rich Texan is ever going to give up trying to get you back."

Maboola spoke. "Well, we'll just keep moving north. Maybe he'll run out of money or run out of men before long."

Mick spoke. "You need a rifle if you keep running. That shot-gun, pistol, and machete are only good for closed-in fighting."

Maboola nodded. "You're right. The truth is, I was going west, kind of looking for you, Mondo. I know your reputation. I was hoping I could trade for a rifle and get a few lessons to boot."

"So you were coming our way, were you?" said Mondo. "Then it wasn't by chance that you came upon us when we were pinned down by those rustlers."

"I was just drifting along Arbuckle Road trying to hit the Abilene Trail and then cut up to your place. But when I heard the shooting and saw an easy white man to kill or two, I decided to try to get me a few."

"Yeah, that's what you said," indicated Mondo. "As long as you try to kill every white man you see, you won't last long and Savanah will wish she stayed with that Jones fellow."

Maboola frowned. "Aren't you glad that I decided to help you? If I hadn't, you three would be dead."

"I agree," said Mondo. "But I'm just telling you that you can't go gunning for every white man you see and expect to keep Savanah alive."

"What business is that of yours?" asked Maboola. "I saved your life, and I was hoping that I could trade for a rifle and you could teach me how to shoot it. Most ex-slaves don't have a lot of experience with rifles. You owe me."

Mondo nodded. "I've got an extra rifle to trade, and I'll teach you all I know. But it's not right for you to go on a killing spree and take this girl with you. You're making it impossible for her to learn how to live free."

About that time, they heard some thunder off to the east. Bear Chaser stood up and looked at Mondo and smiled. After a long day, they broke early and went for rest. Maboola led Savanah out of the compound and disappeared into the trees along Little Beaver Creek. Even though Mondo had showed Maboola about the trapdoor and the escape tunnel under the cabin, Maboola could not stand to be closed in. It was a wet night.

CHAPTER 22

Now there were six people living in Mondo's compound, and that created an uneasy tension that prevailed until the fire. Bear Chaser smelled the smoke first. The spring had become very dry, and a strong wind from the southwest blew the cloud of smoke from the prairie fire miles ahead of the line of blazing grass moving at five miles an hour.

It was late in the evening, and all had come in for supper. Bear Chaser sprung up and ran out of the cabin with Mondo right after him. By the time the other four had come outside, Mondo and Bear Chaser were gathering gunny sacks and buckets and running for the southwest corner of the valley. The others saw the boiling clouds of smoke and gathered blankets, coats, and water containers and followed Mondo and Bear Chaser.

Mondo gave orders. "Maboola, you and Bear Chaser come with me across the creek and meet the fire head-on. The rest of you, get the sparks and floating embers that get through the trees and put them out. Maybe we can save the valley."

The three men soaked their sacks in the creek and began wetting the ground outside the south tree line. Sparks of fire were flashing in the air over the trees and landing on the valley grass. Mick and the two women ran from one burning spot to the next, beating out the small fires before the flames grew. The wall of blazing orange roared into Mondo, Bear Chaser, and Maboola as if they had done nothing to stop the speedy advance of the ten-foot-high blaze.

"Run!" yelled Mondo. The three men jumped the creek and entered the valley the same time the prairie fire sprung up on the inside of the valley and started to advance toward the fort.

The grass was eaten down inside the trees so that the fire didn't get over five feet high, but the blaze moved fast and hot. All six were swinging blankets and gunny sacks and backing off as if in a backward trot. The sparks stuck to their clothes and exposed skin so that half the time, they were slapping out embers on themselves as much as pounding the grass fire and retreating. The fire was fast and too strong. They broke and ran back toward the fort.

Mick stumbled and fell just as a spot of tall grass blazed up right on him. Maboola spun around and ran into the fire, grabbed Mick by the collar, and slung him like a rag doll ahead of the fire. Mick landed with his clothes on fire. Maboola dove on top of him and rolled them both up in a wet blanket as the fire raced over them. Maboola jumped up and ripped the burning clothes from Mick and picked him up and ran through a low place in the fire toward the fort.

Maboola set Mick down, and they all stayed with the flame to keep the walls of the fort from catching fire. The fire seemed to turn right and skipped past the fort and raced toward the horses in the northeast corner of the valley.

As they turned, they saw Skywalker running ahead of the blaze toward the horses, yelling and screaming and waiving her arms. The horses hesitated against the trees. Skywalker forced them down into the creek, and the herd moved westward along the creek and got out of the way of the fire.

By the time the rest of them reached Skywalker, she was sitting down on the ground, breathing in and out as if she couldn't catch her breath. Mick trotted up to her, wearing the bottom half of his long underwear with his chest red as if he stayed out in the sun all day. They turned and watched the fire speed on to the northeast and then looked back at the burned valley and the fort still standing untouched.

Everyone looked around, and Bear Chaser started to laugh. They looked at Bear Chaser like he was crazy, and then they looked at each other. All of them were covered with black stains and tattered clothes as if they had been trampled by a herd of cattle.

Mondo stepped up to Mick. "Are you all right? You look like you've been baked and put outside to cool down. And a lot of your hair is gone like you've been scalped by an Indian who didn't know how."

Mick felt up on his head and smiled. "No, my scalp is still on but my hair is real stiff. I'm burning up, and I don't know what the rest of you are going to do, but I'm going to cool off in the creek."

Mick turned and started for the bathing hole they called Three Rocks. The rest got up and walked after him. At the northwest corner of the creek, they pulled up at the swimming hole. There was a large rock that was on the floor of the creek and one lying flat on the bank and one that partially dammed up the creek so that there was a little clear pond twenty feet long and about twelve feet wide and six feet deep. Mick walked up, jumped in, and went under. One after another, each of them jumped in with their dirty clothes hanging onto their burn-spotted bodies. They started rubbing the black off their clothes and skin and then rested in the cool water. One at a time, they got out and climbed up on the rock on the bank and sat in the sun to dry off. They were all quiet for a while until Mick looked over at Maboola. "I guess I owe you my life. Why did you do it? I thought you would be the last one that would pull me out of those flames."

Maboola looked over at Mick and, for a while, didn't say anything. Then he shook his head as if he didn't know the answer. "I guess I didn't know it was you. I just saw somebody fall, and I didn't want to see them burnt to a crisp."

Mick smiled, "Well, thanks anyway. It would be a shame if you killed me now after saving my life."

Maboola continued to stare at Mick. "Some things do change. I've learned to feel when someone thinks I'm lowlife because I'm deep black. I've been around a few Yankee white men that claim that blacks are equal to whites, but that's not how they look at me or other ex-slaves. When someone thinks they're born better than someone else, no matter what they say or do, you can feel that deep down."

Mondo looked over at Maboola. "You've got that right. I fought alongside some Yankee whites during the war. In the battle, when things were tough, nobody thought anybody was any better than the other. All worked together to save lives. But just as soon as the battle was over, when you ran into them again, you could tell that things were back to normal. They looked at you like you were dirt. It's real simple. No matter what the white man says or does, as long as he thinks he's superior in every way, then you know he's a lying, no-good bastard."

Bear Chaser nodded. "Same with mixed-bloods and full-bloods. Mixed-bloods, even if they are seven-eighths Chickasaw, feel like they are better than full-bloods. It's as if that drop of white blood makes them superior to anybody that doesn't have any white blood."

Mick nodded his head. "I guess I did feel better than you, Maboola. I don't any longer. You are just as much a man as anybody, and I would ride the river with you any day."

"I can feel that. I guess I won't kill you." Maboola smiled.

"Well, it really doesn't matter," said Mondo. "You're not going to change anybody's feelings. As long as they leave you alone, you can live with your own kind. But look around at this bunch-it's hard to figure out who our own kind is. We've got one Irish Texan, one full-blood Chickasaw, and one half-breed like me with a little black thrown in. We've got Maboola who is all-African, we got a woman like Savanah who has a hell of a lot more white blood than black blood, but everybody in the white world says she's all black, and we got one Mexican-Spanish aristocrat who has lived with the Kiowas long enough to be part Indian. I guess if we can learn to live together, anybody can."

Skywalker stood up and looked around at all of them. "Then let's live the right way. We've got a lot to do. We need to round up those horses and find some grass. We worked together good with that fire, but we've got a lot to do."

Mondo jumped up. "She's right. Let's clean this place up and get on with it. We live in a dangerous spot, and the fire isn't the only thing that is going to be after us. But I have a good feeling that we can take care of most things."

Chapter 23

THE TENSION AMONG the six occupants of Mondo's compound began to ease as they got used to each other. The four men and the two women worked well together. The horses were taken care of, a garden was planted and tended to, and there was plenty of meat on the table as all four men enjoyed hunting. Mondo took the time to teach Maboola how to shoot the rifle, and Maboola learned quickly. Savanah was still shy and hardly said anything at all, but her confidence seemed to grow as she worked with Skywalker around the compound. Skywalker looked after her like she was a little sister. By early June, when the weather turned warm, all were sleeping outside the cabin within the four walls of the little fort. Things were going well, and even Mondo began to think that living with this bunch was better than living alone. But then in mid-June, Split Face and his gang of cutthroats arrived.

Bear Chaser saw them coming and got everyone inside the compound. Split Face raised a white flag and rode up to the compound alone. Mondo stood up on the ledge at the top of the wall near the front gate and peered down at Split Face. "Get off my land. You're not welcome here. You've got five seconds to turn around, or I'll blow your damn head off."

"Just hold on a minute. I'm not after you, and I'm not after doing anything to your little fort if you do the right thing. Word has reached Mr. Jones that a darkie called Maboola and that high yellow Negress called Savanah are in your fort. You've got five seconds to turn them over to me or we're going to burn your place down and scalp everyone in the fort."

Mondo smiled. "You didn't bring enough outlaws to get that done. You're right. Maboola and Savanah are in here, and they are in here to stay as long as they want to stay. I'll count to five, and if you're not turned around and out of my range before I reach five, you are a dead man. You think ten sorry-ass bounty hunters are going to be able to bust into my place? I hope to hell you try. One-two-…"

Split Face jerked his horse around and buried his spurs in the horse's side and took off back to the white men waiting with their guns in hand. Even before Split Face reached his men, Maboola fired a rifle shot that took Split Face off his horse. Yelling and cursing, Split Face jumped back on his horse and rode low in the saddle as Maboola fired again and missed.

Mondo looked over at Maboola. "He came under a white flag, why did you try to back shoot him?"

Without changing the expression on his face, Maboola said, "I was afraid that he was going to take your warning and leave. I don't make it a habit of passing up a shot at a black hater like that Split Face. You got to kill those sorry bastards whenever you get a chance, from the front or from the back. If you'd taught me better with this rifle, I'd got rid of one sorry SOB."

Even though the outlaws were at least five hundred yards away, you could hear Split Face yelling and screaming and pointing toward the fort. At once, the outlaws split up and headed for the trees along the creek and surrounded the fort, taking rifle positions on all sides. Each of the men inside the fort took a side to watch through a peephole that had been cut in the stockade walls. The outlaws had really nothing to shoot at but the wooden fence. However, the bounty hunters commenced firing and wasting bullets. For the next five hours, the men inside the fort waited and watched to make sure no one tried to make a run to the wall and get inside the fort.

Toward dusk, four men charged out of the trees on the west side and ran toward the stockade. Bear Chaser was watching on that side. He hollered and rose up and dropped one of the men that was thirty feet from reaching the wall. Before the other three men got to the wall, Mondo and Mick had run to assist Bear Chaser, and all three fired at once, and three attackers went down. Within a matter of minutes, the four outlaws who charged the fort were lying dead, killed before they had even reached the west wall of the compound.

The next time, the attackers waited until dark. The women in the fort relieved the men so that they got some sleep, but there was always a pair of eyes watching and listening during the night. Savanah was on the east wall when she heard the outlaws trying to belly-up to the fort. She warned everyone, and all six people were waiting at the top of the wall when a couple of killers struck a match and tried to set fire to the fort. Four guns roared, and the two attackers died before the fire could be started. The next day, there was no sign of the outlaws. Split Face had learned that it was going to take an army to get inside Mondo's fort.

From the first test of his compound under attack, Mondo learned he had built a compound that could withstand a lot of attackers as long as they didn't bring a cannon and as long as they didn't find the trapdoor and tunnel that would keep Mondo from getting water and maybe even food if someone attempted a long siege.

The rumor of the battle of Fort Mondo went up and down the Chisholm Trail and into Texas, and there were many exaggerated killings told and retold about the big black African ex-slave and the Negro half-bred Indian who hunted and killed white men like they were wild game.

As the Texas longhorn cattle drives went north, they generally passed within two or three miles of Mondo's fort. Many a cowboy rode up on the hill about a half a mile southeast of Mondo's fort to look and wonder about the killers that hid behind the walls. Many rode by just to say that they had seen Mondo's fort.

When the Comanches and Kiowas did not get all the provisions they were promised by the US government in the Medicine Lodge Treaty, the warriors went on the warpath. Many Texas herds were stampeded, and the longhorns were killed for meat. Again, the rumor got started that the Comanches and Kiowas were operating out of Mondo's fort since nobody could believe that people could live on Comanche and Kiowa hunting grounds without being friends and partners and working with those Indians.

After the Comanches had stolen almost all of the extra horses from Red Granger's longhorn cattle drive, the Texan decided to ride over and investigate Mondo's fort and see if he could do business with the occupants since he needed more horses before he could continue the drive, and the horses around Mondo's fort were fine-looking animals.

CHAPTER 24

TWELVE MEN DRESSED like trail drovers eased through Mondo's herd, checking the brands on the horses as they came toward the fort. Mondo left Maboola inside the compound with the women. And Bear Chaser, Mick, and Mondo rode out to meet the cowboys. They wore the hats, bandanas, and chaps that identified them as trail drivers, unlike the bounty hunters that had previously come to Mondo's compound. Five of the cowboys were black. Out in front rode Red Granger identified by his bright red beard. Mick had met this famous trail boss who had ridden up and down the Chisholm Trail several times. Mick remembered him from Red River Station when Mick had won the horses riding Tree Top. Red Granger rode up to the three men and stopped with his well-armed cowboys behind him. "I saw six fresh graves when I entered your valley. On the marker it says, 'Here lies those who tried to take this fort.' Who were those you buried in them graves?"

"Those were outlaws who tried to kill us. If you aim to do the same thing, then we'll just dig more graves," said Mondo.

Without showing any reaction to Mondo's statement, Red Granger continued. "Almost all of my horses have been stolen. We can't drive cattle without horses. This country is full of thieves, some Indians, some white rustlers. Some of your horses had trail driver brands that have been changed."

Mick spoke up. "Don't you remember me? I saw you at Red River Station. I won a bunch of horses on Mondo's Tree Top there. I met you at Red River Station when all the herds got held up by the high waters on the Red."

Red Granger studied Mick. "I thought I'd seen you before. So you're the one that lives with this Mondo character and his father Bear Chaser. I heard there was a big black man that lived in this compound. News travels fast up and down the trail, but sometimes it's not always true."

Mondo spoke. "You're the one they call Red Granger, aren't you? We don't steal horses. We might sell you some, if you want to trade with me."

"I'm kind of particular who I trade with. There's a legal bounty on a big black man called Maboola. I don't deal with killers. Is he here with you?"

"These horses belong to me and to Mick," said Mondo. "You would be dealing with us."

"What I hear, there's a KKK bounty from under the table out for you and for Mick as well as for a Chickasaw they call Bear Chaser. Is that you?" Red asked as he nodded toward Mondo's dad.

Bear Chaser said, "Yes."

Red Granger continued. "It's not a legal bounty. But there's a bunch of outlaws that are holed up south of Saint Jo, Texas, that's led by a guy that everybody calls Split Face. He is big in the KKK. The rumor is that they have put a $200 bounty on each of your heads. But I don't give a damn about them. I don't care if you kill that Split Face. Texas would be better off with that bastard dead."

"Why don't you do something about it then?" asked Mick.

"These Yankee carpetbaggers have moved in a Freedmen's Bureau out of Washington, D.C. These Northern boys are backed by the US Army, and they are there to protect ex-slaves and make sure that they are free to vote. Anybody that fought for the South can't vote. Our old leaders are dead or have no power in Texas. Most people feel that the KKK is the only thing that's stopping ex-slaves from taking over the state. So nobody can or will do anything about an evil bastard like Split Face."

Mondo shook his head. "That sounds like a Texas problem. What's that got to do with me and my compound here in Indian Territory?"

"Your fort is right in the path of all those Texas cattle going to Abilene. We're going to move the cattle because that's the only way we can make any money. Along this trail, we're being attacked from all sides. We don't trust anybody in Indian Territory. The Chickasaws want as much as ten cents a head for eating their grass. It used to be one cent. The Comanches and Kiowas want to steal our horses and kill our cattle like they were buffalo. Then there's those sorry white outlaws like Split Face and his gang. They go back and forth across the Red River, stealing and killing because the Chickasaw Lighthorse Police have no jurisdiction over white men. They have to take anybody they catch to Fort Smith, Arkansas. It's a mess."

Red Granger pointed to Mondo. "And nobody knows which side you're on. As I understand it, your dad is a full-blood Chickasaw and you are good friends with the Comanches and Kiowas. And the worse story is about that white killer Maboola who they say is a friend of yours and may be in that compound." Red Granger stopped talking and looked at the compound. "I ask you again, is that Maboola in there? And do you have cannons in that fort?"

Mondo produced a half-smile on his face, "Cannons are easy to come by. There were just a whole bunch lying around after the end of the war. And who's in my fort is none of your business."

"I'd like to take a look. The other cattle owners told me to check this out and see if your fort is a danger to all the herds coming up from Texas. I'm supposed to find out if Maboola is in that fort and whether you have cannons. Now I can't do business with you until I find out just who you are and what you are about and what you intend to do or try to do to us trail drivers."

"I don't bother anybody. I built this place, and I'm going to stay in this place right here. Everybody keeps coming by and trying to run me off, but so far, nobody's been able to do that. I don't steal horses, and I don't shoot cowboys. But I'd like to trade horses with you if you need some."

Red Granger looked around at the horses and back at Mondo. "You got good horseflesh, and I need horses. I don't trade with murderers, but I've never heard tell of you killing anybody that didn't need killing. I don't care how many outlaws you kill, but if you start stealing cattle, then by God we'll wipe you out. We Texans take care of our own. The US Cavalry out of Fort Arbuckle is just made up of a bunch of ex-slaves, and they can't stop the Comanches or Kiowas, and they can't do any damage to those ex-Confederate outlaws that are roaming through Indian Territory. Therefore we can't trust anybody, and no one is going to stand in our way of moving these Texas cattle to Abilene. I'll trade with you because I have to have horses, but if you'll take a suggestion from me, I'd send your partner Mick down to that new store around Cow Creek and to do your trading there. There's a Theodore Fitzpatrick that's opened up a store. This fort doesn't have a good reputation as a safe trading post. The word down the trail is all should ride a big circle around this here compound. And one other thing, if that Maboola is hiding out in your fort, you had better get rid of him. There's a lot of Texans besides Split Face that want that son of a bitch dead."

Mondo stared at Red Granger for a second. "If you're through with your speech, maybe we can get down to trading."

But Red Granger wasn't through. He looked over at Bear Chaser. "Now I know you're Chickasaw, but I heard you were a good friend of Ten Bears. Ten Bears has always been a reasonable Indian and has been at peace with us Texans for a long time. Can't you talk him into controlling his warriors? First, they ride up and beg for calves to kill, and then at night, they try to steal our horses. And if that doesn't work, they stampede the horses and cattle and just take what they want and go about their business. Some of my men are ex-Confederate soldiers, and they know how to fight. These blacks that work for me are not bothered by anyone. They're tough. If the Indians don't stop this stealing, we're going to get together and do what the US Cavalry can't do and that's get rid of those Kiowas and Comanches and anyone else who stands in our way."

Bear Chaser nodded. "Comanches and Kiowas have always hated Texans. They believe Texans have no honor. Texans called a peace council in San Antonio and then killed the chiefs. I really don't know whether the Comanches and Kiowas hate those so-called man-eater Tonkawas worse than the Texans or the other way around. But right now, the Texans aren't the problem. They know that they can never trust a Texan, but the American government from Washington has made a deal, and the Great White Father is not keeping his promise. The Comanches and Kiowas really had nothing against the Americans until now. It's my understanding that a lot of the Comanches and Kiowas are up north about fifty miles around Fort Cobb, and the US government has not delivered any of the goods that were promised to these Indians at the Medicine Lodge Treaty. The Comanches are not happy with Ten Bears anymore. If the promises are not kept, it's going to be worse before it gets better for anybody coming into this part of the country."

"That's what I thought. We cattle herders have got to look out for ourselves. We're going to move these cattle no matter who tries to stand in our way. That's the only way we can survive." He looked over at Mondo. "So you remember this. If this fort gets in our way, then we'll just get together and destroy it. You really don't have enough help. Do you understand that?"

"I've been receiving threats all my life," said Mondo. "However, a couple of years ago, I stopped paying attention to loudmouthed white men. Now, if you want to trade horses, we will. But if you want to stand around and threaten me, then you better go back and get a whole bunch more cowboys. Those graves you saw when you rode in were what's left of a group of outlaws, about the same number as you have, that rode in to take this fort. Ten came and four rode back to Texas. Now do we trade or do we fight?"

"You're awful uppity for an ex-slave."

"I never was a slave, and by God, I'll never be a slave. I'm a man, equal to all men, and you better tell everybody coming up and down this trail that they're dealing with somebody just as smart and just as tough as they are. If they don't want to come around my fort and trade, then that's fine with me. I'll take your advice and send Mick up to Fitzpatrick's store, and I'll sell horses from there. If they don't want to deal with anybody with black blood, that's fine with me too. Because I don't like to deal with people who look down on me. Now, how many horses do you need? I'm tired of listening to you and tired of you being on my land. So let's trade, or you better be out of rifle range in five minutes."

Red Granger stared at Mondo for what seemed a long time. Then he nodded and dismounted.

"Well, let's see what you got. I need horses, and you sure got some good ones."

The cowboys helped Mick and Bear Chaser move Mondo's herd around in front of Red Granger, and he picked thirty horses that he bought for $100 a head. He reached into his saddle bag and gave Mondo $3,000 in gold coins and rode off with the horses.

Later, the six of them gathered to discuss what they had learned from Red Granger. The more they thought about the increase in cattle drives that would be coming up the old trail, carved out by Jessie Chisholm, on the way to the Abilene railroad yards, the more they thought they would have a good chance of selling horses especially since the Kiowas and Comanches and the white outlaws kept trying to steal the horses from the trail drivers. Mondo really didn't want the Texas trail drivers to come to his fort for horses. He wanted to keep his privacy. Therefore they all agreed that Mick would take about twenty horses and go to the Fitzpatrick's store on Cow Creek and try to make a deal to sell horses out of the store. The store was about eight or ten miles southeast of Mondo's fort.

Mondo also knew from what he had heard from Red Granger that as long as Maboola stayed in his compound, that the bounty hunters would be coming to his place. There was a big reward out for Maboola's head and the capture of Savanah. Maboola had saved their life, and Mondo had given him a rifle and taught him how to shoot it. He didn't think he owed Maboola anymore. He discussed Maboola's leaving with Mick and Bear Chaser. Bear Chaser felt that Mondo was already lumped with Maboola, and no matter whether Maboola stayed or whether he left, there would always be trouble from men like Split Face. Bear Chaser said that crazy men like Split Face, who didn't reason like everyone else, would never give up because Maboola and Mondo had bested Split Face, and that only added fuel to the fire of hatred that Split Face had for anyone with Negro blood.

Mick felt that as soon as the Yankee carpetbaggers left Texas, the people would regain their reason, and the hatred for the ex-slaves would die out. The fact that the Yankee carpetbaggers were forcing the Texans that fought for the South to live under their iron hand was causing a lot of the problems. The Freedman Bureau backed up by the US Army had raised taxes to support schools for ex-slaves. Money was scarce, and a lot of Texans were losing their property because of the increased taxes. The old Texas Rangers had been disbanded, and the new bunch were all Yankees or Yankee lovers. There was no strong local legal enforcement group in Texas. Until there was law and order, people like Split Face and other Texans who wanted to keep the Negroes in their place would have a free hand. Therefore, Mick thought that it would be ten years before people like Split Face could be controlled.

Mick thought it was a good idea if Maboola was asked to leave the compound. Mick also thought that Maboola shouldn't endanger the life of Savanah by taking her along when she was such a beautiful girl that could pass for white. Mondo needed to talk to Maboola to try to do the best thing for him and Savanah and for the other people in his compound.

Chapter 25

Split Face waited outside Purify Jones's study for what seemed an hour long. A black servant dressed like a gentleman finally opened the door and stepped way back to let Split Face enter. All servants backed off any time Split Face got near them. The ugly KKK leader got a thrill out of their fear.

Purify Jones slowly rose from behind his huge desk and glared at Split Face, who expected another cussing from the little rich man.

"What the hell happened this time?" boomed Purify Jones, who had a voice ten times bigger than his body.

Split Face ducked his head and then forced his eyes up to stare at the glare of Purify Jones. "You haven't seen his fort. It's built better than those damn Yankee forts. We lost six men trying to take it. We've got to have cannons and more men to knock the walls down and get those people like you want."

"Jesus S. Christ. This Mondo is no Robert E. Lee. You're trying to tell me that we need a whole army fully outfitted with cannons to take one black Indian, an ignorant African giant, and a full-blood Chickasaw? There's only one white kid in the whole bunch who would have any brains. Now isn't that right? I sent you and nine ex-rebel soldiers who fought in the war, and you can't take these inferior savages and a young white man with no battle experience at all? You have to do better, or someone else will get the job."

"It don't take brains to shoot straight. They can fire them rifles as good as anyone. Even the women know how to shoot. So there's six guns instead of four," answered Split Face.

"Women, my ass! I'm going to send some men next time. You act like a bunch of girls. You can't handle this. Savanah can't shoot. She's a lady. I want her back, and I want her back right now. I'm going to find some people, by God, that will get the job done."

"It isn't as easy as you think. You sent that old Texas Ranger to Wildhorse Creek last month, and he didn't get that Maboola. He was a great Indian fighter who the Yankees fired because they wouldn't let any ex-rebs be rangers. He couldn't get past those river rats and those Negroes at Wildhorse Creek. I heard he killed the wrong black and claimed that they all looked alike to him, as if there was anyone who looked like Maboola."

"I can't believe that those ex-slaves know how to organize and lead. There's no trained leaders among them, and we can't allow any leaders to develop because that might happen in Texas. Fear must keep all blacks apart, and all potential leaders must be eliminated. I have even hired the Pinkerton Agency out of Chicago, Illinois, to get me information from what's really going on in Washington, D.C. I need to use these Yankee detectives to find out anything about the activities of ex-slaves. The Freedmen's Bureau and occupying Yankee troops in Texas are trying to protect ex-slaves. I thought that an ex-Ranger like Old Scalper could slip in and kill Maboola while he slept, and he killed someone that he thought was Maboola, and Old Scalper won't go back. So I guess you're right. We've got to raise an army. I can get some information from the Pinkertons, but they refuse to go in and kill anybody but Maboola. I've got a lawyer in Gainesville that I'm going to send in with some protection to keep him safe and see if we can buy Savanah back."

"I tried that, and she wouldn't come," said Split Face.

"I've got a spy hired that keeps an eye on that fort owned by Mondo Hobbs. The spy is a Shawnee Indian who can move around freely in Chickasaw and Comanche territory. So I know what's going on."

Split Face didn't answer.

Purify Jones continued. "I've tried sending you and twenty-five men against that Wildhorse Creek settlement, and you got run off and got chased back by one black man."

"I'm telling you, we didn't know there was just one man chasing us. We thought the whole Chickasaw Lighthorse Police and all those darkies were trying to catch us."

Purify Jones shook his head in disgust. "That Maboola hung another white man by his feet without a head. We can't let anyone know about that. I can keep it out of the papers, but gossip and rumors are hard to keep down. If the ex-slaves in Texas hear that they can get together and fight back, we'll never get control over them again. We don't want a war. We want ex-slaves to do what we say as we've always done, and we will as long as we've got the KKK scaring the crap out of them. The Yankees will go home soon enough. Washington, D.C., will run out of money and get tired of messing with us. But wild stories like one Negro running off twenty-five Texans will give them savages courage to rise up and take over without the Yankee help. When the Yankees leave, we have to have the black people broken down like they were still slaves or we will lose all power and control over them and the whole state. Do you want to live in a state run by darkies?"

Split face nodded in disagreement and stood without speaking a word since he had heard all of this before from the little rich man.

"And we can't have no white Texans even thinking about helping those Negroes. We've got to scare them off too. No do-gooders can be allowed to side with those non-humans. Any white who helps ex-slaves must be dealt with the same as a black. Fear must control both blacks and those whites who think about trying to help them. That's why I gave you and the rest of those ex-rebs a lot of money to run off those kind of people at night.

For instance, the spy tells me there's a guy by the name of Mick O'Ryan who is a white Texan. He's living with and helping those blacks. That ain't right. He must be killed too. I can't keep stopping those stories coming out of Indian Territory about black people and Indian people kicking around white Texans. That's got to end. I've told you that over and over again, and you don't seem to understand or able to take care of it."

"What do you want me to do?"

"Go talk to some ex-Southern officers that have war experience and explain to them the problem of taking Mondo's fort. Get some advice on the number of men and artillery necessary to get the job done. Listen to what he says and try to act like a professional instead of a no-good outlaw. Do it right and be smart about it, or I will get rid of you. Do you understand? I'm going to try a few other methods and get the Pinkertons involved and get information myself. But I want you to go talk to these military men and find out how to take a fort and don't go back again without talking to me and getting everything straightened out so you will know how to win. When you get all that you need to get the job done, then we will take care of this matter properly, and we won't have to try to do it again."

Split Face nodded yes but turned and stomped out quickly so he wouldn't hit the little rich man. He would take plenty of time to get the job done. He would check on the necessary information and be slow about it. Jones wanted plenty of men, and Split Face wouldn't go until he had soaked Purify Jones clean through. Jones wants an army, and he'll get an army. No matter how much it costs, and Split Face would get some of that money too. Split Face hoped he could take a whole year of raising men and cannons so that when he crossed the Red River with an army, he would have enough guns and people to take care of anyone and everyone.

CHAPTER 26

MABOOLA ADDED DANGER to Mondo's compound. There was enough peril without Maboola. Mondo dreaded talking to him. Not being accepted and being looked down on by people was something that Mondo understood very well. The main reason Mondo came out to this compound was to get away from the people that did not treat him as an equal. And here he was, trying to run off Maboola just because his actions against those who hated the color black brought great danger to his fort. Mondo also told himself that Maboola was really a killer. Maboola hated whites as much as some whites hated blacks. Also, Mondo felt that if he lived alone, he would feel more like keeping Maboola in the fort, and together, they could take on the world. But there was Skywalker, Savanah, Mick, and his dad that Mondo had to think about. Then it would make Mondo mad to think that he now felt the responsibility for others. He had come out here to live alone and stay here alone forever. How things had changed!

When Mondo was by himself or with his dad part-time, there was nobody that could slip up on him, but since so many others had moved in and the atmosphere had changed as to smells and noise, his intuition in feeling danger had almost disappeared. But on the other side of the coin, Mondo had to admit to himself that he was beginning to really enjoy the comfort provided by six people working together. Savanah had joined right in with Skywalker and turned his fort into a very clean and comfortable place. They had a garden, and they had fresh vegetables.

His cabin was spotless, and meals were delicious. They had dug a small cemetery on the south end to close off the area between the east and west creek banks where the bounty hunters were buried with a quote, "Here lie men who tried to take this fort." That helped make his place safe. And their herd was growing into fine-looking horses. There were so many people looking after the horses that it seemed that each horse had individual care. Even the conversation after the evening meal when they all sat around and just talked was pleasant and very comforting. There was Bear Chaser who sat back and enjoyed the talk of everyone, and when it got touchy or when a subject that might bring anger or embarrassment to anyone came up, Bear Chaser always tried to change the subject or make a joke or keep the negative or unpleasant statements from entering the discussion. Mick talked all the time about anything, but he always had an upbeat attitude, a smile, and was never negative or critical. Maboola never said much, but when he spoke, everyone listened. He certainly wasn't dumb. Skywalker had a sharp tongue and could be very critical, but she cared for everyone, and that was very apparent. Then there was Savanah who at first said hardly anything, but her head began to lift, and she began to study people by looking directly into their face with those coral-green eyes. It was almost like doubt was leaving her personality. Savanah began to participate in the conversations and ask questions, and they were good questions. As people went, Mondo felt like this bunch was pretty smart and basically pretty nice. It was as good as any company he had been around. He felt like Maboola had to go, or his and everyone else's danger would be multiplied because of the large bounty and the hate for Maboola possessed by Split Face and other whites, led by the rich Texan, Purify Jones. Maboola was the symbol of the great fear that all Southerners felt that the ex-slaves would rise up and kill them all for the ill treatment that the slaves had suffered for hundreds of years. Maboola had no fear, and he appeared to love killing white men, and that was not good for ex-slave owners.

It was on Independence Day, 1868, on a hot evening, that Mondo had the courage to take Maboola aside and have the talk with him about leaving. After supper, Mondo asked Maboola to go out to the corral with him. They leaned on the fence, and Mondo brought up the subject that he dreaded. "You've been a great help to me. And I sure feel a lot safer with you by my side, but I just don't think that all of us would have the trouble from those Negro haters and Purify Jones if you weren't living here."

"Are you wanting me to leave?" asked Maboola.

"I don't want you to leave, but I think it would be best for everyone here if you did leave."

"Do you really think that the race haters are going to stay away from you when I'm gone? Twice you have been seen with me when I've killed white men, and you've killed too. If you don't think those white trash don't have a grapevine, then you're not being very smart. All those sorry bastards talk about is what they're going to do to keep the Negroes in their place. I know. I've talked to a lot of those house servants that had to listen to those whites talk,and those ex-slave owners fear any kind of a man that might bring about an uprising. Whites want to get rid of anyone who might lead a rebellion. The race haters consider me a dangerous man that could cause a savage, out-of-control killing of ex-slave owners. They think I could cause other blacks to start killing whites. They consider you a dangerous man with a rifle or a pistol. And most of all, they consider you a friend of mine, which makes you a white killer."

"But I'm not. The first white men I ever killed outside of the war were those outlaws attacking our fort a couple of months ago. Before that, I've knocked a bunch of them whites in the head, and I've drawn on a few, but I never killed one until they came after you, and they trespassed on my place because you were here."

"Well, I think you're wrong. Purify Jones will offer more money for Savanah. Besides, I don't think you'll ever escape what the haters think about you, and this place will always mean rebellion to all whites. First of all, the word is out that you fight with the Comanches, and since those Indians let you live right under their noses, there has to be some truth to that. Secondly, you're a Negro who has protected both Indians and blacks and one who keeps a white killer like me protected behind these walls. Face it, Mondo, you're going to die young just like me, and you better take a bunch of whites with you so that our race as a whole will get enough courage to stand up on their own two feet."

"Killing just brings on more killing. For every white coward you kill, many more white cowards will lynch a bunch of innocent ex-slaves for no reason at all. There's nobody stopping men like Split Face. And the way he figures it, for every white man that a Negro touches, hits, or kills, there should be twenty-five Negroes strung up. Now you may get a kick out of killing white men, but don't tell me you're helping the Negro race by doing so."

"We've got to have heroes, Mondo. Negroes have got to have somebody to look up to. Ex-slaves have to see somebody that, by God, can kill white men and not the other way around. Our people have to see the 'man' as a real black man."

"Not everybody is as big or as tough as you. It's too early for killing. Do you think the US Army and the Freedmen Bureau are going to stay in the South forever? It might take about ten years, but soon, all the Southern whites will be running their own states again, and they won't forget that the Yankees tried to force them to live equal with people that they felt were animals."

"'Well, whatever we say really doesn't matter if you think that you can avoid trouble by getting rid of me. But I'm kind of like you, Mondo. I don't stay where I'm not wanted. Me and Savanah will be gone tomorrow."

"Oh, I don't think you should take Savanah. I told you before, you're going to get her killed. You can't protect her because you can't protect yourself forever. Where's your gang? No matter how many whites you kill, Split Face and his kind will always come back with a lot more men. Those cowards gather in great numbers, and they only feel bravery in a group. They don't move in on anybody unless there's twenty-five-to-one odd. Where's your gang of followers? Where's your army? How many black people followed you when you left Wildhorse Creek? You're going to fight alone, and you're going to die alone, and you are going to take Savanah with you."

"For your information, there were a bunch of people that wanted to come with me from Wildhorse Creek, but I said no! A mob is too easily seen and too easily tracked down. I can slip through and move around and not be caught and shot if I'm by myself. Even though my size makes me hard to hide, if I move at night, I might stand a chance out there."

"Exactly. That's what I'm trying to tell you. Why are you taking Savanah? You're not alone with her. She's no gunman. She'll just slow you down, and she will always attract a lot of attention. Maybe not as much as you, but she's too pretty to go unnoticed."

"She wanted to come with me. She's my girl. I treat her right. I don't ask her to do anything that she doesn't want to do. When I first saw her, when she wasn't playacting like a rich white woman, she was so afraid that a bird singing would scare her. Nobody scares her when I'm around. I'll let her decide. If she want's to stay, that's fine with me. If she wants to go, then she'll go with me. I'm in love with her, but you'd probably tell me that if I loved her, that I would leave her here."

Mondo nodded yes, and they started for the porch to talk to Savanah. As they neared the porch, Maboola reached out and gently took Mondo's arm and turned him around to face him.

"There's just one thing that I want to know. Are you trying to keep Savanah here for your own? I thought you wanted to live alone and didn't want company. And here you are, trying to make me feel bad for taking off with the gal I love. I think you've got feelings for her whether you admit it or not. She would really be safer if she left both of us and went way up North and just became a white person. You know that's true."

Mondo studied him for a while and then looked away. "She's got to learn to feel better about herself deep down and to make some decisions on her own and not playacting white before she can really know who she is. She's getting better, but she still looks down at the ground a lot like she was still a slave."

"So you're going to teach her to be a real true white lady, is that it?"

"No, I'm not. But Skywalker was raised a lady. She was one of those rich rancher daughters that claimed to be more Spanish than Mexican. She went to school. Savanah should stay with Skywalker, and then Savanah would be ready to go back North and pass as a white person without acting, if that was what she wanted to do."

Maboola smiled at Mondo. "You've got it all worked out, don't you? You're doing everything for Savanah and nothing for yourself. I'm not dumb, Mondo. We both know you've got to travel a thousand miles to find any girl as pretty as her. So stop kidding yourself and feeding me bull. You don't want her to go with me because you want her to stay with you."

Mondo shook his head no and nodded toward the cabin. "Well, let's just go see what she wants to do."

The men both walked up to Savanah, and Maboola spoke first. "Mondo says I ought to go. He also says that I shouldn't take you with me. Do you want to go or stay?"

Savanah's eyes widened in surprise, and she blushed, then she looked down and shook her head. She looked back at Mondo and then at Maboola, and then tried to speak but only mumbled and stuttered so that nobody could understand her.

Skywalker grabbed Maboola by the arm and spun him around and glared at both men. "You big bullies don't know how to talk to a woman. You don't just charge up to her and glare down at her and yell at her to stay or leave. Now, let's sit down and discuss this like civilized people, and she might be able to come up with an answer."

All six of them found their usual spots for the evening discussion. Mick on an old tree stump and Bear Chaser in the old rocker that he had bought at Fitzpatrick's store. Mondo sat on the porch with his feet hanging over the side, and Skywalker and Savanah sat together on a bench. Maboola never sat down but always stood and leaned his back against the side of the cabin with his right hand near his holster.

Skywalker looked at Mondo. "Why do you think Maboola has to go?"

"We've already discussed that, and I think Maboola agrees with me. There's a bunch of dollars on his head, and there's a lot of poor starving people in Texas. So whether they are KKK, horse thieves, or fast gunmen, they're going to come after Maboola if he stays here. You heard that from Red Granger. Everybody knows about Maboola. If he's gone and we can convince those killers that he's not in the fort, then they won't attack us. They're not going to sacrifice a bunch of lives on us, but for a pile of gold, half of Texas would risk death."

Skywalker frowned. "Do you really think they are going to leave you alone and leave us alone if Maboola's gone? No matter how much they want Maboola, we're viewed as his and your gang. Red Granger said there was a secret bounty on you, Bear Chaser, and Mick. They may want Maboola more, but for whatever reasons, when they come for Maboola, they'll not pass up a chance to get you three. And Purify Jones wants Savanah back real bad. If she doesn't leave with Maboola, then the bounty hunters will come for the money to bring Savanah back alive."

"Well, I don't see it that way," said Mondo. "Savanah's not a threat to whites. Jones will give up someday. Mick's here, and he's a white Texan. Bear Chaser's here, and he's full-blood Chickasaw. The white Texans and Chickasaws will finally accept my place here and leave us alone. And we're friends with Ten Bears, and we made a deal with the Kiowas. Besides, the Kiowas are afraid we'll make them take you back." Mondo was serious, and Skywalker glared at him.

"Leave me out of it. We're talking about Maboola and not me. I've told you before, trading me around is long over, and it will never happen again."

"I know. I know," said Mondo. "I'm just trying to tell you all that we might be able to cool everything down, and we might be able to stop all this senseless killing and attacks if Maboola's gone."

"You need Maboola's rifle on the fourth side of the wall," said Bear Chaser.

"Hell, Skywalker can shoot, and she's teaching Savanah. We could put the two girls on that wall," said Mondo.

"I thought you were trying to save Savanah. Now you are going to stick her on the wall ducking bullets?" said Bear Chaser.

"Now you stay out of this, old man. This is my place and this is really something between me, Maboola, and Savanah."

"I guess Skywalker and me don't have anything to say about it either," asked Mick.

"No. Everybody can speak up. They might as well. I started out wanting to be alone, and all of a sudden, there's a whole damn tribe living in my fort. It's like having a boarding house or a hotel. Let's just vote on this. Everyone wants to take part. We'll make this settlement a democratic tribe. The majority rules. Hell, I've lost control of this damn place a long time ago," spoke Mondo as his voice rose in anger.

"Just like a bunch of backward, savage men," said Skywalker. "Everybody spoke their mind except the one that it concerns the most. Nobody has let Savanah speak. It was nice of you to let the women vote, Mondo, but this is not a majority decision. This is only Savanah's decision."

All five looked over at Savanah. She finally spoke. "I have felt safe for the first time in my life when I was with Maboola. I was happy at Wildhorse Creek. When more and more white men with guns came after Maboola and me, I was frightened again. I want to go and I want to stay." She looked over at Mondo. "Please don't make Maboola leave."

"I'm not making him leave. He can stay forever for all I care. I'm just trying to make it safer for all of us."

"I'll be gone tomorrow," said Maboola. "And Savanah is going to stay here." With that, Maboola stomped out of the fort and headed for the trees on Little Beaver Creek.

CHAPTER 27

B EFORE ANYBODY GOT up the next morning, Mondo heard Maboola getting ready to leave. He got one of his better horses and led it over to Maboola.

"Get all of the supplies you need, and here's an extra horse."

"Thanks," Maboola said. "I enjoyed the stay. Take care of Savanah. If and when I find a place where it's safe, I'll send for her or come back myself to get her."

"I'll watch out for her. She'll be fine. You take care of yourself. As soon as you get over the thirst of killing all white haters, you may find it nice to live free in this world. I'm sure there's some place besides Africa that you can fit in. Watch your back and don't worry about Savanah."

Mondo helped him gather a week's supply of food, and they loaded it on the extra horse that Mondo had given Maboola. As he mounted, he looked over at Mondo. "Have Skywalker see to Savanah's learning to be free. She's been afraid all her life, and she has no idea how pretty she is. She needs a little of what Skywalker has. She needs to feel good about herself and not take anything off anyone. I feel I can trust you, Mondo, even though you have very little African blood." He smiled and tipped his hat and started North.

Mondo watched him ride away and knew at once that he was going to miss the giant. Even though he had thought he had wanted to live alone, the last couple of months had been pleasant and real secure. Maboola could damn sure hold his own against anybody and anything regardless of the number of men who came at the people in his compound. He felt regret at Maboola's departure and felt responsible for making sure that Savanah was safe. Also, he knew that he and Skywalker had a duty to help Savanah grow. He really didn't think he would ever see Maboola again. There were too many bounty hunters after his high-priced head. He hated the decision to ask Maboola to leave, but he knew that if Maboola didn't go, that his compound was guaranteed to be attacked from a lot of white people who hated Negroes or loved money, or both.

As he turned back toward the cabin, Savanah ran out holding her things. "Is he gone? He's watched out for me for the last six months, and I've never felt safer. I've got to go with him, Mondo. I owe him my freedom. I can't think about him dying all alone. Go stop him."

"I promised to take care of you. I'll keep that promise. Maboola's doing what's best for both of you. He doesn't want you running and hiding all your life like you were still a runaway slave. He's right. You've got to stay."

"Do you think you can protect me? Mr. Jones still has a lot of money. A lot of tough men will be paid to bring me back. You're right. It's probably better for Maboola that I'm not with him. But you still got a problem with me and Mr. Jones who wants me back."

"Well, if you and Maboola both think you're better off separated, then you don't have a choice but to stay here. Maboola's doing this for you, and you are doing this for Maboola."

Savanah looked at Mondo and Mondo continued. "Let's give it a try. Maboola trusts me, so you better trust me too. If and when he finds a place where you both can live safely, he'll send for you, or he will come back for you. Let's ride this out and see how it works."

Savanah stared at him with those green eyes. Mondo felt himself stir and knew that he would do everything to keep his promise to take care of Savanah. Savanah finally nodded yes and went back into the cabin.

The next couple of months, through the hot summer of July and August of 1868, things passed smoothly. There were no attacks on the compound, and life went on in Mondo's compound as if Maboola had not left. Mondo spent a lot of time with Savanah trying to make her feel safe, and the rest of the group noticed Mondo's increased interest in the beautiful tan-skinned woman.

In late August, Ten Bears of the peaceful Comanche bands rode by and stopped in to report that the US government out of Washington, D.C., had not lived up to their agreement to provide supplies and food to the Comanches. The Comanches had gathered at Fort Cobb and had become so hostile that the agent, Colonel Levenworth, had run off back to Kansas. The Comanches had lost faith in Ten Bears because of the failure of the US government to do as promised. He was shunned for the first time in his life, and he rode by to advise Mondo that any protection he may have provided Mondo was no longer good. He said that a lot of Comanches didn't speak to him, and he really had to leave Fort Cobb for fear that he would be done in by the angry young warriors. He said more raids by his tribe had occurred all over Colorado, New Mexico, Texas, and the Chickasaw Nation. He told Mondo to be on the alert because the young Comanche warriors knew that Mondo was Ten Bears's friend, and this worked against Mondo now.

Soon thereafter, the chief of the Pickens County Lighthorse Police, Hurbert Dixon, rode by, looking for Comanche raiders and stopped at Mondo's fort. He again advised Mondo that Mondo shouldn't deal with the Comanches at all. He said the young warriors stole many Chickasaw horses and killed some Chickasaws, and the Fort Arbuckle garrison of black soldiers had to ride to Fort Cobb to try to restore order. He also heard that the US Army was going to build a new fort in the Wichita Mountains near Medicine Bluff since Fort Arbuckle was too far away to control the Comanches and Kiowas. Dixon told Mondo that if that new fort were built twenty miles west of where Mondo's compound was located, that Dixon was pretty sure that the US Cavalry would make Mondo abandon his compound unless he could prove that he was on Chickasaw land. Mondo showed him the papers that his father had acquired for him, and Bear Chaser explained that the land was, in his opinion, located in the Chickasaw Nation and that Ten Bears had allowed Mondo to live here if his compound was on Comanche land. Again, without a survey, they didn't know where Mondo's fort was located, but Mondo anticipated a visit from the US Cavalry.

At first, after Maboola had left, Savanah moved around as if she was afraid. She kept looking through the entrance of the fort, hoping and expecting to see Maboola return or fearing another attack by Purify Jones's outlaws. But after a while, she began to relax as Skywalker spent a lot of time with her, keeping her busy, and trying to make her feel at home. Mondo watched out for her and never left the compound for a long period of time. It wasn't long before Savanah was smiling and looking people in the eyes when she talked to them. She would watch Skywalker, and she began to try to imitate her in every way. Pretty soon, everybody settled in as a family again, and even though Maboola was not forgotten, his absence didn't seem to bother anyone left in the compound. The August heat drove them outside, and even the girls slept in the open and not in the cabin. It was still hot by September, but the evenings began to cool off, and they started gathering at sunset and talking for a couple of hours before they went to their bedrolls.

Mondo began to sit by Savanah and glance her way even when somebody else was talking. Without realizing it himself, Mondo began to give most of his attention to Savanah. She began to think and act like Mondo was her protector, and she had found a replacement for Maboola. Mondo was leaning over, whispering to Savanah, when Skywalker frowned and spoke. "I wonder what Maboola's doing now?"

Mondo and Savanah both looked up and stared at Skywalker. Mondo frowned. "Well, let's hope he's not cutting white people's heads off," said Mondo.

Savanah looked over at Mondo. "Maboola said he wasn't going to do that anymore. He's trying to quit. He said he was going to try to find a place where we could live in peace. He'll be back."

"Sure he will," said Skywalker. "And we all promised Maboola we would take care of you until he got back."

Skywalker glared at Mondo. He shook his head in agreement. "That's right. That's what we're all going to do, and Maboola will probably be back. I'm just not sure if he's ever going to find a place where they both can be safe. Three hundred dollars will drive a lot of those bounty hunters crazy. They'll go around the world twice for that much money. Besides, Maboola sticks out like a sore thumb no matter where he lives. He's so big and scary that he couldn't disguise himself if he wanted to. Every white man will be afraid of him, even if that man didn't have it in for all Negroes. For the ones that hate Negroes, he's the man that they all have to kill. Those Negro-haters don't want to fear anyone with black blood. And if Maboola thinks it's going to change when he goes up North, then he's lying to himself. I heard those Yankee soldiers talk. They may be against slavery, but they're not for equality with the black man. For most all whites, freedom means blacks are no longer slaves, but not equal to whites."

Mondo looked over at Mick. "Tell her about your father and how he was treated up in New York when he came from Ireland."

"He was treated like a skunk. The New York people avoided him like he smelled. As far as the people in New York were concerned, there was no difference between a black man and an Irishman. Most Yankees would have thrown both of them back into the sea. That's why my dad came out here. If you think those Yankees don't feel superior to everybody around them, then you've never met one."

"See there," said Mondo. "Where's Maboola going to find a place where the two of them can live safely? And if he can't live safely, he can't protect Savanah."

"That's kind of between Savanah and Maboola, isn't it?" stated Mick.

Skywalker stood up. "Nothing's always safe on this earth. What about me? I had a real nice life in Mexico, and all of a sudden, I was a Kiowa slave. There's no guarantees, and there's no safety net covering anyone. You just take it day by day the best way you can and go from there. It's obvious that Savanah misses Maboola and wants him back."

Mondo shook his head. "It's not obvious to me. She looks a lot happier to me since Maboola left."

"Hey, what's the matter with you?" snapped Skywalker. "Are you trying to move in on Maboola's girl? What kind of man are you? He left her here for you to protect, not take over."

"What do you mean take over? We're just good friends, that's all. I'm just trying to tell the truth about Maboola. He probably won't come back. Now what is Savanah supposed to do?"

Savanah put her hands to her face and began to cry softly.

Skywalker put her arm around Savanah and glared at Mondo. "See what you've done! I can't decide whether you are more cruel than stupid. You either like to hurt women, or you don't even know anything about women. You think you're protecting Savanah by being nice to her, but that's not the real reason. You're just like every man I know. You're out for what you can get."

Mondo jumped up. "You're the most know-it-all woman I've ever met. You must have an evil mind because everything I do or anybody else does, you seem to think it's for bad reasons. I'm a friend of Savanah, and you need to keep your evil thoughts to yourself."

Mick stood up. "Now, Mondo, you're saying a lot of awful things to Skywalker. It's obvious to me and everybody that you've been giving a lot of your attention to Savanah. And everyone knows you promised Maboola to take care of her. But it appears to me you're trying to take care of her too good."

Mondo spun around on Mick. "Now that isn't your business. Skywalker was way out of line. She's been trying to say some things that aren't true. I know Savanah is a very beautiful young girl, but she's Maboola's girl, and that's the way it's going to be and going to stay, and I mean that."

With a doubtful look on his face, Mick stared at Mondo, and then Mick nodded his head in agreement and turned to Skywalker. "Mondo has a point there. What difference does it make to you one way or another whether Mondo likes Savanah more than a friend or whether Savanah likes Maboola or whether Maboola's coming back? You act like you're jealous of Mondo."

This time, Skywalker flew to her feet and charged over and stuck her face into Mick's face. "Don't you think I have any taste at all? The only man around here that knows anything about a woman and who is nice all the time is Bear Chaser. You keep staring at me with those mournful begging eyes like I'm not being fair if I don't go to bed with you. And neither one of you understand Savanah at all. She needs my help. And Maboola told me to look after her too. Maboola told me to teach her how to feel good about herself. Good enough to look people in the eye and talk straight at them. So I've got some things I'm supposed to do, and I'm going to do them." She spun around and stomped into the cabin.

Savanah looked around at the three men. "I didn't mean to cause all this trouble. It's all my fault." Then she broke down and cried as she got up and charged back into the cabin.

Bear Chaser looked at the two stunned young men. "You young bucks got to learn a few things. If you're not sure about how people are going to take what you're fixing to say, then you might think twice about saying it. We were all getting along fine like a happy family, and you two start moving around and acting like you were stud horses in need. If you'll just try to keep your mind off what you're thinking about doing to these two girls and just let life flow free and easy around here, everything would be a lot better, and you both would be a lot happier."

Mick said, "Mondo had no business getting all over Skywalker. Maybe she is a little outspoken, but like you say, Mondo shouldn't have said it. Mondo, I never knew you to talk so much and say so many things wrong until those girls came. I kind of agree with Skywalker and Bear Chaser. You don't know anything about girls."

Mondo glared back at Mick. "And I don't want to know anything about girls. If it was just the three of us and there was no women in my fort, we wouldn't be having this word fight right now. Life would be a lot easier. We three get along okay, but you throw in those two girls, and everything falls apart. That's all I've got to say, and I'm going to have to figure out something to do about those two girls, especially Skywalker. I could sure see why those Kiowas got rid of her. They should have given us horses to take her off their hands."

Mondo spun around and went off to bed down. Mick turned to Bear Chaser with a questionable look on his face. Bear Chaser raised his hands. "Leave me out of it. You young bucks got to learn to live in close quarters around females without coming to blows."

CHAPTER 28

That night, Chickasaw Killer, Baby Killer, and two renegade Comanche outcast warriors struck. It had taken several months for Chickasaw Killer to find the hiding place of Baby Killer and his two companions. Ever since Mondo had knocked out Chickasaw Killer in front of his whole band after the horse race, Chickasaw Killer had sworn revenge and had tried to persuade other warriors to attack Mondo's fort. The warriors in his band refused to go because they all thought that Chickasaw Killer deserved to be struck by Mondo. Chickasaw Killer had violated a sacred rule by attacking a visitor who had been accepted as a guest. When Chickasaw Killer realized he could get no one to go on a war party against Mondo, he struck out on his own and searched for four months until he finally located Baby Killer.

It didn't take long for Chickasaw Killer to realize that Baby Killer was hopelessly insane, and the love of killing was the only thing that kept Baby Killer going. Chickasaw Killer had brought several horses and promised at least ten more horses if Baby Killer would help him get rid of Mondo. The horses didn't seem to entice Baby Killer, but the more he had heard about Mondo and the more he heard about the fort and the fine horses that Mondo owned and most of all, the heroic deeds that Mondo had performed in protecting his horses the more it appealed to Baby Killer to go on the raid. It was September before the four Indians rode into Mondo's valley.

Baby Killer was not a large man or a smart man, but he was a man that had no fear of death and that made him a very dangerous man. All four of the Comanches knew that they had to get inside the compound before being discovered, or they had no chance at all. It took them an hour to crawl on their bellies across the fifty yards from the creek to the stockade wall. They listened for ten minutes before they tossed a rope up onto one of the logs supporting the gate and eased up the outside wall. On top of the entrance, the four Indians eyed the ground in the darkness until they located all three of the bedrolls lying near the compound's gate. Without making a sound, they eased around till they were above the three men sleeping on the ground. As they leaped from the wall, Mondo woke, yelled a warning, rolled away, and drew his gun; but before he could fire, two of them were on him trying to bury their axes in his skull.

Baby Killer's tomahawk glanced off Mondo's head and dug into his right shoulder, and Mondo's gun flew out of his hand. Chickasaw Killer's war ax glanced off Mondo's rib cage as Mondo twisted away, tearing the skin off his left side, exposing his ribs. Mondo was stunned, and both Chickasaw Killer and Baby Killer raised their axes to finish him off when two quick shots rang out and the two Indians fell backwards. Before Skywalker turned her rifle on the other two, Bear Chaser had already broken the neck of the Comanche that had jumped him, and Mick had managed to get his hand on his pistol and kill his attacker. Four Comanches were dead in a few seconds, and of the five living inside the compound, the only one that was hurt was Mondo.

Skywalker ran over to Mondo and started to cry when she saw all the blood. She then picked up the tomahawk and crushed the skull of Chickasaw Killer and then drove the ax into Baby Killer's head and left it there.

Before Mick and Bear Chaser could get to Mondo, Savanah was there, and both women were tearing off Mondo's shirt and examining his wounds.

Mondo was unconscious, and Skywalker was still crying.

"Don't you die on me, damn you!" she shouted and then turned to Bear Chaser and Mick. "Give me some help here. We've got to get him inside and see how bad he's hurt." They carried him inside and set him down on Skywalker's bed. Skywalker was giving orders as Savanah boiled water. Skywalker tore off cloth to wrap and stop the bleeding. All the time, she was talking to herself in Spanish as if nobody was there. "I finally find a halfway decent man, and he gets himself chopped up like a chicken. He'll probably die, and we'll never be together. He's too stupid to know that I care for him."

Savanah brought the hot water, and Skywalker continued to doctor him as tears flowed from her eyes.

"I should have left you before I fell for you. And you eyeing that Savanah like she was a ripe plum. I ought to let you die," Skywalker said in Spanish.

Mondo was still unconscious and didn't hear a word. But the rest of the three stood back in stunned silence as Skywalker carried on about Mondo. Mick knew enough Spanish to understand some of her words, and the other two understood she really cared for Mondo by just watching her. It wasn't until she had bandaged him and he had opened his eyes did Skywalker start to behave like her normal self. She stood up and looked down at Mondo.

"You're going to live." With that, she turned and walked away.

Mondo looked around the room at the others and spoke. "Anybody else hurt? What happened to those raiders? Did they get away?"

Mick seemed too stunned to answer as he stood back with a frown on his face. Bear Chaser stepped up to Mondo.

"There were four, and they're all dead. They were Comanches, but I don't recognize any of them. I got one, Mick got one, and Skywalker got the two off you."

Mondo looked over at Skywalker, "Why does she look so mad? Is she sorry she saved my life?"

Skywalker dried her tears. "No, but I told you that men are going to keep raiding this fort until you're dead. If it's not those bounty hunters, it's those crazy Comanches or Kiowas. And the next ones will be the US Cavalry coming from that new fort over by Medicine Bluff, and you're either too stupid or too stubborn to move. Let's get out of here and follow Bear Chaser's advice and move back toward his place where it's safer."

"Well, I guess I owe you for saving my life, but that doesn't mean that you're going to tell me where to live. I'm no damn quitter. I've told you before, I am staying here, and I may die here, but I'm not leaving."

"I'm leaving," said Skywalker. "I can't stay here anymore." She turned to Mick. "Mick, you've always said you would take me out of here. I'm ready to go, but I'm going to stay until Mondo's well. Will you take me to Fort Worth when Mondo gets on his feet?"

Mick frowned and looked over at her, "I'm not taking you anywhere. You don't need my help anyway. You just killed two Comanche warriors to save Mondo's life. Let him take you, or you can stay with him forever for all I care."

They were all stunned at Mick's anger, but Skywalker ignored Mick's statement and looked over at Bear Chaser, "Will you take me to Fort Worth when Mondo's well?"

"I'll always help you, Skywalker, but this is not the time to make all these decisions. We almost got wiped out, and everyone is kind of shaky. Let's sleep on it and then we can talk about it in the morning."

Mondo looked over at Mick. "What do you mean Skywalker wants to stay with me? You're the one that bought her."

Skywalker charged over to Mondo and looked down at him. "I don't care if you're hurt or not. If you bring that up again, I'm going to kill you myself." She pulled out her dagger and pointed it at Mondo. "I've told you from the beginning that no man was going to decide for me anymore. Everyone here but you knows that Mick doesn't own me. You act as if you want me to be Mick's slave."

Before Mondo could answer, Bear Chaser interrupted. "We're going around and around on this kind of talk. Let's everybody cool off and take it easy. Mondo needs to rest. He's in a lot of pain, and he can't think straight, and you, Skywalker, had a big scare tonight, and you just killed two Comanche warriors. I don't think you can think straight either. Everybody needs to settle down, and we need to try to find out who those warriors were."

Savanah finally spoke. "Do you think there's going to be more Comanches trying to kill us?"

Bear Chaser shook his head. "I'm not sure. I think these four were just a bunch of renegades and couldn't get any more warriors to go with them. I think one of them might be that warrior they call Baby Killer. There's some small scalps on his belt. Ten Bears had described him to me, and I think he was one of the warriors that Skywalker killed."

At the sound of the insane warrior's name, Skywalker turned white.

Bear Chaser looked at her and replied, "There's no Comanche, not even relatives, that will avenge his death. He always lived outside the band. I wouldn't worry about a bunch of Comanches coming after you or Mondo over his death. I don't know the other three, but if they were with Baby Killer, they probably weren't important or even well thought of."

Before Bear Chaser finished, Mondo's eyes shut. They all looked at Mondo, and the conversation ended.

The next day, Mondo was better, but everything had changed in the compound. After breakfast, Skywalker called the four of them together outside of Mondo's presence. "I acted foolish yesterday. I think I was just scared. I would rather nobody mention anything to Mondo about what happened when he was unconscious."

"Do you love him?" asked Savanah.

"No! I just kind of got used to him, and I would hate to see him die. I don't love any man, and I don't think I ever will. As soon as he's better, I'm going home."

"I'm leaving right now," said Mick. "Tell Mondo I'll come back after a while and pick up my horses. The partnership's over. It's time for me to move on."

Bear Chaser gently grabbed Mick's arm. "You and Mondo make a pretty good team. If you think you have to leave, then you have to leave. Time has a way of taking care of most problems. Stay away until you feel you are ready to come back, and things might be right again then."

Skywalker pointed her finger at Mick. "Don't go because of me. What I may have said when I was worried about Mondo doesn't mean a thing. I've got too many things I need to straighten out before I settle down with any man, if I ever do. Please stay with Mondo. He needs both you and his father."

Mick shook his head no and walked off. Within two hours, he rode out of the compound and headed south.

CHAPTER 29

As Mick rode south toward Red River, his anger grew. Somehow he thought his partner stole his girl. The girl he bought and paid for. And Mick had treated her like a gentleman should. If he had been a Kiowa or a Comanche, he would have taken her the day he bought her. But no, he wanted to treat her right, and look where it got him. She had fallen for Mondo, and Mondo had treated her like dirt. Mondo was the one that kept reminding her that she was a five-horse woman or less. And it was obvious that Mondo had his eye on Savanah. And Mick knew he was the only white man in the whole compound. Things did not make sense.

Mick had taken his share of the gold from the sale of the horses to Red Granger, and his pockets were full of money. He hadn't been to Texas for over a year, and he hadn't been to a wide-open town like Fort Worth in more than two years. Mick was ready to have some fun. It had been awful hard to live with two beautiful women and only be allowed to look but not touch.

Mick reached the Red River by nightfall and crossed at Red River Station. He rode until midnight before he camped out. He hit Fort Worth early in the afternoon on the third day. He had run into several cattle drives still moving north in late September 1868, and he could see that the trail-driving business had caused Fort Worth to grow. There was construction and a lot of activity.

Mick entered the first bar he came to. He was both thirsty for a drink and a woman. A long stretched-out bar ran about forty feet from the front to the back. He needed a bottle of whiskey and then a female to hold, long and close. He stopped to look over the people. It was early, and the bar was nearly empty. Three girls sat at the bar, talking to themselves. A big bartender who looked more like a bouncer glanced up to see who had come in. A poker game was going on between two cowboys and a man dressed like a professional gambler.

As Mick walked toward the bar, he smiled and nodded as if talking to himself. *There's not many here*, he thought, b*ut there's enough*. All three girls looked up and smiled at the young, good-looking blond-haired cowboy, a real cut above most.

Mick moved toward the girls and said, "Drinks for all. It's on me. If anybody is as thirsty as I am, then they'd drink like they were in a desert." He laughed at himself as he eyed the three girls at the bar.

The poker players glanced over and nodded thanks, without taking their mind off their cards. The taller blond barmaid moved over close to Mick and eased up against him as Mick put his boot on the foot rail at the bar.

The bartender interrupted Mick's pleasant thoughts. "What's your pleasure, cowboy?"

"Yeah," the blonde girl said. "What is your pleasure?" She reached out and gently stoked his arm.

Mick looked at the bartender. "A lot of good bourbon whiskey." Then he turned. "About anything from you would certainly do for a bunch of pleasure."

The tall blond threw back her head and laughed a little too long and a little too loud, but Mick still felt good about watching her laugh. She was just a couple of inches shorter than Mick and big in all the right places with plenty of size up front above her waistline. Mick shifted his gaze to the other two girls watching him. Both were younger, but neither moved closer to Mick, allowing seniority to have the first crack at the dusty, horny-looking cowboy. "You act like it's been awhile," said the big blonde. "Been on the trail too long?"

"Too long and too lonely. I'm both thirsty and hungry for love," said Mick as he smiled and leered at the blonde's large breasts.

"Do you want to feel them or chew on them?" asked the blonde. Mick laughed like he had heard the funniest thing in years.

"You've got me figured out from the get-go," said Mick as he slid his arm around her waist and pulled her up really close. She put her arms around his neck and hugged him back. Mick immediately responded to the soft feel of her body smothering his senses.

"Here's to all that ride on the lonely trail," said Mick, and the three girls tilted their drinks, and Mick threw down the whiskey in one gulp.

"Been to Fort Worth before, cowboy?" asked the blonde.

"Once or twice, but it's been at least two years since I've been back. Things sure have changed. It's almost a full-grown town now."

"It's a cow-boom-town right now. Herds coming through to Kansas about every day. Lots of thirsty men getting fortified before they head through Indian Territory and fight off wild Indians up there."

"What's your name? And how long have you been around?" asked Mick.

"My name is Millie, and it seems I've been around all my life. Came west from Georgia with my folks at the end of the Insurrection. Moved around until I landed here about two years ago. Been home ever since. Are you a born-and-raised Texan?"

"Yeah," said Mick. "I lost my mom in Indian Territory when I was about three. Was dealing horses with my old man, and he joined the Southern cause. He never came back. I've been bouncing around North Texas and Indian Territory ever since my dad went off to fight in the glorious war."

"Have you sold some horses lately so there's enough money to take care of me?" she asked.

"Don't worry about that. My money will last longer than you will. I've been living with a bunch of dark-haired people in Indian Territory. I haven't seen a blonde in so long, I forgot how good one looks," Mick said as he stroked the back of her thin, short barroom costume. "I barely can remember how good a woman feels."

The blonde kissed his lips, and Mick hardened when she stuck the tip of her tongue in his mouth. Fire raced through his veins, and he knew at once he was going to have to get this over with as soon as possible or he wouldn't be able to do anything else. The girl looked into his eyes, touched his pants, and felt his great need. Without another word, she led Mick into the back room where a double bed with wrinkled covers and dirty sheets awaited them. Mick didn't mind the dirt. He wanted a release from the pain of doing without too long. She kissed him and undressed herself. Mick tore off his clothes. It was over before it really got started, but Mick bought a second ride real quick, and it lasted a little longer. The third time did them both some good, and Mick lay back, fully satisfied at last.

That night, he drank a bottle of whiskey, lost some of his money in poker, and went at the blonde again. The next morning, he woke up with his head hurting so bad he didn't get up from the hay in the horse stable even though the smell made him sick. It wasn't until late in the afternoon that he struggled on his boots and walked back to the bar. This time it was crowded. A large longhorn herd had just hit town, and there were about fifteen cowboys having a last drink before they struck out for Indian Territory. It was so loud that after two drinks, Mick bought a hotel room and slept through the night.

The third day, he felt a lot better, and after eating a good breakfast and a good lunch, he went back to the bar and bought another ride from the tall blonde. As they walked from the back room, Mick suddenly stopped and stared hard into the eyes of the man with the divided face. The blonde froze and surveyed the four men glaring at Mick and moved quickly to the bar. Mick shuddered as Split Face walked up close and leaned into his face.

His eyes looked cold and dead. The red scar that ran from his forehead right down between his eyes and cut through his nose and upper lip looked as ugly as Mick had remembered. Mick had seen some beat-up men that came back from the Civil War, but none looked as terrifying as this man with the half-and-half face. His nose dripped out all over each side of the slit and ran down his face. Split Face tried to smile, but the effort only opened up the crevice in his upper lip. Mick thought that this man shouldn't be allowed out in public, and probably the only place he needed to be was buried. Then the smell hit him. He had smelled festering wounds before, but not added to a real horrible breath. It was almost enough to knock him out.

The three goons with Split Face moved in closer, and they all waited for Mick to make his move. Even though Mick was scared, he started to smile because he thought to himself that no man should have to look at these characters unless he was blind drunk. Monsters from hell.

Mick laughed and tried to joke the four men out of killing him.

"I didn't wear old Millie out. She's still good for some more rides. Help yourself."

Mick looked around the bar, but no one laughed. All looked scared. Mick knew he was all alone in this one. The four men continued to glare at Mick. Finally, Split Face spoke, and slobber touched Mick's face with each word. "We meet again, darky lover!" The added stanch from his breath mixed with the festering wound on his face and the overwhelming body odor caused Mick to gag.

Mick straightened up, then asked, "Why are you bracing me? I thought you all stayed hid out around Saint Jo, Texas, until after midnight. I heard you all were cowards ducking behind hoods and just sneaked around in the dead of night."

Split Face glared even harder. "I got word that you were here. I've got spies all over North Texas looking for you and that deep black jigaboo and that yellow woman. Those two stupid darkies are a lot smarter than you, boy. They know better than to come south of the Red River. Are they still at that little fort?"

Mick shook his head. "That's Mondo's fort. Maboola and Savanah took off. They're going up north to get away from assholes like you."

Split Face threw a right cross at Mick's jaw, and Mick ducked under the punch and drove his fist six inches into Split Face's stomach. Before Mick could withdraw his right hand and regain his balance, the three thugs with Split Face were all over him. Two grabbed an arm on each side and the third slammed his fist into his nose. As Split Face rolled around on the floor gasping for breath and holding his stomach, the three men dragged Mick out the back door and into the alley. Mick got a few blows in, but he took three times as many as he gave. When he finally went down, he could feel the boots driving into his ribs and into his skull. Before he passed out, he was hoping they would shoot him so the pain wouldn't last. He knew he was going to die, but he wanted to be dead sooner than later.

CHAPTER 30

MONDO FELT USELESS staying in bed. Bear Chaser, Skywalker and Savanah stayed busy keeping the place going. Bear Chaser stayed with the horses, and Skywalker took care of the garden while Savanah was in the cabin most of the time, cooking and cleaning while Mondo lay in the bed and watched her. Mondo was upset that he couldn't help and didn't understand why Mick took off. He had asked Savanah, and she avoided answering him. As Savanah worked around the cabin, she and Mondo would have long conversations. Mondo noticed that Savanah was developing a confident personality, and she smiled a lot more than she looked down at the floor.

Savanah had made some curtains for the small windows that Mondo had built so that no man could crawl in, but he had a good view to shoot at any intruders. He shook his head and laughed.

"Now that beats all. When I built this place, I never thought there would be curtains on those gun ports. Those were made to look out of and shoot and not to be covered."

Savanah turned to Mondo and smiled. "When you built this place, you didn't know that you were going to have two women living here. Skywalker and I are determined to make this a nice-looking place to stay."

"This cabin is beginning to look more like a boarding house instead of a fort. Now, I realize that without the three of you living here, I would not be alive, but I sure don't want you two women to ruin everything that I wanted to do when I built this place."

Savanah put her hands on her hips and smiled. "Mondo, I've watched you closely. I don't say much, but I see a lot. You think you are a man who wants to be alone, but that's not true. You're not as hard and tough as you act like you are."

"I was tough and I was hard, but look at me now. Nobody touched me the first year I lived in this place. Now I'm beat up like I've been a dog in a fight with wolves. Maybe I was a little bit lonely, but it's a lot better to be lonely and alive than to be happy and dead."

"Skywalker tells me this place was filthy when she came. And you ate like a stuffed bird. You can't tell me you haven't liked the food, the fresh vegetables, and the good company."

"Oh, I admit I like it, but I've become soft. I came out here after the war to keep living and stay out of trouble. Now I might have had trouble whether I had all this company or not, but it's sure a lot easier just to take care of me than worry about you and the rest. Maboola told me to take care of you, and I'm going to do that. But it's not going to be easy."

"Are you just being nice to me because of Maboola?" she asked.

"Well, I like you. I'd probably make sure you weren't harmed even if I hadn't promised Maboola."

"I'm learning to take care of myself like Skywalker. She's been through a lot, and so have I. She had to make the best out of whatever happened to her, and she did. She can sure shoot too, or you wouldn't be alive today."

"Yeah, that's right. Skywalker is hard and tough. She's hardly a woman anymore."

"So you don't think a woman should be able to shoot a gun or speak her mind? That's not what Skywalker is trying to teach me."

"I'll teach you how to shoot just like I taught Maboola how to shoot. That's the least I can do and about all I can do right now. I've got to feel useful. And if you listen to me, you'll be able to shoot as well as Skywalker ever did."

"I'll take you up on that. I want to be just like Skywalker. I'm learning a lot from her. In fact, I can doctor now. Skywalker says you can't live with a man until you can live without a man."

"Women are the weaker half of people. Everybody knows that. It makes a man feel good to take care of a woman. That's the way it's been, and the preachers tell me that's what the Bible says. You may not ever have a man if Maboola gets killed because most men I've known only like women that need looking after."

Savanah shook her head and smiled. "Well, what I've picked up by watching everybody around here is that I really don't know if you understand women. You don't pick up on things about Skywalker. You're so busy looking out for people slipping up on you you don't pay attention to those inside here."

"That's not right. I'm paying too much attention to you women. I know what's going on. The only thing I can't really figure out is why Mick took off. I mean, we were friends. We've been friends a long time, since we were children. We've had a few arguments before, but this was his horse-trading business too. I thought he liked Skywalker. The next thing I know, he took off. I think he got mad because he thought that I was trying to mess around with Skywalker."

"I think he does like Skywalker very much. I think it had nothing to do with you or what you did, but I think he found out that Skywalker didn't like him as much as he liked her."

Mondo shook his head. "Well, he'll be back. He's still got a bunch of horses in our herd. He probably just needs to get away for a while and blow off some steam. He's young, and he'll get over Skywalker. I think Skywalker is just off men. She'd rather stab them than be with them. Mick shouldn't take that personal. He's still got some growing up to do. He'll be back. and we'll work it out."

About that time, Skywalker walked in with some vegetables she'd pulled from the garden. She looked at both of them and then set down the produce.

Savanah spoke. "Mondo's going to teach me how to shoot. He says that I'll be as good as you after he gets through with me."

"He can't teach you how to shoot. He doesn't even have a right arm. Besides, he needs to stay in bed for a while longer. He's still too weak."

Mondo got up out of the bed and picked up his rifle. "I can teach her how to shoot. I'm well. I don't have to be able to shoot to tell somebody else how. Why don't you teach her how to stab a man with that dagger you wear under your skirt?"

Savanah smiled and reached under her skirt and pulled out a knife. "She's already taught me. She says this is the only weapon for a man if he wants to do something that you're not ready to do."

Mondo shook his head. "Just like I said, if something happens to Maboola, you're going to be too mean and scary to catch a man. Look at Skywalker. Who would feel safe living with her? With her temper, she's liable to wake up after a bad dream and just drive that dagger right into a man's heart."

The two women looked at each other and just laughed. Savanah looked back at Mondo. "Just like I said before, Mondo, you don't know anything about women. Why don't you go talk to Bear Chaser? Your father failed to teach you anything important about girls. He knows a lot more than you think he does."

"Who taught you about men?" asked Mondo. "Mr. Purify Jones? Did he beat you?"

Savanah and Skywalker looked at each other and then shook their heads. Savanah spoke first. "Mr. Jones did not want a scar on my body. He wouldn't let anybody touch me, only him. I guess he liked what he saw because he tried to keep me all to himself. I'm the only one who has seen Maboola without a shirt. His back looks like raw meat with little hills and valleys from top to bottom. It's horrible. No. Mr. Purify Jones didn't damage his play toy."

Skywalker shook her head in disgust. "One of my Kiowa husbands tried to beat me, and I spooked his horse. The Kiowas didn't know for sure whether I killed him or not, but everyone in the band left me alone after he died. Nobody else tried to beat me."

Mondo pointed at her. "See there, I knew you were a husband killer. The Kiowas knew deep down that you were a murderer. That's why they were so happy to get rid of you. Savanah, you said I worried about people attacking the fort so much I didn't know what was going on in here. You're right, but it's not only people attacking the fort. I worry about being in the same house with Skywalker. I'm always on the lookout. I've learned that you can't let down your guard for anyone, or you're going to die. You don't want to be like Skywalker. She's going to die alone, an old spinster with a murder reward on her head."

Skywalker stepped up close to Mondo. "Look whose talking. I've never seen a man who thought he wanted to be alone more than you. You're afraid of people. And you're really afraid of women. If you live to be old, remember what I'm telling you right now. You're going to die a lonely hermit, and there won't be anybody coming to your funeral."

Mondo started to say something when Bear Chaser rushed into the room. "They're here. The US Cavalry is riding up to the gate. I knew they'd be by soon. We better go see what the Federals want to do about your fort, Mondo. So far, you've talked your way around the Comanches and the Chickasaws, but you haven't talked to the boys in blue from Washington, D.C."

CHAPTER 31

MABOOLA MISSED SAVANAH before he got ten miles from Mondo's compound. He rode north mostly at night, staying away from any campfires or trails so that he would not be seen. Generally, he traveled about five to ten miles west of the Chisholm Trail where the Texas cowboys were driving longhorns to Abilene, Kansas.

He ran into no one until he crossed the Kansas line a week after he left Mondo's. He had ridden through the darkness until two o'clock in the morning before he finally stopped and rested. When he woke up, he saw four Cheyenne warriors decked out in war paint, smiling at him as if they had found one big scalp of glory before breakfast.

It was the first time that Maboola had ever seen Cheyenne. They were taller and bigger than the Comanches and Kiowas. They carried no guns, and each one of them held a tomahawk or a knife in their hands as they waited for Maboola to get up. They acted like they were going to have some fun with this big man before taking his scalp. The Indians could tell Maboola was big, but they didn't realize how big until he eased to his feet. Even then, as the four warriors looked up into Maboola's eyes, they were not afraid and seemed to look forward to playing games with Maboola before killing him.

Communication was useless since neither could speak the others tongue. What was said was said through the expressions on their faces and the intensity in their eyes. Maboola could see that the four Cheyenne were looking forward to killing such a big black man. The Cheyenne had seen a few Negroes, but they had never seen anything like this giant. But the Cheyenne were over sure of themselves as warriors. Size didn't bother them. A big black scalp would be a nice prize. The body language of all four oozed with confidence.

Maboola went for his pistol, and the holster was empty. He looked up in shock, and the four warriors began to laugh. Maboola noticed that all his weapons were stacked on the ground about fifteen feet away. The Cheyenne were so sure that four of them could take any man no matter what his size. They had elected not to use his pistol, rifle, or shotgun. Maboola thought maybe they didn't know how to use the guns, but he couldn't believe that they had slipped up and disarmed him in his sleep and then tossed the guns away like the shooting weapons were not necessary.

The four spread out and circled Maboola. They were smiling and having fun. The biggest Cheyenne lunged forward with his knife and stepped back with a cocky smile. For a second, Maboola thought about the many times before the war the slave chasers had surrounded him with dogs, pistols, whips, and plenty of rope. He almost laughed at the fact that there were only two knives and two tomahawks that were going to be used to try to kill him. He couldn't hold back the laughter. Maboola let his head roll back, and he grabbed his stomach and let out a big belly laugh that stunned the Indians to silence.

The Cheyenne stopped and stared at Maboola like he was crazy. Here was a big black man that was unarmed and surrounded by four Cheyenne warriors who had killed before and were famous in their warrior society. Each Indian had at least two scalps hanging on his belt. By tradition, the Cheyenne warriors did not attack crazy people. They looked at each other and spoke in Cheyenne, trying to determine whether this big black man was insane or whether he did not understand the fierceness of a Cheyenne warrior.

Suddenly, the largest Cheyenne with the dagger crouched to attack again. But before the warrior moved a muscle, Maboola struck. Two hundred and sixty pounds was behind the arm that drove his fist smashing into the warrior's face. The bones in the Cheyenne's face splintered on contact and drove into the Indian's brain before the Cheyenne started flying backward. The sound of the blow froze the other three Indians. The noise sounded like a skull being crushed by a large stallion horse landing with both its front hoofs on someone's head.

When the Cheyenne hit the ground, there was no sound from the already dead Indian except the movement of his body skidding across the prairie. Maboola sprung out in the place that was now left by the dead Indian and faced the other three and smiled again. This time, the three Cheyenne warriors knew why he smiled. They also knew that they had met their match. This big black man was laughing, acting as if the three Cheyenne were not enough to do him any damage. As one, the three turned and fled to their horses and disappeared, leaving their companion's body dead on the plains.

Even in the summer of 1868,when there were a lot of Cheyenne war parties out looking for victims, Maboola rode through Kansas unharmed by this tribe. The word of his barehanded killing of a famous warrior spread through the Indian raiding parties, and the Cheyenne left Maboola alone.

By the time Maboola reached the Nebraska line, he was ready to go back to Mondo's. He was lonely for Savanah, and he had to admit that he enjoyed staying at Mondo's. He felt bad that he brought the white haters of Negroes down on Mondo and Savanah. They needed his help. He almost turned around and went back, but then he began to think about his future with Savanah. Maboola felt that if he could find a place that they could live an honest and safe life, then he wanted her as a wife, and he wanted children like other men. He still hated whites, and he never met a white man he could really trust. He also still thought that ex-slaves had to kill a lot of whites before Negroes could receive equal treatment. Fear was the equalizer. And fear of whites was what controlled the ex-slaves. But the odds were against him because of the population advantage of whites, and there were way too many whites that knew how to use a gun and not enough Negroes. It was obvious to Maboola that the Yankee army and the Freedmen's Bureau, and all other groups and societies that wanted to force the South to accept the Negroes, would not stay in the South forever. And when the Yankees went home, the Negroes would suffer the payback for the insult of losing the war and being ruled by white Yankees. For every ex-slave that tried to act like he was as good as a white man, there would be ten blacks killed by the night riders of the KKK. All the Southern whites thought for one reason or another, they had to keep the Negroes in their place. It was still a moral issue and an economical issue for the great majority of Southerners. For every good Southerner that had white skin and wanted to do the right thing, there were fifty Southerners waiting and ready to silence those few good white men. Realistically, Maboola knew that he was way ahead of his time. He felt it would probably take a hundred years before there were enough unafraid Negroes that would challenge white dominance in the South and enough reasonable white men to hold off the insecure, stupid bigots.

Maboola wanted to give the good life a try. He wanted to find a place where he could live with Savanah and raise a family. He did not want to go back into the swamp and live with the alligators. He wanted a place where he and his family could be reasonably safe, and his children could get an education.

It was still warm at the end of the summer of 1868 when Maboola rode into Omaha, Nebraska. This was a boomtown where anybody could get a job. The Transcontinental Railroad was extending west and they were hiring anybody that was strong enough to lay the track.

As he rode down the main street of Omaha, he noticed the looks that he always got from white people. No matter whether a white hated blacks or not, Maboola's size put fear in everyone, black or white. He was told once that the average height of a man in the United States was five foot three. Maboola had been measured at six foot six, which made him over a foot taller than most men in the United States.

Maboola thought that everyone stared at him initially because of his size, but then their eyes turned to fear when they saw his deep-black color. It appeared to Maboola that he represented the fear of all white people. Maboola was the potential payback for slavery. Whether the white people he ran into believed in slavery or not, all whites deep down felt the guilt of allowing slavery to exist in this country. That guilt showed in their faces, and the punishment that they expected from God or someone seemed to be reflected in their eyes when they looked at the big black giant. Even other Negroes didn't like to be around Maboola. When other Negroes saw the fear in the eyes of the white man as they looked at Maboola, the Negroes knew that Maboola was walking trouble. The whites would have to kill Maboola and every black that hung around him. The other Negroes feared that even if the whites didn't kill Maboola, when Maboola left the area, the fear and guilt that he represented would be taken out on the blacks still around. Maboola was a freak of nature that caused fear mixed with guilt in white people. The look in Maboola's eyes did not invite company, and even if he smiled all the time, his size and deep-black color caused a nervous apprehension in everyone around him.

Maboola dismounted and stepped up on the sidewalk and almost ran into a white man in a suit and a smile on his face. The white man stuck out his hand for a handshake, and Maboola hesitated.

The white man smiled and spoke. "Are you looking for a job? My name is Ben Morgan. I run several construction gangs laying track about a hundred miles west of here. You look like you could do the work of three men. Are you interested in working for the railroad?"

Maboola frowned at the man and looked at him in a suspicious manner. "I've never been offered a job by a white man. What would you want me to do?"

"You look too big and strong to do an average man's work. I'll tell you what, I need a troubleshooter. I need someone that goes where there is a size problem. I mean, if something can't be lifted or moved, I bet you could take care of that. I've never seen a man bigger than you. I'll pay you double Negro wages. You can catch the train going west tonight at six. I'll pay you as much as I pay any white man. We don't pay the Negroes or the Chinese as much as we do our white workers, but I figure you can do more than most anyone. What's your name?"

"My name is Jones. Robert Jones," Maboola said. "And, I'll take you up on that job. I want to take my horses. They stay with me."

"Sure, you can load them in one of the boxcars and take them along with you. I'll meet you down at the train at six o'clock tonight. I will ride out with you. See you later, Mr. Jones."

At that, he turned and walked away, and Maboola didn't know what to think. He'd heard about the Transcontinental Railroad and the effort to build a track connecting the east to the west across America, and he knew there were jobs laying tracks. He could earn some money and then find a place up north for him and Savanah to live.

That night at six, he met the foreman, and they rode the train together. The foreman sat down beside him in the railroad car, and Maboola got a few looks from the other passengers, but it didn't seem to affect Ben Morgan.

Maboola didn't feel comfortable sitting next to the foreman and didn't say much. Other than having very little room left on the seat, the foreman didn't seem to mind sitting next to a colored man. He looked up at Maboola and spoke.

"I'm from Maine. Been working out here for about six months. Were you a slave that was freed at the end of the big war?"

Maboola looked at him and nodded. "I was born free and got away at the end of the war. I've never been back east. How is it back there, I mean for a big black man like me?"

"Well, unfortunately, the end of the war hadn't equalized everything for the Negro back east. My family were abolitionists. They have been fighting slavery for many years. But the thing that has surprised me is that being against slavery and being for equality is not the same, even in Maine. Most people go through the motions of treating Negroes right, but there's not very many Negroes in Maine. White people there don't have to worry about being around many blacks. They don't live next to black people. There's just not very many colored people. But I fought in Mississippi during the war, and there's a lot of darkies in Mississippi."

Maboola nodded his head. "I'm not looking to be white. I just want to be left alone. If the white man will stay out of my way, then I'll stay out of the white man's way. But I want to have a chance to raise a family and not be bothered by white people. Would that happen in Maine?"

"Oh, I think so. There's a Negro settlement down by the railroad tracks in Portland, Maine where I live. There's no night riders or KKK running around. Both groups leave each other alone. The Negroes stay in their part of the town, and the whites stay in their part of the town. You and your wife could live down there in the colored section and wouldn't be bothered."

They discussed living in the east for a while, and then the foreman fell asleep. The sun was coming up when they arrived at the end of the track. They got off and walked down to where the men were starting to drive the spikes. It looked like a thousand men of various nationalities were busy doing one thing or another to lay the rails west as fast as possible. As Maboola walked behind the foreman, the first man at the end of the line stopped driving his spike and then the next man stopped and the next and pretty soon, the entire line pulled up and stared in silence at the six-six, 260-pound black man walking a step behind the foreman.

"Get back to work!" yelled the boss, and at once the sledge-hammers began to hit the spikes, but you could see the men glance up after each stroke to eye the black giant walking down the railroad tracks.

The big-boss foreman pointed to an area of tents and shan-ties off by itself and told Maboola to go find a place to stay down in the colored section. Maboola got his horses and started them toward the area where the Negroes lived. The big boss called to him and walked up to Maboola. "I forgot to tell you something, Jones. You're a scary man. Did you notice the work stopped when you walked by? You attract a lot of attention, and you cause a lot of fear to everyone who works here, especially the ex-rebs and Southerners. Everyone has a gun, and so do you. I want you to put your guns away. I want you to watch what you say and do so you won't get shot. I need your size, and you can earn a lot of money, but you've got to be on your best behavior."

Maboola frowned. "Are you trying to tell me to act like I was still a slave? You want me to 'Yes, sir, no, sir' and bow and scrape to all these ex-rebs around here? If they can carry their guns, then I'm going to carry my guns. I'm not going to cause any trouble, and I'm not going to start anything, but I'm not going around smiling and acting afraid of those crazy bastards that almost beat the life out of me when I was a slave."

The foreman stared at Maboola for a long time and then shook his head. "I sure hope you last. I'm afraid that with your attitude, you're not going to be here long. And I sure need you and your strength. We handle stuff all day that's too big for the average man. You'll just be on call to go do the heavy lifting. That's not too much to ask. That means that you won't be work-ing all the time. You'll be standing around like a specialist. And your specialty is strength, and we're going to pay you white man wages for that strength. Now, if you really want to get a wife and settle down somewhere, then you need money. You need this job. So don't you go around acting superior or mean and get yourself shot. You can make a bunch of money. Do you understand me?"

Maboola didn't answer but led his horses down to the shanties and to the colored section of the railroad builders.

CHAPTER 32

H IS FACE WAS on fire and he hurt everywhere. Mick tried to open his eyes but the sun kept them closed. He was either blind or his eyes were glued shut. He tried to turn and the pain shot through him. He smelled garbage and filth. Mick couldn't remember where or why he was laid out in what felt like dried mud. He rested his mind and then tried to relax his body so that he could remember. The pain all over made him know he wasn't dead unless this was what hell felt like.

In short flashes and fuzzy pictures, events crept back into his head. The bar, the girl, and then Split Face the monster came into his thoughts. He shuddered. Three men charged him after he hit Split Face. "Darkie lover" was all that he had heard.

Finally he was able to open up one of his eyes, then opened his mouth and forced out a word. He could hardly hear the "Help!" that he tried to yell. He tried again and forced the other eye open. The back of a two-story wooden building was what he first saw. He was lying in the mud and garbage that was thrown out the back door. He fought through the pain and rolled onto his side. He felt his face and could tell that loose skin hung around deep cuts soaked with dried blood, and it hurt like hell.

There was not a place on his body that didn't produce pain when he tried to move. He finally managed to push to his knees and struggle to his feet. He stood while the dizziness left his head. He looked down at himself. Blood and filth covered his body. His gun and gun belt were gone. All he had was a torn shirt, pants, and boots. He felt for his wallet, and that was gone too.

Mick managed to stagger toward the opening between the two buildings, and each step brought a new sore place. He'd been in losing fights before but never like this. When he managed to struggle out onto the street, he recognized the entrance of that Fort Worth bar. He leaned against a wooden hitching post and tried to think what he should do next. He managed to look up to the sun and guessed it was mid-afternoon. He needed to lie down and heal. The men who beat him the night before might still be in the saloon or in town.

He spotted a livery stable across the street and struggled over to the open door. No one was around, and his horse was gone. He walked over to a pile of hay and eased down into the grassy softness and forced himself to sleep away the pain.

It was the next afternoon when he opened his eyes again. He was real thirsty. Mick struggled to the horses' trough and doused his head and drank some water. He washed off some of the blood before he struggled to that saloon. He entered that saloon and looked around. The same bartender and three girls were at the bar. That was all. The bartender looked mad, and the girls looked frightened. He stepped over to the bar.

"Why did you let me rot out in the alley?"

The bartender poured Mick a drink and set it down in front of him. "The constable stopped Split Face from killing you. He didn't want Split Face to shoot you while you were lying on the ground. Everyone thought you were going to die anyway."

"Why in the hell does the law let an ugly bastard like Split Face tell him what to do?"

"Split Face is the head of the night riders. The KKK. They've got everybody afraid around here. But they keep the Negroes in their place. There's a lot of people riding with Split Face. People don't mess with them. Even the law."

"Does he live around here?" asked Mick.

"Yes. And as you know, he hates Negroes big time. I think some runaway slave put an ax in his face before the slave died from the bullets put into him by Split Face. He has a reason to hate a lot. He's a real dangerous man. A lot of people think he's necessary to keep the Yankee officers and the Freedmen's Bureau from turning this country into a Negro-run government."

"What did he say about me?" asked Mick.

"He said you were running with the Black Death named Maboola. They said you and a Chickasaw Negro live in a fort in Indian Territory and you all make raids across the Red River to kill white people."

"I partner with a Chickasaw named Mondo, who does have a little Negro blood in him, but Maboola is gone. He left and went up north. We don't raid in Texas."

"Well, Split Face convinced everybody that you were helping that Maboola kill whites. The constable made a deal with Split Face. Nobody would help you, and everyone would let you lie there, and Split Face wouldn't gun you down while you were unconscious in the alley. If Split Face hadn't already thought you were dead, he never would have agreed not to shoot you. Split Face warned everybody in town that if anyone helped you, they were dead. People believe him and know Split Face does what he says he will do."

"Where's my stuff?" asked Mick. "I had a pistol, a rifle, a saddle, two horses, supplies, and some gold. I guess the constable didn't make Split Face leave that for me, did he?"

The bartender shook his head no. "That was part of the deal too. The constable gave Split Face everything you had just to save your life. It wasn't so much that he wanted to save your life. The constable just didn't want any more shootings in Fort Worth. Some of the trail bosses might not let their men come into town if there's any more killings. The trail bosses don't like their men to get drunk and shoot up the town until they've made it to Abilene. The cattlemen can't afford to lose riders. The constable has been warned to cut down on the shootings. I'm sure that the constable would have let Split Face kill you if it hadn't been bad for business. Now, I've said more than I should. We don't want to be seen with you. You need to get out of the bar and get out of town as fast as you can. If Split Face finds out that you are alive, then he won't keep his side of the deal, and you're going to be dead real quick."

Mick glared at the bartender and looked over at the girls. "I never thought about riding with the Black Death, but I'm thinking about it now. You tell me where this constable is and I'm going to have a little talk with him."

The bartender raised his sawed-off shotgun from behind the counter and stuck it against Mick's belly. "Take my advice, young man. You better move out while you can. If you can run, I'd run, but don't hang around here. Your life is hanging by a thread, and it wouldn't take much to cut that thread by any of us. If you're not out of this bar before I count to three, there's going to be a huge hole in your belly."

Mick turned and limped out of the bar, looked around, and, realizing there was no one to help him, he wandered up the street.

CHAPTER 33

ALL FOUR WALKED out of Mondo's compound and waited for the soldiers to ride up. There was a major leading a small detachment of black cavalry. A lieutenant rode behind the major. Both officers were white, and the ten troopers were blacks. They slowed to a walk and eased up about ten feet from Mondo and stopped. The lead officer looked at the four people waiting for them and then looked over the compound and then slowly dismounted. The lieutenant and the black troops remained in the saddle. The major walked up to Mondo and stopped. "Are you in charge here?"

"This is my compound," said Mondo.

"How long have you been here? When was this built?" asked the officer.

"I've homesteaded this place for a couple years under my father's name who is a full-blood Chickasaw."

"What are you called?" asked the officer.

"I'm called Mondo. What are you called?" asked Mondo.

"I'm Brevet Major General Benjamin H. Grierson, colonel of the Tenth Cavalry sent from Fort Gibson to locate a new post. I'm here by orders of the US Army, and who gave you the right to be here?"

"This is Chickasaw land. My father is a Chickasaw. I've got a written permit from the Chickasaw Nation to stay here," said Mondo.

"This isn't Chickasaw land. This is Comanche, Kiowa, and Kiowa-Apache land. I don't know a lot about surveying, but I can damn sure read maps. I can tell you right now you are west of the Chickasaw Nation, that ends at the 98th meridian. It's not been surveyed yet, but you're not on Chickasaw land, and you're too damn close to the new fort at Medicine Bluff the army's going to build."

Bear Chaser stepped forward. "You may be right, but you may be wrong. Until the survey is complete, nobody knows for sure. The Chickasaw Nation and myself as a Chickasaw are right now treating this land as Chickasaw land."

Colonel Grierson turned to Bear Chaser. "On the map, Little Beaver Creek is just a little west of the 98th meridian. I know that's guesswork, but it's good guesswork. The Comanches and Kiowas are raiding again, and they have joined the Cheyenne to hit white people all around this country. General Custer is right now swinging down the Washita, looking for the renegades that are killing white people. You must know the Comanches hate forts. They remember the forts that pushed them out of Texas. The young warriors are demanding that you get off of their land, and the army can't keep them from burning you out. I don't really give a damn if they do."

Mondo said, "Have you been ordered to remove us?"

"No. Not yet," said Colonel Grierson. "I've been sent down here to find a location for a new post close to all this raiding and killing. The army will probably close Fort Arbuckle and move us over near the Wichita Mountains. But just as soon as I report back to my commander, I'll probably be ordered to remove this illegal settlement you've built."

"We have permission from Ten Bears," said Mondo. "So whether it's Chickasaw or Comanche land, I have a right to stay here."

"The young warriors don't listen to Ten Bears. They're all mad because they think the Comanches are due food from the Medicine Lodge Treaty. And by the way, my scouts saw ten graves at the south end of this valley that said, 'Here lie men that tried to take this fort'. Who were those men?"

"Those were six white outlaws from the South that rode here to kidnap this young lady." said Mondo, pointing to Savanah. "The other four were renegade Comanches that attacked us."

"So you say. You just admitted that you've killed Comanches. That's reason enough for you to be taken in right now. We're here to protect the white people, but we're supposed to enforce the treaty, and no one is allowed to come on the Comanche and Kiowa land between the Red and Washita River and the 98th meridian and the Texas Panhandle. Now, I think that applies to Negroes, Chickasaws, Mexicans, and white people," said Grierson as he looked at each person, indicating that Savanah represented the white race.

Mondo answered, "Until you prove this is Comanche land, we have a right to be here, and we have a right to defend ourselves. We were attacked, and we killed some of the people who tried to kill us. You wouldn't even think about arresting white people that killed attacking Comanches or attacking members of the KKK. Just because I'm Chickasaw and part-Negro, you're trying to run me off of my own place."

Major Grierson shook his head no. "It has nothing to do with who you are. It's where you are. And what about these two women. Are they captives?" Colonel Grierson looked at Skywalker and then at Savanah. "Speak up. I won't let these men harm you."

Skywalker smiled. "I'm here right now because I want to be here. These men got me from the Kiowas. I was a captive of the Kiowas for three years. I'm from Mexico. I may want to go back home some day, but right now, I will stay until Mondo is completely healed from his injuries, and I sure don't want to go back to the Kiowas. They don't want me back either. I'm stuck here for right now."

"The army will help you get back home. We sent some other Mexican captives back to Mexico. I would recommend that you let me take you back to Fort Arbuckle, and you can catch an army supply train going south and probably be home in a month or so."

"I will stay here for now. I thank you for your kindness, and I may call on you and the US Army to help me get back one of these days."

Colonel Grierson looked over at Savanah. "And who are you? What's a white woman doing living with a Negro and a Chickasaw Indian?"

Savanah smiled. "Not white. Before the end of the war, I was owned by a man named Jones in Texas. I came here when I was rescued. I don't want to leave."

"Who looks after you now?" asked Colonel Grierson.

"I look after myself. I'm like Skywalker. I'm free, and I can go or stay whenever I want to. And like Skywalker, I'm going to stay here awhile."

"Well, who's married to who?" asked Colonel Grierson. "Are all four of you living up in that little rock cabin together?"

"That's none of your business," said Mondo. "Nobody's married, and nobody's living in sin if that's what you are worried about."

"I'm worried about everything concerning this compound. I'm worried about where it is and what it stands for. I'm worried about the people that are staying here. I'm going to have to search this compound."

"Nobody goes into my compound without my say-so," snapped Mondo.

"I'm not going to mess with you about this. Either you let us search this now, or we will bring some cannons back and just flatten this place."

Bear Chaser took Mondo by the arm and kind of walked him back toward the entrance. "Let them look at the place. What can they find? I don't think they will find the trapdoor. And we don't want to give them an excuse to come back and start shelling this fort with cannons."

"I just don't want the army thinking they have a right to come in here anytime they feel like it," answered Mondo.

Bear Chaser shook his head. "Mondo, you're injured. We're down to one and a half men and two women. They've got two officers and ten troopers. Let's use our heads for once and just let them look around."

Mondo stared at Bear Chaser for a while and then walked back to the colonel. "Go ahead. Search it. But you tell your commander this is the last time the army is going to cross into my front door. I'm here by right, and I'm here to stay. If you want to search again, you better bring those damn cannons."

Colonel Grierson glared at Mondo and then nodded his head that he'd heard Mondo. He turned and ordered his troops to dismount and search the compound. Mondo, Savanah, Bear Chaser, and Skywalker stood outside as some of the black troops entered the cabin, and others walked around the fort and climbed up on the walls and checked everything in sight. While the two white officers were out of sight, the black sergeant came out and walked over to Mondo and lowered his voice. "Aren't you the one that took on that evil bastard named Split Face?"

"Me and a few others," said Mondo. "That's six of his men out there six feet under."

"Is the one the whites call Black Death hiding around here somewhere?"

"No. You're talking about Maboola. He's been gone for a while. He went up North."

"That's too bad. I sure wanted to meet that man. I hope we never have to take him on or you for that matter. My name is Sergeant Omar Culberson, by the way."

"They call me Mondo Hobbs. Nice to meet you." They shook hands. "How do you like the army? Do they treat you right?"

"It's a lot better than being a slave. The US Cavalry is not freedom for anybody, except maybe for the generals. But I like it. You usually get fed regularly."

"You're with the Tenth Cavalry, aren't you?" asked Mondo.

"Yes. It's an all-Negro cavalry unit."

"Are you going to be stationed in that new fort the army is talking about building over by Medicine Bluff?"

"That's what I hear. In fact, I think we're going to be the ones that will build it. I don't think that Colonel Grierson is really going to try to burn you out. He talks tough, and he has a tough job with the Kiowa and Comanche raiding everywhere, but he has a lot more to worry about than your little compound."

"That's good to hear," said Mondo. "I sure wouldn't want to kill colored soldiers." Omar nodded in agreement. "You're right. What have we got if not each other? Is Maboola going to come back?"

"If he does, he'll just come back to pick up Savanah and head up North. I think Maboola wants to settle down. If it wasn't for Savanah, I think he probably would keep on fighting until he finally went down for good. I think he's ready to try to live a peaceful family life."

"Well, he's being smart, but to tell you the truth, we kind of enjoyed the fear that we heard in white people when they talked about him. Just for once, it was nice to see a little fear coming from the other side."

"Maboola couldn't win. He was fighting a losing battle. He knows that," said Mondo.

Omar nodded in agreement. "By the way, I found that trap-door. The white officers won't know about it though. I think it means something you staying out here no matter what everyone is trying to tell you to do. Not many colored folks live long standing up against 'the man.'"

"Thanks," said Mondo. Before he could say any more, Colonel Grierson came out of the cabin and walked up to him.

"I will report to the commander that I found no cannons. You do have a lot of guns and ammunition though. I'll be back just as soon as I get my orders."

With that, he turned and ordered his troops to leave the fort. Mondo walked out to watch them leave. As the troops turned, the black Sergeant Omar Culberson dipped his hat to Mondo, and they rode off.

CHAPTER 34

T HE WORD WAS out. Every place Mick turned, people looked at him like he had a contagious disease. Fear leaped into their eyes, and a lot of them just plain took off walking fast in the other direction. The night riders or the KKK controlled by Split Face had everyone afraid. No one would help Mick.

He struggled down the street with nothing but his shirt, pants, and boots. He walked about a block when his legs gave way, and he sat down on the boarded sidewalk in front of the largest general store. He hurt all over like he had been run over by a stampede of longhorns. His mouth was dry, and he needed a drink. People walked by and ignored him like he wasn't even there. The horse trough held water, and it looked awful good. Mick crawled over to the horse trough and drank the cool water. There was pain all over his body, and he felt cold. He crawled back and sat on the board sidewalk and hugged himself while he shivered and thought about his predicament. He had to get out of town. He had no family, and the only place that he could call home was Mondo's fort. He had enough horses there to sell and replace all the things that were stolen from him. Somehow in the middle of November 1868, he had to get from Fort Worth to Mondo's fort, which was about 130 miles. There were no cattle being driven up the Chisholm Trail toward Kansas because the weather had turned cold. He really didn't know any cattle owners that used the Chisholm Trail during these winter months.

Then the ugly picture of Split Face flashed in his mind. A feeling of hate came over him like he'd never felt before in his life. It produced so much heat that his shivering stopped. Split Face was almost like a dictator in a country that was supposed to be free. He ruled with fear, and even those so-called "good citizens" were afraid to do anything about his murderous ways. There was very little law in Texas. The Yankee troops, the Yankee commissioners, and governmental people along with the Freedmen's Bureau were trying to force the Texans to change their way of life. Texas was a defeated country with occupying troops. The government and courts were run by the hated Yankees. All was taken over by the winning North army, and the rules for Texas came out of the US Congress in Washington, D.C. Only in the darkness of night could some of the whites feel some kind of control. Daytime was controlled by the Yankees, but the nighttime belonged to the KKK, who still tried to maintain their way of life by fear and intimidation. The whole town of Fort Worth was so scared of Split Face and his night riders that no one would help Mick. This certainly was not the real Texas way. Before the war, if you needed help, you usually got it. Now if you were a Yankee, you were the enemy, and if you supported anything the Yankees stood for, you were an enemy no matter how long you had lived in Texas.

Mick shook his head and almost cried. Why was he such a fool to think that he could run with Mondo and be with Maboola and not expect this treatment by Split Face and the people who sat back and wouldn't stop the night riders? It was the only organization that wasn't controlled by the Yankees and the only way a lot of whites could protect themselves from what they believed was total destruction of their way of life. There was no law enforcement and all feared the many ex-slaves would run-a-mok and punish all white people.

"Is that you, Mick?" came a voice from the street.

Mick looked up through blurry eyes and tried to recognize the man that sat on the horse. When he saw the red hair, he recognized someone who was afraid of no one.

"Yeah, that's me. Is that you? Red Granger, is that you?"

"Damn, boy, horse trading must be real bad or you lost eve-rything horse racing. I thought that was you drinking out of this horse trough like a dog. What the hell happened to you?"

"I've been beat up and left for dead. That sorry Split Face and his gang got a hold of me, and I'm supposed to be thankful that the local police wouldn't let them kill me. I feel like every bone in my body has been busted up twice."

"Why don't you get some help?" Red Granger looked around as two men walked by and looked away from Mick as if he didn't exist. "Is this whole damn town afraid of that sorry, no-good Split Face?"

"That's right. People are treating me like I've got the black plague. If you want to do business in Fort Worth, you better stay away from me."

Red Granger just nodded, dismounted, and tied his horse to the hitching rail and reached down and helped Mick to his feet. "I've survived three big battles in the Civil War, seventeen stam-pedes, and lost three men drowning in the Red River. I've been shot at a hundred times and hit five of those times. Nobody in this little piss-ant town scares me. As far as I'm concerned, there's no worse outlaw than that ugly bastard with the scar down the middle of his face. The only thing that run-a-way slave did wrong is he didn't bury that damn ax deep enough to split his brain instead of only his face."

"I know, but you risk everything by helping me. Why?" asked Mick.

"Because, by God, it's right. Come on. The first thing we're going to get you is a coat."

Red Granger helped Mick into the general store and walked over and grabbed a coat and put it on his back. Everyone in the store stood and stared without saying a word. Finally, the store owner walked over and shook his head no.

"Do you know who that is cowboy?" he asked.

"Damn right I know who he is, and do you know who the hell I am?"

"I've seen you come through here before. You're one of those trail bosses on the cattle drives."

"I'm a trail boss, and I own all the cattle that I bring through here. My name is Red Granger. Ever heard of me?"

The man took a step back and shook his head yes. "Yes, sir. I have heard of you. Have you ever heard of Split Face?"

"I've heard of that ugly murderous son-of-a-bitch. He's the sorriest man in Texas. And the next sorriest people in Texas are the sons-of-bitches that let him get by with killings, robberies, and the spreading of fear. Now, if you want me to pay for this coat, you better let me know what it costs. And we need a few other things before we leave. If you don't show them to me, then we'll just take them and walk out of here. It's your choice. Do you want me to pay you or just take this stuff?"

"All right, I'll sell them to you." He looked around at the people in the store. "I want everybody in here to tell the people that will go find Split Face that I had to sell these things to this man. He threatened my life, and I know he has a bunch of men that work for him." He turned back toward Red Granger. "I know Split Face is no angel. But by God, somebody has to stand up to those Yankees. They won't let an ex-Confederate vote, hold office, or enforce the law. They raised the taxes on the people that didn't have any money after the war and are trying to take all our land. I don't like what Split Face is doing, and if it was normal times, we'd stop him, but this ain't normal times. You don't sound like a Yankee, and you don't look like a Yankee, but you damn sure act like one."

"I fought for the South, and I got wounds to prove it. But the damn war is over. We lost, and we got to take a little shit from these Yankees before we get back to being regular Texans. Just because the carpetbaggers are acting like a bunch of assholes doesn't mean that we have to forget everything about decency. Any people of any town that let a bunch of evil bastards like Split Face come in here, beat up this kid, and leave him for dead, ought to be run out of the state of Texas. Now, let's start acting like what Texans are supposed to act like. If you don't, I'll gather up enough cowboys that come through here and spend money in your damn town and we'll just burn this son of a bitch down. We cattle owners have formed an association to stop rustling. We're against outlaws. We're the only non-Yankees that have any money in this state. Are you going to treat this man right?"

The owner dropped his head and then looked back up. "Take what you need. There's a doctor in town that you might convince to look at this young fellow."

Red Granger outfitted Mick, and they checked in with the doctor. Word was out that there was another madman in Fort Worth, and it wasn't Split Face. As much as the town feared Split Face, the town had heard of Red Granger. Red Granger got a room for both of them in the downtown hotel, and they laid up overnight so that Mick could gain enough strength to ride a horse. Red Granger told him that he was heading for Indian Territory to meet some Chickasaw representatives at the Fitzpatrick's store near Cow Creek. He told Mick that the trail driver association had picked him to discuss the per head price for longhorns coming through Chickasaw lands. The Cattlemen's Association wanted to get a fixed price and a method of counting the herds since there was going to be a lot of cattle moving through in 1869. Red Granger informed Mick that the charges per head varied and were collected off some and not collected off others. Since the Chisholm Trail to Abilene, Kansas, ran about one hundred miles through the Chickasaw Nation, the Cattlemen's Association wanted to work out details on how the taxes were to be paid and hoped that they would keep the price to not over ten cents a head if all the Cattlemen's Association agreed to pay the tax without protest. Some of the cattle bosses had fifteen or twenty ex-Confederates that had been through the war and were not afraid of dying and would not pay the fee. The Chickasaws either had to shoot it out with these men or try to arrest them and take them to Fort Smith, Arkansas, for trespassing without paying the per head fee for cattle. Therefore, Red Granger was going to meet with the Chickasaws to try to clear up the problem and work out an agreement that would benefit both sides.

The next day, Red Granger and Mick rode north out of Fort Worth, headed for Fitzpatrick's store on Cow Creek, about fifty-two miles north of Red River. Mick was still sore, but he started to feel alive and was very thankful that Red Granger helped him out of town.

After they crossed the Red River, Mick started to feel like his old self and began to talk and ask questions.

"Why don't the Cattlemen's Association just go kill Split Face?" he asked.

"There would just be somebody else to take his place. Texas has never lost a war. Texans are bad losers. One way or another, they are going to try to do what they want to do no matter what the Yankees say. The KKK has a lot of crazy Texans that are members. People in Texas don't think that the Yankees that occupy Texas know one thing about right and wrong. Until the Yankees go back home, there will to be a lot of night riders trying to keep ex-slaves from raping and killing all the whites, or at least that's what they think and preach. They're trying to get so called justice at night which is really revenge against the carpetbaggers that now run Texas during the day."

"Life's going to be real bad for the next few years," said Mick.

"If Lincoln hadn't been killed, things might have been different. He was smart enough to know that you can't punish the South, you have to work with them. Before that revengeful Congress passed all those laws in regard to ex-Confederates having no rights, and the Freedmen Bureau came out and tried to get the ex-slaves to run Texas when they couldn't read or write, and could hardly speak English, things might have worked out over a period of time. Some counties in South Texas had more Negroes than whites. After the war in Colorado County, all the cotton growers that were left got together and entered into contracts with the slaves that picked the cotton. They agreed to certain rules of no beatings and for reasonable working hours. One owner tried to beat one of his workers and the rest of the owners rode by and straightened him out. Those men were smart and they were reasonable. They knew they had to have the cotton pickers and they knew that the cotton pickers were no longer slaves. The ex-slaves worked with the white leaders and a plan was agreed on that over the next twenty years, all Negroes would be allowed to go to their own schools paid by taxes. Things were going pretty good, then Congress up in Washington, D.C. decided to take all the rights away from the ex-Confederates and sent down Yankee troops to punish. That ended all progress and negotiations with the black people down in that county. Before the war, the Democratic party controlled about eighty percent of the vote. After Congress cut off the ex-Confederate soldiers' voting rights, the Negroes joined with a lot of German Immigrants, who mostly did not support the South and the Republican Party in Texas became a majority. Since ex-Confederates couldn't vote, forty percent of the population of that county controlled ninety percent of the voting. The war battles have ended, but there's going to be a lot of hard and bad times in Texas for the next ten years until the white landowners take back control of this state and get rid of the KKK."

"Hell, it's a lot safer in Indian Territory. As much as the Texans hate the Kiowas and Comanches, I'd rather deal with them Indians any day than that crazy Split Face and all the people that support him or won't stop him."

"Well, I'll have you home pretty quick now. And, come spring I'll be back up the trail. I'll stop by and see how you are doing."

"I'll give you some horses for what I owe you. When we get to Fitzpatrick's, I can borrow a horse from him. He's Irish too. I've been trading my horses out of his store for the last few months. It was your idea and it's paid off. When spring comes, we'll be ready to take care of the horse needs of all the trail bosses coming up the trail. Get the word out for us. I'm heading for Mondo's and I may never cross the Red River into Texas again unless I'm going to try to kill that sorry son-of-a-bitch called Split Face."

CHAPTER 35

THE RIDE FROM Fort Worth wore Mick out. Theodore Fitzpatrick had to help Mick get to Mondo's compound. Savanah and Skywalker eased Mick into the cabin, and after examining him, they determined that Mick had busted ribs and a cracked bone in his right leg. Mondo wasn't much help for he still couldn't use his right arm and wore it in a sling.

As the cold days of winter approached, Bear Chaser took care of the horses and handled all the other chores that Skywalker and Savanah couldn't do. The compound looked like an army hospital for the walking wounded. Mondo went around with one arm, and Mick hobbled around with a cane on one good leg.

By the middle of December 1868, the young Comanche warriors began to gather at Mondo's fort. At first a few rode in and set up camp at the north end of the valley. About once a day, they would get up on their horses and ride crazy stunts around the compound, yelling war whoops and calling the people in the fort all types of insulting names. Each day, a few more young warriors came until there were about thirty gathered around Mondo's fortress. The more Comanches that moved into the camp, the closer they rode around the fort. Their daily routine consisted of challenging the occupants of the compound to come out and fight and making threats and insults. The young Comanche warriors were trying to entice Mondo and the other people in the fort to do battle. The rest of the Comanche Indians who signed the Medicine Lodge Treaty were waiting for the goods and supplies promised by Washington, D.C. They were gathered at Fort

Cobb to see if the US government would live up to its promises. Located on the Washita River, Fort Cobb was forty miles
north and about fifteen miles west of Mondo's fort. The more the
Comanches waited, the more restless the young warriors became,
and Mondo's fort that was built in their territory was again the
symbol of the white man's encroachment and destruction of the
Comanche tribe. The fact that Mondo had great warrior status
and was respected more than many of the young warriors of
the Comanche tribe added fuel to the fire of the warriors' anger
toward Mondo and a good cause for notoriety if the warriors won
in a battle with Mondo.

Inside the fort, the cabin got tight and closed in. Over a hundred horses were inside the walls, and there was enough winter feed stored to take care of the horses for about two weeks.
The occupants used the secret trapdoor to replenish their water
supply. By this time, Savanah had learned to shoot, but not very
well. Someone had to stay up through the night to watch for an
attack. As Bear Chaser said, "Besides me, we have one woman
that shoots like a man, one woman that barely shoots, and two
wounded half-men that might match one good Comanche warrior." Therefore Bear Chaser took the north wall, watching the
campfires of the gathered Comanches. Skywalker had the west
wall closest to the creek. Mondo took the east wall, and Savanah
and Mick had the south part of the compound. It became like an
old-fashioned castle siege because the inhabitants in the compound were running low on food and the horse enclosed smell
tested their noses. They were trapped with a hundred horses,
two wounded men, two women, and Bear Chaser. Each day, the
Comanches built up more courage and rode in closer to the main
gate. On the twelfth of December, they fired arrows that were
burning into the fort. Bear Chaser and the women moved around
fast enough to put out the fires, but they knew time was running
out. The attack was going to come. There were about forty young
warriors gathered on the north end of the valley, and each day,

they built each other's courage up to attack the symbol of the white man's encroachment into their territory.

Early the next morning, they heard the war whoops and they saw the young warriors chasing another Indian toward the compound. The young warriors would ride up and touch the Indian with their tomahawks, rifles, or bows and then ride off laughing. Bear Chaser recognized Ten Bears, his old friend, and opened the compound enough for Ten Bears to ride inside.

Ten Bears was exhausted and had been scratched and had bleeding marks on his body like he had been beaten with a whip. Bear Chaser helped his old friend off the horse and looked at him for an answer as to why the old chief was chased into the compound by his own brethren. Ten Bears looked sad and angry at the same time. He raised his eyes and looked at Bear Chaser. "The big chief in Washington has lied again. By the Medicine Lodge Treaty, there should have been two deliveries by now of food and supplies. The young warriors blame me for accepting once again the white man's lies. They say I should die in a fort with the enemy and not out on the plains like a Comanche warrior."

Bear Chaser patted his old friend on the back and told him that he had to get back up on the wall and see what the hotheads were going to do next.

Mondo helped Ten Bears to the porch, and the old Indian sat down.

Mondo asked Ten Bears, "What are they doing? Are they going to attack or are they just trying to starve us out?"

"I think they'll attack in the morning. Some white bootlegger sold them a bunch of whiskey. They will do the war dance tonight and get their false courage from the whiskey bottle. They're angry at the lies of the white men. Your fort just happens to be in the way of their anger. They blame me for listening to the white man's lies over again many times. Your compound is the weakest fort located on their hunting grounds."

"How many will attack?" asked Mondo.

"Well, right now there's about forty young Comanches out there. I don't think all of them will attack. But after they dance all night and drink plenty of that firewater, they'll be all hot and ready and probably will come at you."

"Will they try to kill you too?"

"If I help you, then they will have a good reason to kill me. The young ones want to kill me anyway."

"Do what you think is right," said Mondo.

Mick limped out of the cabin and sat down near Ten Bears.

Ten Bears looked over at Mick. "The young warriors also know that you have a white Texan as a partner. The Comanches hate Texans, and they hate forts. With all the lies from Washington, they don't need whiskey to build up their hatred for you and this place. If they don't come tomorrow, they will come the next day or the next."

Mick looked up and asked, "If I leave, will that stop a raid?"

"They would kill you if they saw you leaving, and if you left without being noticed, they wouldn't know you were gone."

"Mick's staying," said Mondo. "I can shoot left-handed with a pistol well enough to get a bunch of those hotheads. If we kill a few, their anger will die down."

Ten Bears frowned. "I've been told for about the tenth time that the US government is sending supplies from Kansas. I had a reliable scout ride in and say there's a big wagon train moving across the territory to Fort Cobb. If the food gets to Fort Cobb, the young warriors might leave your compound and go back there to get food. They are awful hungry."

"Where's the US Army?" asked Mondo.

"They're scattered around Kansas, and some troops are coming into Indian Territory looking for the Cheyenne. The Cheyenne have killed a bunch of white people in Kansas, and the Comanches and Kiowas have raided in New Mexico, Colorado, and of course in Texas. The golden-haired one they call Custer is in the Panhandle of Texas, looking for the raiders. The army is finally bringing supplies with one hand and sending the army to kill with the other hand. The trouble is, the army never knows peaceful Indians from warlike Indians, or whether an Indian is Kiowa, Cheyenne or Comanche. All Indians are all lumped together. And all Indians are considered bad Indians."

Ten Bears continued. "Custer is out to kill any Indian. If that happens before the supplies get to Fort Cobb, these young warriors will come after you and burn this place down. If I were you, I'd slip out at night and either get to Tishomingo City or across the Red River and find a safe place for a while. I'll stay and make enough noise where they think you are still here."

Mondo nodded his head in agreement and called Savanah and Skywalker over to the fence where Bear Chaser was watching the young Comanche warriors. Mick limped over to join the group.

"This is how it's going to be. I'm staying, but the rest of you are going. Me and Ten Bears will make enough noise that they'll think that everybody is still in here. Bear Chaser, you're going to help Mick and lead Savanah and Skywalker out the trapdoor tonight and head for Tishomingo City."

There was silence as everyone looked at each other and then looked back at Mondo.

Mick was the first to speak. "I think he's right. We've got to save the women. There's no use everybody getting killed. These warriors got whiskey. They're going to do something for sure. I think we ought to make a run for it."

Skywalker put her hands on her hips and snapped at Mick. "You mean you'd walk out and leave an old man and a half a man to take on all those Comanche warriors? Well, you can go ahead and take Savanah. You and Bear Chaser can slip off like a bunch of cowards, but I'm staying. Besides, the chance of you slipping through those Comanches and finding any horses to ride are zero to nothing. Do you really think you can walk out of Comanche country with all those hotheaded young bucks looking for scalps? Bear Chaser could probably do it by himself, but Mick can hardly walk, and Savanah has no experience slipping around in Indian country." She looked over at Mondo. "Sometimes, Mondo, I don't think you have a brain in your head."

Mondo turned red and stepped up close to Skywalker. "There you go again. This is my place. And I am ordering everybody out but me and Ten Bears. That's it."

Bear Chaser hollered down from the wall. "It's too late. They're all in their war paint and gathering for an attack."

Mondo crawled up on top of the wall with the help of Bear Chaser and looked out. About twenty-five warriors were hollering and screaming and yelling insults as they passed a jug back and forth. The whiskey was giving them more courage. All of a sudden, the shouting stopped. Mondo and Bear Chaser looked over to the west, and from the creek rode a lone warrior. He rode out, turned, and faced the Comanches that were preparing to charge the fort.

"I know that warrior," said Mondo. "That's Storm. What's he doing here? His band mostly stays in the Panhandle of Texas."

Ten Bears answered. "Well, that's him, and he's here now. All those young hotheads sure know who he is!"

Storm slowly rode his horse up to the Comanches. There was a conversation that Mondo and Bear Chaser couldn't hear from the compound, but the Indian voices were angry. The young warriors shouted and made threats and argued with Storm who sat calmly on his horse as if he was in no danger. Soon, the young warriors turned and rode back to their campsite. Storm waited until they were all dismounted and then turned and slowly rode back toward Mondo's compound.

Mondo opened the compound door, and Storm rode in and smiled. He looked at Mondo. "You spent the last winter with me. You told me to come by any time. Well, I thought it was time. When I arrived here, I noticed that you had a problem. I convinced those young drunkards that you were my blood brother and that an attack on you would be an attack on me and my band. They don't want any trouble from us Antelopes."

Mondo smiled and reached up and helped Storm down.

"You're sure a sight for sore eyes. I can't believe you convinced them to back off. They've been here about a week, raising hell and drinking whiskey. Ten Bears was sure they were going to attack."

Storm looked at Ten Bears and nodded and turned back to Mondo. Then he looked up into the sky. "The reason the young drunkards were attacking now and not waiting until in the morning is that everybody knows a storm is coming."

The people in the fort looked up and could see the clouds drifting in and the north wind picking up. Mondo realized that the weather was changing for the worse. Storm continued. "I reminded them of my medicine. I told them I didn't need anybody else from my band to kill them all in a blizzard. They have heard enough about me to know that was probably true. So you can really thank the weather."

Mondo smiled and hugged Storm. They both laughed. Bear Chaser hollered down from the north wall. "They are breaking camp. They must be going for shelter to get out of the storm's way."

Storm shook his head. "That's not the only reason they are leaving. I gave them word that Custer wiped out an entire Cheyenne village and killed over a hundred, mostly old men, women, and children. I told them if they really wanted to get the people responsible for their problems, they better ride out and face the cavalry instead of trying to attack two old men, two cripples, and two women. I found out your condition in the fort from a good friend who keeps an eye on your place and was with that bunch at first. I kind of insulted them as warriors. I told them if they wanted to be brave, why didn't they go chase down Custer and his army? After the US Cavalry destroyed Black Kettle's village up near the Texas Panhandle on the Washita River, a lot of Kiowas and Comanches are joined up with the Cheyenne looking for war. I was with a few who got some of Custer's men. And besides, I got word that the supplies going to Fort Cobb just crossed the South Canadian River, and the food is only a day away from being delivered to Fort Cobb and the peace-loving Comanches. They're hungry. They really weren't afraid of me. I kind of talked them out of attacking this place."

Before he finished, the snow started to fall. Mondo introduced Storm to the rest of the occupants. As they entered the cabin, Storm pulled Mondo aside and whispered. "I see you're not shy anymore around women. Those two are your wives, aren't they? Now, you remember last winter I offered you the choice of my wives because you were my honored guest? Now that's the Indian custom, and you're more Indian than anything. I think I prefer that light-skinned one. That other one that walks around with her nose in the air looks kind of mean. I could do great things with that one you call Savanah, but I don't know that I'd feel real safe going to sleep next to that Skywalker woman."

Mondo glared at Storm and then smiled. "You don't waste any time, do you? Neither one of them belongs to me. But I have to admit, you've got good judgment when it comes to women. That Skywalker would just as soon stab you as hump you, and that Savanah is one real good-looking gal."

Storm shook his head in disgust. "Who do they belong to?"

"Skywalker belongs to no man, but Savanah has a man," said Mondo.

"Who is Savanah's man?" Storm asked.

"He's gone up North, but he left his woman in my care," answered Mondo.

"Are you taking care of her?" Storm asked then smiled.

"Taking care of her means keeping men off her. No one's lying with her. If I let you have Savanah, we'd both be killed if her man Maboola came back. Have you heard of the man the white Texans call Black Death? That's her man."

"Yes. I've sure heard of him from the Cheyenne. That's too bad. It's going to be a cold winter staying with you."

Chapter 36

That night, it got colder. There was a fire going in the fireplace, and after eating a bite, the seven people in Mondo's cabin gathered around for conversation. Since Storm and Ten Bears spoke only Comanche, they talked in Comanche, which caused Mick and Savanah to be left out of the discussion. Bear Chaser, Mondo, and Skywalker could all speak Comanche fairly well. At first, Mondo wanted to know why and how Storm had suddenly appeared at the compound and headed off the Comanche warrior strike.

"Word got back to my Antelope band that Chickasaw Killer had finally found somebody to help him seek revenge on you. I was ashamed and embarrassed when he attacked you in our camp last winter. Nobody in our band would ride with Chickasaw Killer against you. He finally found that crazy snake that kills babies. When I heard about what they tried to do, and that you were hurt, I came to see what I could do to repay you for their bad behavior. Since someone in my band caused injury to my friend, it was a point of honor to come make it right."

"We sure needed you today. If it weren't for you, we would be fighting off Comanches right now. How did you find out who was in this fort and that Mondo and Mick were hurt?" asked Bear Chaser.

"You all live in Comanche country. There's always some warrior watching your fort. The Comanches know everyone who comes and goes around here. Every day, there's some young warrior who rides out and tries to get the courage to take you on or at least get your horses. Anybody that counted coup on you or touched you in battle while you were still alive would become famous overnight. A young warrior would make his name for life if he got your scalp. So the young men are always prowling around, seeing who's coming and going and thinking about catching you alone. Chickasaw Killer won't be the last one to come after you. You're too famous, and Ten Bears cannot protect you anymore." Storm looked over at Mondo. "By the way, the story is that you killed both Chickasaw Killer and Baby Killer. Is that true?"

"No. Those two chopped me up like a piece of firewood before Skywalker shot them both dead. To tell you the truth, a young warrior would probably get more glory scalping Skywalker than taking me on." Mondo looked over at Skywalker and smiled.

Skywalker glared at them and said, "I should have let them scalp you, Mondo. And, Mr. Storm, I have seen you giving Savanah and me the eye. If Mondo hasn't told you yet, we both sleep with daggers, and we both know how to use them."

Storm raised his hand and laughed. "You sure don't have these women trained right, Mondo. For someone who has such a reputation of being a great warrior, it looks like to me you get pushed around by these two women."

"They are not like normal women, and they will be gone soon."

Storm shook his head. "What a waste. Who do they belong to? Where are they going to go?" Storm looked over to Bear Chaser. "Are you the one taking care of these two?" He nodded toward Mick. "Surely this pale, skinny Texan isn't the one that's humping both of these pretty women."

The four men that could understand Comanche laughed out loud. Skywalker frowned and looked over at Mick and Savanah who sat over by themselves looking confused and upset at not knowing what was said.

Skywalker looked at the two and spoke English. "Storm was wondering who has been servicing Savanah and myself. He didn't think a Texan was man enough to do the job."

Mick sat up straight and glared at Storm. "That savage doesn't understand honor. He still lives like a caveman. Whenever there's a woman around, he thinks somebody should be doing it to her."

Bear Chaser raised his hands and smiled. "He's just making a joke. He didn't mean any insults. Storm just believes it's a real waste for two beautiful women to be sleeping in a small cabin with four men and nothing happening. He was raised in a small teepee where the main activity on a cold winter night was snuggling up close and enjoying each other."

Storm didn't understand Bear Chaser's explanation and asked Mondo in Comanche. "You didn't answer me. Who does the one you call Savanah do it with?"

"Nobody," said Mondo. "I've already told you that, but you don't believe me. She has a man that's a real warrior. You said you've heard of him. Maboola. He's a great big black man. I've been through a lot, and I'm not very afraid of anybody, but I guarantee you, if you saw Maboola, you'd leave that Savanah alone."

"There's a story that came from the Cheyenne that some kind of black giant killed with his fist one of their big tough warriors. That just happened earlier this year. I guess that's the one you call Maboola."

"There's nobody else like him. He's real big, and he headed North earlier this year. If the Cheyenne tangled with him, I bet they lost no matter how many were after Maboola."

Storm shook his head and looked sad. He nodded toward Savanah. "Poor thing. Nobody to keep her warm at night. Why do you think he will ever come back?"

"Like you said, she's beautiful. If he stays alive, I think he'll be back. No sane man would assume that he was dead and try to take advantage of Savanah. However, if he dies, there will be a long line trying to take Maboola's place with that girl," answered Mondo.

Savanah frowned. "That's rude. I know you're talking about me. I can't understand a word you're saying, but I don't like the looks that I'm getting. I agree with Mondo's biggest gripe. This isn't a hotel, and there's too many men sleeping in this cabin. Be sure to tell this young warrior that Skywalker and I carry knives, and we know how to use them."

Bear Chaser patted her on the arm. "Don't worry. He's been told. He knows how everything stands. Ten Bears is too old to bother you and Storm will not try anything that will dishonor his friend Mondo. You're safe."

Mick spoke English. "Mondo, I agree with Savanah. I know you're Indian, but your not Comanche Indian. Old Ten Bears is nice enough, but this new one acts like he's happy all the time, but there's something in the look of his eyes that makes me not want to go to sleep when he's in the same cabin with us."

Mondo answered. "Just like my father says, there won't be any trouble. I'm just explaining to Storm how things are with the women, and he won't try anything. I stayed with him last winter, and he's a man of his word. He came here to help me because one of his band attacked me while I was his guest. And that's the same guy that Skywalker killed. By attacking me, Chickasaw Killer dishonored Storm. The Comanches take a lot of pride in doing what is proper and doing the honorable thing."

Ten Bears had understood enough English to nod his head. "Mondo knows the Comanches. Honor is a great thing. But times are changing. The young warriors dishonored me today. The white men's intrusion is changing our way of life. I was a young warrior in Texas when they poured in and forced us out of that state. The white man has no honor. But the Comanches can't defeat the white men. The young warriors don't understand that, and I didn't understand that when I was a young warrior. They blame me because I tried to deal with the white men so that we could have some peace with honor and survive as a tribe. But the white men always lie. If what Storm said is true about the supplies arriving at Fort Cobb, then I may save some face. In the morning, I'm going to ride up to Fort Cobb and see. Maybe the whites will finally try to honor the terms of the Medicine

Lodge Treaty. But even if the terms are carried out by the US government, I don't think the young warriors will ever listen to me again."

Ten Bears bowed his head and disappeared into his own thoughts. Bear Chaser and Mondo both felt sorry for their old friend. His tribe had turned against him because he was the Comanche leader at the Medicine Lodge Council and was the main spokesman for the Comanche tribe even though he had very little authority over most of the Comanches.

About that time, the north wind got stronger, and the snow picked up to blizzard proportions. The wind howled, and the temperature dropped. Everyone moved closer to the fire except Storm. The more the wind blew and the snow fell, Storm became very quiet. He disappeared from the conversation. Mondo looked over at him and saw that he was almost in a trance-like state. Mondo remembered that Storm went on the warpath when a storm hit, and he became worried. He moved over and touched Storm on the shoulder, and Storm looked up at him.

"I know your medicine," said Mondo. "Are you going to kill all of us during this storm?"

Storm smiled and shook his head no. "Tonight, I see game in my vision. I'll go now. We'll have plenty of meat tomorrow."

At that, Storm gathered his weapons, put on a buffalo robe, and went out into the blizzard.

"What's he doing?" asked Skywalker.

"It's his medicine," said Mondo. "He does better when it's storming, whether it's killing an enemy or hunting game. Bad weather is what makes that warrior go into action."

"He's crazy," said Savanah. "There's something wrong with your friend, Mondo. No sane person would go out on a night like this. He'll never make it back."

Mondo smiled. "You don't know Storm. When someone believes the Great Spirit will protect him and help him during a storm, then that someone can overcome anything. He'll be back, and he'll be bringing fresh meat."

"Should we bolt the door?" asked Bear Chaser. "If we don't, it's liable to blow open in this storm."

"Sure," said Mondo. "I've seen this man in a storm. Nothing is going to happen to him. He'll let us know when he wants back in."

Soon after Storm left, everybody bundled up in buffalo robes and lay around the fire. Nothing happened during the night, and the next morning, Bear Chaser had to break the ice in the creek for the horses. The sun came out about ten in the morning, and Storm rode up looking as happy as if he'd stayed near the fire all night and dragging a big buck deer. Despite the warning from the others about the bad weather, Ten Bears rode off toward Fort Cobb to be there when the supplies arrived. By noontime, everyone was back in the cabin, and soon they ran out of conversation. Mick and Savanah always felt left out when the other four spoke Comanche, and Storm knew no English.

Mondo thought to himself, *This is going to be a long winter. What a mixture. An Irishman from Texas, a full-blood Chickasaw, a full-blood Comanche, an ex-Negro slave female, a Mexican that lived three years with the Kiowas, and me. And I thought I wanted to live alone, and now look what I've got. Strange people live in strange places. I'll never understand how so many different people ended up in my cabin. Tight quarters with so many different people always bring trouble. I remember again why I wanted to live alone.*

CHAPTER 37

THE NEXT DAY, the weather warmed, and Mondo was examining one of his horses that was sick and thinking about putting the horse down when Skywalker rode up. She dismounted, looked over the horse, and stood up with that look on her face. Mondo had almost accepted that she was the boss inside the cabin, but right off, he decided that she wasn't going to try to tell him how to run his horse business. She might be good at people medicine, but she didn't know horses.

"You have that bossy look again. You're fixing to tell me what's wrong with that horse. I can take a little bit of your ordering everyone inside the cabin but not out here. What do you know about horses?"

"People and horses are animals. You doctor one, you can doctor the other. What do you think is wrong with this horse?"

"I think he's got poison in his system. He's down and he can't get up and he's been that way for about twenty-four hours. It's time to put him out of his misery."

"Wasn't this horse in the compound for about a week and then you let him out on this fresh green grass?"

"That's right. What's that have to do with it?"

"Everything. This horse has just got gas. It's eaten all that winter grass you planted, and he's got the bellyache. We need to get it up and walking. You were fixing to kill a horse that has a stomachache?"

"You're so smart, aren't you? You think you know everything. I can show you snake bites on its leg. This horse stepped into a hibernating den of rattlesnakes. It has poison, not gas."

"You're wrong as usual. You judge horses about like you judge people. No wonder you want to live alone. Anybody that can be so wrong about horses and people should live alone."

Mondo turned, drew his pistol, and aimed at the horse's head, and Skywalker threw herself into him and drove him to the ground. His pistol flew from his hand.

Mondo couldn't believe that she had knocked him over. At once, he thought of the dagger. She had her hands around his throat and was trying to choke him. Mondo was feeling under her skirt for the dagger. She tried to knee him in the balls, but Mondo blocked it with his right forearm. *My God*, he thought, *for a tall, skinny girl, she's really got some power.* He tried to bump her off, and she rode him like a stallion. She went back to choking him, and he was having a hard time breathing and swallowing, and still he was frantically searching for the dagger with his right hand and holding her off with his left. He knew she was going to kill him, so he was going to have to knock her off him. He swung with his right hand, and she ducked under his fist and, this time, did bring her knee up between his legs, causing him much pain. *Damn, this girl's going to bust my nuts if I don't do something*, he thought and grabbed her around the neck to push her off. She twisted her head free and bent down under his right arm and planted a kiss on his mouth. All Mondo could think of was, *she's trying to distract me so that she can get to her dagger.* His left hand finally found the knife attached to her thigh. By this time, her mouth was open and her tongue was in his mouth; the fighting had stopped and he was kissing her back. His hand let go of the dagger. Her skirt was pulled up around her waist, and the inside of her thigh felt smooth and soft.

Before he could think about what was happening, both of them were coming out of their clothes at the same time as they fumbled and wrestled around on the ground. If anyone had been watching, it would have been comical, but Mondo and Skywalker weren't laughing because four hands were busy peeling off clothes. The clothes were moved around enough to expose the important parts, and it was over quickly in an explosion. Panting deeply, Mondo rolled off her. He tried to figure out what the hell happened. He rose up on his elbow and looked into her face.

"Why did you start kissing me? Were you trying to get my mind off that dagger so you could kill me, or did you really want to do what we just did?"

She shook her head. "I'm not sure, a little of both I guess."

"I'm not sure what really happened."

"If you don't know what happened, then you are a lot less experienced than I though you were," she said.

"I know what happened. I just don't know why it happened. I mean this is crazy. We're not even good friends. We were having a good fight that was long overdue, and you just took advantage of me since I hadn't had a woman."

"If that's what you want to think, then go ahead and think it. If you didn't want to do it, then why were you so determined to pull up my skirt?"

"I wasn't trying to pull up your skirt. I was trying to find that damn dagger."

"I wasn't going to use that dagger. I just wanted to knock some sense in you. You never listen, and the only thing you understand is a good kick in the balls."

"I guess it doesn't matter why it happened. It happened. But it can never happen again. That felt damn good, and that's a real problem. But I came out in this faraway country to get away from all those kind of people problems. And the next thing I know, I have a house full of a strange mix of people. Now what is Mick going to think? He thinks you belong to him, and Bear Chaser has taken a shine to you also. All I need is a woman causing a bunch of trouble inside my place. We've got enough problems from the outside without having a bunch of fighting going on in the inside. And when a man starts up with a woman in these close quarters, all kinds of bad things happen. There is damn sure a shortage of women in these parts. It makes a man a little crazy."

Skywalker jumped up and put her hands on her hips and glared at Mondo. *She sure looked good half-naked*, thought Mondo.

"Listen to me, Mondo. We'll try to forget about what happened. And you can live alone and without anybody for the rest of your life. I don't need you, and I don't need any man, especially one who wants to live and die alone in his little cabin, in his little fort, and inside his little valley. That makes you a little man despite your size."

Before Mondo could answer, the sick horse rolled over, struggled to its feet, and slowly walked off. Skywalker gave Mondo that look again, like she was always right and he was always wrong.

Mondo jumped to his feet and moved in close to Skywalker with the initial intent to shake some sense in her. But when he got close, he just grabbed her and kissed her real hard. Then the next thing he knew, they were on the ground again. This time, he was so amazed that afterward, he just sat there feeling awful good but not understanding what had just taken place once again. Many things went through his mind, and finally, he looked over at Skywalker. "If there's a baby, I'll keep it so you can go back to Mexico without a bastard child."

"Mondo, don't you know that you don't always get pregnant every time you do it? And besides, if there's a baby, you won't have to do anything about raising the child. I wouldn't leave a baby here for anything in the world. Who would take care of it the right way?"

"Well, I guess Bear Chaser could help me raise it."

Skywalker jumped up and started putting on her clothes and Mondo did the same. After they got dressed, they rode toward the fort without saying another word, acting as if nothing had happened. Before they entered the compound, Mondo stopped and looked at Skywalker. "This didn't happen. It won't happen again. We just have to avoid each other."

Skywalker shook her head in disgust and rode on into the compound.

Bear Chaser was outside chopping wood and straightened up to study them. He looked over at Mondo, and Mondo ducked his head. Bear Chaser sighed and went back to cutting wood.

That evening in the cabin, things were very quiet. Everyone sensed some kind of change, but most of them didn't know what had occurred. Mondo and Skywalker went about their business without looking at each other. Bear Chaser looked worried, and Mick was still acting quiet and rather sad. Ever since the beating, Mick had become the opposite of what he was before he went to Fort Worth. He used to smile a lot and talk a lot, but now, he did neither. He moved around and did his chores, and the scars on his face seemed to keep him from smiling.

Storm kept looking at everyone, trying to figure out what was wrong with these non-Comanches. He was the only one in the cabin that looked happy and wanted to talk. Most of the time, Storm tried to entertain Savanah through Bear Chaser, the Comanche interpreter. Savanah sensed something was wrong, but she didn't know what it was either. Storm was beginning to doubt the story that Mondo had told him about the huge black giant that was in love with Savanah. If such a giant did exist, Storm tried to convince himself that the giant would never leave such a prize. Savanah was beautiful and all alone. Storm felt there was a woman not being taken care of properly, and it was his job as a great warrior to remedy this problem.

Storm finally asked Savanah through Bear Chaser how she came to be with this black giant who he had never seen and only existed in tall tales.

"Did the big black warrior steal you from another tribe?"

Savanah answered, "No, it wasn't another tribe. Before the war, I belonged to a white man who used me for his pleasure. After the war, he was so afraid that I'd run away that he always had a man guard me wherever I went. One day, I was coming back from the store, when I looked up, there was this big man standing there with his machete. The guards tried to kill him, and he killed one and took the arm off of the other. Right then, I knew that this man could help me escape. So we took the horses pulling the carriage and headed for Indian Territory."

"So, you went with him willingly, and you lived with him as his wife?" asked Storm.

"Yes. I was like his wife."

"Is he going to come back?"

"If he can, he will be back. He's trying to find a place we can live and both be safe and have a family."

"Mondo says if he comes back, he'll be killed."

"I've been with him for about a year now, and let me tell you, he's hard to kill."

"Until he gets back, you need someone to look after you," said Storm. "It's not good for you to live alone without a man. Out in this country, a woman has to have a man to look after her and keep her safe from the wild men that roam around, looking for unprotected women."

Bear Chaser stopped interpreting, glared at Storm, and spoke in Comanche. "She has plenty of men to protect her. Mondo, Mick, and myself all promised Maboola that we would look after her."

Storm frowned. "It's a waste. She should be with a man. It's well and good that the three of you protect her, but someone needs to keep her warm during the winter nights. She needs to make many babies."

Bear Chaser did not relay Storm's message to Savanah. "That's not the way we do things, Storm. I know you mean well, but just because she's here doesn't mean she has to share her bed with a warrior. You are a guest, and we'll honor you while you are here. But you must honor our rules. That does not include letting you have your way with Savanah."

Storm got to his feet. "I feel a storm coming on. I need to go hunting. This time, I won't be hunting animals. I'm going to find me a nearby Comanche camp and visit some of my cousins and look for some warmth from a woman. I'll be back in a few days."

With that, Storm left the cabin and rode off as snow started to fall.

Mondo rose and looked at Skywalker. "I better go and check the horses. One of them has been pretty sick. Skywalker, why don't you go with me?"

Skywalker turned to Mondo with a look of surprise and then nodded her head yes. Mondo grabbed one of the buffalo robes as they both went out into the snow, walking to the horse shed together. When they came in the next morning, Bear Chaser, Mick, and Savanah knew something was going on between Mondo and Skywalker. Mick walked up close to Mondo and glared at him as he spoke. "You owe me five horses."

Mondo stared back at Mick before he replied and then he said, "Take ten, she's worth every one of them."

With that, Mick slugged Mondo and knocked him back out the cabin door. Mick limped after Mondo and was on him in a second and tried to hit Mondo while he was on his back. Mondo was bigger and stronger and rolled Mick off, and Mondo ended up on top. Mondo raised back his one good arm to drive his fist into Mick's face and Bear Chaser grabbed Mondo's arm and pulled him back off Mick. Before Mick could attack again, Savanah and Skywalker were both between the fighters, yelling for them to stop.

Skywalker faced Mick. "It's not Mondo you want to hurt," yelled Skywalker. "Ever since that Split Face almost beat you to death, you've never been the same. Don't take it out on Mondo. He's not the one you hate. You need to forget about that beating. Don't take your revenge out on your friends."

Mick stopped and looked at Skywalker and thought for a minute and then turned and went to the corral, and while the others watched, he saddled up and rode out the compound gate.

That night, Bear Chaser and Savanah slept in the shed to give Mondo and Skywalker some privacy. In the wee hours of the morning, Savanah moved over next to Bear Chaser, and they made love for the first time.

CHAPTER 38

THEIR FIRST TIME making love came about almost by accident, but an accident that was certainly enjoyed by both parties. The shed was mostly hay in a six-by-eight-foot wooden structure where they laid their blankets and settled in for the night. The last winter storm in the late spring hit that night, and Savanah got cold. Almost in her sleep, she rolled over close to Bear Chaser, and Bear Chaser felt her breasts against his back and responded. He sat up and looked at the beautiful Savanah.

"Hey, I'm old, but I ain't dead," he said. "We would both be better off if you rolled back over on the other side of the shed."

Savanah shook herself awake and smiled. "Don't tell me you're afraid of women just like your son. No wonder Mondo can't get around women without getting nervous. He was raised that way. I'm just cold and thought it would be warmer if we snuggled up together."

"I know you're trying to find out something about yourself, Savanah, but you still don't know very much about men either. You can't snuggle up with me without me having a reaction to your warm body next to mine."

"You act like you're twenty-one years old. I thought you said and acted like you never thought of me that way. You don't look at me like the other two look at me. I know when a man wants me, you can tell by the look in his eyes. You've never looked at me like that."

"Well, any time it comes into my mind, I throw it out," said Bear Chaser. "I think too much of Maboola as a man, and besides, I think that guy would kill me if I slept with you."

"Well, Mondo says Maboola's gone and won't be coming back. I don't know, and I think I love him, but he's no longer around. I'm not saying that I want to have sex with you. I'm just saying that I'm surprised that you even think about wanting to have sex with me."

"Any man that's alive would think about how it would be to lay with you. You don't realize how beautiful you are. Now, I think you better roll on back over to your side of the shed and stay there or things are going to happen that we both don't want."

Again, Savanah laughed and rolled back on her side of the little house.

They both drifted off to sleep, but almost without her making a decision whatsoever, she got cold and rolled back over against Bear Chaser. This time, Bear Chaser was not awake and turned and took her in his arms as if it was a dream. At one point, both of them realized what they were doing as they start kissing and stroking each other. They both treated it as a dream and not as something real that was actually happening. Feeling their rising passion woke them up, and they knew it was for real. Both thought about it and tried to stop at one time or another, but neither managed to cool down their passion as they slowly but surely began to explore each other's bodies.

Bear Chaser took his time as if he really didn't want to go all the way and was giving Savanah a chance to say no since he couldn't stop himself. Therefore they both progressed slowly like they were waiting for the whole process to end before the final step was achieved. So the ending took awhile but was very explosive. They were both shocked at the extent of their overpowering and long-lasting climax that left them breathless and drained. Savanah thought to herself that she didn't realize Bear Chaser had such wonderful hands.

After it was over, they lay side by side in silence without looking into each other's eyes as thoughts of guilt seeped into the glow that enveloped their senses.

Finally, Bear Chaser asked Savanah how she felt.

She looked into his eyes, smiled, and replied, "I don't think I've ever felt so good, but I don't think we should have done this."

"Probably not," answered Bear Chaser. "But I haven't felt so good for a long, long time. I really didn't think that this would have ever happened again with so much feeling and so much satisfaction."

"Well, what are we going to do now? It's happened, and we're going to be tempted in the future. I'm old enough to know that," said Savanah. "Are we going to try to act like it never happened and not do it again because that's going to be hard. I know that. Are we going to fight our desire for each other with the thought of Maboola coming back? You're the wise one. What do you say? Is this the first and last time? Should I leave? I don't know. I'm still trying to figure out how to make decisions on my own, and I don't know an answer for this one."

"I'm the guilty one. I know that you are used to a man protecting you. And the man that was protecting you is gone. So the only available one besides Mondo was me or Mick. Mondo ended up with Skywalker, and Mick took off mad. Therefore I was the only one left. I think that you allowed this to happen because of my desire and you're uneasiness that you were going to be left out and not have a man to look after you. You were trained to depend on a man, and you probably felt like you had to do this because you were trained that sex was the way that you kept a man protecting you."

"I don't know. I was afraid and lonely. I'll admit that. But you have to admit that what happened between us was wonderful, and it can't be destroyed or avoided by a lot of questions as to why we did what we did. It's done, and we don't know for sure how this happened, other than we are both human and we were both together and it was cold and I was lonely and possibly afraid and it happened. I think it's a human thing and both physical and mental. It was natural and probably something that we should not feel guilty about. If Maboola comes back, then we'll have to deal with it. If he was right here and I had to choose, I don't know how I would choose."

"Well, if I was your age and a young buck like Mick and Mondo, I could probably say that I couldn't help myself and that was just the way things are. But I've grown through the stage where my thoughts were controlled by my desire. I lived with a woman, and I loved that woman and we were very happy, and then she died. After that, I didn't think about love, but occasionally I took care of my needs with anybody that was available whether I paid for it or not. I never expected to fall in love again, and I'm not sure that I love you like I loved Mondo's mother, but I know that there's more to love than sexual desire and I know that I care about you more as a person as you've grown and developed. You are not simply a beautiful woman who takes care of my sexual needs. So I'm going to leave it up to you. I'm a lot older than you, and I don't know that I could ever protect you like Maboola, but I promise I will treat you right, and I think that since we are together and since what we just experienced was so wonderful, that no matter what we say, do, or try, we are going to be doing this again, and I don't think we can do anything about that."

Savanah smiled and moved over close to him. "I think you're right. Let's not worry about it. Let's enjoy each other while we can and deal with the future and any problems in the future as they arise. I think I chose you because I wanted you and not because I needed a man to protect me or that I was lonely. I'm starting to make my own decisions now, and I think I decided to sleep with Maboola and I think I decided to sleep with you. I think you're right. Let's make the best of it and move on. We'll deal with the future when the future comes."

With that, they looked at each other as they lay back down together and took each other in their arms.

Chapter 39

Happy times existed in the compound as summer approached except when Mondo tried to try to figure out the relationship that he had with Skywalker. Bear Chaser and Savanah seemed to enjoy each other without worrying about it. They were happy to be together and didn't want to ruin it by digging into it too deep. However, Mondo wanted to know why he had ended up with Skywalker. Most of the time, Mondo walked around like he was in a love-sick daze and couldn't get enough of Skywalker. Then he would think about where he was and what he was doing and would have to sit down and analyze his supposedly undeserved bliss.

Skywalker knew her man and did not try to explain things to him. She just let him talk himself out, and then they would make love. It seemed to Skywalker that Mondo was having problems trying to adjust to this major change in his life. Mondo would explain how he had come out to this territory between the Chickasaws and Comanches to live alone and to avoid the trouble caused by human contact. Now, he found himself in a relationship with Skywalker and felt he never wanted to be without her. He began to think about a family. He didn't want his child to go through the prejudice that he faced. This was against all his goals. The more Mondo talked about his problem of adjusting to his new life, the more the other three ignored him. It was as if Mondo thought he didn't deserve to be happy, and at the same time, he was so afraid that his love for Skywalker would end and he would be alone again. He seemed to be fighting his own happiness. He was so wrapped up in his own thoughts that he didn't even notice that his father was sleeping with Maboola's girlfriend until Skywalker told him. His immediate reaction was that this was not right and he couldn't let this go on in his own house. He charged up to his father.

"Is it true? Are you having your way with Savanah?"

Bear Chaser gave Mondo a look like he was still a child, and this made Mondo even madder. Then Bear Chaser smiled and answered, "What's between Savanah and myself is really not your business. You're having a tough enough time adjusting to your life with Skywalker. Don't waste time worrying about us. What Savanah and I are doing is our concern and our concern alone."

"My God. Didn't you promise Maboola to look after Savanah? Is it because he's a black man that you don't think you should live up to your promise? You remember that Maboola saved our lives. Don't you think you owe him something?"

"Don't you think Savanah has a say in this? Do you think I'd be sleeping with Savanah if she didn't want me to? Haven't you learned anything from Skywalker? Do you really think that just because a man decides a woman is his that she belongs to that man? Son, I know your values are all screwed up, but you are old enough to know it takes two people to have a good life with each other, and Savanah and I have a good feeling between us, and we don't try to ruin it with a lot of questions of why we are together and what's going to happen in the future."

"Well, you better worry about the future. If that Maboola comes back, he's going to cut your head off and maybe Savanah's too."

"Now, you're talking like he's a savage. Do you think the only thing Maboola knows is how to kill people? There's a lot more to that man than cutting people's heads off. Didn't he leave Savanah here for her own good and safety? You ought to have learned by now that you never know about tomorrow, especially out here. A thousand things can happen the next day and then nothing is the same. You've got to accept changes, and everything changes.

I'm a full-blood Chickasaw, and I was born and raised to live a life that disappeared. When and if Maboola comes back, we will have to settle some things. Right now, I'm very happy, and I think Savanah is very happy too. You worry about your own relationship with Skywalker. Don't worry about me and Savanah."

Before Mondo could answer, they heard, "Hello in the little fort." Mondo and Bear Chaser walked to the open gate and looked out and saw a well-dressed man on horseback. He had on a business suit and looked just like a city slicker. He waved with a big smile on his face and hollered. "Can I approach the gate? I'm from over at Gainesville, Texas, and I'm a lawyer who represents a man by the name of Purify Jones. I've been asked to come here and negotiate a deal with you people. I'd appreciate it if you would allow me to come forward and let me speak."

Mondo looked over at Bear Chaser and then back at the man.

"Sure, come on forward, but keep your hands away from your pistol." Mondo looked over at Bear Chaser and saw a firm but determined look in his face. Mondo knew Bear Chaser was thinking about Savanah's ex-owner.

The well-dressed Texan rode up with a big grin on his face. He took off his hat and bowed toward Mondo and Bear Chaser.

"Howdy, my name is William Hopkins Jr. I have been paid well to ride a long ways to try and strike a deal with you, gentlemen. I would be much obliged if you would allow me to dismount and discuss a financial arrangement that would be beneficial to us all."

"Go ahead and get off your horse and let us know what you've got to say. I don't see anybody behind you. Are you alone? You better be or I'll drop you like you're a fat squirrel sitting in the sun," said Mondo.

The smile left Mr. Hopkins face as he dismounted. "I'm sorry you don't trust me. I had some escorts who brought me safely through this heathen country, but they were instructed to wait for me at the south end by your graveyard. You have several graves that probably contain most of the men that tried to take this fort. Mr. Split Face failed. Mr. Jones is a good businessman and a smart fellow, and he has hired me to try to settle a matter that has caused great concern to Mr. Jones before there is any more unnecessary bloodshed."

"Would that matter be a nice-looking light-brown girl named Savanah?" asked Mondo.

"That is correct, sir. You are way ahead of me. It seems that Mr. Jones was very fond of this ex-slave called Savanah. He is concerned that she will be injured or, worse, killed in her association with the outlaws and bandits that now prevail in Indian Territory. He wants to protect her and to make sure that she lives a long and happy life. Mr. Jones was very fortunate during the late war for Southern independence because he had a way to sell cotton through Mexico. He's very intelligent and has a lot of influence in Texas. He was able to amass quite a fortune before the unfortunate hard times after the war caused by the Yankee occupation of troops and federal bureaucrats. Mr. Jones is tired of war and doesn't want Savanah hurt in any way, shape, or form. Therefore he has authorized me to pay one thousand in gold to any man who delivers Savanah to me so that I can escort her back to her rightful home."

"What makes you think that Savanah is here?"

"We have reliable information that the big black buck that stole Savanah from Mr. Jones has gone up North. Mr. Jones hired some Pinkerton detectives to find this white-man killer that some call Black Death. Just recently, Mr. Jones got word from the Pinkerton Agency that there was a black giant working on the Transcontinental Railroad in western Nebraska. And Maboola did not have a female with him. Mr. Jones has assumed that he left her at this fort. This has been confirmed out of Tishomingo City by the Lighthorse Police. Therefore I know that she's here, and I know that Black Death is no longer keeping her from her freedom. She really should return to Mr. Jones."

Bear Chaser nodded and said, "I'll go get her. If she wants to go back, you will not need to pay the thousand dollars in gold."

He turned and walked back into the fort.

Mondo looked into the lawyer's eyes. "She's not going back. And none of us here will accept that dirty money from Mr. Jones. Why doesn't he give up? Why does he think that Savanah, who was forced to have sex with the old fart, wants to go back and lay down with the bastard some more?"

William Hopkins smiled. "Son, let me tell you something that you probably don't understand so early in your young life. Mr. Jones thought that Savanah was in love with him. And nothing you or I can say or do would make him change his mind. He brought the girl up and treated her like a queen. He raised her like he wanted a wife to be. She had everything and could have had anything she wanted. Mr. Jones was in love with Savanah. She never gave any indication to him that she wasn't in love with him. Now, this man that you refer to as the old fart has everything he wants in the world except the woman he loves. And he's willing to put down a thousand in gold for her to come back peacefully or he's willing to put a lot more money down to bring her back by force. He's hired Split Face to purchase cannons and repeating rifles and gather up as many men as necessary to come across the Red River and destroy your fort if I'm not able to bring Savanah back to him. Now, I'm telling you like it is. You can accept it and send her back, or you better get the US Tenth Cavalry, the Comanche Nation, and the Chickasaw Lighthorse Police to guard this place and even they won't be enough. Mr. Jones can send a big army. There's enough hungry kill-crazed ex-Confederate soldiers running around, starving to death, so that he could raise an experienced army of five hundred in a week. So, I would suggest to you that you convince that ex-slave called Savanah that it's good for her and good for you and everyone living here that she go back across the Red River with me and rejoin this rich and powerful Mr. Jones."

Before Mondo could answer, Bear Chaser showed up with Savanah and Skywalker by his side. The lawyer looked over at Savanah. He took off his hat, bowed low, and then put his hat back on and smiled at Savanah.

"It's such a pleasure to finally meet you, my dear. I've heard many, many reports of your great beauty, but to witness it in person is more gratifying than what men have said and described to me of your wondrous good looks. It is easy for me to see why my client, and dear friend, Mr. Purify Jones wants to protect and save you from injury and possibly death."

Savanah frowned and pointed her finger into William Hopkins face, who looked shocked and surprised that a black female would even look him in the eyes let alone point an accusing finger at him.

"Mr. Jones does not want to protect me for me. He wants to protect me for him. He will use me as his play toy." She stepped up and put her arm through Bear Chaser's arm. "Bear Chaser treats me like a lady. Let me tell you something, Mr. Lawyer, if you've never been a slave, then you don't know what freedom is. Mr. Jones did treat me good as long as I did exactly what he told me to do. I did have more than any other slave. I had a good life compared to most Africans, but even with all the dangers that existed when I took off with Maboola, the wonderful feeling of being free and on my own grew and grew. For a while, I listened to Maboola and did what he said and didn't make any decisions on my own when I wasn't playacting like I was white. Then I came here and met Skywalker and found out that as a woman, I could use my mind to do what I wanted to without obeying a man. That feeling is greater than all the big plantations, fine dresses, great meals, and the rich, easy life. Once you've tasted freedom and independence, you would kill yourself before you went back to the life that I had with Mr. Purify Jones."

William Hopkins stared at her a long time without saying a word. Then he smiled and shook his head in agreement. "I think

I might understand, young lady. Those Yankee carpetbaggers and Freedmen's Bureau are giving us Texans a taste of slavery. I don't like it and will not be happy until those Yankees clear out of Texas and give us back our state. I see you've changed. You no longer act like an ex-slave. Maybe you are happier, but you better enjoy it now because I don't think you're going to live very long. Your ex-boyfriend that stole you away from Mr. Jones is going to be killed. Mr. Jones has paid the Pinkertons a bunch of money to get rid of him. He's as good as dead now. And I see you've found a new boyfriend as quickly as most beautiful women do. But surely you remember how determined Mr. Jones is as a man, a man with great wealth in a state that has no money except carpetbagger money. Have you ever seen the man they call Split Face up close? If you haven't, you've at least heard of him. He's an evil bastard. We all know that. But right now, he's a necessary evil. Mr. Jones will finance an army of black haters and all those bitter losers that fought and lost in the Civil War. They have hate running out of their ears, and they have experience at killing, and they like it. If you care anything about these two brown-skinned men standing next to you, you'll go back with me for them. You've already lost Maboola, and by going with Maboola, you signed his death warrant. Now are you going to kill these people too?"

Before Savanah could answer, Bear Chaser reached out and grabbed the lawyer by the collar and pulled his face up so close they were nose to nose. "Savanah gave you her answer. You represent the worst of white men. You're a smooth-talking tongue twister that will do anything for money. You're probably looked up to in your community. It was evil men like you that have no honor and whose word means nothing that have driven the Chickasaws from their homeland. Take your thousand pieces of gold and stick it up Purify Jones's ass."

With that, Bear Chaser shoved him back, and the lawyer almost lost his balance before he regained his footing and stood up and straightened up his suit and tie. He placed his hat on his head and looked at Savanah. "I'm leaving, but I'm warning you that you just started another war. If you care anything about these people, you'll come with me no matter what they or you say or think. If you want to kill these people and destroy this fort, stay here."

With that, he stared at Savanah, and she stared back at him. After a few seconds, Mr. William Hopkins, attorney from Gainesville, got on his horse, looked back sadly at Savanah, and then rode back toward his guards who were waiting to guide him safely back across the Red River and to the plantation of Mr. Purify Jones.

CHAPTER 40

MABOOLA MANAGED TO work for six months in Nebraska and saved his wages so he could afford a place to take Savanah and live safely. Everyone left the giant alone, even the African Americans. Even though the black workers were proud that Maboola had a certain amount of pride and was independent, they also knew that there was fear and hatred in most of the whites that looked at Maboola. History had taught them that to side with a proud Negro only brought disaster to themselves. So even though Maboola lived near the "colored section," as it was called, which was nothing more than a campsite of tents and put-together rickety shelters, Maboola camped out alone, away from the other blacks.

Maboola felt that if he lived alone in a swamp, he would have had as much company as he did working for the railroad. He was lonely, and he missed Savanah. Sometimes at night, a brave black worker would find Maboola in his campsite, which he moved every day. The workers would talk to him in awe and be nervous in his presence. The black people who visited Maboola were always looking around to see if any white person saw them with the giant who demanded and got respect from everyone, even the whites.

Every time Maboola walked down the railroad line, work stopped and people stared. The Southerners who still believed that a Negro was no more than an animal looked at the giant in silence and burned with guilt and fear at the size and strength of this animal.

Maboola was called in for any heavy job that couldn't be handled by normal men or even the oxen. One day, some of the ex-rebs got together and schemed to make Maboola look bad. A large boulder could not be moved by any of the men and the oxen.

Maboola was called, and he walked down the tracks toward the huge stone that blocked the building of the railroad track. The word had gotten out that the big black giant was going to get his "comeuppance" with the large boulder. Men gathered around and snickered as Maboola tried to move the boulder. The foreman ordered some men to help him, but the ex-rebs had threatened to hurt anyone if they assisted Maboola. The white workers refused to help.

Maboola tried to move the boulder, and it wouldn't budge. He heard the snickers and laughter as all work stopped, and the white workers gathered to watch Maboola fail. As his eyes went around the circle of men, the laughter stopped and the crowd feared that Maboola might leave the boulder and turn on them.

Maboola looked back at the boulder and glared. He closed his eyes and concentrated on the strength he would need. The bulging muscles tensed and tightened and grew around his shoulders, and he let out a loud roar that caused the gathered crowd to step back. Maboola went low and grasped the underside of the boulder, and the noise grew louder as muscles expanded all over his body. After a few seconds, it appeared that nothing was going to happen, when all of a sudden the great boulder started to roll forward as Maboola leaned into the rock and tumbled it out of the way.

The feat of strength shocked the gathered whites, and you could have heard a pin drop. But off to the south where a group of Negroes had gathered to view the feat, a huge roar went up from them, and all the whites turned away from Maboola and glared at the cheering Negroes.

That night, there were several beatings; two black men died, and others showed up for work the next morning with cuts and bruises on their face and body. However, no one touched Maboola. After that, Maboola carried a sledgehammer everywhere he went. It was always slung over his shoulder as he walked to work with his head held high and without a glance to his left or right.

Again at night, Maboola would sleep alone. He would go back to the colored section and then after dark, he would slip off and set his bedroll in hidden places. He could feel the hate and danger that faced him as more and more of the white workers looked at him like they wanted him gone for good.

The Pinkerton Agency out of Chicago had worked for the US government during the Civil War and had gained notoriety for their ability to infiltrate, spy and intimidate the enemies of the North. After the war, the Pinkerton Agency became the enforcement bureau of big business. If you had the money, you could hire almost anything done. Purify Jones had the money, and he employed the agency to find and destroy Maboola. The Pinkerton agent assigned to the task was too smart to try to back shoot Maboola. He knew it wouldn't be a problem to get plenty of ex-rebs to carry out a "good old boy" Southern killing. The agent paid a man from the south to help him infiltrate the ex-rebs and set up the murder. It wasn't long before the agent was good buddies with a group of Southern boys that hated all blacks and wanted them all dead, especially Maboola. The Pinkerton agent had trailed Maboola and knew his habits. Each night before he slipped off to a hidden sleeping place, Maboola always went down to the swimming hole in the creek and bathed. He cut through a dense thicket of trees along the creek back toward the colored area. That night around the ex-reb's campfire, the agent set up the kill.

"I got the word on that big black bastard that walks around like he owns this place. He's from Texas, and he decapitated some ex-Confederate soldiers."

"What's decapitated?" asked one of the ex-rebs.

"Cut their heads off. Took a machete and just wacked their heads right off. And that ain't all. You know he goes by the name of Robert Jones? Well, that uppity darkie took the last name of the man whose wife he stole. He kidnapped a white woman and raped her all the way to Indian Territory. And I don't know what he's done with her. She's probably laid up dead in Indian Territory."

"Why don't those damn Yankees arrest and hang the son-of-a-bitch?" asked one of the ex-rebs.

"They say he's free and he's like any other white man. If he wants to marry a white woman, he can. He raped and killed his way all the way from Texas to up here, and nobody will do anything about it. Everyone is afraid of him."

"I'm not afraid of the son-of-a-bitch. He's big yes, but by God, he'll die just like a big bull with a bullet between his eyes," said another worker.

"No, no. You can't do that. If you shoot him, then they'll arrest you and try to put you in jail. It's got to look like a fair fight. The big boss knows there's trouble and fights between the blacks and whites that work here and it happens every night somewhere. So it must look like just another fight and the guy that the whites call the Black Death just got bested."

The six ex-rebs around the campfire looked at each other and back at the agent. "Who's going to take on that guy? He's too big to fight fair. You'd have to club him in the back of the head before he sees you coming."

The agent shook his head in agreement. "I know how to do it. He takes a bath every night down at the creek and walks back through a thicket of trees along that creek near colored town. He's always alone. It's real dark in those trees, and there's no moon tonight. He always carries that sledgehammer, so you six, you need to take your sledgehammers or pickaxes and surround the path that he walks on. When he comes up, you all jump him. He won't be able to see you, and you can clobber him for good, and it'll look like just another white-black fight, sledgehammer against sledgehammer, and the big black lost."

"It'll be as easy as eating pie," said one ex-reb.

Another reb spoke up. "Sounds good to me. Somebody's got to do something about that son-of-a-bitch. If we don't stop him, every damn colored man in this camp will be walking around like he's white. I mean, when this guy walks, you have to get out of his way. That ain't right. And he never looks down like he's supposed to. If you get in front of him, he'll look you in the eyes so hard that you can just feel that damn sledgehammer coming down on your head. He has got to die, and die now, or there will be color-eds killing whites like mad dogs."

"You're damn right," said another ex-reb. "If we let him get by with raping a white woman, then every white woman in America will be raped. Those animals will be going across the country defiling our daughters."

That night, the six of them gathered in the path cutting through the forest. Like the agent had said, the moon was covered with clouds, and the trees that branched out across the path made it total blackness. Three stationed themselves on each side of the path and waited for Maboola to come along. They didn't have to wait long. As he entered the wooded area, all six of them knew that it was Maboola by the size of the dim outline of the very tall man as he entered the blackness of the trees.

They waited as the sound of his footsteps got closer. They couldn't see Maboola, but they could hear him. They had no pre-arranged signal, so one of the six stepped up to the path early, and Maboola heard the sound.

The man swung the sledgehammer at the invisible shadow, and Maboola bent down and felt the swish of the sledgehammer as it passed over his head. Maboola rolled to his left where the sound had come and ran into the legs of the man that swung the sledgehammer. The other five raised their sledgehammers. The first attacker went over the top of Maboola and fell in the middle of the path. Maboola slowly rolled away and stepped back against a tree. The other five rebs came down on the sound of the body that hit the ground. For about three minutes, all you could hear was the screams of pain and agony as sledge-hammers drove into the ex-reb that had fallen over Maboola.

Maboola's first thought was to wade into the sound of the attackers and try to get as many as he could with his own sledge-hammer. But he didn't know how many there were. He also knew that fighting in total darkness was a matter of luck. His advantage of size and strength were lost if you couldn't see the targets. The way the sledgehammers were swishing through the air and crashing down and the screams that followed, Maboola knew that they were striking each other. For the first time instead of attacking, Maboola eased back into the trees and silently slipped away into the night.

After a few minutes, the noise of the striking blows stopped, and for a second, there was no sound. Then someone hollered, "Let's get out of here," and Maboola could hear them rushing through the woods. Maboola again stood silent and heard someone rush by him, and Maboola did not strike. Instead, he made the decision that it was time for him to cut and run. Besides, the winter up North was too cold for his blood.

Maboola slipped back to camp and gathered up his things and then headed for the manager's office. He broke the door down and took some gold coins that he thought was owed to him for back wages. He mounted up and headed south for Savanah.

The next morning, they found two dead ex-rebs on the path through the forest. The four alive rebs that had attacked Black Death and the Pinkerton agent approached the railroad officials and explained that the two men had gone into the woods and Maboola had gone in after them. They all swore that they had seen Maboola come up behind the two ex-rebs and club them to death with his sledgehammer.

When the payroll officer noticed that some of the gold was gone that they had kept in the manager's office, stealing was added to murder, and a warrant went out for the arrest of a man named

Girt Taylor called Maboola, alias Black Death, alias Robert Jones. The Pinkerton men put up a reward of five hundred dollars, dead or alive, and a posse was formed with some of the best frontier trackers, and the posse left south in pursuit of the Black Death.

CHAPTER 41

AFTER MICK HAD left Mondo's, he rode to Theodore Fitzpatrick's store on Cow Creek. He felt bad about hitting Mondo when he found out that Mondo took the woman he bought. Ever since he had received the beating in Fort Worth, he got angry a lot easier. He seemed to go around in a fog of shame and revenge and he hit his best friend all because of being rejected by a Mexican gal.

The faster Mick rode toward Fitzpatrick's store, the more he felt like a coward for not crossing the Red River and going after Split Face. He knew his problem was not Mondo and Skywalker. No man took a beating almost to death from a sorry coward like Split Face and left it alone and still felt like a man. Before he went to Fort Worth, the good outweighed the bad in his life. He liked most everybody he ever met, and he laughed a lot. He knew what Skywalker told him was right. He was moody, he was depressed, and he took it out on his friends. Not only was he ashamed of himself, Mick was overcome by the hatred for Split Face and the desire to get even.

Theodore Fitzpatrick was born in Ireland in 1830 and had come to the United States and had fought in the US Army in the Seminole Indian War in Florida prior to the Civil War. After he had spent time with the Indians, he came to like them and eventually left the army, moved to Indian Territory, and had married a Choctaw woman. When Theodore Fitzpatrick married a Choctaw, he had legal rights in the Chickasaw Nation by a mutual agreement between these two close tribes. Therefore,

Theodore Fitzpatrick had settled on the far western edge of the Chickasaw Nation and built a store on Cow Creek in Pickens County where the north-south Chisholm Trail intercepted the east-west road connecting Fort Arbuckle with the new fort the US Army was building at Medicine Bluff on the eastern edge of the little Wichita Mountains.

Mick had made a deal with Theodore Fitzpatrick to sell horses from his store. The venture had been successful for both of them since he paid a portion of his profits to Theodore for allowing him to keep his horses in the corral near the store. Both Theodore and Mick's father came from the same part of Ireland, and Mick and Theodore knew many stories about the old country. They enjoyed having a drink or two and talking about Ireland, the old days, and the great opportunities in America.

Theodore welcomed Mick, and he stayed the next few months at the store. Mick drank a lot of Irish whiskey, and when drunk, he would eventually get around to talking about how he was going to kill Split Face. Mick built a new corral and shed for the horses that he sold to the cattle drivers. Mick even got a five-dollar-a-year permit from the Chickasaws to use some of the land around the store for feeding his horses. He legally settled on land near Fitzpatrick's store.

Mick was embarrassed to ride back to Mondo's, but he knew when the spring of 1869 came, he would have to go back and round up the horses that would be available when the cattle drives started again from Texas to Kansas.

Mick traveled around with Theodore Fitzpatrick and met the few other Chickasaw settlers that lived east of Cow Creek and even went to Tishomingo City a couple of times with Theodore. He got to know most of the Chickasaw and white settlers between Cow Creek and east, all the way to the Washita River near Fort Arbuckle. White people could settle if the Chickasaws approved the terms of a lease or rental agreement. The more he experienced Theodore Fitzpatrick's life, the more he thought that it wouldn't be a bad idea to marry a Chickasaw woman and get the right to graze as much land as he could utilize in the Chickasaw Nation.

It was around the middle of March 1869 when Mick turned twenty-two that he decided that he better ride out and face Mondo. When he arrived, Mick knew at once that the fort was occupied by two very happy couples. He was a little jealous, but he was also happy for his friends. After a few hugs and pleasant-ries, Mick called Mondo to the side to discuss their partnership and the future of their herd.

"Mondo, I've been living with Fitzpatrick, and the word is out that there's going to be a lot of cattle driven through this area. Fitzpatrick has stocked up his store, and I think we can sell a bunch of horses. I'd like to take about thirty head and put them in a corral that I built down there on Cow Creek near the store. I can just come back for more when needed. We'll just split the profits fifty-fifty. And after this season, we can just divide up the horses we've got left and go our separate ways."

"Mick, I sure hate to end the partnership. I thought we got along real well, and we made some money. I guess we kind of let Skywalker come between us, and I'm sorry about that. I hope that isn't the reason we're splitting up."

"No. I've kind of accepted that. I know it's not your fault, and I know, and I guess I always knew, that she cared for you more than she did me. I'm kind of surprised that Savanah has hooked up with your dad, but that's life. Besides, I'm getting serious about business and maybe making some money. I want to make my own way. I think I'm going to try to do just what Theodore Fitzpatrick did. He married a Choctaw gal, and he's going to make some money around here. You know, I never had nothing against Indians, and by golly, I think it's good business to marry for a profit."

Mondo smiled. "Well, you're probably right. There's a lot of good Chickasaw women around. In fact since the war, there's a lot more women than men. You could probably get a pretty good pick if you take your time and look around. Hell, I hope you settle down close by. We can still trade with each other and make deals, and you're welcome at my place any time. You're my friend and you'll always be my friend, and I hope we'll continue to cover each other's backs."

Mick nodded yes, and the two guys hugged and shook hands, and Mick was gone before he even had a meal with the two couples. He had to admit that he was a little envious of the happiness of the four people left at Mondo's fort.

When Mick got back to the store on Cow Creek, the area was surrounded by a large herd of cattle. The first drive of longhorn cattle had stopped at Fitzpatrick's store.

The building was a twenty-by-thirty-foot log cabin with supplies on shelves along two walls and a small bar with a couple of tables and chairs in one corner. Along with Mick's large corral, there was an outhouse and a small blacksmith shop nearby. As Mick entered the store, Red Granger stood up from the table and approached him with his hand out.

"Hey, you look a lot better than the last time I saw you. You still got a few scars on your pretty-boy face, but you'll pass for a real man now. I guess you're still selling horses?"

Mick shook his hand and smiled. "Yes, I am. Good to see you. I never did thank you properly for you bringing me here. I really wasn't in any condition to think or talk. Are you the first bunch coming up the trail?"

"Yes. I always try to be first. We've got thirty-five hundred head we're trying to drive up to Abilene and get there while the market is running high. I want you to meet my new headman and foreman," said Red Granger as he turned to a stocky black cowboy that rose to his feet and extended his hand.

Mick walked over and shook his hand, and Red Granger pulled out a chair and told Mick to have a seat.

The three men settled in and Red Granger continued. "You just shook hands with the smartest cowboy on the trail. This here is Delaware Hunter. He rides hard on the herd and all the men too."

Mick nodded. "I've heard of you. You're quite famous. Aren't you the one that crossed the Red River when it was up and nobody else would try it and you made it without losing a man or any animals?"

Delaware smiled and nodded. "I was lucky, and I had some good people pushing the herd." He spoke with a soft voice, and a person almost had to lean over to hear what he was saying. By speaking softly, anyone who wanted to know what he was saying had to really listen.

His boss, Red Granger, bellowed out as he usually did and talked loud as if he was talking to people inside the store and outside too.

"That was him, all right. If you'll look around and notice, most of my cowboys are ex-slaves. Some of the white men quit when I made Delaware a foreman. I just got about three white cowboys riding with me this time. It seems a lot of those ex-rebs just don't like to be bossed by a Negro."

Mick looked over at Delaware. "Do you find that you have some real problems when you give orders to the white cowboys?"

"They always hold back a little at first. But I've found if you work hard and do anything they can do and do it better, they'll start to listen to you, and things go fine after a while. That doesn't mean they are going to sit down and eat with me, but when you start working together and everyone has the same idea as to what needs to be done and that is to get as many cattle alive to Abilene as you can then the color line seems to fade a bit."

Mick nodded. "Do you think you'll live long enough to see the day when all white Texans treat all black Texans equally, work-wise and socially?"

"Nope," said Delaware. "Neither will my grandson. It will take over a hundred years. It will probably be some outside force, either politically or through the courts, that brings about true equality. Hate is taught and passed down, and it will continue to be taught and passed down just because the South will never admit they were wrong, and they damn sure hate to be losers or told what to do by Yankees."

Red Granger nodded. "The worthless, lazy, dishonest cheaters that we refer to in our terms as white trash can't live with equality. They don't like themselves, and they don't like losing jobs to ex-slaves, but they always tell themselves that no matter how bad things get for them, they are still better than the so-called lowlife with African blood. They always tell themselves, 'At least we're not black. We are not at the bottom of the barrel.'"

Delaware spoke again. "And the white people with money in the South want to keep the cheap labor. You know, money always bends morality in this country. They've got to keep some group doing the dirty jobs that nobody else will do."

Red Granger nodded in agreement and continued. "And the South is stubborn. The more the Yankee carpetbaggers and the vengeful Congress force punishment on the South, the more that the South is determined to send the Yankees back home, and the ex-slaves will suffer because of the hatred the South has for the North. The South is still trying to fight the last battle and win one for their self-esteem. I'm afraid the last battle is going to be the ill treatment of all ex-slaves."

Mick shook his head in disbelief. "Are you trying to tell me that intelligent, reasonable, good businessmen that are supposedly good Christians and good Americans are going to continue to allow riffraff like Split Face and the night riders that some call the Ku Klux Klan to ride and terrorize black citizens? I've seen you stand up to those crazy haters in Fort Worth. If there were more like you or if you could even organize a bunch of good men, you could put the KKK out of business in a minute. That's what I don't understand. Whether the ex-Confederate leaders can vote or not, they know right from wrong, and even if they are afraid to admit their treatment of the slaves was immoral, they've got to know, or really feel deep down know, that it's a sin to allow the KKK to lynch another human being."

Red Granger nodded his head. "You've got that right. I've had some good friends that were good people and good Christians that went to church every Sunday that damn sure beat their slaves. They thought they were so-called Southern gentlemen. I've seen a many of them die in anguish, thinking that their soul was going to burn in hell. I've seen them free their slaves and pray to God that the fires of hell don't scorch them for the rest of eternity. I don't care what anyone says, deep down, men know and feel right from wrong, even if it's hidden in the back of their minds. Sometimes I think those superior-acting Christians go to church to try to pray away their guilt. Even if the Southern white doesn't admit it openly or to himself, he knows that when he harms a fellow human being, he is committing a grave sin. Some white Christians stick their nose in the Bible and say, well, there were slaves when Jesus was around, and Jesus didn't try to abolish slavery. They use the Bible as a crutch and a place to hide so they can continue to make a lot of money on the suffering of black people. But every sane white who mistreated black people that I've seen die, died with fear and horror in their eyes. So the real question is, how long can these so-called good Christian leaders of the South allow the poor white trash and ignorant criminals and psychopaths to commit horrible crimes against the ex-slaves before they come to their senses and as a group put a stop to these crimes? If they don't, there will be a lot of good Christian Bible thumpers go to their graves with fear of the torture in hell on their minds. They will not die in peace. Guilt may be hidden from their minds, but it is felt deep down in their souls."

The whole room went quiet when Red Granger finished his outburst, and his speech had echoed to everyone inside and outside the store. Most of the people in the store and standing around out in the front were ex-slaves. After a short pause of silence, they started clapping as if the ex-slaves had heard the first sane statement from a white man and it showed on their faces. Mick could see hope that if one white man knew right from wrong, there must be others.

Red Granger looked around in surprise at the hand clapping, and Delaware patted him on the shoulder and spoke. "Unfortunately, you are a minority of one. When it comes to color, ignorance runs everywhere through this part of the country and talk like that will get you killed by your own kind."

Mick looked around at the faces that stared with admiration at Red Granger. He thought to himself that Split Face and his crew better not come after Red Granger because there would be many ex-slave cowboys that would die to protect their boss. When he thought of Split Face, the hate boiled through his body, and he leaned over to Red Granger.

"On the way back from Abilene, stop in here. I've got a proposition for you. I've got a bunch of horses I will give you if you and your cowboys will ride with me across the Red River and hunt down that Split Face so I can kill the son-of-a-bitch."

CHAPTER 42

R ED GRANGER AND Delaware Hunter left Fitzpatrick's store and moved the herd from the valley to Cow Creek. The cattle were driven across the creek at the rock bottom where there was no mud, just a hard surface as if God had built a bridge at the bottom of the creek so that the chuck wagon's iron wheels wouldn't bog down in the mud.

Delaware Hunter counted the herd by fives as animals moved up the east bank onto the trail heading northwest around the thick post oak forest that swung the Chisholm Trail east for about two miles before turning north again and heading toward Kansas. There was 3,568 head, which was more than the normal herd of around 2,500 cattle that most of the Texans drove to Abilene, Kansas.

The lead bull, called Old Blue because of his dark bluish color, had been up and down the trail a dozen times and knew the way better than most of the cowboys. The herd stretched out for a mile and resumed a steady walk, grabbing bites of grass as they moved by so that most of the herd gained weight as they slowly moved north through the Chickasaw Nation.

After they had gone about five miles north, Delaware Hunter rode up to Red Granger. "Interesting statement that young Mick fellow said as we were leaving."

Red glanced over at Delaware. "Yeah. He's real bitter about the beating that he got from that crazy Split Face. Who would blame him?"

"It sure would be a shame if that rich bastard sent a bunch of killers and wiped out that fort that Mondo has."

"I expect Mick will try to help his friend. They've been good buddies a long time. Mick may get a crack at the ugly Split Face if that Purify Jones sends that scarred bastard back north across the Red River again."

"Don't you think Split Face will bring an army the next time he crosses the Red River?" asked Delaware.

"I suppose so. Do you think Mondo will get any help from anybody?" asked Red.

"Not from the law. That's for sure. What law and police there is, ain't for the black man. I really don't believe the Chickasaw Lighthorse Police or the US Cavalry will get involved. As usual, the black man and his friends will be all alone when the white boys come."

Red Granger shook his head in disgust. "That's bad. Someone ought to try to stop them crazy bastards from killing that bunch in that little fort."

An Indian war whoop came out of nowhere, and before Delaware and Red could react, ten young Comanche warriors charged into the herd and started a stampede. The middle of the herd spread out and broke east, running into the cross timbers, scattering and being lost in the thick matted trees while others broke north, running as if on fire, along the timber line, kicking off a terrified dash of cattle toward the front of the herd. Only Old Blue held steady as if nothing was going on and watched as the cattle scattered in all directions and started a mad dash for nowhere.

At first, the drovers took a few shots at the Comanches who seemed to disappear in the dust of the wild stampeding herd and headed into the cross timbers to pick up some strays. The drovers forgot about the Indians and tried to get the terrified cattle under control. The experienced old hands drew their pistols, fired shots to turn the herd from the edge of the woods and try to get the lead stampede circling so that the front would slow down and turn and eventually run into the rear and get into a slow circle.

By the time Delaware and Red had reached the front of the stampede, the old hands were already swinging the charging cattle around toward the west. Old Blue came walking up as if he was waiting for the herd to stop running and settle back down behind him so they could get on toward Kansas.

Delaware Hunter and Red Granger were glad that the stampede occurred in the daytime and not at night. At night, the cowboys would have to ride full speed in the dark without knowing if a cliff or ditch or tree was in their way. They had to depend on their horses' ability to avoid the pitfalls that threw a rider under the hoofs of the cattle and stomp the rider to death. At night, a stampede almost always spilled a few riders, and if they landed in the middle of the herd, those riders usually did not come out alive.

Red bellowed orders that carried over the sound of the cries of terror coming from the animals and the drumming of thousands of hoofs beating on the prairie floor. The drovers managed to get the cattle turned into the rear and slowing down. Soon, the whole herd was moving into a slowing-down circle until the cattle stopped and started to graze as if nothing happened.

"Get into those woods and find those strays before those damn Comanches get them," hollered Red Granger.

Most of the drovers poured into the short, thick trees and disappeared. The noise of the riders crashing through trees and tearing vines and branches off made about as much racket as the stampeding herd had made just a few minutes before the cattle finally stopped.

Off to the west, Red Granger saw the men they had been talking about riding toward him and Delaware. Bear Chaser and Mondo were pushing about twenty steers toward the grazing herd.

"Looks like we got some help from that Mondo fellow and his dad," said Red Granger.

Mondo and Bear Chaser pushed the cattle into the herd and met Red Granger and Delaware Hunter riding up to them.

Red Granger smiled at Mondo. "Well, I knew you weren't a cattle thief, but I didn't know that you would help us round up these stampeding strays. Where did you find them?"

"We were out working our horses when we heard the commotion and headed this way. These twenty broke west toward our place. I didn't want them to get any of my horses' grass," said Mondo and smiled.

"Much obliged," said Red Granger. "Any help you can give us will be appreciated. We've probably got a hundred or so head running around in all directions. If you give us a hand, I'll give you one of these steers so you can have some good meat for the next month or so."

Mondo shook his head no. "I'll help you round up the strays, but I don't need anything from you. I can tell by looking at your crew that you are a good man and don't look down on a man of color."

"That's true," said Delaware Hunter. "I'm the foreman of this bunch, and I think I'm the only Negro foreman in all of Texas."

Mondo smiled. "Well, I hope you do good. There's not very many people who think a black man could handle that job. What caused the stampede?"

Delaware Hunter shook his head in disgust. "Bunch of Comanches raided the herd and started them running. They chased quite a few of them into the cross timbers there and then went after the strays. They probably got ten or twelve head already hidden out somewhere, and we'll never see them. Aren't you a friend of Ten Bears and some of those Comanche warriors? Don't you think you could keep them from hitting our cattle?"

"Oh, I have enough trouble keeping them off of me let alone trying to keep them from trying to take a few head of cattle. They're starving. The supplies haven't come in from the US government like they are supposed to, and they are having trouble finding buffalo. Besides, those peaceful Indians that came up from Texas don't go very far from this area, and there's certainly no buffalo left around here. So those Indians are taking on your cattle like they used to take on a herd of buffalo."

Red Granger frowned. "Are you trying to tell me that an Indian can't tell the difference between a buffalo and a longhorn? I mean, it's stealing, and you know it. I'm getting sick and tired of the Chickasaw tribe being paid money as we go across their property and the Comanches, Kiowas, and the rest of those wild Indians stealing like this was an open free-roaming buffalo herd instead of longhorn cattle beef being driven to market."

"When a man is hungry and can't feed his family, he might grab something to eat any way he can," answered Bear Chaser.

Red Granger looked over at Bear Chaser. "That's true. I've been hungry before. I walked all the way back from Chicago, Illinois, after I was captured during the Civil War. I was hungry plenty of times, but I didn't steal anything. I asked for food, and I got some food from some Yankees."

Mondo spoke. "That's a story I'd like to hear someday. I've heard of that Yankee prison in Chicago. Bad place."

Before anybody could continue the conversation, five drovers rode out of the thick timber with guns on three young Comanche warriors and rode up to Red Granger and the rest of his men.

The young Comanche warriors were only boys about twelve or thirteen years old, and they looked wide-eyed and afraid as the drovers aimed their guns at them. One of the drovers rode up to Red Granger.

"We caught these young 'uns. They had about five steers and were slipping down the creek trying to get away. What shall we do with them? Hang them?"

Red Granger looked over at Mondo. "Can you speak Comanche? If so, ask those boys why they steal our cattle and who's decision it was to stampede our herd."

Mondo looked over at the three young men. "Who led this raid? What did you want to do with these cattle?"

The oldest of the Comanches answered. "I led the raid, and we were trying to get something to eat. Our families are starving."

"I thought so," said Mondo. He turned to Red Granger. "Just like I said, they have nothing to eat, and these young fellows were just out trying to get food for their family."

Red Granger stared at the young boys for a while and then looked over at Mondo. "Tell them that they don't need to stampede the herd. We've got lots of cattle. Every day, there is a bunch that get crippled or get sick, and we have to turn them loose. Tell them that if they'll come by and talk to me when I come through, I'll give them four or five head. Every time they stampede our herd, we lose twenty, twenty-five, thirty head. If they'll just come by and talk to us, we can give them the cast-offs. We don't need this problem. If we pay the Chickasaws ten cents a head, then by golly we can give a few of the ones that ain't going to make it to the Comanches."

Mondo turned and told the boys what was decided. They all looked relieved like they had expected to be shot or hung.

Red Granger turned to the drovers and said, "Check out the cattle. There's always some that are crippled after a stampede. Turn them loose to these Comanche boys and let them take them back to their families."

Mondo explained what was going to happen to the young warriors, and they rode off with a drover as they found a few injured cattle and turned them over to the Comanches. As the Comanches started pushing the cattle east toward the Wichita Mountains, they broke into a war cry, drew arrows, and started firing them into the cattle that had been given to them. The cattle went down like buffalo, and from the east came some women that had been watching the whole process hidden off in some trees. The white men watched as the Indian women dismounted and started butchering the cattle immediately. The warriors got down and cut out the liver and ate the liver. Within twenty or thirty minutes, they had skinned the cattle, cut up the meat, and moved on, and the drovers looked at the process in disgust.

Delaware Hunter looked over at Mondo. "Why do they eat that raw liver? That's the most bloody thing I've ever seen. Why don't they butcher those cattle and cook the meat like it is supposed to be handled?"

"The liver gives them something their bodies need. A hundred years or so ago, some medicine man figured out that they needed to eat that raw liver without cooking it because it made them more healthy. That's all I know. And you ask why they butcher them like that? Well, it's real simple. They've never dealt with cattle before. They always dealt with buffalo, and that's the way they do buffalo, and so they are treating those longhorns as a replacement for the buffalo, and that's all they know."

Red Granger shouted some orders and returned to Mondo and Bear Chaser. "You guys want to help, you can. We still got a bunch of strays to round up. Why don't you give us a hand and go through the timbers and help us look for those lost cattle and we'll treat you to a big steak tonight. We're going to find some more cripples and we'll just cook it up and have a big old meat eat. What do you say to that?"

Mondo nodded in agreement, and he and Bear Chaser rode into the timbers.

By dusk, they had gathered up most all of the strays and counted the herd. Counting the five head that they had given to the Comanches, they had lost twenty-five. Two or three of the injured cattle were being cooked over the fire place. All the men on the drive and Bear Chaser and Mondo settled down around the campfire and enjoyed a big steak.

Mondo looked over at Red Granger. "Tell me about this story of you walking back from Chicago. I want to hear this."

Red Granger smiled and nodded his head in the affirmative. "Yeah, I was captured in the Civil War and spent about a year in Chicago. We had a big breakout. There was a lot of shooting and killing, and I just slipped off from the group and made it out of town. It took me three months to walk back to Texas, and all the way back I didn't steal a thing. I'd go up to a farmhouse and I'd say, 'look, I'm from Texas and I'm through with this war. I'm trying to get back home. I'm not going to hurt you, and I'm not going to steal anything. But if you'd give me something to eat, I'd appreciate it.'"

"It was toward the end of the war and people were tired of fighting and ready for the war to end. I think the North knew they had us whipped, and most of the people appreciated my honesty. And I was given something to eat all the way back, and I'll never forget it. Just as soon as I get my ranch all situated and get myself back in a position of having a little bit, I'm going to get a bag of gold and I'm going to ride back up North and I'm going to stop at every place that helped me out and give them a gold piece. You know, Yankees are Americans too. I just don't have the hate that a lot of Southerners do. We fought. We lost. And there's nothing we can do but try to make the best of the situation. Just as soon as I got back from the POW camp, I freed my slaves, and Delaware was the first man I turned loose. I grew up with Delaware and knew him as an honest, hard-working man, and I felt good after I freed my slaves. All of them are still working for me for wages and have been loyal, honest, and good hands."

Red Granger stopped for a second in deep thought and then looked at Mondo. "I'm not going to be like a lot of my friends. They take out the loss of the war and the loss of their slaves on the black people. Most of those people that are encouraging white trash to scare or hurt blacks were also bad to their own slaves. We've got to learn to live a different life, and the sooner the better. I'm afraid I'm a minority, and most of the Texans I know don't go along with me. I think that they don't want to admit that slaves are human beings because they don't want to admit that they kidnapped and held real people against their will. It will take a long time, but the sooner we straighten out our way of thinking, the better off we will be as a state and a people."

Mondo turned to Delaware. "Is that how you see it?"

"You're damn right. What he says is what he did. I was lucky. He recognized me as someone who could get something done and has never looked back on the fact that I was black. The men he freed and the men that work for him would die for him. He's a straight shooter like a lot of Texans were before the Civil War. Now, we've got a bunch of bad losers that want to blame their loss on the color of the skin of the ex-slaves. There's nothing like your fort in Texas. The KKK and the bitter losers of the South are making sure that there's no rebellion by black men. Do you think that they're going to let you survive in that little fort? That fort represents to the white man a symbol of rebellion, a symbol of human qualities of the black man. A symbol of equality that the South won't let stand. Everybody in the Indian Territory and Texas has heard about your fort. The news travels from mouth to mouth all over Texas. There's this Maboola who takes no crap from any white man, and there's this Mondo who is both part-Indian and black who stands up to the white man. If the Chickasaws and Comanches don't burn your fort down, the KKK from Texas will damn sure make a try at it."

Mondo answered. "Well, Fort Mondo has stood so far, and I'm going to stay there even if I die there. It has nothing to do with slavery, and it has nothing to do with Texas. I'm half-Chickasaw, so I consider myself more Indian than anything, and this is Indian Territory. The fact that I get along with the Comanches better than the Chickasaws has nothing to do with it. After the war, I decided that I was going to raise horses in Little Beaver Valley, and that's what I'm doing. I've got a woman now, and I'll probably have a family pretty soon. If I start out by running, then my son will be a runner too. It's good to meet you guys and break bread with you. Thanks for the good steak. It's getting dark, and Bear Chaser and I've got to get back to my place. We've each got someone to protect back there. When you come back through from Abilene, stop by, and we'll give the whole bunch of you a good feed. It might not be steak, but it will be a good meal anyway."

Red Granger and Delaware stood up and shook hands with Mondo and Bear Chaser. Red Granger spoke. "I'll stop by, that's for sure. If you ever need any help, you can call on me and my crew. You and that little fort are bucking the wind, but I hope you make it, and I'll stand by you if you ever want or need any help."

With that, the men shook hands, and Bear Chaser and Mondo rode off for Fort Mondo.

CHAPTER 43

THEODORE FITZPATRICK INTRODUCED Mick O'Ryan to several unmarried Chickasaw maidens who were available for courting. The closest settlement besides Fort Arbuckle and the Wildhorse Creek community was a valley and store where Rush Creek ran into the Washita River known as Pauls Valley. The valley had been settled by Smith Paul, a white man who had married a Chickasaw woman back in Mississippi and had come to Indian Territory with the tribe. Fitzpatrick knew Smith Paul was an influential man of the tribe and was accepted as one of the leaders even though he was all white.Smith Paul claimed the valley between Rush Creek and the Washita River and built a store there to provide necessities and essentials to the settlers. He shared his valley with others that came there so that the entire thousand acres in the area was being farmed on very fertile land. Quite a few Chickasaw Indians and white people came in and made a deal with Smith Paul to farm the area, and Smith Paul became a well-to-do person in the area.

Fitzpatrick had taken Mick O'Ryan to a picnic celebration in the spring of 1869 and introduced him to a Chickasaw family that had two daughters in their late teens. While Mick was conversing with the two young ladies, he noticed another very attractive girl who was surrounded by two or three young men, and she seemed to keep them all entertained and laughing as she was the type that would stand out and control the view of all people with her sparkling personality and beautiful smile.

Mick excused himself and went over to get some cider and stopped to talk to a young man he had met through Theodore Fitzpatrick, a fellow by the name of Sam Paul, the son of Smith Paul.

"Who is that girl over there, Sam? She seems to have the attention of all the young men around here."

"Isn't she something? That's Lucy Johnson. She's quite the catch, and everybody is after her. I don't like sharing time with all those other young fellows who are trying to get her attention."

"How long has she been around here? Is she Chickasaw?"

"Her family moved in about six months ago. They've got a farm down on Rush Creek. They made a deal with my dad as tenant farmers. She's half-Chickasaw. I think her mother is Chickasaw and her father came east from North Carolina or some place."

"Fitzpatrick is trying to fix me up with the McClure girls. They are nice enough all right, but that Lucy is really something. Is she spoken for?"

"Nope. She plays them all. She's like a queen around here. She's spoiled. I don't have time to put up with her playing the whole field wide open like she does. She's available, but you'll have to be lucky to get her attention at all. Some of those guys hanging around her have got quite a few acres under cultivation. I think she might be looking for a husband and a home, and she want's a big home, and she'll probably get it."

Mick excused himself and got some cider from the punch bowl and moved over to the group that surrounded Lucy Johnson. The three young men talking to her glared at Mick as he walked up, and Lucy looked over with a peculiar look on her face.

"Hi. I'm Mick O'Ryan. I got a place down by Fitzpatrick's. I understand you are Lucy Johnson. Can I get you some punch?"

"We have not been properly introduced, Mr. O'Ryan. You're pretty bold to come walking over here like you've known me. These three men I've known for years, and I've never met you. I think you are interrupting us."

"I sure am interrupting you. That's what I came over here to do. You are a sight for sore eyes, and my eyes are sore. I'll ask you again. Can I get you some punch?"

"Absolutely not. You're rather rude."

With that, Lucy turned her back on Mick and began to converse with the three young men standing there.

Mick didn't leave but stood there and waited. After a few minutes, she realized he was still standing there, and she turned back to him.

"Are you still here? Can't you take a hint? I am not going to have anything to do with you until we are properly introduced. That Fitzpatrick's store is where all those cowboys come riding in, pushing those cattle north. It's a wild place, and the people down there live right up against the wild tribes. You don't look like somebody that has settled down. You've got fighting scars on your face."

"Are you saying you are too good for me? I was just going to say hello. I didn't ask you to marry me."

She blushed and stomped off, and the three guys faced Mick like they were fixing to whip him real good. Mick laughed out loud, turned, and walked back over toward Fitzpatrick. That was the first meeting with Lucy Johnson. But it wasn't the last meeting, not even the last meeting for that day.

After they had sung some songs and played some games, and the sun was setting to close out the evening, Mick again approached Lucy Johnson. This time, he brought Theodore Fitzpatrick with him.

"Hold on a second, ma'am," said Theodore Fitzpatrick. "My partner here, Mick O'Ryan, has indicated to me that you are refusing to talk to him because you have not been properly introduced. Well, let me introduce you to Mick O'Ryan."

Lucy Johnson turned and looked at Theodore Fitzpatrick. "I know you, Mr. Fitzpatrick, but I don't know this man, and I'm not sure I want to be introduced to him."

"That's why I'm here. I'm going to introduce you to Mick O'Ryan. Lucy Johnson, I want you to meet Mick O'Ryan. He's a fine young man that sells horses out of my store. He's been in the horse business a long time, and he has a fine reputation. Is there anything else you want to know about him before you can talk to him?"

Lucy looked over at Mick and finally smiled. "I guess that takes care of the introduction. Yes, I'll talk to him. Thank you, Mr. Fitzpatrick."

Theodore Fitzpatrick nodded, turned, and left the couple standing and staring at each other. Mick cut her one of his best smiles. "You're sure a hard one to get to know. I was determined to get past this introductory business. Now, will you talk to me?"

Lucy Johnson nodded in agreement. "What have you got to say?"

"Well, I've got to say that you are the best-looking girl here for one thing. Another thing, you've got the sweetest smile I've ever seen. Other than that, I don't know enough about you to say much. Where are you from and how long have you been here?"

"My dad's people are originally from South Carolina. He came out to Indian Territory after the Civil War and married my mom. My dad is farming some land for Smith Paul. That's about it. What else do you want to know?"

"Well, I'm fixing to settle down myself. I've got a deal with Fitzpatrick to sell horses out of his store, and I'm going to go to Tishomingo City and get a permit along Cow Creek where I plan to settle in, farm a little, ranch a little, and sell a bunch of horses."

"Well, that's a good business, Mr. O'Ryan. Now if you will excuse me, I have to get back to my folks."

"Sure. I'll excuse you, but you haven't seen the last of me. I'm going to come calling. I hope you will accept me and listen to me because I'm going to make you my girl."

Lucy Johnson smiled. "You know where I live. Come by next Sunday, and I will introduce you to my folks. You got off to a rocky start, but I'd be glad to see you along with the rest of the young men that keep coming by every Sunday."

She turned and walked away, and Mick felt like he'd met the girl he wanted to marry, and he hoped that he had a chance to wed her.

After Mick O'Ryan had ridden back to his leased property near Theodore Fitzpatrick on Cow Creek, he couldn't get the thought of Lucy Johnson out of his mind. The harder he worked to forget her, the more he thought about her smile and laugh and the more he wanted to see her again. Therefore he started making the trip at least once a week back to Pauls Valley to see her.

She was polite and nice to him and seemed to enjoy his company, and the more he saw her, the more he forgot about the beating given to him by Split Face. Slowly but surely, Mick's laugh returned, and he smiled a lot and he relaxed and became very interested in the prospect of marrying Lucy Johnson.

When he decided to pop the question to her, he had purchased a gold ring from Theodore Fitzpatrick and had ridden over to propose. When he got there, the excitement and anger showed in the people around Pauls Valley. Small Pox had struck the area. In the early summer of 1869, people were dying of the disease that ran rampant through the area.

Lucy Johnson was very sick. Mick O'Ryan did not go back that night or the next and stayed with her and helped those that bathed her hot face with a cool rag, and he prayed for the first time in a long time that she would live. The more the disease spread and the more the people passed away, Mick realized that they had no answer for the disease. Lucy Johnson had sunk into a coma, driven that way by the ravages of the small pox epidemic in the valley.

Early on the third morning, Mick O'Ryan rode as fast as his horse could carry him to Mondo's fort and talked Savanah and Skywalker to come back with him to help him save Lucy Johnson. Mondo was reluctant to have Skywalker go when he heard of the small pox epidemic, but Skywalker assured him that she had been through this before and had contracted the disease as a child in

Mexico, and it was her understanding that once you've had the disease, you built an immunity to the disease, and she would not have a serious bout the second time.

Savanah and Skywalker rode over to Lucy Johnson's place, and Mick convinced Lucy's mother and father to allow Skywalker to apply her own remedies. Skywalker had learned some medical treatment that the Spanish had brought to Mexico while she was in Mexico City, and even though the Kiowas were not very experienced at treating the white man's diseases that were brought over from Europe, they had developed the treatment for high fever that had hit the tribes before the white men brought all the various new diseases from Europe.

Day and night for two days, Skywalker and Savanah worked on Lucy Johnson with the home remedies and roots and herbs that they gathered, and Lucy responded to their treatment. She lived, and Mick O'Ryan was very relieved and happy and didn't waste any time in proposing to Lucy Johnson for fear that he would lose her again to some kind of disease or accident. After Lucy got well, she got to know Skywalker and Savanah the few days that they stayed to visit with her prior to returning to Mondo's fort. A close friendship was blended among the three women, and Lucy said yes to Mick O'Ryan's proposal.

In the early summer of 1869, there was a wedding at Ben Johnson's house, and a lot of the residents of Pauls Valley and the residents of Pickens County that knew Theodore Fitzpatrick and Mick O'Ryan were present. Mondo and Bear Chaser brought Savanah and Skywalker to the event that lasted most of the day. At one point, Mick and Lucy were able to sit down and visit with Bear Chaser, Mondo, and the women that came with them.

"I guess you are all going to settle down on Mick's place on Cow Creek as soon as you get through with the honeymoon?" asked Bear Chaser.

"Well, we're not going on much of a honeymoon. We have too much to do. We'll probably ride down to Tishomingo City and stay at that new hotel they built for a couple of days and then get on back to Cow Creek," answered Mick O'Ryan.

Lucy Johnson, now Lucy O'Ryan, looked over at Bear Chaser and Mondo. "You two need to come by next Sunday. We'll be home by then, and we'll be having a barn-raising. I understand you built quite the place over on Little Beaver. We don't have to have a protected barn like your cabin—your famous rock cabin that is—but we need a barn for the animals in the winter and to store some hay and stuff. I guess we can count on you. Come on over, and I'll fry some chicken, and we'll have an all-day event."

Mondo smiled. "Sure thing. I wouldn't miss some good home-made fried chicken for anything. We'll be over. We'll help you get started and get settled in. I'm glad that I've got some neighbors close to me, even though you are still about five miles from my place and you are on the other side of the Chisholm Trail. We'll do whatever we can to get you all started."

Skywalker spoke. "Are you still feeling good? You seemed to come out of that small pox sickness in good fashion. You look like you can handle a barn-raising pretty well."

"I'm fine," Lucy said. "We are ready to get started, and we look forward to being your neighbors."

With that, they moved on to other guests, and about two hours before nightfall, Mondo and Skywalker rode with Bear Chaser and Savanah back to Bear Chaser's house, and Mondo and Skywalker went on to the fort. It looked like that the civilized settlements were moving farther west, encroaching on the Kiowa and Comanche land but giving Mondo some neighbors reasonably close.

CHAPTER 44

Split Face rode through the back entrance of Purify
Jones's plantation where the servants were required to go,
and again, Split Face felt anger at being treated no better than
the Negroes that worked for this rich man. The grounds were
immaculate, and wealth showed all over the place. He had looked
at the plantation from the front, but he had never been allowed
to ride through the gates where the upper-crust people entered.
This plantation was a larger version of the famous James Madison
mansion that Split Face had seen in books. Negroes were all over
the yard working to keep the grounds perfect. The black workers
recognized Split Face and eased away from the ugly man as if he
was the devil himself. This made Split Face smile.

He got down from his horse and knocked on the back door.
A black servant opened the door and immediately stepped back
with fear on his face. He turned without saying a word to Split
Face and walked toward the interior of the house. Split Face
entered and went to the library where he knew Purify Jones
would be waiting. The servant opened the door and allowed Split
Face to enter and then shut the door tight.

Purify Jones was working at his desk, and he didn't even
bother to look up as Split Face waited for the rich plantation
owner to finish what he was doing. Finally, Purify Jones looked
up and stared at Split Face without saying a word. The little plantation owner didn't stand over five-two, but he acted like he was
big enough to take on anything and feared nothing. After a few
seconds of silence, the little man finally spoke.

"Have you found the necessary number and right men for the job this time?"

"You wanted thirty of the best in Texas, and I found twenty-seven that would go for five hundred dollars a head. I still think we need some more. I went down there with ten men that were damn good, and I left six of them there. I keep trying to tell you that this is a strong fortress and the men in there can shoot and so can the women. "

"Savanah can't shoot. I didn't teach her to shoot. I taught her to be a fine lady and how to use her charms, not arms. She was a perfect woman, and perfect women don't shoot a gun, dammit."

"With all due respect, Mr. Jones, I saw the two women fire down on the men that were trying to scale the walls of the fort. They didn't hesitate to put a bullet right through them. The Savanah you know and raised ain't the Savanah that's living out there in that fort with those headhunters. The natural savage has come out in her."

"Damn it, I know Savanah. I know her better than any person in the world. I raised her right and made her a lady. She would do anything in the world for me. And that big black bastard stole her away. Now, by God, I want you to listen and do what I tell you this time. I sent you across the Red River twice, and you've come back with dead bodies of the wrong people, and none of them have been that damn Maboola. I want Savanah alive and Maboola dead. Now if you do what I say, we'll get Savanah back. The Pinkertons will take care of Maboola."

"I still think we need a hundred men. And I don't like the idea of a siege. If we surround that fort and try to shut them down and starve them out, everybody in Indian Territory will know what we're trying to do. We've got to take the cannons, shoot down the damn walls, charge them, and wipe them out."

"By God, I told you if you harm a hair on Savanah's head, I'd hang you from the tallest tree and leave you there until the buzzards pick your bones. All you have to do is to surround that fort with thirty of the best cowboy gunmen and ex-Confederates that know how to shoot cannons and don't let anybody in or out, and they'll give up Savanah. Just fire the cannon over their heads a few times and set up camp. Don't be charging that damn fort across those open fields, or you'll lose again. Now, did you get some men who know how to fire cannons?"

"I got some men that know how to fire the cannon, and I got twenty-seven in all. All but three of them are ex-rebs who fought in the war and know how to kill and know how to fight. We can set up in the trees along the creek with that cannon and our rifles, and we can keep everybody in or out. But you got to remember, about twenty miles west, the Yankee cavalry is building a damn fort with a whole bunch of colored soldiers. Hell, they'll probably hear the cannon shots, and you know how those coloreds are. They run together like a pack of wolves. You can't let them run in gangs."

"You do what I tell you. The US Cavalry is not going to come. I've gone through the Pinkerton Agency, and we've put out some money to the right people, and there will be orders going down to the white officers that nobody helps anybody in Mondo's fort. So you don't have to worry about the Tenth Cavalry. They're going to stay in the fort and let me and my army take care of our mutual problem of an illegal fort on the Comanche reservation."

"What about all those ex-slaves that live at Wildhorse Creek? If word gets out, they're liable to come and help Mondo. I don't want a bunch of Indian ape savages slipping up on us and back-shooting us while we're surrounding that fort. Especially if I have less than thirty men. Also, the word is that this here Mondo has a good friend that the Comanches call Storm, and he is a hell of a warrior, and a lot of Comanches might follow him. We just can't hang around there for seven to ten days trying to starve them out and not be worried about people coming up behind us."

"The Comanches don't care about that Mondo. They don't want that fort there. Besides, I've paid the generals in Washington,

D.C. enough that word will come down the line that not only are the Tenth Cavalry to stay away from Mondo's, they're going to prevent any Comanches from coming up on your backside. And you don't have to worry about the Chickasaws. The Lighthorse Police want Mondo and that fort gone too. They're having a lot of trouble with their freedmen and all the ex-slaves that ran into their nation. Mondo and that damn Maboola are a symbol of armed resistance that civilized people can't have anywhere, and the Chickasaw government is white enough to know that."

"Have you got word from the Pinkerton men that Maboola's dead?" asked Split Face.

"Not yet. He got away from the railroad camp, but there's about ten of the best trackers and hunters trying to run him down before he gets back to Indian Territory. He's got a long ways to go across Cheyenne country, and he's got some good people after him. The Pinkertons say he'll never make it back to Mondo's fort."

The little man finally stood up, and Split Face again marveled at how such a small skinny man could have so much power. Purify Jones walked around the desk and walked up real close to Split Face, and Jones looked up at Split Face as if he was looking down on him. "I don't want any mistakes this time. I know you hate anyone with color, and you know that Savanah has a little bit of color. But she's my woman, and I'm going to live with her the rest of my life. Offer a thousand dollars in gold to the man that brings her out alive. And offer a thousand dollars in gold for the head of any man that kills her accidentally or not. If you kill her, Split Face, or you allow somebody to kill her, I'm going to lynch you like you were a damn monkey yourself. If you can't get the job done, I can afford to have others do it. There's hundreds of ex-Confederate killers running around here as broke as a son-of-bitch. Through the KKK, you have a lot of influence and people are scared of you. But I ain't people. I'm Purify Jones, by God, and you're nothing but an ugly piss ant that I can step on and squash any time I feel like it. So don't let your damn hate get in the way of what you're supposed to be doing. Do you understand me?"

Split Face was breathing hard now, and air was coming out of both sides of his face. Purify Jones acted as if the evil smell coming from Split Face didn't affect him at all. Split Face wanted to kill the little bastard so bad that he had to clinch his fists to hold himself steady. If it wasn't for all the money that the fifty-five-year-old man poured into his KKK organization, Split Face would have killed him right there and then.

Purify Jones seemed to feel the hate in Split Face's eyes, and instead of backing off, he jammed his finger into Split Face's chest. "You want to kill me, don't you? I used to be pushed around a long time ago. But you know, I made a fortune during the war. I can do anything I want anywhere I want to anyone I want. You just think of me as the king of North Texas. And the king wants Savanah back and wants that Maboola dead. I'm giving you one more chance to get the job done, or you're going to be dead. Think of Savanah as my white wife and you're saving her from those damn black animals you hate so much. Now, get out of here. I can't stand the sight of you anymore."

With that, Purify spun around and dismissed him as if he wasn't there at all. Split Face started to lunge forward and kill the little man, but held back. He hated a lot of things, but what he hated most were the uppity coloreds that ran loose and free and acted like they were white. He knew he couldn't carry out justice aimed at the ex-slaves if he didn't have Purify Jones's money. But once he settled the Negro issue and Texas took back control of those people, then he was going to turn on the rich bastards like this Jones fellow. Someday there would be justice when the right people ran Texas again.

Before he reached the door, Purify Jones hollered. "I want this done this summer. You've been fooling around too long trying to get ready. You've wasted a lot of my money. And I don't let anyone waste my money. If you're not on your way by August, then I'll get someone else and get rid of you."

Split Face slammed the door to the library and marched out of the house, knocking down the black servant that was attempting to get out of his way. In his head, Split face was dreaming of the glory he would achieve if he rode back to Texas with the head of Mondo and the rest of those black-skinned animals. He swore that even if he had to die trying, the head of Mondo was going to come back across the Red River without his body. And as for Savanah, he'd bring her back to Mr. Jones, but he was going to have his way with her before they entered Texas. If Split Face became a hero, Purify Jones couldn't talk to him like he was nothing. And who would believe the word of a Negress like Savanah over him? For now, Mr. Jones would get what he wanted as usual, but Split Face was also going to get what he wanted and needed and what the state of Texas needed before Purify Jones tasted his little sexual delight.

CHAPTER 45

I T WAS IN the middle of April of 1869 that Ten Bears showed up at Mondo's compound to visit his old friend Bear Chaser. The old Comanche Indian looked sad, but he was still in pretty good health. Bear Chaser welcomed Ten Bears into Mondo's fort, and they all went to the rock cabin to visit and get caught up on the latest news. Deep wrinkles in Ten Bears's face showed his age, and his eyes showed disappointment in his efforts to bring some kind of peace between the Comanches and the US government.

Ten Bears brought them up to date on his activities. "After Storm showed up and headed off that attack by the young Comanche warriors, I went directly to Fort Cobb to wait for the supplies to arrive to feed all the starving Indians waiting for some help. There were about 1,700 Indians, 700 of them Comanches, the rest were Kiowa, Cheyenne, Kiowa-Apaches, Arapahos, and even some Caddos. Major General William B. Hazen was in charge, and there was no civilian Indian agent there. A Civil War general named Sherman was the main general over everything, and he also sent another general named Phillip Sheraton to take care of all of the warlike raiding Plains Indians that wouldn't come to the fort in peace. Sherman let Hazen provide $55,000 worth of food and rations for the Indians that had been around Fort Cobb waiting to receive something to eat. That money was supposed to be here last spring to take care of farming equipment and seed so the peaceful Comanches and Kiowas could get started farming. But since we didn't get to plant anything, there was no food to eat. The money for farming had to go for food."

Bear Chaser frowned and asked, "What happened after you got back to Fort Cobb? I heard there was a bunch of run-ins between the Comanches and the US Cavalry under General Sheraton."

"You know that crazy Custer wiped out Black Kettle's peaceful Cheyennes. But before that, did you know that Black Kettle had come to Fort Cobb? And General Hazen said he had no power to make any deal with the Cheyennes, and so Black Kettle went back to camp on the Washita River and was killed by Custer. There is no talking at all between the army and the civilian Indian agents, and it's just a mess. On what the white men call Christmas Day of last year, General Sheraton attacked a bunch of peaceful Comanches at Soldier Spring at the western end of the Wichita Mountains near the North Fork of the Red River and killed twenty-five Comanches."

"What are you going to do?" asked Bear Chaser. "And what about that new fort they are supposed to be building over by Medicine Bluff?"

"Well, they're working hard. Those buffalo soldiers are building rock buildings and plowing fields for farming. The army plowed one thousand, two hundred acres for more than a hundred small garden patches, and three hundred acres of corn were planted. There are some Comanche men working with the women in the fields, but most warriors won't do women's work."

"Have the Comanche raids stopped?" asked Bear Chaser.

"No. There's just not very many raids around close by since there's a lot of soldiers over at Medicine Bluff. There's still not enough rations to feed all the peaceful Comanches, and I've heard Washington has changed the whole policy, and the new president Grant has signed some kind of law where Quaker medicine men are taking over as Indian agents. I was told that these Christian agents are taking the power away from the army. This might be a good change. The young warriors don't like the soldiers, and they might be persuaded to come in and farm if these Quaker medicine men work some magic."

Mondo looked over at Ten Bears and asked, "Are those young warriors still against you?"

"Oh, the young warriors that want to fight to the end are not around the Medicine Bluff fort. Only the peaceful Indians are hanging around and getting rations. Things are still bad, and there's not enough to eat, but at least the ones that don't want to make war on the army are not after my scalp."

About that time, they heard shots off in the distance, and all five of the people in the compound ran out into the yard and to the gate. Off in the distance, they saw a rider approaching fast with several men firing at the lone rider coming for the open gate.

Bear Chaser was the first to recognize the fleeing rider and hollered, "That's Hudson Greer. He's that freedman from Texas that lives over at Wildhorse Creek. I can't tell who's chasing him, but he's a friend of ours, and we should let him in."

"Sure," said Mondo, and the men got ready to close the gate as Hudson Greer rode into the compound and dismounted. The gate was closed, and the men jumped on top of the fence to see who was chasing Hudson Greer.

Captain Hurbert Dixon and the Lighthorse Police of the Chickasaw Nation reined up at the gate and shouted for Mondo to open up. There were at least twelve Chickasaw Lighthorse policemen with Captain Dixon. They were all armed and looked determined.

"Why are you after Hudson Greer?" asked Mondo.

"He's a Texas freedman that came across the Red River, and we're getting rid of all those foreign ex-slaves and sending them back where they belong," answered Hurbert Dixon.

Hudson Greer crawled up on the ledge and looked over the wall at Hurbert Dixon. "I was born a slave of Chickasaw owner Daniel Colbert. I was sold to a Texas man right before the Civil War. I have family that were Chickasaw freedmen, and since I was born a Chickasaw slave, then I have the rights of a Chickasaw freedman."

Hurbert Dixon answered, "You have no rights here. Ex-slaves keep pouring across the Red River and into the Chickasaw Nation and causing trouble. They can't get work like a Chickasaw freedman, and so they steal. The Lighthorse Police have been assigned the task of getting rid of all that are in the Chickasaw Nation except freedman of the Chickasaw people that were slaves here at the end of the war. The US government is going to move the real Chickasaw freedman. Soon there will be no freedmen in our nation."

"What about black people who have Chickasaw blood but were never slaves?" asked Mondo.

"There's no law about them people, and since the only black people now allowed in the Chickasaw Nation are Chickasaw freedmen, then I would say to you, Mondo, as one of those people, that we've got to run you out too."

Bear Chaser shook his head and laughed. "The last time you were here, you said we were on Comanche land and not Chickasaw land. If so, you don't have any authority here. I don't think you want to lose a bunch of your men trying to interfere with Hudson Greer or Mondo Hobbs, my son."

Hurbert Dixon glared at Bear Chaser. "We're dealing with the Chickasaw freedman, and we're doing a good job of it. All former Chickasaw slaves were required to choose an employer and make a written wage agreement with the employer before a Chickasaw judge. Any black person that doesn't have a written wage agreement is to be arrested and their services sold to the highest bidder, and the freedmen will be compelled to work off the bid amount, and if they're troublesome, they will be run out of the Chickasaw Nation. Also, the money we get from the bid for services of the arrested black person is put into a special fund for the support of any ex-Chickasaw slave in need of financial assistance. We're taking care of our own, and we will continue to do so, but we can't take care of every ex-slave that comes running across the Red River and tries to settle on our land and tries to become a

Chickasaw citizen by lying to the US government. They're all claiming to be ex-Chickasaw slaves. And the Federals are trying to force us to give Chickasaw freedmen membership in our tribe, but we won't, and according to the end of the war treaty, the US will find them a new home away from the Chickasaw Nation."

Hudson Greer spoke up. "We don't want to leave. I'm trying to get tribal rights. About fifty Lighthorse Police raided Wildhorse Creek looking for me. I barely escaped. There's lots of ex-slaves that are not Chickasaw freedmen that the Lighthorse Police are leaving alone. They're after me because I petitioned the US for some tribal rights for me as a Chickasaw freedman."

"We've talked enough," said Dixon. "We've rode fifty miles trying to run this intruder down, and now that we've got him, we're not going to let him go. Either you turn him over to us, Mondo, or we're going to crash the gates and, if we have to, kill every son-of-a-bitch living in this fort."

Mondo bristled and aimed his thirty-thirty at Dixon. "Every time I've run into you, Dixon, you make threats on my life. I'm not the only one here and we've got women to protect. I'd just as soon shoot you now as later but I'm giving you a chance to turn around and ride away and buy a little more time for your sorry life. I don't want to kill you or any other Chickasaw. I just want to live peacefully. But you're not going to ride in here and force me to turn over my friend and guest, Hudson Greer. Now, if you want shooting, just start shooting 'cause you're going to be the first one to die."

Dixon glared at Mondo and then looked over at Bear Chaser. "I know you, Bear Chaser. You don't want to do battle with your own tribe. You're full-blood and you've got rights. You should have known better than to breed with black blood. All rights were lost for your son when you did that. Now, I would go ahead and kill Mondo right now even if I lost a few men, if it weren't for you. I don't kill Chickasaws if they haven't committed a crime. I'm going to turn around and leave, but I'm going to come back with more men and some cannons. I suggest you turn over Hudson Greer to me right now because he's nothing but a troublemaker, and he's causing unrest among ex-slaves in the Chickasaw Nation. We want him dead or out of our country. Don't make me come back and bury you and everyone in this place. I'll count to five, and if Hudson Greer's not out the front gate, then I'll promise you, I'll be back and if I have to, I'll bring the US Cavalry with me. Mondo never did have any right to stay here, and I don't know why you haven't been run off before now."

Mondo smiled. "We stay here because I said I would never leave. And you better bring all the Indian police and the US Cavalry if you come back again. You and this bunch riding with you are not men enough to take this place. I don't want to kill any Chickasaws, but I damn sure can, and I damn sure will, if I see your face again."

"One...two...three...four...five," counted Hurbert Dixon, and when nothing happened, he jerked his horse around and led his Lighthorse Police away from Mondo's fort.

Mondo looked over at Hudson Greer and shook his head. "I don't know why every refugee that's on the run seems to find my fort. What made you bring all these Lighthorse Police down on us?"

"I had no place else to go," said Hudson Greer. "I was hoping that Maboola was here. I heard he'd moved North, but since you gave Maboola protection in your fort, I thought you might be able to help me."

"Well, come on in and have a bite to eat," said Mondo.

As they entered the cabin, Mondo thought to himself. *Everyone swears Split Face is coming with a bunch of ex-rebs to wipe us out. I guess I can't count on the Chickasaw police to help us at all. Maybe it's time for me to take Skywalker and get out of here.*

CHAPTER 46

WHEN MABOOLA LEFT Nebraska, he thought that some men may be trying to chase him down, so he rode hard and fast and tried to cover his tracks. He was in the saddle at night and slept during the afternoons. He picked up some Cheyenne tracks and had to change his course and swing to the east and then to the west to make sure he didn't encounter the fierce and warlike Cheyenne that were raiding throughout Kansas. Maboola had no idea that the ten men coming after him were expert trackers and experienced plainsmen who caught up with him soon after he crossed into Kansas. The trackers intended to kill the man known as the Black Death, who now had a thousand dollars on his head.

Around three o'clock in the afternoon, the lead scout of the ten bounty hunters slipped up within fifty yards of Maboola and spotted him sleeping under a big cottonwood tree down in a dry creek bed. When the scout got back to the approaching bounty hunters, they completely surrounded the creek and all ten men moved in for the kill. They were all supposed to fire at the sleeping Maboola at one time. Captain Bones, the leader of bounty hunter hired by the Pinkerton Agency with Purify Jones's money, was to signal the attack with the first shot.

Maboola's eyes jerked open when the sounds of the birds stopped. He was near a water hole in a dry creek bed, and he'd been put to sleep by the chirping of the many birds that flew in to get a drink of water. As the ten men crept forward toward Maboola, the birds picked up the sound of creeping men and flew away. The stillness of the air around him caused Maboola to snap his eyes open, as if a cannon had been fired. He had a contingency plan in case the Cheyenne spotted him and tried to slip up on him like they did when he came through Kansas the first time. He was not going to be caught asleep again. He immediately rolled to his right as ten guns exploded and the bullets dug into the ground where he had been sleeping. As he had planned, Maboola fell six feet off the bank into a sandy bottom of the dry creek bed. He rose and ran down the creek bottom toward a hidden low area where he had picketed his horses. The ten men that had surrounded Maboola could not see but flashes of him as he ran through the bottom of the creek. They fired and charged, but by the time they neared the creek, Maboola had mounted his horse and was riding low in the saddle between the dry banks of the creek so that only the three men on the east side of the attacking bounty hunters had any kind of shot at Maboola. As Maboola came out of the creek bed, they all fired, and two of them struck Maboola but did not take him from his saddle.

By the time the men ran back to their mounts and started riding after Maboola, he was at least three hundred yards ahead. The trackers spotted blood and knew that they had wounded Maboola. The trackers thought they could run him until Maboola dropped or wore his horses down. Thus the bounty hunters started a horse race across central Kansas toward Indian Territory.

Maboola soon let go of the second horse with his supplies as he needed all the speed he could muster to stay ahead of the bounty hunters. The pain in his shoulder and his thigh began to throb, and he knew he couldn't ride until darkness because he was growing weaker with each mile. He looked back and he could tell his pursuers were experienced plainsmen. They were riding in an organized manner and were preserving their horses. The bounty hunters knew they would eventually wear Maboola down. They were in no hurry, and they didn't want to waste ammunition on long shots. Soon, Maboola would be too weak to fire back. They were going to ride him down and kill him, and Maboola knew it.

Maboola rode on looking for any place to hide or a hill or some place he could have an advantage and might be able to hold off ten men. The Kansas plains were flat, and he could see for miles. The ten men chasing him were spread out like a prairie fire and moving slowly in on him, gaining ground on each stride of their horses. Maboola knew that the men were not going to take him on physically in hand-to-hand combat. These guys would stay back and finish him with a rifle. They would not get real close until they were sure he was too weak to fight.

Maboola felt like it was the end, and he didn't want to die. If it hadn't been for Savanah, he probably would have just turned and attacked and got as many as he could before they got him. However, he really had, for the first time, someone to live for, and he wanted to see Savanah before he died. He had been beaten, tortured, and almost killed by white men so that all he wanted to do was kill as many whites as he could, but that was before he met Savanah. It seemed so unfair that when he finally decided he wanted to live and live with someone and to raise a family and to stop killing, he was going to be killed. He counted the white men he'd killed in his day, and it numbered ten. He guessed that was justice. He killed ten and ten were going to kill him.

The pain in his thigh and shoulder increased, and he could see the blood leaking out from under his shirt sleeve and dripping from his hand. The early spring sun made him dizzy, and the heat increased as his horse slowed down. Maboola's body slowed down too. He felt weak, and he could hear the horses pounding across the plain, getting closer and closer by the hour.

He had to stop, and he again searched for any place that gave him a little cover. There were no trees, no creeks, just flat plain. Then he saw a buffalo wallow, like a small man-made pond that held no water in the middle of the flat countryside. In the past, buffalo would wallow in the mud after a hard downpour and leave a dip in the level floor of the flatland, two feet deep and ten to fifteen feet in width and length. It wasn't much of a cover, but it was something. Maboola guided his horse toward the buffalo wallow, pulled up, and forced his horse down. He drew his rifle and dropped behind the animal.

The ten bounty hunters immediately stopped out of rifle range and sat down to wait for darkness or to wait for Maboola to pass out so they could shoot him. The bounty hunters were smart, and Maboola knew it. If they charged him, he could get more than half of them before they got him. If they tried to creep up on him, it would take them a long time, and Maboola would get some of them before they got him. But if they just waited, then Maboola would have to go for water, and they would catch him on the flat plain without any cover. The ten men circled the wallow out of rifle range and surrounded Maboola and waited for him to choose his method for death.

The first real hot day of spring sun beat down on Maboola, and he had to strip off some of his clothes. The sweat got in his eyes, and his wounds continued to hurt like hell. He tore up his shirt and wrapped his shoulder and his thigh tight enough to slow down the bleeding. He had a canteen full of water, and he drank two swallows every hour as darkness approached. The bounty hunters waited and watched.

Maboola's horse rested, and just as soon as it got dark enough, Maboola was going to jump on his mount and try to run for it again. He had regained some strength, and his dizziness had left him. He peered out over the wallow to the north where four men had been waiting in the tall grass about a hundred yards apart. Now, he could only see two. He turned to his left and right and then turned around and counted a total of six men barely visible sprawled in the grass, waiting for him to move. Maboola strained his eyes and looked everywhere across the plain to see if he could spot the other four crawling along on their bellies, trying to slip up on him. Maybe the four were sleeping so they could be ready for a nighttime rush at him.

He was looking off to the east when all of a sudden, two figures sprung from the grass and took one of the bounty hunters down so quickly that Maboola wasn't sure that he saw it happen. Then he realized what was going on. The Cheyenne had spotted the ten bounty hunters spread out and alone. The Indians had been creeping up on each one of the bounty hunters. The Cheyenne had bellied across the flat plains and taken them out. The other bounty hunters must have thought that the ones disappearing were just resting. The spring grass was already high and could conceal a man easily.

By the time the shadow of dusk had covered the area and he could barely see the outline of the bounty hunters waiting for him, the number of whites were down to four. Each of the other six bounty hunters were dead, hidden by the Kansas grass. The Cheyenne had slipped up and taken the men so quickly and so quietly that the other white men had not noticed that their numbers were being reduced.

Maboola was glad that his pursuers had been killed and he had only four to contend with, but he knew just as soon as the Cheyenne had finished off the last four, they would be after him. They were probably getting rid of the white men so they could get to Maboola. After he had killed the Cheyenne warrior last summer and the word had gotten out about the great black warrior, and the size and strength of that warrior, the young Cheyenne warriors wanted his scalp more than any white man's scalp. So basically, Maboola figured that the Cheyenne were just killing off the bounty hunters so that they could get to him. There were a lot more than four warriors this time, and the Cheyenne wanted revenge.

Maboola was weak, but he was determined. He didn't want to be tortured to death in the slow manner that the Cheyenne sometimes dealt with their enemy. He would prefer a bullet between the eyes than to be put to the fire.

Maboola jumped on his horse and rode hard to the south. At the same time, Indians rose all around the four bounty hunters, and he could hear the shooting and the screaming as scalps were taken and at least thirty Cheyenne moved in and finished off the bounty hunters, and at least five mounted Cheyenne warriors started after Maboola. This time, Maboola decided that he was through running and he would meet them head-on. He stopped, turned his horse, and waited. And again, the Cheyenne's did not fire guns or arrows at him but raised their axes and charged toward Maboola. These Cheyenne were gallant warriors, and they did not like to kill at a distance. They wanted to count coup just like the Comanches and Kiowas, which meant that they wanted to touch a live enemy first and then kill him. And they wanted to touch Maboola with their tomahawks buried inside his head. No greater honor could be had than to kill by hand-to-hand combat this large black warrior.

As they approached, Maboola fired his rifle and took one off the back of his horse and then drew his pistol and fired twice, knocking two more down. Maboola charged as they came near. There were two Indians riding full speed, and Maboola came on right at them. Maboola dove forward off his horse and spread his arms and took the two Indians with him to the ground. Before they could get up, he cracked their heads together so hard that they broke like watermelons. In less than five seconds, he had killed five Cheyenne, and he stood alone on the prairie as his horse raced off. He turned and roared a challenge at the rest of the Cheyenne riding toward him.

Maboola pounded his chest and signaled the Indians forward, begging them to take him on. He had a pistol in one hand and his machete in the other. He screamed curses and threats at the Cheyenne. Twenty-five Cheyenne warriors rode up and stopped about fifteen yards from Maboola to study the big black giant stomping around, screaming curses, and mocking them to charge him as blood dripped from his arm and leg. Four of the Cheyenne had rifles, but most had bows and arrows. However, not one of the Cheyenne raised his weapon. They looked at the five warriors that were dead and looked at the bloody black giant that was challenging all twenty-five of them. Some circled Maboola and stared wide-eyed at the deep crevices of red scars on his back. The Cheyennes had torture ceremonies where the bravest warriors swung from ropes tied to their chests that left proud marks of courage, but none had seen so many deep scars as was on this man's back. The ones behind Maboola described the scars to the leader. The louder Maboola yelled, the bigger he seemed to get. The Cheyenne wondered if their bullets or arrows could even harm him. They could see the blood running from his shoulder and the blood painting his pants red from the hip wound, but Maboola moved about as if he had no wounds. They had never seen a man covered with so many marks of bravery. The Indians began to think of Maboola as either totally insane or some great black spirit that the gods protected.

Maboola got tired of waiting. He raised his pistol and fired at the Indians then charged them. The leader of the Cheyenne's yelled, "He is a devil god. He can't be killed." With that, the leader turned his mount and drove his heels in his horse's side and took off away from Maboola. The rest of the Cheyenne followed, revealing a strange sight on the Kansas plains. There was this large black ex-slave trying to run down on foot twenty-five Cheyenne warriors riding their horses away from him as fast as they could go. Maboola couldn't believe it. Here he was, ready to die and to die as a man and a warrior and he couldn't get a fight out of twenty-five Cheyenne. He finally pulled up and stopped and started to laugh. The retreating Cheyenne warriors could hear his loud laughter, and they knew not only was Maboola a spirit devil, but he was crazy too. They didn't even take the time to pick up their dead but scattered for their village and would report what they had seen and done, and the news would go throughout the Cheyenne tribe and to other Indian tribes that the man known as Black Death by the whites was a crazy god devil who couldn't be killed, and when any Indian saw the big black giant, they better run and hide or they would be destroyed. Twice Maboola had faced the Cheyenne and twice he had acted so quickly and so viciously that he had at once become a legend that was supposed to be protected by the Great Spirit. There was no other explanation. None of the Indians had seen anyone so big or so black and with so many deep bravery scars. They thought Maboola was a ghost that had his back burned raw. This one black man was more dangerous than all the whites pouring into their country. He must be avoided at all costs. He was death walking, riding, and living amongst them. In May of 1869, Maboola weak and bleeding started south toward Mondo's compound. There were no more white men chasing him in Kansas, and there were no Indians that would dare bother him again.

CHAPTER 47

When Mondo arrived with Hudson Greer at Fitzpatrick's store, the last thing on his mind was the thought of drawing his pistol. He was a happy man. Things were going well in his compound. Hudson Greer had stayed with Mondo a few days and had decided to go back to Wildhorse Creek. Mondo had wanted to talk to Mick about selling more horses, so he saddled up and rode with Greer the seven miles southeast to Fitzpatrick's store on Cow Creek in Pickens County, Chickasaw Nation.

Hudson Greer felt obligated to go back to the Negro settlement. Even though he thought the Chickasaw Lighthorse Police would probably be looking for him, he belonged with his people. No rights were going to be obtained by the blacks in Chickasaw Nation unless they stayed together and were led by responsible leaders. Hudson Greer knew he was a responsible leader.

When the ex-slaves arrived at the Wildhorse Creek settlement from Louisiana and Texas, they had no idea what to do or where to go. All they knew was they were going to get out of Louisiana and Texas where their experience as slaves was not good. Since most freed slaves had never been anywhere other than a mile or two from their master's home, their experience and knowledge of the outside world was very limited. After the war, plantation owners entered into contracts for labor with their ex-slaves and worked them in conditions that were barely an improvement from their lives as slaves. So the ones with courage left and looked for something other than a life that resembled their previous existence.

Hudson Greer had joined with others to form a community and divide responsibilities. Even though on one side of town there were bars and drinking and gambling were wide open, the Wildhorse Creek community developed a beginning of a town with elected leaders and governmental functions. It was hard to maintain restrictions on the freed ex-slaves since to them, freedom was freedom to do anything they wanted, when they wanted, and anywhere they wanted. Therefore the first thing they needed in the church side of Wildhorse Creek was some kind of law and order, and Hudson Greer was elected mayor. The church side community began to live a more civilized and organized life. Hudson Greer was needed at Wildhorse Creek to keep the development growing to a full, responsible, civilized community.

Mondo was as relaxed and content as he had ever been. Even though he still feared and expected the attack from Purify Jones led by Split Face, Mondo lived from minute to minute and day to day with a smile on his face and with his love growing for Skywalker. He knew he had given up part of himself to her, but he still felt good about it. Even though he added responsibilities with more people living at his house, he also shared a feeling with Skywalker that made him comfortable and relaxed and secure for the first time in his life. He still had doubts about how long this good life would last, but he intended to enjoy it as long as he could. It was a happy and secure Mondo who rode into Fitzpatrick's store with Hudson Greer on a warm June day in 1869.

The first person they saw sitting out on the porch was Omar Culberson, the sergeant of the Tenth Cavalry stationed at the new fort being built at Medicine Bluff. Hudson Greer told Mondo that Omar had a girlfriend at Wildhorse Creek, and every chance he got to leave the post, he rode the sixty miles to the Negro town. Omar always stopped at Fitzpatrick's store to talk to Theodore Fitzpatrick and Mick O'Ryan. Omar stood up on the porch and waved at his two friends.

"Now there's a couple of good people. Come on in and I'll buy you a drink," hollered Omar.

Mondo and Hudson climbed off their horses and shook hands with Omar. The three of them walked into Fitzpatrick's store and found Mick sitting at the table by himself, playing with a deck of cards.

Mick jumped up with a smile on his face and welcomed the three men. "Good to see you all. Theodore has gone over to check his gardens and left me here to watch the store. Have a seat. The first drink is on Theodore," said Mick with a smile. Mick shook hands with Omar and Hudson Greer and then hugged Mondo. Mick went over to the bar, got three whiskey glasses, and brought them back to the table. He poured a drink for all. Everyone settled down around the table.

Mick smiled. "I know where Omar is going, but why are you two here?" asked Mick looking at Mondo and Hudson.

"I'm headed back to my town," said Hudson. "I got run off by a bunch of Chickasaw Lighthorse Police. I made it to Mondo's, and Mondo got them off my back."

Mick frowned and asked, "Why in the hell are they running you off? I didn't think they'd dare ride into Wildhorse Creek. They must have had an army with them. Word is out among the whites that you better be black to go back into Wildhorse Creek. Maybe it's not as mean since Maboola left."

Omar answered, "It's just like any other town. They got some saloons and some whorehouses on one side, and on the other side they got a church and a bunch of nice people and one damn pretty girl."

"More than one," said Hudson Greer. "I'd say right now we may be the biggest town in Pickens County. The Saturday night before I got chased out of town, I counted over five hundred people in Wildhorse Creek."

"It's a funny town," said Omar. "I don't think there's hardly anybody who can read and write, is there, Hudson?"

Hudson shook his head no and frowned, "No. Most of the ex-slaves that can read and write went north and got a job. We sent off for a reading black man and we're paying him to come to Wildhorse Creek to teach school and keep our records so we can set up a real legal, written-down community."

"How can the Chickasaw police chase you out of your town? Where was the so-called Freedmen's Bureau that them Yankees sent down south to protect ex-slaves?" asked Mondo.

"They're in Texas, not in Indian Territory," said Hudson Greer. "They came through and said we weren't having any problems with the Chickasaws. There's a report by the US Army that said there were forty-nine murders of ex-slaves in 1866, but the same officer that gave that report came back in 1867 and said there was no racial problems in the Chickasaw Nation. That same officer that wrote the report resigned and entered into contracts with the Chickasaw Nation. So even though they are trying to protect ex-slaves in Texas, they're not doing anything in the Chickasaw Nation. Besides, the Freedmen's Bureau wouldn't have any legal rights to prosecute anybody unless they took them to Fort Smith, Arkansas. So blacks don't have any protection here."

"I thought you, an ex-slave, could enter into a contract for labor with a Chickasaw citizen and you could work for wages. Isn't that true?" asked Omar.

"Only if you were a slave owned by a Chickasaw citizen. And most of the Chickasaw freedmen have entered into some kind of contract with Chickasaws, but that doesn't cover anybody that wasn't a Chickasaw slave before the end of the war. All the ex-slaves from Louisiana and Texas are not governed by any law in the Chickasaw Nation. The whites can get permits to work and live in the Chickasaw Nation, but if you have a little bit of color, you can't get a permit. Therefore the blacks that are here now that weren't ex-Chickasaw slaves don't have any place to turn. We have no courts to go to. The US government says I'm a Texas citizen, and the Texans say I'm a Chickasaw citizen, and the Chickasaws say we're not Chickasaws," said Hudson Greer.

Omar scratched his head and looked over at Hudson Greer. "Hell, if you've got five hundred black people down there living in Wildhorse Creek, it looks like to me that you could kind of say who was coming in and out of your place. I know you have guns and other weapons."

Hudson Greer shook his head. "We have some. When I get back, we'll get better organized, and the Lighthorse Police will think twice before ever coming in there again. Maybe we don't have any legal rights in the Chickasaw Nation, but rights or no rights, if you ain't got black blood, you better act right if you come into our town in the future. Guns make the laws out west, more than people."

"If you get organized and get some guns, maybe we can work out a deal to help each other out," said Mondo. "As you know, Savanah is living at my place, and we've been warned that Split Face is going to bring a bunch of killers up here to get her back. It would be nice if I could work out a way to get word to Wildhorse Creek so you people might come riding across to my place and help out when Split Face attacks."

"Sure," said Hudson. "We all got to stick together if we're going to make it. Just as soon as I get back to Wildhorse Creek, I'll send a message to you, and we'll try to set up some way where we can get in touch with each other if there's ever any trouble."

Mondo reached over and shook hands with Hudson Greer and then looked over to Mick. "Mick, I need to talk to you a little bit about some horses. If you two will excuse us, I'm going to go out with Mick and look at our stock. We've got some business deals to discuss."

With that, Mick and Mondo got up from the table and walked out of the store and over to the corral where about thirty horses were penned in and waiting for buyers.

"Are all these horses our horses?" asked Mondo.

Mick shook his head yes. "I've also got about forty of my own over on my place about four miles east of here in a clearing. You need to come by and see it real soon. Lucy and I got our place fixed up real nice."

Mondo smiled. "That's good. You can get that place all legal and use as much land as you can take care of since you married up in the Chickasaw tribe," said Mondo.

"I notice you asked for help from the Wildhorse Creek settlement, but you didn't ask help from me. You know, if Split Face comes over here with a bunch of those damn killers, I'll be there. I have a personal grudge with Split Face, and I live a lot closer to you than Hudson Greer does."

Mondo put his hand on Mick's shoulder. "I don't know, Mick. You probably should stay out of this. Since you married into the Chickasaw Nation, you're going to have a lot of rights and you don't want to be on the wrong side of the government here or anywhere. You've got to remember that Texas is just a good rock throw across the Red River. We trade with a lot of those trail drivers coming through. If you get to be known as one who helps black people, then you're liable to have no Texans or no Chickasaws talking to you. It would probably just be best for you to stay out of it."

"I'll be there, Mondo. I hate Split Face and all his kind. I was a stupid kid to let my feeling for Skywalker get between us. We've been friends for a long time. If you need help, just holler. I think I can count on the same from you."

Mondo nodded yes. "That's good by me. We'll be friends to the end, and I hope that's not soon. I'll watch your back, and you can watch mine. Besides, we're going to be close neighbors in this country even though we're at least ten miles apart. Your place and Fitzpatrick's store are the closest settlements to my compound."

About that time, a gun roared in the store, and both Mondo and Mick took off around the corral and headed for the front door. They saw four new horses tied up in front of the store. They busted through the door and froze as four dusty-looking cowboys had guns drawn and aimed at Omar and Hudson, who both calmly sat at their table. Three of the cowboys turned their guns on Mick and Mondo before they could draw their own weapons. The biggest cowboy turned back to Greer and Omar.

"The next shot will be for one of you. What did you do with the white owner? I know this ain't a colored store and this ain't a colored town. A man named Fitzpatrick owns this place, and I want to know where you all buried him."

Omar slowly straightened in his chair and squinted at the cowboy doing the talking. Omar nodded toward Mick. "There's the man in charge. His name is Mick O'Ryan and he's in partnership with Fitzpatrick. Fitzpatrick has gone off to check his farm."

The cowboys turned and looked at Mick. "Is that right?"

Mick nodded his head. "That's right. Those two at the table are customers. I'd appreciate it if you'd put your pistols up and we'll be glad to take care of your needs." Mick smiled.

The three young cowboys holstered their pistols, but the leader a tall, thin cowboy with sandy hair and a slight beard kept his gun pointed at Omar and Hudson. He was older than the other three cowboys and obviously was the one that did the talking. The tall cowboy studied Mick for a while and then looked over at the two black men at the table. He turned back to Mick.

"If you're in charge, get rid of them darkies. I don't go into any place where there's coloreds. Now this is either a white place or a slave place. And if it's a colored place, then I'm going to leave, and I'm going to tell everybody else that comes up and down this trail that this ain't a white man's store no more."

"They are my friends, and they don't have to leave," said Mick. "Now, if you don't like the way this store is run, then you can get out. We don't need your business, and we don't even want your kind in here," said Mick.

"Well, you're a damn darkie lover," said the slim cowboy. "You don't know what's going on in Texas. Them ex-slaves are running all over the place like they was white. They are stealing and raping and killing, and it's not safe for anyone. Now, you're either with us whites or for them black monkeys, and if you are for them, by God, you'll be lynched too."

Mick shook his head no and started to speak as Mondo eased up close to the cowboy talking who had turned his pistol toward Mick. The tall Texan cocked his pistol and extended his arm toward Mick's head. Mondo drew his pistol and cracked the cowboy's skull in one quick, smooth movement, and the man fell backward, landing in a heap on the floor. The three young men started to draw their pistols but stopped as they heard the click of other hammers as Mick drew and so did Omar and Hudson Greer.

Silence lingered, the three young cowhands looked at the faces in the room and saw that the men holding pistols on them were calm but dead serious about killing them. Then they looked at each other and lifted their hands away from their guns and raised their hands.

"Take that son-of-a-bitch out of here and don't come back again," said Mick. "You don't know how close you all came to being laid out dead. Now get."

The three men grabbed their unconscious friend and carried him out the door, tied him to his horse and rode away.

Inside the bar, Omar and Hudson Greer walked up and shook Mondo's hand and then Mick's. Then Hudson Greer spoke. "I hope this doesn't kill Theodore's business and yours too, Mick. I don't know whether you realize what has happened here. Even though Mondo did the hitting, Mick, you stood by and didn't fight for your own kind. There's a war coming and everybody is going to have to decide where he stands. Will a white stand up for what's right? And if a white does the right thing, will he be treated worse than the blacks? Mick, we want to thank you for allowing Mondo to cold cock a sorry white man, but I'll guarantee you, that was bad for your business and probably worse for your health."

CHAPTER 48

As Mondo rode back to his compound, he felt dread and sadness. It seemed like every time he met new people, trouble happened. He had initially built the compound to be away from others. But no matter what he did, trouble found him, and trouble came and stayed. He didn't like to fight because he knew deep down anger or fear settled by fists or guns did not soothe those feelings. At first he wanted to live alone, and now he had Skywalker. He had never been so happy in his life and he didn't want this to stop, but he knew that Split Face was coming with a lot of killers.

Should they run and hide to keep their happiness? Where could he and Skywalker go? Was there any place that was free and safe for a man with some Negro blood and Indian blood to live in this country? If he was a man, and acted like a man and stood up for himself and his family, there would always be people in this country that would try to put him down and make him bow and scrape and become no man at all.

What about Mexico? He'd always heard and the word came from reliable people that in Mexico a man of color, whether black or Indian, received equal treatment. Although life in Mexico was a life of peasants and poor people for most Mexicans, they weren't mistreated because of their color. Skywalker was Mexican, and maybe they could head for Mexico and live a safer life. He knew if he stayed at his fort that there would be one battle after another. If Split Face came and he defeated Split Face and ran him off, there would be others. The US Army would not stay in the South forever. At some point, they would go back North and then through law or by fear and intimidation, the Southern whites would try to put people of color in their place, which was at the bottom.

When he first came to the area and built the fort, he was willing to stay there by himself and die by himself if necessary, but he now had Skywalker and he wanted a family. Could anyone raise a child when the future would be hard for a person with Negro blood to hold his or her head up high and live like an equal and free person? Would his kids inherit this fear and live without pride?

As he entered his valley, he saw his fine horses grazing between the banks of the encircling Little Beaver Creek and felt pride in his herd. He had come a long way in two years. How long would this place last for him and for Skywalker? He rode into the compound and immediately saw a beautiful black horse with a Spanish saddle covered with silver. At once, Mondo knew he had either a rich Mexican visitor or a rich rancher with Mexican blood from Southern Texas. As he walked in the door, Skywalker jumped up and gave him a hug and turned and introduced him to a tall, nice-looking Mexican man about forty years old that was dressed in splendid clothes. There was just about as much silver on his pants, belt, and shirt as there was on his saddle.

"Mondo, look who showed up. This is my third cousin from Mexico, Juan Gonzalez. Word reached Mexico through the US Cavalry that I was alive and living in Indian Territory, and he rode up to take me home."

Fear jolted through Mondo. He hesitated before he reached out to take the hand of Juan Gonzalez, who was facing him with a big smile. Mondo did not smile back. The fancy-dressed Mexican spoke English well.

"Thank you for saving my cousin. Everyone in the family was surprised that she was still alive. It's been over three years since the Kiowas captured her and wiped out her entire family. It's an unbelievable story. God is great."

Mondo glanced at Skywalker, and she had an undecided look on her face. He could already tell she was thinking about going home.

Mondo straightened and growled. "Why have you come this far to take her back?"

Skywalker patted him on the shoulder and forced a weak smile, "Let's have a seat and Juan will tell you the whole story. It's really unbelievable that word got back to what's left of my family, and there sure has been a lot happening in my country."

Mondo glared at Skywalker when she mentioned that Mexico was still her country. He had assumed that her country would be his country. He thought it strange that he'd been thinking about going to Mexico right before this distant cousin showed up. He sat down but said nothing.

Juan Gonzalez smiled at Mondo and spoke. "Yes, sir. Good things are happening in Mexico. The republic has returned. The French Army came in and made a Frenchman the king of Mexico during your Civil War. But he didn't last. Juarez is back in power, and the people of Mexico are free and running their country again. Juarez is building schools and bringing Mexico up to the standards equal to a modern country in Europe."

"What's that got to do with Skywalker?" asked Mondo.

"She's a big part of this. After her family was wiped out, some of her other cousins took over her father's property. He had lots of land, and their ownership is questionable since Skywalker is still alive. Juarez guaranteed a strong federal court where Skywalker will be able to receive justice and regain her family's lands. And I intend to take her back and help her do just that."

Juan Gonzales reached over and laid his hand on top of Skywalker's and gave her a big, sweet smile. Mondo reached down and removed his hand and leaned over close to the Mexican.

"She's not going anywhere without me. She's my woman now, and I don't care if you are her cousin. You don't touch my woman without permission from me."

Skywalker glared at Mondo and shook her head in disgust. "Ownership! Men always think they own women. Mondo, we get along great, but I think of it as working together equally and you don't own me."

Juan Gonzales leaned back in his chair and looked at both Mondo and then at Skywalker and then back at Mondo. "Are you married, senior? Out here among the Indians, it's my understanding that social customs and legal requirements of marriage are many times ignored. I'll assure you that this lady is a woman from a fine family and a religious family, and whatever has happened to her because of her kidnapping means nothing. She's a lady of considerable wealth, education, and high standing in our community. Even though you may have saved her life, you have no legal rights to prevent her from going where she needs to return. If she hadn't been stolen away by the Kiowas, she would never have considered talking to you let alone ever marrying someone of your class, at least not in our society."

Mondo's chair flew back as he stood up and drew his gun and put the barrel on the nose of Juan Gonzales. There was dead silence as the two men glared at each other and Skywalker shouted, "Mondo, put that gun down. That won't solve anything. We'll discuss this matter later."

Bear Chaser and Savanah walked into the cabin and halted. Bear Chaser stepped forward and put his hand on Mondo's shoulder.

"Slow down, son. This man is a guest in your house. You remember when you were a guest of Storm and that Chickasaw Killer insulted the band by attacking you. Please learn to act proper, like an Indian should. This man didn't come to harm you. This man came to help Skywalker, and he's come a long ways. Let's sit down and talk about this."

Mondo looked at his father and then placed the pistol in his holster and sat down. They all pulled up chairs and sat around the table. For a few moments, nobody said anything. They just looked at each other wondering who would say something first. Bear Chaser looked over at Juan Gonzales.

"As I told you, Mr. Gonzales, Savanah and I are staying at Mondo's for a while because of possible trouble. I'm his father. What do you plan to do for Skywalker if she goes with you?"

"I want Skywalker to retrieve the fortune that has been stolen from her. I think she can get it back, and it amounts to a lot of money and land."

"How much money and land do you have yourself?" asked Bear Chaser.

"Oh, I do fine, but I feel sure that Maria will compensate me for my time and effort if she recovers her fortune. She'll be very rich. And she will able to choose her husband from the many eligible bachelors that will be able to take care of her land."

"And I suppose you're available," asked Mondo.

"I am single. That is correct. And Maria will need a strong man to look after her and her future children. I am such a man. But there are others for her to choose from. She will need to marry someone equal to her own social standing."

Mondo leaned in close to Skywalker. "See there, Skywalker. He's trying to take you back to Mexico so you can get your fortune and then turn it over to him."

Mondo looked back to Juan Gonzales. "By the way, Mr. Gonzalez, does the law in Mexico allow the husband to have total control over the wife's property on marriage?"

"Of course. A strong man must protect his wife and their property." Juan glanced at Skywalker and saw her glaring back at him and cleared his throat. "However, I have no intention of exercising any control over Maria's property, unless she wants me to and unless, of course, we get married."

Mondo laughed. "Skywalker, do you think this guy would have ridden all the way up here if he didn't think he could get his hands on your land and money? By the way, Mr. Gonzales, I assume that you didn't get any of that property that Skywalker's father owned before he died. I guess some of your relatives cheated you as well as Skywalker. I bet if you'd have gotten your share of the spoils after her family was wiped out, you wouldn't be up here at all."

Juan Gonzales swelled up and shook his head no. "I'm not that kind of man. I'm a gentleman. I did not steal her family's property, but I do have some ruthless cousins on my mother's side of the family that would steal from a blind man. I came here with good intentions, and I intend to leave with my cousin, Maria and you, sir, cannot stop me."

Bear Chaser laid his hand on Gonzales's arm. "I think you should realize that you are not in Mexico. I don't think that people care whether there's a French king or some Mexican named Juarez who runs your country. You're a long ways from home, and I don't think you should act like you have any control over people here. There's only one person that's going to make a decision about your offer, and that's Skywalker. And if she decides she's going to stay, she'll stay, and you, sir, will go."

"Why would she stay here?" said Gonzales. "I mean, you're right out in the middle of a bunch of wild Indians in a little old broken-down fort, and all this Mondo got is a few horses. If she goes with me, she'll have thousands of acres of land and much gold. She'll have an army of tough men that she could call on. Why would she stay with an Indian after what the Indians did to her? And this Indian has Negro blood in him. That's not good in this country, and she'd be at the top of her class in Mexico. To me, there's no choice involved here. She'd be crazy to stay here, and it would be best for her to go and everyone here knows it."

This time Mondo didn't rare up and pull his gun. He just looked at Skywalker. Skywalker looked back at him. He waited for an answer, but she said nothing. Finally, she spoke.

"I want to talk to both of you alone. There's some questions I want to ask my cousin and there's some questions I want to ask Mondo. Juan, let's step outside."

The two rose and walked out of the cabin, and Mondo felt like he had been shot in the heart. She acted like she would leave him.

He thought she loved him and any decision by her would include him. If she decided to go to Mexico, would he go with her?

Mondo got up and paced the cabin as Bear Chaser and Savanah watched him. It seemed like forever, but after a few minutes, Skywalker returned to the cabin and Juan Gonzales waited outside.

"Mondo will you go back with me and help me look into this matter? I don't want to leave you, but I don't want to stay here and die when Split Face brings his killers down on your fort. If you go along with me, then I think I can maintain some control over what happens. You're right, this Juan Gonzales would not have come all this way to fetch me unless he thought I could help him get his hands on my family's money either by rewarding him big time or marrying him. If I go back by myself, I'll just be absorbed into the family by a bunch of men relatives and forced to do what they say. With you, I'd be able to keep my independence and live a life where I can control what I do and what's being done to me. Will you go back with me?"

"Go back with you as what, your bodyguard? I can't speak Spanish. Do you want me or do you want my gun? To tell you the truth, I was even thinking about going to Mexico to get away from Split Face. But I wasn't thinking about going back with you as bodyguard or servant or some kind of lover so you could fit in to the Mexican society that you left a long time ago. You know damn well, I'd never fit in. They would never let me in, and for you to get anything, you'd have to get it without me sharing it with you as an equal."

"No, that's not right. What if we married before we went back? Then you would be my legal husband."

"Yeah. And you'd sure fit in married to a man of color and an American Indian. That's high society, I'm sure. No, I'm not going back like that. You've got to decide whether you are going to be with me or you are going to be with him and return to the life you once knew."

"You're trying to make me decide whether to go back and pick up a bunch of money and land or stay here and fight with Split Face and all his gang of killers. Do you think that's fair? Just because you swore that you'd never leave this place doesn't mean that I should die here with you. Mondo, you don't own me, and I don't own you, but you are acting like you won't sacrifice anything at all for my good."

Mondo stared at her for a while and then turned and started toward the door. "I'm going to check on the horses. You decide. When I come back, you'll either be here or you won't. You know damn well I can't fit in to your way of life back in Mexico. If you love me, you'll stay with me, and we will fight whatever comes together."

Mondo walked out of the cabin and mounted his horse and rode out to check his herd. He stayed out there for a couple of hours but kept his eyes on the compound. After a while, he saw a lone Mexican rider leave the compound and head south. Mondo felt relief and love for Skywalker and again thought to himself about how he was going to protect her from Split Face and the rest of the people that hated anybody with Negro blood.

Chapter 49

The loss of blood from the wounds that Maboola suffered made him weaker each day that he rode toward Mondo's place. He tried to stop the bleeding and was unable to close the bullet holes in his shoulder and thigh. Pain didn't bother Maboola, but growing weaker couldn't be stopped. As he continued south toward Mondo's, he slipped into a delirious state where he remembered the past and remembered the beatings he got when he was a slave. Each time he ran away, he was caught and his foreman would apply the whip. Before he was fourteen years old, he had tried to escape six times and had been beaten so bad that he almost died three times. The desire to run away, to be on his own, kept him going no matter how many times he suffered the whip. Maboola got so that he could put his mind on other things and forget the lashes no matter how deep the whip bit into his back. He would dream about his life back in Africa, of roaming the country as his own boss and not having to take orders from the white man. Maboola had once felt free. When he turned sixteen years old, he had made up his mind that he was either going to be free or die trying to get there. That's how he felt as his horse took him South.

Maboola was about thirty miles from Mondo's fort near the Washita River when he passed out and fell from his horse. He laid there unconscious, and even when thunder, lightning, and hard rain began to hit him, Maboola didn't wake up. Frightened by the lightning and thunder, his horse ran off, and the black giant lay dying as the storm rolled over him.

The Comanche warrior called Storm had been lost until the rain came and then he saw his way clear as if he had lived in this area forever. Where others went blind in this weather, Storm saw with clarity. He was south of the Washita about three miles when he came upon Maboola's horse. He immediately recognized the animal as the one described by the Cheyennes ridden by the big black giant who had been proclaimed a God by the Cheyennes north in Kansas. He also knew that this big warrior was a friend of Mondo's. Storm took hold of Maboola's horse and started backtracking through the rain. He saw the tracks as if it was a clear day. The Great Spirit again helped Storm to see all things and know all things as if Storm was a God himself in bad weather.

Storm found Maboola unconscious, and it took him a while to get the big man slung over Maboola's own horse. By the time Storm reached Mondo's fort, the sun was out and the sky had cleared. As he rode toward the gate, Mondo rode out to meet him. Mondo recognized Maboola and jumped from his horse and examined the body and found that Maboola was barely alive. He looked up at Storm. "These look like bullet wounds, and you don't have a rifle. At first I thought that you were the one that took him during the storm. That's the only way you could get Maboola. Where did you find him?"

"I found his horse first. I back tracked and found him. He's in pretty bad shape. He's lost a lot of blood and he's real weak. We had better get him inside."

As they started toward the compound, Skywalker and Savanah came running out. They both recognized the big man slung over the horse. Maboola's size seemed to make the horse carrying him look like a small colt. His feet and head were nearly touching the ground as he lay across his mount. Bear Chaser came riding in from the south where he had been checking on the herd.

Mondo looked at Storm. "What are you doing down in our part of the country?"

"Oh, I just came to check up on you. Besides, I'm kind of hiding myself."

Mondo glanced down at the blond-haired scalp that was hanging from Storm's belt.

"Is the reason you're hiding the fact that you've got a blond scalp?"

"Yeah, I was with a group of Comanches and Kiowas that killed some of Custer's men after Custer murdered over a hundred Cheyenne, mostly women and children of Black Kettle's band. Custer left some of his men behind and took off. We killed them many times real good. I came to your house after that, but I didn't tell you about me being involved in the attack and I hid my only scalp."

"Well, you should have stayed out in the Texas Panhandle and hid in the canyon with your band. We've got lots of troops around here. They are even building a fort over at Medicine Bluff, and the military activity from Fort Arbuckle east of here and Fort Washita northwest of here is heavy. This is no place to hide."

"I wanted to see how you were doing. I've heard rumors all the way out to my country that a whole bunch of white killers out of Texas are coming after you. Is that true?"

"That's what I hear too. As you recall there's a crazy rich white man that is in love with Savanah and wants her back real bad. Savanah still doesn't want to go. She and my dad have been living together lately. I'm not sure what Maboola's going to say about that if he lives through these last bullet holes."

Storm nodded in agreement. "I'll stay around a while. I'd like to see what happens. Besides, I've got a girl who lives with the peaceful Comanches, so I'll be in and out. I want to be here when those white devils from Texas come."

When they reached the cabin, both men jumped down and pulled Maboola from his horse and carried him into the house. As soon as they laid him down on the cot, Skywalker and Savanah were all over him, tearing off clothes, cleaning his wounds, and placing bandages on him to stop the bleeding. Maboola looked almost green as he moaned and then faded away into darkness.

Savanah and Skywalker cared for him day and night. His shoulder wound smelled awful, and it looked like gangrene had set in. Maboola was unconscious and moaned in his sleep and mumbled Savanah's name as he struggled to stay alive. Savanah was at his bedside around the clock and changed and dressed his wounds after cleaning them with boiling water three or four times a day. Bear Chaser and Mondo did everything they could to assist the women in taking care of Maboola.

Savanah's devotion to healing Maboola made it clear to Bear Chaser that she hadn't gotten over the giant. Bear Chaser had fallen in love with Savanah, but he knew that life changed, and this was something that he would have to deal with as soon as Maboola recovered. He was old enough and mature enough to know that it would be better for Maboola to live than to die. Savanah would have to choose between them, but if Maboola died she would always feel guilty about being with Bear Chaser. Bear Chaser didn't get to talk to Savanah about his feelings because she seemed to be caring for Maboola with all her waking time. Bear Chaser knew she cared deeply for both of them. He had learned to accept life as it came and not expect to control those things that would be controlled by others. He even admitted to himself that since Maboola was nearer Savanah's age and she wanted children, Maboola would probably be better for Savanah.

At the arrival of Maboola and the need to help him, Mondo had put off talking to Skywalker about her Mexican relative. At first he was afraid to talk about whether she was going or staying, and he let things ride. She was still here, but he didn't know for how long. She never told him that she was not leaving and even though her cousin had left, Mondo still worried about her deciding to return to Mexico. Also, she didn't like to sit in an enclosed fort and wait for the armed outlaws to come for them. Mondo knew if she could go back and establish her inheritance, she would be a high-class wealthy Mexican woman with a very soft and easy life. He couldn't offer her more than a dangerous place to stay in the middle of land that was surrounded by turmoil. The only people that really wanted him to stay in this area were the ex-slaves that lived on Wildhorse Creek about fifty miles east. The blacks were surrounded, outnumbered, and resented by all the Indians and the whites that kept pouring into the Chickasaw Nation after the Civil War. Mondo knew that he was here to stay, but he wasn't for sure that he had a right to ask Skywalker to join him. One hot, dry evening in July, Skywalker cornered Mondo and said she wanted to talk. As usual, she was direct and to the point, and things changed at once.

"I'm pregnant," she said as she sat down on a log outside the cabin.

Mondo had thought about all the different angles and the problems he had to face, but for some reason, he had never thought about Skywalker getting pregnant. He was speechless. At first, joy went through him and he seemed to have a good feeling about having a child, but then he realized that he was keeping not only Skywalker but their baby in a very dangerous place. He felt real fear for the first time. He'd always been a little afraid about dying himself, and then when Skywalker came along, he was afraid more because there finally was a person in his life who meant more to him than himself. Now all of a sudden, there was a third little person. So with mixed joy and fear, Mondo finally smiled and nodded his head in approval.

"That's great." He walked over and kissed her on the forehead. "I guess we'll have to get you out of here as soon as possible. You and our baby can't live here until this thing with Jones is settled."

"Settled? What do you mean settled? It's never going to be settled. There's going to be a lot more Jones's in the world. Do you really think we can bring up a son or daughter around here? You have to come back to Mexico with me."

"Do you really think I would fit in down there? Look, you lived with those people and that high-class society, and how many people with Negro blood were members of that society?"

"Mexico is part-Indian almost exclusively. There's very few Spanish families that don't have Indian blood. And Mexico allowed slaves to come and be free during the Civil War and after the Civil War. They are not as prejudiced as the people are north of the Rio Grande. They would not try to kill you. You might not fit in to high society, but those upper-class people don't let anybody fit in if they weren't born in that class. You wouldn't be any different than if I'd married some Mexican peasant. They wouldn't accept a peasant as a husband, and they probably won't accept you. What difference does that make? You never were accepted by anyone. You ran your own life and you were your own man and that's one of the things I love about you. You don't really let others control your life if they don't accept you. But you've got to come back with me for the sake of our child. Our child will have a chance, and we will both be alive. Our child will be much better off if we both stay alive. You know that and you know that if you stay here, eventually you're going to be killed. Just like you told me about Maboola. He can't live in this world and neither can you. The whites have to take 'the man' out of any nonwhite. Why do you think they call everybody boy? You've heard them talk. All black men are called 'boy', and mostly Indians are referred to as a child or some heathen or savage when they come in contact with the white world. It's not the question of whether we should go. It's the question of when and how soon. And you know very well that we better leave now or we may never be able to leave."

Mondo sat alongside her and put his arm around her shoulders. They looked into each other's eyes and didn't say anything for a few seconds. He finally smiled.

"Do you really think that I could be happy in Mexico? You're right. I don't give a damn what they think about me anywhere. It's what I think about myself that counts. I've been pushed around and mistreated most of my life, and when I got out of the army, I said that was never going to happen again. I told myself that I was coming here and that I was going to stay here and I was going to die here if necessary. And since that time, things have been lucky for me. I've never been happier in all my life, but I'm afraid that this will end just as soon as I tuck my tail in and run with you down to Mexico. Then I would feel like a boy. A man stays and fights for what is his and when he becomes a coward, then he no longer can live with himself or anyone."

Skywalker sadly shook her head and looked back into Mondo's eyes. "Then I'm going to leave. I've got to do this for our baby. My cousin is waiting for me at Fort Worth. He said he would give me thirty days to get down there."

"Did you know you were pregnant when your cousin got here?"

"Yes. But I had to settle things with you. I knew I was going. I was hoping that I could get you to go."

Mondo breathed a sigh of disgust and then answered her, "There's two things that can happen. When I finally get to where I know that I can stay and nobody is going to run me off, then I'll come after you in Mexico. Or secondly, you go and have the baby in Mexico, and I'll send word when it settles down around here and you can come back. If I'm able to pound out a peaceful existence here in this compound, then you and the baby can come live with me. Civilization is going to come to this country someday and I don't know how I will end up, but we will see how well an Indian with Negro blood fits here in Indian Territory. If it looks okay and you come back here, we can still make a decision to go to Mexico later if people look down on our child. If we don't have a good place to raise our child without the child being hated because of the color of his skin, then I'll go back to Mexico with you."

"Are you saying that you want me to go and you're going to stay?"

"I don't see any other way. Now that you are pregnant, I don't want you anywhere around here when those bounty hunters come and I can't leave and face myself each day."

"You don't love me or the child enough to abandon your male pride? It's time you grew up and decided that our family is more important than your own feelings of worth. Just as soon as Maboola gets well enough to get around, then I'm going to leave for Mexico. And that has to be within two weeks because my cousin is going to be leaving Fort Worth in two weeks."

Mondo bowed his head and swallowed. "I guess that's it." He got up, turned, and walked over to his horse, mounted, and rode out the gate. For some reason, he couldn't stand himself. He wondered if he was letting his past treatment stand in the way of making a good decision for his future. It was as if his mistreatment by society had turned him into a person who couldn't make a decision based on love. If that was the case, he was no better than Maboola who let his hatred rule his life and ruin his life to the point that everyone knew he was going to be dead soon.

CHAPTER 50

S TORM WAS IN and out of Mondo's compound, spending some time observing how other people lived and riding off to stay all night with the peaceful Comanches around the new fort being built on the east end of the Wichita Mountains. Storm knew that the bunch gathered at Mondo's was not a typical white man settlement. He knew very little about non-Comanche life and was trying to figure out the differences between Indian tribes and how the various tribes dealt with the white invasion.

Over the last thirty years, the Panhandle Comanches had seen the influx of different kinds of people. The Spanish and Mexicans had been known by the Antelope band for a long time. The Comanches had raided Mexico for a hundred years and captured many Mexicans and made many of them part of the tribe. The first blacks as a group were seen when the black troops came to Indian Territory within the last year. The white Indians, or the mixed-breeds, made up most of the ruling leaders in the Chickasaw Nation. There was a lot Storm didn't know about the mixture of people who were closing in on his Antelope band.

Storm also liked to observe what was going on in the compound as the people living there tried to get along and live together as an unusual mixture of color and ancestors. All but the Indians of the plains were a strange group of people to Storm. The Comanche felt a tension between Bear Chaser and Savanah that had something to do with Maboola.

Storm also observed Mondo and Skywalker with amused interest. Something was going on between them, and even though it was obvious that they cared a great deal for each other, something stood between them. Since Storm understood very little English, he couldn't keep up with the conversations, but not being able to speak the language allowed him to observe their body language and facial expressions in order to interpret their feelings. Therefore, not having to listen helped him to keep track of feelings between the parties more than someone who spoke the words.

Storm felt the strain in the rock cabin. He knew that something was going to have to give. He couldn't stay long in the compound before he got nervous and had to ride away and spend the night with the peaceful Comanches and find a willing young woman to get his mind off the conflicts at Mondo's. It seemed to Storm that the people at Mondo's seemed to take small problems and blow them out of proportion. Instead of accepting things as they were, his friends seemed to live under some expectation that wasn't realistic. It was pretty basic as far as this Comanche was concerned. If Skywalker was about to have Mondo's child, then Skywalker should stay with Mondo. Why would she want to go back to Mexico? After Mondo explained what the problem was between Skywalker and himself, Storm just couldn't understand it. And when Storm found out that Maboola had finally realized the truth by observing Savanah with Bear Chaser, Maboola seemed so upset that he couldn't wait to regain his strength and get out of bed and take on Bear Chaser. Even though they were both great warriors and friends, they appeared to let a woman come between them.

This happened in Comanche villages also, but it was never or hardly ever settled with the killing of one of the warriors. The Comanches needed warriors too bad. The families settled the disagreement over the ownership of a wife with property exchanged or the women ran off with one of the other men and they joined another band. No killings.

Besides the problems in the compound between man and woman, Mondo also explained to Storm the problem with the coming attack from the white men who hated people of color. Storm understood this problem because the white Texans had attacked the roving bands of Comanches for years. Pure whites hated darker skin. Among Indians, color was not a problem. The Cheyenne had been the Comanches' big enemies in the North until about twenty-four years prior when the Comanches and Cheyennes had made peace. Also, the Apaches had agreed with the Comanches not to kill each other about thirty years ago. However, the Tonkawa, the Caddo, the Osage, the Pawnee, and the Utes in Colorado had always been the Comanches' enemies; but most of all the white Texas Rangers were the killers of Comanches. Storm did not like these Texas whites and decided he wanted to be here when the Texans hit Mondo's fort.

Maboola was getting stronger, and madder every day. Skywalker and Savanah continued to treat him, and his wounds were healing. Since he was still too weak to take on Bear Chaser, he decided to confront Savanah. One morning when she walked in, he sat up in bed and looked her square in the eyes.

"Did you think that I wasn't coming back?"

"I wasn't sure. I hoped that you weren't harmed, but I knew that there were a lot of white people that wanted you dead."

Maboola reached out and took her hand and eased her onto his cot. "I don't think we can find a place where we could live in peace in this country. We probably ought to go to Canada. But I did come back for you. I think you were surprised to see me return."

"I was surprised and happy that you returned. I have not forgotten what you have done for me. I care a lot about you."

Maboola frowned. "But you also care a lot for Bear Chaser, don't you? I know this. I can see it in his eyes, and I can see it in your smile. Has he taken my place?"

"Nobody could take your place. He has been good to me. I like to be with him. I had to think about my future. Are we going to stay here and fight the killers? Are we going to go off together and run for the rest of our lives? I could settle with Bear Chaser and have a pretty good life in this Chickasaw Nation. It's not that I care more for Bear Chaser, but I think he offers a better life for me. You and I both know that there's a lot of armed men that want you dead. You and I both know that you're some kind of symbol to the white that fear the ex-slaves will want to punish their ex-masters. You are the one that represents the great white fear. The whites fear they will get what they deserve if the ex-slaves remember every whiplash and return in the dark of the night and cut the throats of every ex-slave owner. That's what you represent to the whites, and they know that they have to kill you or other ex-slaves will remember what was done to them and will follow your example and turn on the whites with vengeance."

Maboola shook his head and smiled, "You've come a long ways since you were the scared little slave girl that I found in North Texas. You only knew how to playact as a white woman. You've been watching and listening to Skywalker. What you say has a lot of truth to it. However, they haven't killed me yet. We can make a dash for it. If we can get to Canada or even go to Mexico, we'll have a lot better life than in this country. It's my understanding that Skywalker plans to leave for Mexico as soon as I am well. Let's go with her. I've heard stories that they treat ex-slaves a heck of a lot better than around here. I like Mondo a lot, and I would like to stay and help him, but I think you're right. We don't have a chance. There's enough ex-rebel gunslingers that will keep coming, and they're going to finally burn this place down and kill everybody in it. I wouldn't mind dying side by side with Mondo as long as we took about twenty or thirty black haters with us. But I think I have changed a little bit. I want to be with you. Now, the question is, do you want to go with me to Mexico or do you want to stay here with Bear Chaser? I don't think I want to live if I don't live with you. I don't want to fight Bear Chaser, but if you turn to him, then I probably can't stop myself from getting after Mondo's father."

Before she could answer, Bear Chaser walked into the cabin and looked over and saw Savanah sitting on the bed with Maboola and they were holding hands and looking at each other like two love birds. Bear Chaser started toward them, stopped, and then turned around and walked out. He really had nothing to say. He was old enough to know that it was Savanah's choice whether she stayed with him or with Maboola. She was herself and finally old enough and wise enough to make her choice. He was not going to fight Maboola over Savanah. He cared a lot about her, but he cared about his own life and Maboola's too. Maboola was no one to fight, and even if Maboola had been short and skinny, Bear Chaser had learned that as far as women were concerned, they eventually made the final choice, not the men. If you forced a woman to live with you when she didn't want to, life could be hell. He had seen this many times before in a male-dominated society. He knew he could survive and go on without her, but it sure wouldn't be as nice.

Mondo hardly noticed that there was tension between Bear Chaser, Maboola, and Savanah. Mondo was worried about his own problems. He knew that Skywalker meant to leave and that she was a stubborn woman, and she acted like her final decision was already made and there was no more to talk about. She wasn't going to hang around and take the chance of losing their child when the killers came.

Mondo was torn between leaving with her to Mexico and living as man and wife south of the Rio Grande where mixed races were treated better or staying here and fighting to keep his place and to die like a man. Mondo knew that if he left and ran, that he would feel like a coward the rest of his life. A half-breed with Negro blood couldn't act like a coward and live with any pride. When he had come to this place, he had made up his mind that he was going to stay or die. So far, he had been lucky and he had gotten a lot of help from people that he did not consider as being his friends when he first came. His father had definitely helped him and had convinced Ten Bears to keep the Comanches from killing him. Then there was Mick, who helped him build a ranch and sell horses and who assisted him against all odds, but Mick was gone and Mick was living in the half-white Chickasaw world. Even though Mick was close and still a friend, Mondo didn't know whether he could count on Mick to help him when Split Face came. One thing was sure, if Maboola got well and Storm stayed, they would have a pretty good fighting force against a whole lot of ex-rebs. No matter what Savanah decided, Mondo was sure that Maboola would stay and fight and fight to the death. His father would stay also. He had begun to appreciate and love his father more and more, and Mondo knew he could depend on him. However, Mondo felt an obligation to Savanah too. Even if they all died, Mondo didn't want the bounty hunters to take Savanah back to Jones, who was financing this whole raid. Mondo knew that unless it was really bad weather, he probably wouldn't get great help from Storm. The Comanche Indian lived by his medicine and would fight by his medicine. Storm believed that the gods allowed him to fight and win any time it was storming but believed he was real vulnerable if he disobeyed his medicine and fought during a clear day. Therefore, Mondo didn't know whether he could rely on Storm all the time or not. Mondo would almost have to pray for rain just to get Storm ready to go against the white killers.

Mondo knew he was a hell of a lot better off than being alone. He had some good fighters, and he had some good people that would die for principle. And he knew that the whites better bring some cannons, and that they better be tough as hell and good shots. Mondo figured that Maboola, Bear Chaser, Storm, and himself were good enough to take on at least six or eight men easy. Skywalker and Savanah could take care of their share too. The more he thought about it, the more he realized that realistically without more help, they could kill a lot of whites but couldn't win if twenty or more ex-rebs with cannons came to wipe them out.

Mondo thought he needed a warning system to get the message out for help. He needed to talk to Hudson Greer so that the ex-slaves that lived along Wildhorse Creek might come in time. Mondo also knew he needed to check with his friend, Omar, the sergeant of the black soldiers at the new fort being built near Medicine Bluff. If the sergeant could slip away and bring some cannons, then Mondo would be able to fight the ex-rebs on equal terms. Mondo knew that the army would not take sides and he knew that the white officers would not order an attack on the whites since there was no legal right for Mondo to be on what the army thought was Comanche land. The US Army had told Mondo to move. Also, if Mick would come and bring a bunch of his friends that had settled in the Chickasaw Nation, there might be enough men to hold off an ex-rebel raid for a while.

If it wasn't for the fact that Skywalker was having his child and Mondo wanted to survive for her and that child, he would have fought them in the fort with the people staying there now. To have a good chance to win and be able to hold his own and chase the whites back across Red River, Mondo decided that he needed to ask for help, and he needed to see who his friends really were and find out who was willing to help him at the risk of their own lives. So Mondo rode off first to the west toward Medicine Bluff to find Omar Culberson and check with the buffalo soldiers that lived about fifteen miles from his compound. It had been a long time since Mondo had asked for help from anyone, but this was life and death for him, his love, and his future child. This was not for Mondo alone; this was for Skywalker and his child-to-be. Mondo knew that if he didn't get help, they would all be killed if he kept his family here. If he got enough help, maybe he could convince Skywalker to stay.

CHAPTER 51

Mondo found Omar Culberson in his tent near the rock fortress the army was building south of Medicine Bluff. The black troops were constructing the fort right off Cache Creek up against the Wichita Mountains, about fifteen miles west of Mondo's compound. Omar stood up with a big smile and extended his hand.

"Glad you came by. I had a few things that I wanted to tell you. How are things going back at your place?"

"Well, Maboola is recovering. I guess you heard about him."

"Yeah. Word's out. It's my understanding that the Comanche called Storm found him and brought him to your place about half-dead."

"Yeah, but he's hard to kill. Skywalker, with the help of Savanah, is doctoring him up real good. He's coming along fine. He's already moving around kind of slow and easy. I think in about a week or two, he'll be almost back to half strength, which is stronger than most men. What did you want to tell me?"

"I've heard a bunch of rumors. Word's out that a big party of outlaws are heading to your place. I even went and talked to the lieutenant about trying to give you some help."

"What did he say?"

"He still says you're trespassing and you're on Comanche land and that we are supposed to keep white intruders out and protect Comanches from invaders."

"Well, I'm Chickasaw. Aren't the troops supposed to protect other Indians besides Comanches, and what do you mean protect Comanches? The army's still fighting the Comanches."

"That's just it. We're still having lots of trouble with the Kiowas and Comanches, and there are troops running all over the place. That's why we are building this fort. We want to set up right down in the middle of those warriors that won't come in and live in peace. The lieutenant says you're in Comanche territory and you aren't supposed to be there, and therefore, we can't protect you from those black haters south of the Red River."

"Well, I still say that I'm living on Chickasaw land. The army is supposed to protect the Chickasaws from the Comanches, so why can't the lieutenant protect this Chickasaw from those ex-rebels?"

"He said it's not in his orders. He's talked to the higher-ups, and the general says that you have no right to be where you are, and your fort is causing trouble with the Comanches and we have to try to settle those Comanches down."

"I get along with Comanches. Most have no problem with me, and the Kiowas aren't too bad. At least they are not raiding us. They're leaving us alone. I just can't figure out why the army wants to leave me out there undefended when word is out all over the place that there's a bunch of killers coming up from Texas that want to wipe us out."

"Politics, I guess, Mondo. I don't understand it either, and if I could get away, I would help you. But the man knows how I feel about it and the rest of the white officers know how all of the black troops feel about it. We all want to help you. There are no black officers, and I don't want to be kicked out of the army. I like it, and it's one of the few steady-paying jobs for Negroes, and I sure don't want to lose this job because I disobeyed orders."

"Well, I understand that. I don't blame you. I'm worried about the cannons the raiders are supposed to be bringing. You've got cannons here. If they bring cannons, the walls of my fort are going down. Is there any way you can slip off with a cannon and with some of your men that know how to fire it and come when you hear their cannons are blasting away at my place? I'm sure you can hear the cannon fire from where my place is located."

"I don't think I can come. We've talked about it, and there's a lot of my men who want to go and there's maybe some that will go anyway. They know what's going on here. They know that so far, you and Maboola are the only ones who have stood up to those Negro haters. You're the only one along with Maboola that has told those bad whites to go to hell. There's nobody else really trying to put a stop to the midnight raids and the Ku Klux Klan and all that going on in the South and here in Indian Territory. The Yankee troops try to hold them off, but there's not enough troops. And the KKK is roaming around at night in robes, and all the whites say they don't know who's doing it, but everybody really knows. You know what I mean? Nobody will tell who the night riders are."

"I've heard that's what is going on in Texas and all through the South. But these killers are coming across the Red River for money because a rich man wants his ex-slave on his bed. The troops are supposed to maintain peace in Indian Territory, and there's not going to be any peace for us in the compound when those KKK-type people hit our fort."

"I'll tell you what. I'll go back to the lieutenant, but I think it's no use. He's determined to stay out of this fight. He says he's too busy with the Comanches and he can't let a bunch of black troops get in trouble by trying to protect you. He's afraid that Washington will get rid of black troops if we try to help you. He's determined not to interfere and that's what he's been ordered to do."

"Let me tell you what I think, Omar. If it's true that we are the only resistence or people standing up to the KKK that is causing fear in all ex-slaves and those type of haters are lynching ex-slaves for any reason at all, then I think that if we don't get together and stand up as a race, then just as soon as the Yankee army goes home, we're all in for hell."

Omar nodded his head in agreement. "I think you're right. I don't think the Yankee troops will stay in the South for more than five or six years longer. At some point, they're going to let each state in the South run its own state government. And if there is no organization protecting ex-slaves, then the police and sheriffs of the South and all the crazy whites who hate black people are going to turn against us and make it impossible for any black person to live with any kind of freedom and without fear down in the South."

"Of course you're right, and we both know it. That's why I want you to try to come to my aid. We can't hold out by ourselves, and if we don't work together, then nobody is going to look out for any man of color. All those righteous talking Yankees back east won't do a thing when the US troops are called back North. When the North politicians get as much money as they can from the South, they'll abandon this area and let the Negro suffer."

"Have you gone to the Wildhorse Creek settlement? There's some pretty tough ex-slaves living over there, and they've got guns and they can use them."

"That's where I'm going next. I'm going to go talk to Hudson Greer and see if he can send some people over to my place. The rumor is running wild through the countryside that those raiders are on their way and they will be here in the next week or two. If I don't get some help, then we'll get wiped out. Those Southern boys will take their loss of the war out on us. They couldn't beat the Yankees, but just as soon as the Yankees go back North, they'll start making the Negroes pay for the South's loss."

"I know that, and I'll see what I can do. I'll go back to the lieutenant, but I don't think he'll budge. I'll also talk to some of the troops. There's a few around here that might go no matter if they are court-martialed or not. It's just that I don't know whether we would have a chance even if I could talk eight or nine black men to ride with me when we hear the raiders fire their cannons."

Mondo stepped forward and shook Omar's hand. "Well, just keep us in mind. I'll hope that you can get away with some of your friends and bring a cannon without getting into a whole lot of trouble. And If I don't see you again, it's been good knowing you, and I wish you luck in the army."

With that, Mondo rode away from the construction site of the new fort and bypassed his compound and headed east. As he approached the wagon road of the Chisholm Trail, he stopped at Fitzpatrick's store. When he entered the store, he saw Mick sitting over by himself as if he had nothing to do.

Mondo walked over and shook Mick's hand and sat down. "Why are you sitting around doing nothing? Have you got your place so fixed up and working so good that all you have to do is sit around like a rich plantation owner?"

Mick smiled and shook his head no. "I just brought some horses down to leave with Fitzpatrick so we'll have more available for the cattle drives in case some of those trail drivers need more mounts. I'm glad I ran into you. I was just fixing to ride over to your compound. I heard some bad rumors when I got here. Some of the cowboys that came through a couple of hours ago said they saw an army of whites coming this way. Everybody thinks it's that bunch that's going to your place to get you, Maboola, and Savanah."

Mondo stood up and questioned, "You mean they're already on their way?"

"The cow punchers said they are camped out on the other side of the Red River. The cowboys said the raiders had a cannon and they were going to ferry the cannon across at Red River Station."

"Then they will be here by tomorrow afternoon," said Mondo. "I've got to ride like hell to Wildhorse Creek and see if I can get some help. How about you, Mick? Can I count on you?"

"Sure. Damn, I wish Red Granger was back from Abilene. He's due any time. He's the only other white man we can count on. His cowboys are mostly black, and they came through here a couple of months ago and are overdue on the way back to Texas. He said he would stop by when he passed back through. He's got some tough colored cowboys riding with him. I'll ride up the trail and look for them."

Mondo shook Mick's hand, and they both mounted up and went off in different directions. Mondo almost rode Tree Top down, but he was at Wildhorse Creek in about four hours. He saw Hudson Greer at once when he rode into the makeshift village that had a few buildings but mostly shacks and tents set up along both sides of the creek. He dismounted and walked over and shook Hudson Greer's hand.

"Looks like you rode hard," said Hudson, "I think I know why you're here. Rumors have been spreading all over the place. The river rats say there's a big raid coming from Texas and heading for your place."

"That's right, and they were spotted on the other side of the Red River a few hours ago. They'll be at my place by tomorrow and they've got a cannon. I need help, and I need help now. Do you think you've got some people that are willing to ride over to my compound and lend a hand?"

"There are a few that want to go, but most of them say we have no business going into Comanche territory or starting another war with white Texans who live on the other side of the Red River. Some say as soon as they get Savanah, they will leave us alone. Also, we have no real fight with the Comanches, and once we cross over to your place, we're probably on their land. Mondo, you've got to understand something. We've carved out a little community here, and most of the time the white people leave us alone. This is an all-black town and we are running it by ourselves. So far, we've been able to keep most trouble out of here. If we start going out and taking on white men or the Indians either one, and we leave this place to do battle, then the battle will come to us. That's the opinion of most people here. Now, I'm not so sure I agree with the majority's opinion, but that's the thinking. We've talked about this before, and you and I believe that if we don't all get together, white people are going to tear us apart especially after the Yankee troops leave. But most hope they will leave us alone if we leave them alone. I doubt it. I think we all have to stick together. We've got black troops over by your place, but they're run by whites. We ought to be able to get some help from some place. The Chickasaw tribe ain't treating us right, but they're not white, so they've got to deal with the Yankees too. This ain't a state. It's Indian Territory and we're located in the Chickasaw Nation, who fought for the South. So the Chickasaws have to walk quietly. The Chickasaw freedmen, the ex-slaves of the Chickasaw, have no status. The Yankee government is telling the Chickasaws to make them a member of the Chickasaw tribe, and the tribe is not going to do that. Ever. So we are kind of not existing. We're not a citizen of anything. We have no protection and no rights. I guarantee we've got some numbers. There was about a thousand Chickasaw freedmen, but there's been another two thousand ex-slaves come from Texas and Louisiana and other parts of the South. We can't split off in a bunch of little black communities and not stick together if we want any rights at all. We can make a difference if we pull together. Therefore, I want to help you. I want to take some people with me. I don't know how many will go, but I promise you that I'll be there even if it's me and me alone."

Mondo smiled and shook his hand. "Good. I knew I could count on at least one person from here. We'll need you and any-one else that you can bring. I've heard numbers as high as fifty but no lower than thirty of those raiders are coming, and we need all the help we can get. You alone are more than welcome, and if you can bring some more, that will be great. Right now, I've got to ride back to my place real fast. Hopefully, I'll see you soon."

"I hope I can bring a bunch from here. But you've got to understand, these people are ex-slaves. They've never made any tough decisions on their own and they've always been taught to be afraid of the white man. It's a big jump for them to decide to attack a bunch of armed whites. It takes time to build confidence and courage. Most are just learning to think on their own. Freedom and responsibility for one's self cannot be obtained overnight. It's a slow process. I'll bring as many as I can."

With that, Mondo mounted a fresh horse that was provided by Hudson Greer and rode as fast as he could back to the compound. As Mondo rode, he realized it was too late to make any decisions about going to Mexico. It was too late to try to make peace. It was too late to run. Now it was him trying to protect his wife and baby. It all came down to this fight and they couldn't lose. Within the next few days, everyone would be dead or there might be a future for his family.

CHAPTER 52

MONDO LOOKED AT Skywalker, and they both actually smiled. No decision would have to be made! They were here to stay, and they were here to fight. Bear Chaser and Savanah helped Maboola from the cabin, and the five people in the compound closed the gate, crawled up on the wall, and watched. The attackers formed up in the south of the valley and rode around the west side of Little Beaver Creek, pulling the cannon as if they had no worries about destroying the small fort.

Mondo felt a lump of fear knot in his stomach, not for himself but for Skywalker and their baby. There was no way out. He knew Skywalker would not agree to turn over Maboola and Savanah. It was too late to run. Then anger poured through him. Why did he have to defend his and Skywalker's life from ignorant whites who were bought off by a love-crazed rich man? If one had black in his blood, he seemed to fight fools alone, and Mondo needed help. Would there be anyone who would ride to their assistance? Government help would not be there. These killers could kill without interference from the law. And where were his black brothers or his red brothers? Was it fear, lack of learning through books, or just plain inexperience in making decisions or no leadership learning that kept the Negroes or Indians from coming together to defend their own kind? The white man knew enough to keep the black man separated and living in fear in order to continue to completely control them. Any organized effort by blacks for real independence and freedom had to be put down immediately with intimidation and leaders identified and hung on false charges of sexual advances toward white women. This was something that any reasonable smart person could understand. It took education to develop most leaders, and that was the big reason why whites so opposed education of the Negro. The few natural leaders who were born with the ability to understand human nature by observation, experience, and common sense had to be identified and eliminated. There were no Southern whites who would dare stand up to the great majority of all whites and try to prevent the total control of all blacks.

All five watched the perfect military formation as the attackers rode along the west bank of Beaver Creek.

"Look at those rebs," said Mondo. "They still think they're in a war."

"They are," answered Maboola. "A war against all ex-slaves. They really feel that God has sent them to clean out mad dogs like us."

Mondo counted twenty-seven riders, a wagon full of supplies, and a cannon being pulled by a team of horses. Mondo knew his dream place was finished. The cannon would tear down his walls and blast open his front gate. The ex-rebs were riding tall in the saddle as if they had no worry about the people in the little fort. *Well, if we have to go, we'll take a bunch of those bastards with us,* thought Mondo.

"They act like they want one last victory so they'll feel like winners and not losers that they really are," commented Skywalker.

Mondo turned to the others. "Here's the way this is going to happen. When they open up with the cannon, Dad will take the girls into the tunnel. Maboola can fire his guns if we help him on the wall. He and I will hold them off. When it gets dark, you three will slip out the tunnel to the creek and head for Fitzpatrick's store."

Maboola nodded and smiled. "Sounds good to me. I'll get my share before I go down. A few less black haters will make this world a better place to live."

Bear Chaser frowned. "Wait a minute. The girls can slip off. That's fine. But I'm staying. No warrior runs from the last battle. I'm not too old to get my share. You don't tell me what to do, Mondo."

Skywalker shook her head. "Forget it. Savanah and I've talked it over. We're staying, and that's the end of it."

Mondo stared at Skywalker and looked at the others and just shook his head. "I see you've made up your mind, and who am I to change it?"

He looked back at the moving attackers through the trees as they reached the point parallel to the gate about two hundred yards directly west on the other side of the creek. Split Face called, "Eyes right," and the formation turned and gave the occupants of the fort a big smile of anticipated killings.

Bear Chaser laughed. "I recall when the Yankee troops drove us from Mississippi to Indian Territory. They rode like gods pushing us into hell. I should have fought to the death back then. No more white men are going to move me again. I was just age ten when driven here, but I'm old enough and not too old to fight this time," he said.

Skywalker shook her head in disgust. "Men! They all seem to want to die instead of doing the practical thing. Anybody with a lick of sense wouldn't look forward to fighting to the death just to prove they had big balls. You're old enough to know that, Bear Chaser. I thought you at least had outgrown the need to prove your courage. Mondo and Maboola are young, but you should have learned that family is more important than showing off your bravery. Courage doesn't make you happy, it just makes you dead!"

Bear Chaser laughed. "You're right, of course. It's just the old warrior spirit in me that's creeping out. A big fight we can't avoid is coming on, and that powerful feeling for the love of battle seems to overtake me. It makes a man think about winning and the love of out doing your enemy. You'll notice that brave talk starts spewing forth to build up the feeling you can't be hurt.

Big medicine begins flowing from your brain through your whole body and leaps forth from your mouth."

Bear Chaser let loose with an ancient loud Chickasaw war cry that boomed across the creek and broke up the perfect formation of the outlaws. Some whites reined up, others couldn't keep their mounts from shying away from the noise. Mondo followed with his own challenging cry for battle that sounded part-Comanche and part-Chickasaw and an imitation of the rebel cry of the Southern troops during the Civil War.

Then Maboola came forth with an African war cry that he had been taught as a boy that really caused all the animals as well as the ex-rebs to lose control and scatter about in confusion.

Split Face rode around in circles, yelling at his men to regroup, but his troops dismounted and turned the cannon toward the fort.

"Hold up, you sorry bastards" yelled Split Face. The rebel veterans who most looked to be in their midthirties glared at this nonofficer and weren't about to take orders from a man who didn't even fight in the great war. Split Face drew his pistol and cocked the hammer before the ex-rebs loaded the cannon.

"Stop! Or you will die!" hollered Split Face. "The only real general left in the South is Purify Jones who has all the money and power, and he ordered me to save his bed toy. He's offered one thousand dollars to the man who brings her back alive. Not dead! Most of you poor bastards would kill your mother for that much money. Don't blow up that compound and kill Savanah or you'll ruin your chances for a soft life as long as you live. Are you with me, or do I have to start shooting my own men here and now?"

The bounty hunters froze, stared hard at Split Face, mumbled a few curses nobody could really hear, and then backed off from the cannon.

As the raiders stood back from the cannon, Maboola saw a clear line of sight through the trees about 175 yards away. He looked at Mondo and Bear Chaser.

"Mondo, even I can hit those stupid men from here. I got a clean shot through the trees. They're just standing there in rifle range. We're not going to get out of this without a fight, so don't you think we should get a few of them while we can? They might not think we can shoot or we are afraid to shoot."

They all looked at each other, and without a word, the three men and both women raised their rifles and took careful aim. "Split Face is moving around on his horse. Let's get those standing still. Start with the one just right of the cannon and go to the left. Shoot in the order we're standing. One...two...three...fire."

Five rifles barked as one and five raiders fell backwards, one with no eye, one with no mouth, one with the top of his head gone, another with a penetrated lung, and the fifth twisting in pain with a gut shot.

"Maboola, I taught you better than that," said Mondo. "You shot your man in the belly."

"I hit what I aimed at. I want that white bastard to suffer like his back was whipped to the bone before he bleeds to death. If you had never been whipped, you wouldn't understand."

The white killers scrambled for cover behind their horses. Split Face ordered quick retreat. The raiders hooked up the cannon, mounted up, and rode out of range. There were now twenty-two attackers and they had left a gut-shot victim twisting in pain. They rode to the north end of the creek and prepared for battle with more hate in their blood than before their comrades were killed.

CHAPTER 53

THE FIRST CANNON shot was long and the second short, but the third took out the gate of Mondo's compound. The Confederate veterans could hit what they aimed at, and they all wanted Savanah alive and Maboola dead. The night after taking out the entrance to Mondo's fort, the raiders got down on their bellies and started crawling up to the opening in the dark. Bear Chaser could hear them, but no one could see them on a cloudy night with no moonlight. Skywalker and Savanah refused to hide in the tunnel leading to the creek, so they all waited silently as the war veterans closed in for the kill. Then outside of the fort they heard a cry of pain cut off by the abrupt stillness of death, and Mondo knew that somewhere out there in the darkness, a friend was taking out the attackers one at a time.

The raiders froze, stopped bellyingup in the blackness and waited for orders. Then a sound of thrashing bodies interrupted the soundless void as a white man began to shout.

"He's got me. Help me…help…." as the crier's voice was choked off and the dreadful noise of a weapon exploding a human skull brought deathly silence again.

Storm had come before the storm started, and he was not as confident as usual since he was going against his medicine. It was not a good time to attack, but he knew his friends needed him. As Storm slipped over toward the next attacker and raised his ax to cave in his head, Split Face yelled for a retreat.

The attacker rolled away from the tomahawk, and Storm drove the weapon into the ground.

Split Face knew there were Indians among them. He could smell their presence. The bear grease used to keep mosquitos off their bodies stank to high heavens to most whites.

As the ex-Confederates rose to retreat, one ran into Storm and the two tumbled to the ground.

"One's got me. Help!" hollered the raider and two of his buddies ran to the noise of the struggle.

Storm rolled with the white man and raised his ax to finish him off when two more bodies crashed into him and took him down.

"We've got one. Help us!" yelled one of the whites.

Mondo thought it was Storm. He saw the clouds and was hoping Storm's big medicine would prevail. When he heard the whites holler, he jumped up to help his friend, but Bear Chaser grabbed him.

"Don't go! If it's Storm, he'll know what to do. If you go out there, you won't be able to see who to help. You might kill Storm yourself."

Mondo held up and then hollered in Comanche. "Storm, is that you? Let me know where you are and I'll help."

"Stay! There's just three of them. I'll be there shortly," answered Storm and his voice indicated that he was in a struggle as he spoke.

Storm broke free as one of the whites fired his pistol into the darkness, aiming at the noise and hit one of his own men in the leg, who then let out a roar of pain followed with some real cussing.

"Are you hurt?" shouted the shooter.

"Damn right, you idiot. You shot me in the leg. Help me get out of here."

Mondo raised his rifle and fired at the noise. There was a weak cry of ending the pain and the sound of a body hitting the dirt.

"Don't shoot. It's me, and I'm coming in," came back in Comanche.

The raiders took off in a panic run and left three of their own for dead. Storm slipped through the entrance to the fort and hugged Mondo.

"Thanks. I needed help. It wasn't raining yet."

Mondo laughed and then wiped the smile off his face as he looked into the serious expression of Storm. Mondo knew that medicine from the Great Spirit was not joked about.

"Come on in and join our little outfit here. We need all the help we can get."

Maboola stepped forward and offered his hand. "Thank you for bringing me in. I've heard I owe my life to you. If I was well enough to do any good, I'd been out there helping you the first time we heard you jump them bastards."

"How did you know that we were attacked?" asked Mondo.

"I heard the cannon take out your gate. I was south of here on East Cache Creek with a band of Comanches camping there. The sound was not coming from the west where the army is building a fort near Medicine Bluff, so I figured white men were trying to destroy you and your fort," answered Storm.

"How many did you get?" asked Bear Chaser.

"I think I killed two and Mondo shot one. I was hoping those attackers would think a whole tribe of Comanches were slipping up on them, and I believe that's why they ran. They'll be back. How many are there anyway?"

"There were twenty-seven when they first came, but now they're down to about nineteen, the way I figure it. What we ought to do now is build a barricade from the torn-up gate while it's still dark and those night riders think the whole Comanche tribe is waiting for them in the dark."

Mondo repeated his suggestion in English and all six got to work stacking pieces of the front gate across the opening so that the raiders would not have an unobstructed path into the fort and Mondo and his friends would have a shield to hide behind and shoot at the attackers.

Meanwhile, Split Face had gathered his men at the far north curve of the creek behind the wall of trees where their camp had been established.

"How many Comanches were there?" Split Face asked.

The men shook their heads, and some guessed a dozen or so, but it was clear that nobody knew for sure how much help the occupants of the fort had received.

"It looks like we've lost eight men already. Let's set up a perimeter and guard against an Indian attack until first light so we can tell what's going on. I've decided to hold off for a few days and set up a siege. They've got to have water. It's a hundred degrees in the day. If we put snipers out ten at a time, we can keep them from getting water from the creek. In three days, they'll be making a dash for water. Let's try to force them out to satisfy their thirst. If that doesn't work, we'll go back to destroying all the walls with our cannon. I don't want to lose any more men. We don't know how many Indians may want to help them. You know that Comanches want to kill Texans for any reason or no reason at all. So we'd better find out how many Indian friends these people have before we expose ourselves out in the open again. If we can't slip up on them in total darkness, then we have to be careful on any attack. Remember, we want that little Savanah Negress alive. She's worth big money to us all. Let's find out how much water they have inside the fort."

The raiders agreed and set up guards so they could get some rest.

After Mondo and his friends had finished the barricade, they settled in themselves with Mondo and Storm left to watch for another attack.

"Thanks for coming to help," Mondo said. "We were in a bad way when the cannon took out our gate. They were slipping to the opening, and the clouds kept us from seeing them in the moonlight. What made you decide to move in on them when it wasn't storming?"

"It was cloudy. It smelled like rain. I usually wait until it's pouring down, but I could see you needed help. None of you could see them like I could. There was too many too close. So I crawled in among them. Almost got killed because I went against my medicine. It's the first time that I've violated the direction from the Great Spirit. My vision when I spoke with the Great Spirit instructed me to go against an enemy only in a storm. If it hadn't been for your lucky shot in the dark, I think I would have been killed. So we are even. I saved you and your people and you saved me. But what are you going to do now? Those attackers didn't leave. They're still camped out there waiting to finish you off, and they've got that cannon."

"Well, I guess if they open up with their big gun and blow up my compound, we'll try to escape through the creek tunnel and fight our way out. We've also got ten of our fastest horses inside, but they've already killed two with the cannon. We could make a run for it, but a lot of us would die if they caught us out in the open. Besides, there's something inside me that says stay no matter what they do. It's like your Great Spirit and my Great Spirit is telling me I must fight to the end to be a man. Crazy, I know, and especially since Skywalker is going to have our baby. It's not smart, but it seems I have to stay."

"I understand. Most of my Antelope band has the same feelings. They will stay and fight to the death. The last stand. I believe what you told me when we first met. There's just too many whites and not enough Comanches. But we will never come in and farm like a woman."

"So you decided to die here instead of out there with your band? Thanks for your help, but you'd better go back. This isn't your fight. You'll have some years left if you go live where the white man doesn't want the land yet."

"This is a good place to die. With a good friend, against a good enemy. Why not? If this is the beginning of my band's end, I would just as soon not be around when we go under. Die like a Comanche warrior with my head held high and not hanging down like the defeated peaceful Comanches. I'll stay, not because of you, Mondo, but for me. I'm here to stay. This is my ending. I don't want to be around when the last of my tribe goes under."

CHAPTER 54

O MAR CULBERSON MET with Lieutenant John Lincoln of Boston, Massachusetts, because Omar knew that the officer was from a long line of ancestors who pushed for the freedom of slaves. The lieutenant requested to be transferred to the Tenth Cavalry to be a part of the African-American unit. He was white but defended blacks against the prejudice that weighed heavily on the minorities' shoulders. Most all the Negroes, who the Indians referred to as the buffalo soldiers because of their curly black hair, could hear the cannon being fired at Mondo's fort, and they felt they should help. The white KKK raiders had crossed into Indian Territory. The area that was supposed to be policed by the Union troops, but the big brass in Washington had issued strict orders to stay out of the conflict, which was termed a domestic dispute between a US citizen whose white wife had run off with a Negro called the Black Death because of the number of white men he had killed.

Omar knew the truth and wanted to protect Savanah and to defend the right of black people to live without fear, and intimidation from the South who supported the secret KKK made up of insecure men who loved to harm African-Americans for the sport of it, kind of like coon hunting.

"Sir, my men have been working on this new fort for a long time without any proper military training lately. I think we need to drill some. Any time now, a full-scale Indian war could break out. Many of the black troops think we were let into this man's cavalry just for the manual labor. We can damn sure lay the mortar to these rocks, but can we fire a cannon with accuracy. I think the US government is afraid to teach us how to use modern weapons for fear we'll turn them against the whites. Is that true?"

Lieutenant Lincoln sighed and shook his head in disgust. "I'm not sure. President Grant just hasn't decided what to do with these Indians. It's not the blacks that he's restricting. It's the Quaker organizations that are trying to convince President Grant to remove the Indian reservations from the control of the army and let the Quakers handle the pacification and civilization of these Plains Indians. Meantime, we got to build this fort first. You'll get plenty of military training before your enlistment is over."

"I understand, sir, and I wouldn't want to disobey any orders from Washington, but a few of us would like to take some artillery practice. Maybe take two or three cannons and go off where it's safe and see if we still know how to fire them."

Lieutenant Lincoln frowned. "I know what is bothering you people. I've heard the artillery firing from over at that Mondo Hobbs's fort. You've got to remember that those attackers are trying to arrest a crazy white-man killer. The information we've got seems to indicate that Mondo is aiding an ex-slave who kills whites. We can't have that."

"I'm not trying to protect no murderer. I'd turn over Maboola, the one the whites call Black Death, if I captured him. It's the wrongness of what's happening at Mondo's fort. We are told to keep whites out of Indian Territory if they plan to break the law or steal horses or try to kill Indians or hunt buffalo. We've run off a bunch of horse thieves and killers, and yet we won't protect a Chickasaw Indian because he has Negro blood. That's not right."

"It's not that at all. Mondo's trespassing. He's not on Chickasaw land, he's on Comanche-Kiowa property. He's illegal. That's why we can't protect him."

"Sir, with all due respect, I'd have to disagree with you. We are supposed to settle things by the law in courts. Normally, we'd enforce the law. We've arrested Texans and other white men who broke the law in the Chickasaw Nation and over here in Comanche-Kiowa land. But now, for some reason, we're letting a bunch of crazy KKK-driven white men ride within fifteen miles of this new fort we're building to break the law and kill ex-slaves, and we are doing nothing about it. We're going to let these killing night riders slaughter three men, two of which have Indian blood, and two women because we've heard a black who kills whites is there. Now some of my colored troops don't like that. And you've always said your family fought slavery for a hundred years. Well, you can't quit now. You've got to take a stand for what's right. Are you just a talker about freedom for Negroes, or are you a doer who stands behind the words coming from your own mouth? Let me take a few men and a cannon and ride east fifteen miles and practice firing. You can tell your supervisors that we didn't want to go north, south, or west for fear of stirring up the Comanches and Kiowas who are camped all around us except back east. Be a man for the underdog. Equal freedom has not been reached."

Lieutenant Lincoln dropped his head and thought for a full minute then looked Omar in the eyes and straightened. "Go ahead. You're right. Your troops need practice, and you don't want to be firing off that artillery piece near any camps where there are Plains Indians. Ride east and good luck. I hope your people can shoot straight, but don't hit anything you shouldn't hit, and if you do, I don't want to know about it."

After getting permission from Lieutenant Lincoln, Omar Culberson called his platoon together to see who wanted to go and who wanted to avoid trouble and not go to help Mondo and the people in his little fort. There were twelve young black men who gathered to hear from their sergeant.

"You've all heard the cannon fire over at Mondo's fort, and you know what's going on there. I had a scout ride out and look it over and they are surrounded by a bunch of white KKK people and they've got a cannon that will tear down Mondo's walls. I've just come from a conversation with Lieutenant Lincoln, and he's going to turn his eyes away from what I plan to do. We're going to go on a cannon practice and we're going to go east of here. I want volunteers, and I want people who know why we are going and what the consequences may be. I plan to have an artillery exercise where we are going to take a cannon to Mondo's and try to get rid of the cannon that the white attackers are using against his fort. I need volunteers, and I know some of you have talked about going. I want to hear what you all think about this mission."

A tall lanky corporal, who was second in command, spoke first. Corporal Thomas unwound his long lanky figure and stood up. "I think we have to go out. I'm in. We're hearing stories all over the South about lynching coming up from across the Red River in Texas. If we don't help them, nobody else will. What I've observed is that American white people respect power. If you don't show strength and together form some kind of power to protect yourself, then the people that have the power and have the strength will run all over you. I'm not even sure it makes a difference if you are black or white or brown or red. This is rough country, and there are rough men all over the place. Some of the men that came west didn't come because they were very successful where they lived. Most of the people who came out here were trying to make something of themselves because they didn't do any good where they left from. These are tough people. These are mean people, and a lot of people were criminals on the run. So you've got a bad element out here west, whether they are in Texas or Indian Territory. You've got some tough, mean people of different colors. The only thing they respect, the only thing they look up to, the only thing they will obey, or the only thing that will make them be halfway decent is the gun, and we've got a big gun right now. There's some people in Mondo's fort who are standing up for what is right and are trying to hold off the killing of the people with color. By golly, I think it is our duty to move on them. We have to show these ignorant KKK and powerful, rich white people who want cheap labor, and for whatever other reason they think they are superior, that we as a group can stand together. If they attack one black man, they're attacking all and we're going to hit back, slap for slap, gun for gun, and we're not turning the other cheek. We're sticking our nose right in the middle and expecting them to behave like good human beings around us or suffer the consequences."

There was a lot of nodding of agreement and mumbling that he was right, but not all seemed to be affected positively by the statements from Corporal Thomas. Some of the negative thoughts came from a few blacks that had frowns on their face. One stood up. "This isn't our fight. We are in Indian Territory, and we belong to the US Army. We've got a good job and it's a steady job and I don't want to lose that. There's Indians down there and there's an African down there. I understand he's not even an American. He came from Africa and he wants to go back to Africa. Therefore, it isn't a black fight. It's an Indian fight and we are hired and fed and kept by the US government to do what the generals say about the Indian problem. And it is an Indian problem. I don't care what you say. You're trying to make this a Negro problem, and it's not. It's certainly not my fight, and I'm not going to get into it. I'm not going to ruin my life. I'm not going to get a reputation in the army of being a troublemaker. I'm not going to slip around and get kicked out of the army. I like this job, and it's the only one I could get and it's one of the best jobs a black person can get in this country. It's just not my fight, and I'm not going."

Some other blacks in the group nodded in agreement and another stood up to speak. "I think you are missing the main point. There's been a big change in our lives and all of a sudden, we've got all these slaves released. I've been a free Negro for twenty years. I was freed before the war, and what I know is that every step is a slow step. Every move is a slow move. Adjustment and changing of the mind and thinking of the white people takes time. We are just trying to move too fast. The change we have to go through is one where we have to be educated. We have to learn to get jobs like the white. We've got to learn to be doctors and lawyers and such. As soon as we gain the experience of the middle-class white and become a contributing individual, we will be accepted. But it takes time, and I guarantee killing whites is not going to speed this up. It is going to set us back. So I don't care what kind of white people they are. If we go out there with a cannon and kill a bunch of them, we're delaying the whole process. We are going to hurt any kind of acceptance at all if we start being war like. Power and strength is not really obtained by the gun. Power and strength is obtained by the mind. As soon as we become what they call successful, then they will accept us but going over there and killing a bunch of them ain't the way to do that."

"I agree," said another black. "For every white man we kill there will be twenty blacks lynched. After the Yankees go home, the good Christian white man of the South will take care of the KKK. The Southern gentlemen will eventually come around and stop the crazy men who like to hurt people. There's a percentage of men, and this is a high percentage in this part of the country that really think being a man is being tough and hurting people. The bigger and stronger and the more guys you whip, the bigger you are, and some of them want to be big. As this part of the country becomes civilized, then the greater percent of good people will try to control those who like to hurt other people. But I don't think we are going to do any good if we join those people who like to hurt people. If we become killers also, then we will be treated like killers by the majority of good people who are not killers and who are against killing."

Omar Culberson stepped forward again. "I think you are all making sense, and I don't know the answers. I think that being weak and afraid is not going to get the job done. If I had a family, I might not go because you all may be right. It may bring down hell on anybody that interferes with the KKK's punishment of so-called Negroes with a bad attitude. Each of you has to make up your mind what you want to do. I'll not hold it against anybody who decides not to go. I'm going and I'm going to take a cannon and I'm going to try to help Mondo and those people in his fort. Maboola's there, and they want Maboola. And he may not be an angel and he may have killed some whites and he may need to hang, but the law ought to take care of that and not a bunch of crazy white people who come over here and try to shoot him down. Besides, there's a rich man in Texas that is paying these outlaws to take the fort because he wants a high yellow woman to live with him. So when you get down to it, we're talking about money and sex. That is important to the white man. It always has been and always will be important. I think we should stand up to show the world that we can stand up and will stand up and this kind of lynching and fear and intimidation has to stop. Now, who's going with me?"

Of the twelve men gathered, six men raised their hand to go and six didn't go. So Omar Culberson knew he had a force that could fire a cannon but not one that could attack the Texans. So his immediate goal was to try to wipe out the KKK's cannon and get back to the fort without losing any men and without trouble from the US Army.

CHAPTER 55

MONDO WAITED FOR the attack that never came. After a couple of days, the six defenders realized that a siege was on and water was the item the attackers were trying to deny them. Snipers guarded access to the creek from the topside, but the tunnel Mondo had dug as an escape hatch provided drinking water. At the exit on the brush-covered bank of Little Beaver Creek, Mondo and his dad had dug a deeper connected tunnel below the main cavern that extended into the creek so that water rose to the small pool inside the main tunnel.

It got up to 106 degrees on August 4, 1869, and the attackers suffered more than the defenders. Water and shade were plentiful for the people inside the compound as they waited for the KKK to make a move.

Mondo called a meeting to discuss his latest thoughts on their entrapment.

"At some point, those damn killers are going to be burned crazy by the sun. They're going to get tired of boiling their strength away and use that cannon. I suspect they are still trying to take Savanah alive and that is the only reason they haven't blasted us into wood chips, rocks, and body parts. When the time comes for the big blasts from their cannon, I want everyone hiding in the tunnel. This rock house will pile up and hide the opening and you'll have food and water to last until they leave. I'll stay up and keep them from overrunning the fort before the house caves in and hides the tunnel entrance. Then you three men can lead the women away from this mess."

Maboola laughed out loud. "You think you're going to get all the fun? Get off your high horse, Mondo. Do you really think this so-called great Comanche warrior, an old Chickasaw, full-blood Indian, and an African called Black Death by the whites are going to hide with the women while you fight alone to save us? The girls will go down in the hole and we'll all get a crack at those *haters* if the cannon doesn't get us first."

Bear Chaser interpreted Maboola's words for Storm, who looked at Maboola, smiled, and uttered a grunt that clearly meant that Storm agreed.

Bear Chaser patted his son on the back and smiled. "That's the way it's going to be, son. When the cannon starts in, the girls go below, and each one of us take a side and kill more whites. Simple. No more talk. You've been overruled."

Skywalker and Savanah started to speak, but Mondo raised his hand. "That's it then. You two will live and we will go down fighting. Skywalker will live to raise my child. No more talk!"

Mondo walked away to think about what had happened. The wait was making him think crazy. He knew that he couldn't be a coward and run away, but he also felt an obligation to Skywalker and his unborn child. If the others weren't here, Mondo thought he would probably try to slip out at night with Skywalker and go somewhere. He could not see himself living in Mexico or living anywhere else, but he really felt like he wanted to live-live with Skywalker and raise his child.

Mondo began to doubt his decision to stay here at all cost. It was as if he was crazy to come out here in the first place. He didn't listen to anybody, and now he was going to die. He had found something to live for, somebody to care for, and a child that he knew he wanted to take care of and to love. And now because of his stubborn youth and his determination to not be looked down upon by anyone, he was going to lose it all. The wait was killing him. He wanted to get it over with before he changed his mind. He had doubts about whether any of his decisions within the last three years had been right. Did he do the right thing? Was it really necessary for him to come out here? Was it really the thing to do to put himself between two tribes that really didn't like each other? Was he asking for trouble all along and wanting trouble all along just to keep proving to himself that he was a young stud?

Now he had not only Skywalker but his father and two good friends stuck in the place he built, and all were fixing to die. His choices may not have been the best for the long run, and for the first time in his life he was interested in the long run and what would happen in the future. But he had committed himself to staying here and he had committed himself to not take anything from anybody anymore. If he left with Skywalker and slipped off in the night, he knew that he could never live with himself. This was not a coward's territory. If you lived where he was born and raised, you fought like a man and died like a man and you didn't duck tail and run. No, this was no place for somebody with a weak heart. You set goals and you lived up to those goals and you fought and died for those goals. Anyone that interfered would have to be taken care of or everyone would try to take advantage of you. This country was only for the strong. With much disgust and regret, Mondo admitted to himself that if he took out a bunch of the outlaws that were going to try to kill him, then he would die as a success, especially if Skywalker was able to escape.

Maboola walked over and sat down in the shade and rubbed his shoulder and thigh. He was still in great pain, but he had forgotten about his injuries in the heat of the battle. He knew he could fight, and he knew he was still much of a man. Even though he was injured, he was going to go out strong. He hoped he could take a dozen or so of these white attackers when he went down. It was funny to him anyway, that he really didn't think about losing Savanah or think about Bear Chaser and Savanah as the end neared. All he could think about now was to pay back the evil men who took him from his home and forced him to do work for them, and when he tried to become free, they had torn his back to pieces. And he had developed hate that was so deep and so strong that it still forced out the power of his love for Savanah. It was while he was sitting there and thinking about the end that he realized that he would not have made a good partner or husband for Savanah. The hate always came back. He would never live long enough to get rid of his desire to kill the people who destroyed his life. He realized that a man could not love if he was covered throughout with hate. Bear Chaser was better for Savanah than he would ever be as a husband.

A warm feeling came over Maboola as he sat there and thought about his death. As long as he took out Split Face and a bunch of the other KKK, then he would have accomplished what he wanted to accomplish in life. He had no future. His future was destroyed by the white man. He would destroy some more white men, and he would then feel like he'd done what he had been put on this earth to do. It really didn't matter whether he was a symbol of power to the black man or whether he gave other Negroes the feeling that they could stand up to the white man. No, that didn't matter to him. His hate, his personal hate, his personal revenge and desire to kill all white men was there, and it would not go away. He wasn't doing this for the glory. He was doing it because he had to do it. He had to kill, and he would kill until he was killed himself. That was his life. That was what he was supposed to do, and he was going to get it done, and he wouldn't have to worry about it anymore. The end would come, and he was ready as long as he ended a lot of white lives.

Storm sat down and thought about his end. He knew he could slip out and run for it and go back to his band in the panhandle of Texas. And he wondered why he didn't do that. What did he owe these people? Nothing. They were friends, and he thought a lot of Mondo, but he was not one of them. He was a Comanche warrior and a Comanche warrior of the Antelope band who had never been defeated and a band that would die before they ever became white like the Chickasaw tribe leaders.

Storm believed what Mondo had told him, and the more he listened and the more he observed, the more he realized that the end was near for the Antelope band. His way of life and his love for that life and his medicine and spiritual guidance and everything that made a Comanche warrior was going to be wiped out. The whites were coming with their armies and their killers and they were going to kill all the buffalo and all the Comanches that stood up against the white take over. The way he was raised and the way that the Antelope band lived was going to end. For some reason, he didn't want to see the end, and Storm didn't want to go back to the band and die with the band and go out with his people. He couldn't stand to see his wives and his children taken over and consumed by the culture of the white man. He'd just as soon die here. It was a good place to die and one where he would not have to witness the total destruction of his culture. Storm seemed satisfied and happy that he would come to an end right here and now. The future was grim. He would just as soon remember the way of life that was in existence when he was a young boy and a young man. He did not want to grow old with what he knew was coming. Today was a good day to die.

Bear Chaser went off by himself and sat down and thought about the conversation they had just had about the four of them dying here in the fort and the girls taking off. He would like to have spent the rest of his life with Savanah, but he knew that probably would not be the case. Even if they survived because of some miracle, he felt that Savanah would choose Maboola and not him. He would be like a grandfather to their children instead of a father. He was too old, and he had the wonderful pleasure of loving once again. He was glad that he had found a second love, which he didn't think he would ever find after his first wife died.

He knew deep down that the real reason that he was staying was because he had been run out of his country and controlled by the whites too many times. Each time he was forced to do something that he didn't want to do, each time he was forced to leave a place he didn't want to leave, and each time that the whites and the half-breed leaders of the Chickasaw Nation made a decision to get away from the past and to get away from the Chickasaw culture, he died a little. He died a long time ago, and with Savanah, he had come back to life. But if he had to see the total destruction of everything again, it wouldn't be worth living and loving somebody like Savanah. She deserved someone that didn't have a defeated spirit. Bear Chaser knew that he was going to stay and that he was going to fight and he was going to die. Even though he had learned a lot and he was an older and a more mature man, he knew deep down that he was not going to be moved again. That he had to stay and he had to fight. And if he didn't, then he wouldn't be worthy of a woman as sweet and nice and beautiful as Savanah.

Bear Chaser smiled and shook his head. "I guess I'm not as old as I thought I was," he said to himself. "I see where my son got his stubborn determination to be some kind of a last-stand man. I guess my son is like me, only just a little younger. We will not be cowards, and we will not be controlled by others. I think my son saw that in me and had sworn that he was not going to be like me. I ran from my tribe and hid in the hunting and exploring and moving around and the relationship I had with Ten Bears and the Comanches because they were still free and that's what I wanted. I ran from my tribe's death. I will not run from mine."

Savanah cornered Skywalker. "Are we really going to run? What do you think about hiding in the tunnel and taking off and slipping out and leaving the men alone to die?"

Skywalker shook her head in confusion. "I don't know what to think. I don't like it, and I wish there was a way where we could convince the men to make a run for it. If I wasn't pregnant, I'd stay and fight too. I'm just not sure what I'll do. I have this feeling that I want to go back to my old life, but I just know it won't be the same. Nothing is going to be the same after you've been through what I've been through. You just can't go back and catch up and regain what you have left after so many years of a different lifestyle entirely. I don't know whether I like it or not, but I'll probably take off, and if we make it, I'll probably go back to Mexico."

Savanah shook her head in confusion. "Well, because of you, I might be able to make it on my own for the first time. I don't want to leave Maboola, and I don't want to leave Bear Chaser, but I don't want to die either. I would love to stay and fight, but it's just not in me. I don't know what I'll do either. If we make it, I guess I'll try to get back North and whether I try to live as a white or as a Negro, I guess it really doesn't matter. You just survive. That's what I've noticed out here. Every day is just to survive. Just to survive that's all. You can make all the plans in the world and you can try to change your life and you can try to go places and do different things, but when you get out here, you're kind of stuck out here. You just can't pick up and go anywhere. You just live from day to day and hope that you don't pass away either by a disease or by a gunshot wound or by raiding Indians or KKK. You know, it just seems to me that every day is a living danger, and I don't know if that wouldn't be true anywhere in the world. I just haven't been around enough. It sounds to me like you at one time had a good safe life and I'm sure you are sorry that you got captured and brought to this part of the country. Aren't you?"

"Well, I've had some interesting times, but it wasn't much fun. I was spoiled as a youngster and really didn't do much for anybody. One thing I learned is how to help people and how to take care of others, and I feel a little accomplishment for doing that. So my life really was a lot tougher but a lot more responsible after I was kidnapped. I guess I really do love Mondo, and I don't want him to die and I would like to stay with him anywhere and raise a family. I guess that's the woman in me and I guess it will never go away. I hate to see them take their own lives when we could probably get out of here and escape if we did it right. I guess you just have to deal with that man idea of proving he's a man every day. They can't be a coward, and they have to fight and they can't take anything off anybody else. It's just part of a warrior attitude, and even though the Kiowas and Comanches are still so-called savages and uncivilized and live out here as they did apparently for thousands of years before non-Indians came, they are still no different from the whites and blacks or anyone else. I just don't know if men are made to conquer or else be conquered. I just don't know whether there will ever be peaceful coexistence as long as there are two men alive. One would probably want to control and dominate the other. I'm not sure we can do anything about that. I mean, we love them to death, I guess, and we will have families with them and we are protected by them, but they are all children forever. Men don't learn to coexist peacefully. I think that we will probably never see the day where there's not some kind of battle, some kind of fight, some kind of disagreement if there are two men alive. So if there's nothing we can do about this battle and we are not going to save our men, I think maybe we should try to get out of here and try to make a life somewhere else for us and as far as I'm concerned, for my child to be. I don't know the answer."

"All right. I'll go with you and I'll try to make it, and I sure hate to leave the protection of these men and this fort but it looks like they can't protect us any longer. I guess that's what women are for is to find someone to protect them, and I was beginning to think that women could live without men or with men, whatever they wanted to do. But what I see now makes me ready to go. We'll try to make a life somewhere else after our men are gone."

CHAPTER 56

O N THE THIRD day, Split Face realized his men were getting burned to anxiety by the hot August sun. They were restless, and Split Face figured that the trapped people must have stored up a lot of water. No one had made a try for the creek. Also, Split Face feared that if they wasted more time, help might come from the buffalo soldiers at the new fort being built or from the Wildhorse Creek settlement of blacks. He had sent out guards in every direction to watch for approaching help, but so far, nobody had made a move to help the people trapped in Mondo's fort.

Omar Culberson and six black troops, pulling a cannon, spotted the guard Split Face had sent to the east before the guard saw them. It took the troops about an hour to crawl up and cut the scout's throat so he wouldn't alert the rest of the Texans.

The troops slipped up on the white raiders, but it took them at least six hours to locate the snipers, the main camp north of the creek, and the cannon hidden under brush. It was dusk when they all convened west of the creek to discuss their plan to try to disable the cannon.

"If we fire more than once, they'll be all over us before we can pull out, and if we try to steal the cannon, they'll run us down before we can go a mile or two," said Omar.

"We can try to Indian-kill that weapon," said one trooper. "Crawl in at night and put it out of working order."

"We'll make too much noise. We'd have to jam up the barrel. Takes too long and sounds too loud," answered Omar. "We're going to have to place our cannon close so we can't miss and fire at the crack of dawn, then blow up our own gun and run for it so we won't leave them a working cannon. We'll fire then block our barrel and fire again and hightail it back to Medicine Bluff. How does that sound?"

"Not too good. First place, we can't miss. And second, by the time we reload and jam the barrel, we won't have much of a head start," answered a corporal who was next in rank.

"I know. But we've got to take that chance. Mondo will go under if we don't get that big gun. It's his only chance. We all talked about this. We've got to win at least one battle on our own if our lives are ever going to be really free. It starts here and now. Those men in that little fort have proven that they've got the guts and the smarts to fight the whites. They've got to survive. We've got to do something to give them a chance or real freedom will go away for all blacks. Anyone who doesn't like my plan can head back to the protection of those white officers. If you stay, we'll try to take out that KKK big gun."

None of the men left and that night they slowly and very quietly moved their cannon into position less than fifty yards from the raiders' piece. They carefully loaded without stirring up the whites and waited for the light of day. The troops had hoped that the raiders would think the guard they killed had deserted and gone back to Texas, but right before nightfall, the attackers found their dead comrade and were on alert in the morning and ready for action when the soldier's cannon fired.

The soldiers sighted and fired a direct hit that temporarily stunned the raiders. Their cannon flew up in the air and the barrel cracked. The KKK recovered quickly, mounted, and charged the black soldiers. The whites knew the black force was small because there were not many tracks found around the dead guard.

Omar jammed their own big gun and fired it, and the gun exploded as he raced for his horse. The battle of the cannons was over in a few seconds, and the race for the fort at Medicine Bluff commenced. The black soldiers knew the best route back that went around the spots of timber and across the creeks at low banks, but the raiders had better horses.

Mondo heard the two explosions and at first sent the girls for cover into the underground cellar, but when nothing hit his fort he realized he was getting help from somebody. Then he heard rifle shots off to the west.

There were at least twelve Texans out front, moving fast and getting into rifle range for a shot at the fleeing black troopers. They opened up and took two of the seven soldiers off their mounts. The other five pulled up and jumped down to help their wounded friends. They fired at the approaching whites who leaped off their horses for cover. Both sides spread out in a line across an open area and lay down flat to avoid the flying bullets. A rifle-shooting contest soon emerged with each side trying to get a lucky shot off at the men pinned down on the ground. Five other KKK whites rode up late and saw the firefight and immediately rode south to circle behind the two injured troops and the five trying to hold off the attackers.

The noise of the rifles firing carried back to East Cache Creek where the soldiers were getting up to the sound of the early morning bugle call. Lieutenant Lincoln saw at once that seven of his men were missing, and since he had heard a cannon fire before all the noise from the rifles, he had an idea of what had happened. He at once ordered his troops to mount up and proceed east toward the noise before his superiors got to the early morning formation. Lieutenant Lincoln felt he had authority to investigate any shooting since he was charged to keep the Comanche and Kiowas from causing more trouble with their raids. He could always say he thought the noise was from the Chickasaw Lighthorse Police chasing some young Comanche warriors. It took him about twenty minutes to get his forty troops on the move, but he ordered a speedy ride toward the gunfire.

Omar didn't know what to do. He saw the white raiders circling behind his position, and he certainly didn't expect help from the US Cavalry. He checked his two injured men and noticed that one could ride and the other was dead. He thought he had about five minutes to remount and flee before he was completely surrounded, but he was wrong. By the time he got the word to retreat to his scattered four troopers, the KKK rode in behind them and took positions that trapped them all. Omar had to turn some of his riflemen to hold off the attack from his rear. Omar lay flat, with his sweat turning the dry ground to mud as he waited out the slow but steady crawling movement of the whites as they closed in for the kill. The shots were more often and closer to each of his men as they cast nervous eyes toward him, begging for a solution on how to get out of this trap.

Omar was about to order his men to run for their horses, mount up, and flee in all directions when he heard the bugle. He saw about forty buffalo soldiers riding from the east and closing in on the whites to his rear, who were caught totally by surprise. The raiders immediately stood up, dropped their rifles, and raised their hands.

Omar ran to his horse, and his men followed as the rifles of the KKK to his back were silent. The whites to the west stopped firing when their comrades surrendered to the buffalo soldiers. Omar met Lieutenant Lincoln, who didn't even ask him what he was doing because the Texans to the east had mounted their horses and were approaching the US troops with a white flag of truce.

Split Face rode up to Lieutenant Lincoln. "What the hell is going on here? Your colored troops attacked us and blew up our cannon. I was told that the US Army was supposed to stay out of this fight? We're just trying to help you people clear out some trespassers on Comanche land."

"Is that why you attacked Mondo's compound? I didn't think you ex-rebs were too happy about ever helping out the US army."

"Well, that Mondo has a wanted killer of white people, like you and I, hidden in his fort. If your colored troops are too afraid to arrest that killer called the Black Death, then we ex-rebs have to do it for you. And we can't get the job done if you let these colored troops run wild like a bunch of savages and destroy our weapons."

Lieutenant Lincoln looked around his troops and nodded to Omar. "Is anyone hurt?"

"We've got one that's slightly hurt and one we left for dead," answered Omar.

Lieutenant Lincoln turned to Split Face. "Mister, I think we'd better let this whole thing disappear. Did you lose any people?"

"Yes. We lost one and our cannon was blown up. And we're not the kind of white men who let a bunch of coloreds attack us and get away with it."

"Well, this time you're going to do just that. We both lost a cannon, and we each lost a man who we'll have to blame on the Comanches since we were told to stay out of this fight. You go on with your business, and we'll go on with our business. You don't want any more trouble from us, and if we both agree to forget about this whole thing, sweep it under the rug so to speak, then we'll both go our way without a big government investigation. Nothing will go in my report except one trooper was ambushed and killed by unknown Indians, and I'll keep my people out of your hair. Besides, without a cannon, the odds are more even at Mondo's fort. My people can live with that if you let this matter drop."

Split Face spit and muttered a few curse words hardly detectible and nodded in agreement, turned his men around, and rode back toward Mondo's fort.

When the cannons exchanged shots at the beginning of Omar's attack, Mondo knew at once that someone had brought help in the form of a cannon. It had to come from Medicine Bluff. The people in the fort rushed out and climbed onto the wall but couldn't tell what was going on. Later, the sound of rifles firing off to the west indicated a fierce battle. Again, Mondo wasn't sure, but he thought maybe Omar had brought a cannon to try to take out the attacker's cannon and was chased off and caught.

Bear Chaser had some binoculars and saw that the raider's cannon had been hit and turned over on its side. Whether the gun was out of commission or not, he couldn't tell. Bear Chaser could see that most of the attackers had left their campsite. Apparently, Split Face had left only a few sharp shooters to keep the fort occupants pinned down. He told this to Maboola and Mondo.

Storm could not understand the conversation between Bear Chaser, Maboola, and Mondo. However, Storm could see and hear what was going on, and without a word, he disappeared into the tunnel and slipped out into the bank of Little Beaver Creek. The August heat had dried out and burned a lot of the green cover in the area, but it didn't take much for Storm to ease through the dried weeds and count the five raiders left guarding the fort. As he eased through the tall grass, Storm could hear many shots being fired west toward the new fort being built.

Storm slipped back into the fort and told Mondo it was a good time for them to attack and make sure that the cannons were down for good. Storm pointed out the positions of the five whites left to guard the fort, and the four men descended out into the yellow tall grass and bellied up on the guards.

Maboola took the first one with his machete without making a sound. Storm cut the throat of the one guarding the KKK's cannon and Bear Chaser and Mondo shot the other three. By the time Mondo and his friends had entered the campsite of the KKK attackers, the shooting in the west had stopped, and Mondo knew they had to move quick. They jammed both the cannon barrels with a piece of iron that had been blown off and then proceeded to ransack the camp, pouring out any food, water, and other items left there. When they heard the approaching hoofbeats, the four men dashed for the creek and made it back into the tunnel before the rest of the killers came back from the fight with Omar.

Mondo felt good about making sure both cannons were out of commission and five more attackers were dead and their numbers were down to fourteen and no cannons. What Mondo didn't know was there was one attacker hidden that they didn't kill who saw them disappear into the creek bed and come out inside the fort without crossing the clearing between the creek and the west wall. He reported his observation to Split Face, and the whites knew there was a secret entrance into the fort.

Split Face gathered up the five dead Texans and buried them and then sat down to organize a search for the entrance into the fort. He told his men he wanted to find the tunnel without the people inside realizing the whites knew about the exit. So Split Face divided his troops and sent two men at a time to ease down the creek bed and carefully examine all covered areas for an entrance to the tunnel. It took them three trips before the hole was discovered and then Split Face gathered his men for a whole new plan of attack where he hoped to carry out Savanah through the once-hidden tunnel and kill the rest.

CHAPTER 57

THE WORD OF the siege of Mondo's fort spread like wildfire across the Chickasaw Nation, and Hurbert Dixon convinced the Chickasaw government to stay out of it. He told Governor Harris that Mondo lived on Comanche land, and it was not a Chickasaw problem. Dixon advised the government that Mondo Hobbs was half-Chickasaw from an ex-slave mother and that the Chickasaws should let Mondo move back near his father's land and take out a lease in Bear Chaser Hobbs's name. Hurbert Dixon went on to tell the people in charge of the Chickasaw Nation that the stubborn ex-Yankee fighter with Negro blood did not deserve any help from the Chickasaw Lighthorse Police who were trying to get along with the Yankee troops about to be moved from Fort Arbuckle in the Chickasaw Nation to the new fort in the Wichita Mountains located in Comanche-Kiowa territory.

Dixon convinced Governor Harris that this was a matter between the whites and the Yankee government and wasn't something that the Chickasaw Nation should get involved in. In addition, the Chickasaw Nation still wanted the federal government to live up to their contract and treaty with the Chickasaw Nation and remove the Chickasaw freedmen from their territory. Nothing was being done with regard to the fact that the time for removal was overdue, and pursuant to the treaty, the United States was to take the three hundred thousand dollars and move all the Chickasaw and Choctaw freedmen out of their nations because the tribes had not made the Negroes that were slaves owned by those Indians a citizen of the Choctaw and Chickasaw tribes.

Right after Mondo left Wildhorse Creek to make the hard ride back to his fort, Hudson Greer started to try to raise a troop of independent black fighters to move on the KKK that was attacking Mondo's fort. He learned that Maboola was there and Maboola was a hero, and he felt like there would be a lot of people that lived in Wildhorse Creek that would assist him and go to Mondo and Maboola's aid. In addition, he wanted everyone to know that the reason Purify Jones was financing the KKK was to get back the beautiful Savanah who had been the kidnapped mistress of the rich ex-slave owner, and that rich slave owner had been giving financial support to the night riders who were terrifying ex-slaves throughout Texas. Greer wanted to make sure that the KKK did not grow and become a powerful force in the Indian Territory. Hudson Greer hoped that maybe in Indian Territory where the whites also looked down on Indians as second-class citizens, the black people might be able to protect themselves without bringing about an immediate death by hanging. Hudson Greer could not understand why the intolerance of the whites to people that were different in any way from themselves was not understood and resisted by all minorities. Indian Territory should be a place where blacks could make a stand against violence and get help from the Indians who also had been receiving the violence of the whites for many, many years. Maybe here a little resistance by all minorities working together might keep the KKK from becoming a power locally.

Hudson Greer met resistance in trying to raise troops. For some reason, he could not get anyone to agree to go with him to help Mondo. The first five men that he asked to go with him were those who he knew would fight for the Negroes' independence and had always gone along with whatever Hudson Greer suggested, but this time, the men looked down and wouldn't stare back into Hudson Greer's eyes, and they all refused to ride with him. Hudson Greer knew something was wrong, and he could not get anyone to tell him why he was being refused assistance.

The bravest and most responsible citizens weren't acting like themselves, and Hudson Greer could immediately feel a conspiracy in the air. The turndowns ducked their head and wouldn't talk to Hudson Greer. Hudson smelled a rat, and therefore he went to the biggest rat in Wildhorse Creek.

Hudson Greer walked to the wild side of town. It was early in the morning and everything was quiet. Hangovers were being taken care of by late sleeping, and there was no one moving about. Hudson Greer entered the two-story whorehouse and saloon and went back to the rear of the building where he knew Tan Bishop had a fancy office. He knocked on the door and was told to come in. Tan Bishop's office looked like a rich white lawyer's office with fancy furniture. There was Tan Bishop sitting behind the big desk in a fancy suit. "Fancy Dan" was all Hudson Greer could think of when he looked at the tall, large, light-colored black man with a big smile on his face. Tan Bishop lived with a smile on his face, but with evil inside his head. He stood up.

"I've been expecting you. I understand you have been bothering all the young men in the community about going on a worthless mission to help out two Negroes that are as good as dead."

"Yeah. I've asked for help, and I'm not getting any and I think I know why. You've got to be involved somehow because it smells like a rat, and you are the biggest rat in town."

"What's the matter with you, Greer? You're always trying to do the most stupid things. Nobody is going to ever help us, and any time we group up for protection, the whites are going to ungroup us. We've got to stay away from people who don't want us around. That's the way it is, and I wish like hell you would finally understand the truth. You're so hardheaded and idealistic, and you are going to get us all killed."

"I know if we don't stick together, we'll be treated like children and never have any say as to what we do. If we don't believe in each other, then who is going to believe in us?"

"Well, you've got one thing right. We've got to stick together and stick together and stay out of the way of the majority. We're in the beginning of learning to be free, and you know what they have done to the Indians. Why do you think they will treat us any different? Those Indians that are still alive have been herded like cattle back to this reservation out of the way of the white men for right now. The whites don't stop taking and killing. Look at history. The people who control this country do not recognize any rights for minorities. We just have to stay out of their way, or we'll not live long. Don't you see that?"

"All you want to do, Tan Bishop, is to keep making money on white man's vices. You let them come amongst us for drink, women, and gambling, and you treat them like they give a damn about us. You don't want to try to gain any real freedom to control our own actions as long as you can make money on those who want us out of society. You are blinded by money."

"That's exactly right. We stay out of their way and out of their sight, unless they want to buy what we've got to sell, and we don't make anything that they want but cheap whiskey, cheap women, and partly honest gambling. We've got to entertain those bastards for money. That is all we've got right now, and entertainment is what I am selling."

"You only prove to the whites that their theory of our worthlessness is true. They think we are animals, and you and your people act like animals. Your life is controlled by money. Do you really think that if the KKK destroyed Mondo and his friends they won't come after us next? Probably just for sport. Just for the fun of watching a black man swing from the end of a rope. If we are going to be able to stay in this country, we've got to show some power and lack of fear. We've got to stand up to the majority and make them recognize us as humans and not animals. We've got to help Mondo and help any other black person that the white haters try to kill. That's the only way we are going to make it."

"That's not true. You won't admit to our place in this country. If we try to do anything against whites or Indians, we'll be
found out at once. We have no law to help us. It doesn't matter
whether we were Chickasaw freedmen or freedmen that came
from outside of Indian Territory. We are all treated like a bunch
of trespassers that the Chickasaws allow to stay because we provide entertainment for their own drunks and the hard-ass whites
who live here illegally. The Chickasaws hope the whites will take
their desires out on us and not the Chickasaw people. We have a
lot of people, white, brown and black, that come across the Red
River to enjoy what we are offering. The Chickasaws try to push
all troublemakers to our community. They want us to take care of
the drunks, the horny, and the gamblers."

"That may be true, but I'm not willing to stand by and do
nothing. If we can't better ourselves, then we might as well be
lynched by those who hate us for the color of our skin. I'm headed
for Mondo's place and I'm going to try to take as many from here
as I can. I know you've done something. Some of the people that
I trust and believe in the most are turning me down. What have
you done? Nobody will help me, and that's bad. And whenever
something turns bad, you are usually the reason."

"If you haven't figured it out yet, then you will never understand about men and men in this country, not just black men, but
all men. Most people don't want to die. Can't you accept that we
are outnumbered and that the smart ones know that they will die
if they ride with you?"

"That's not it. I know some of the men real well. They are not
afraid of much at all, and they know we've got to stick together
and help each other if we are going to have any rights at all in
this land."

"You're a dreamer. You don't know these men deep down, and
you damn sure don't know anything about this country we live in.
I was the big man's main servant back at a big plantation in South
Carolina. I was always standing next to the headmaster and the

owner, and he owned about four hundred slaves. I was a bodyguard, and since I could remember everything anyone said to
him, I always heard his deals. I always heard what was going on
between the rich white plantation owners. I heard it all and saw
it all. There's only two things that mean anything in this country:
land and money. Nothing else matters. To get land and money,
everything is fair in this country. You can keep slavery if it is necessary to keep your land and money. That's the god here in this
United States. The so-called golden rule is for those that don't
have land and money. I learned that and I live by that. While you
were organizing churches and schools, I was showing men what
they really wanted. While you were getting men to fight for their
rights, I was making deals and buying my protection. You never
got to see what was going on between the rich powerful people
in this country, the white people that control everything. I saw it
and I learned and, by God, money is everything."

"What the hell did you do? Have you sold out to the enemy?
Have you become like one of those white slave owners yourself?"

"I entered into a contract for services rendered. I gathered up
or bought those five hundred head of cattle that Purify Jones
lost when he used those animals to slip up on our community. I
negotiated with Purify Jones through a black spy he sent to us. I
paid the spy more than Jones and made a bunch of money. All I
had to do was to keep any of our citizens from riding to Mondo's
aid. Most of the tough ones work for me, but the ones you think
are loyal to you and your idealistic goals have needs that I could
fulfill. Some took cash, some took cattle, some needed a place to
live, and a lot just needed a free poke from one of my working
girls. Money and land will buy most anything in this country.
That's the real god, and the majority recognizes that. Not your
dream of equality, not your Jesus or your education. Just plain and
simple money. And money solves all problems. It will buy you a
place to stay, it will buy you something to eat, and it will buy you
a good piece of ass. That takes care of most men whether they
are black, white, green, yellow, red, pink, or any color. Nobody is

going to ride with you to Mondo's. I made a deal with anybody that's worth a damn and would put up a good fight, and as you know, if somebody breaks a deal with me, I kill them. Those men that live here know that also. I bought off all those that might help you. I am going to keep them away from Mondo's by fear and by purchase. If they ride with you and they made a deal with me, I'll send someone to get them, and they know it. Now, don't waste any more of my time with your dreams of acting as one big black people force who will make those white people treat us right. They'll deal with me because we understand what's what."

"Maboola should have killed you. You're more dangerous to our advancement than Purify Jones. You joined the enemy. You are a traitor to the black race."

"I'm becoming rich. I'm making money. I'm making money mostly off white people. What you don't understand is that black people will be treated equal when they get rich enough to have the power and influence that money brings with it in this country. I don't know how we will get enough rich people, but I know I'm becoming rich by satisfying the lust of the white man for wine, women, and song. We entertain them better than they can entertain themselves. Entertainment will probably make us rich enough to demand and be treated as equals. We'll get equality when we are rich enough to buy it, like everything else in this country."

"You are turning our women into whores. You own them and let the white men use them as if they are still slaves, and you are teaching them to use their bodies for your benefit, and they are not free at all."

"Grow up, Hudson. Look around you and learn what counts. Those of us that will become equal financially will be treated equally. Figure out a way to get rich. Money is god. We can't use force to stop the KKK. The rich whites will put more money down to keep those crazy men who like to hurt people going strong. We have to buy our rights. When enough of us have enough money, we'll put a stop to the KKK, and not until that happens will we have any power to control our own destiny. Don't make it worse on us by taking a bunch of our people to ride with you against the KKK. Remember this and remember this well. For every white bigot that dies, twenty innocent Negroes will swing by the neck from a tree until they are dead. Get rich and save our race."

Hudson Greer stomped out and talked to just about every man in Wildhorse Creek, and he was only able to convince three other men to give up the riches promised by Tan Bishop and ride with him toward Mondo's. He was very discouraged and felt like his goals of equality were impossible to reach as the four men rode toward Mondo's.

Chapter 58

Split Face planned his break-in through the tunnel for a late-night attack. He was going to lead five men through the tunnel as the rest would belly up to the fort, firing away in order to keep the men inside protecting the walls. At four in the morning, August 12, 1869, the attack began.

Split Face encountered no resistance entering the secret passageway, and he and his five men eased through the darkness in silence while the noise of continuous rifle fire could be heard on the surface. Storm, Mondo, Bear Chaser, and Maboola took to the walls, each covering a side as the women went back and forth, reloading the rifles as they were emptied. Mondo and the rest on top of the walls were shooting at the flashes of the rifles going off as the ex-rebs fired and rolled away as they inched forward toward the fort. Storm had the north wall on top of the barricade built in the space of the destroyed main gate. Mondo was on the west wall, Maboola on the east wall, and Bear Chaser had the back or south wall to defend. Split Face had sent most of his men directly at the front barricade but put one man each to slip up on the other three sides in order to keep the protectors in the fort separated and firing so that nobody would be watching the inside of the cabin or, for that matter, the inside of the fort.

Split Face and his five men came out in the dark cellar, found the ladder, eased up until all six men were inside the rock cabin looking out the front door, and saw the two women running back and forth from wall to wall, assisting the men by loading their rifles. It was still dark in the morning, and Split Face could only see the dark shadows moving around. Looking out the front door of the cabin, the attackers could only get a clear shot at Storm, who was on top of the barricade at the north gate barricade.

Split Face looked back at his men and whispered. "You all get out there and grab that Savanah when that other Mexican gal runs around the side of the rock cabin. Drag her back into the cabin as quickly and as quietly as you can. When that Indian turns around, I'll shoot him. Move fast and let's get that Savanah and get her down the hole and out before we go after the other three men."

Storm had just handed Savanah his rifle and she was starting to load the weapon when she heard a commotion and felt hands grab her. The five men knocked her to the ground and one covered her mouth so she could not scream. They quickly lifted her up and started back toward the cabin entrance. Savanah felt fear and immediately bit the hand over her mouth and started kicking and screaming and scratching with all her might like a cornered wild cat. Her mouth came open, and she screamed as loud as she could and kneed and kicked all those around her so that two of the men fell over each other and the grip on her was loosened so that she almost broke free.

Storm turned back from the barricade when he heard her scream and before he could jump off the barricade, a bullet struck him in the chest and knocked him to the ground. He struggled up to his knees and saw the three men dragging Savanah to the cabin door as the two that had fallen jumped up and fired at Storm. A bullet hit his shoulder and another missed, and Storm let out a crazed, but strong war cry and jumped up and charged toward the three men wrestling with Savanah. The Comanche warrior had enough energy to dive through the air and fly into the three men and Savanah, knocking all of them to the ground and freeing Savanah. Split Face and the two men standing all turned and fired shots into Storm before he could rise again.

Mondo heard the cries from inside the fort and the shots behind him and he leaped from the west wall and came running around the corner of the rock cabin and fired his rifle from the hip. Two quick shots dropped the two ex-rebs that had just fired into Storm. Split Face turned his rifle toward Mondo and fired as Mondo rolled back around the corner of the rock cabin to get away from Split Face's rifle fire. Mondo peeked around the side of the cabin and saw Savanah rolling away from the three men that were getting up and moving toward her to capture her again.

About that time, Skywalker came around the corner at a full run, and Split Face fired and missed her. She dove for cover, landing flat on the ground near the cabin entrance where Split Face was trying to keep Mondo off while watching the other three ex-rebs tangle with Savanah in an effort to drag her through the front door of the cabin. They grabbed hold of Savanah again and began pulling her toward the door as Split Face kept firing at Mondo every time he tried to come around the corner of the cabin. Skywalker saw the situation and bellied up close to Split Face then jumped up and ran into him, knocking him back into the cabin door and knocking his rifle from his hand.

The same time that Skywalker was flattening Split Face, Maboola came limping around the east side of the cabin and had one clear shot at the three men wrestling with Savanah, and with that shot, he took one of them out. When Split Face was knocked back into the cabin, Mondo stepped out and fired another shot that took another one of the ex-rebs wrestling with Savanah, and with one trying to hold her, Savanah kicked, scratched, and twisted and finally freed herself from the grasp of the last ex-reb trying to drag her into the cabin.

Mondo and Maboola both shot the ex-reb dead before he could retrieve Savanah. At the cabin entrance, Split Face grabbed Skywalker and lifted her in front of himself so that neither Mondo nor Maboola could shoot at him. Split Face pulled her through the entrance and slammed the cabin door shut.

Right before Maboola and Mondo started toward the cabin door to smash it in and free Skywalker, three men came over the front barricade that had been defended by Storm and open-fired on Mondo and Maboola who had to again seek cover instead of tearing down the door to get Skywalker. Bear Chaser had finally left the south wall and got around to the battle going on in front of the cabin and open-fired on the three men coming over the top of the barricade, and they all dove for cover. But since the walls had been abandoned, the rest of the attackers had climbed up and were now pouring fire down on all of the men and Savanah, and inside the cabin, Split Face dragged Skywalker toward the trapdoor and tunnel.

The three men inside the fort could not even return fire as they were rolling and diving and trying to find some cover from the shots raining down from the top of the wall. There was nothing that anyone could do, and Mondo felt like the end was near. Then a blast from a 10-gauge shotgun blew one of the ex-rebs off the wall and on to the ground inside the fort. The loud noise stopped the firing for a second as the attackers turned to try to find out who was coming up behind them. More shots rang out from behind the ex-rebs on the wall and took a couple more down. The attackers did not know who was firing and how many were firing at their backs, but they immediately dropped off the wall outside the fort and took off in retreat because just as soon as they slowed up firing on the three men inside the fort, Mondo, Maboola, and Bear Chaser fired back at them so that they were being shot at from both sides. These attackers retreated as fast as they could away from the fort.

Hudson Greer rose up from the top of the barricade at the front gate and hollered down for Mondo and the other two to hold their fire. Before Greer and his three friends could get into the fort, Mondo and Bear Chaser climbed over the wall and ran for the creek where the tunnel exited. By the time they had reached the tunnel entrance, they could see where Split Face had carried Skywalker off, and they had been too late to prevent Split Face from kidnapping Mondo's woman. Mondo and Bear Chaser started toward Split Face's camp but ran into the retreating ex-rebs who had joined up with Split Face and Skywalker. Mondo and Bear Chaser feared that if they attacked the ex-rebs, they were liable to shoot and hit Skywalker, and they both felt like Split Face would probably try to trade Skywalker for Savanah so they retreated back to the fort.

When they got back, they saw Savanah, Maboola, Hudson Greer, and his three friends trying to save the dying Storm.

Chapter 59

WHEN THE DUST settled and both sides gathered to decide what to do next, there was a lull in the fighting, and Mondo wanted to attack immediately since the numbers of combatants on each side was beginning to even out. There were almost as many men on Mondo's side as there was on Split Face's side. With the inclusion of Greer and his three men added to Mondo, Bear Chaser, and Maboola, there were seven against Split Face and the eight ex-rebs that were still alive.

Mondo wanted to charge, and Bear Chaser kept saying, "Hold up. Hold up. They are going to try to trade Skywalker for Savanah. You've got to remember that their whole point of being here is to take Savanah back to Purify Jones and get a big money reward."

"Look, Dad, those crazy killers don't mess around, and Skywalker won't sit still. She's a fighter, and she's going to try to kill Split Face with that dagger she has under her skirt if she still has it. She will die and think it is worth it if she can get Split Face. We have to go now."

"Son, the woman is pregnant, and she's got a baby to think about, and you have never been around a mother-to-be. They really start thinking about the child more than anything else. I think she will struggle to stay alive just for the baby. Let's wait a minute and see what happens."

The two men walked back into the fort and saw Storm lying dead. Mondo bent over, and tears swelled in his eyes.

"Well, the weather wasn't right. He really believed in his big medicine, and when he went into a battle with no storm sure enough, he died. But he saved us and I'm going to take him back to his people just as soon as this is over. He was a great warrior, and he deserves the honor of a proper burial. I don't know what we would have done without him. How many times did he save our ass?"

"Well, he came once when the Texans were first here and got a bunch, and he happened to be on the barricade this last attack. Whoever was on the north wall took the shots coming out of the cabin. Let's wrap him up in a canvas, and just as soon as we get Skywalker back you can take him to his Antelope band."

Maboola limped over toward the two men and they examined his wounds.

"How do you feel? Can you go some more?" asked Mondo.

"Sure. I'm fine. I'm a little slow, but I can still hold my own. When are we going?"

"Mondo wants to go right now," said Bear Chaser. "But I know that they are going to try to trade Skywalker for Savanah." He looked over at Savanah. "We're not going to trade you, but my suggestion is that we can get near them and won't have to attack across an open field if we act like we're going to negotiate with them. So let's wave a white flag and get out there. If we can get them out in the open with us, our numbers are such that I think we can take them."

"I think you should do it right now. I agree with Mondo. Skywalker won't let them keep her long. She'll put that dagger in Split Face first chance she gets," answered Maboola.

At the same time that Mondo and his people were discussing what to do, Split Face had gathered the eight ex-rebs that were still alive and was telling them how the last battle was going to go down.

"We are going to trade Skywalker for that Savanah. As you know, Purify Jones will pay us big time if we bring her back. We can't take the fort now without cannons. They know that we know about the tunnel. They will have that blocked. We are down to a number that can't stand up to the help they got from those blacks that came in behind us. So what I think we should do is tell them that we will trade Skywalker for Savanah. It is my understanding that this Mondo is sweet on Skywalker, and I think he will go along with the trade and we will keep the thousand dollars in gold that we got and divide it among ourselves. That will give us plenty of carrying-around money for quite a while. We will tell Purify Jones that we paid the thousand dollars in gold to Mondo. Now let me try to make a deal. You all stay back, and I will go out and meet them and if you see them coming, then you come. I just don't want to lose Skywalker without getting Savanah. If necessary, we will kill them all once they get out of that fort and we get them in the open. Now a bunch of ignorant blacks and stupid Indians are not going to get the best of us. We've been handicapped because they have been holed up in that stupid fort, and we couldn't blow up that fort because we couldn't harm Savanah. Let's get Savanah, split the gold, go back, and get more cannons and more men and then come back and then we can blow the hell out of them. How does that sound?"

The eight men looked at each other and nodded agreement to the deal that Split Face was proposing.

About that time, Split Face looked up and Mondo was walking out waving a white flag, and about ten steps behind him was Hudson Greer and the three blacks from Wildhorse Creek on his left side and Bear Chaser and Maboola on his right side. Walking about twenty steps behind was Savanah by herself.

"See there. Here they come. They want to deal, and this should be a cinch." Split Face grabbed up Skywalker, who was still in a daze after he had knocked her out. He half carried and half dragged her in front of him out toward the middle of the field between the fort and the north end of Little Beaver Creek tree line. The eight ex-rebs followed about twenty paces behind Split Face.

When Mondo got within forty yards of Split Face, he stopped and so did Split Face.

"Turn over Skywalker and we will let you go back to Texas alive," hollered Mondo.

"You turn over Savanah, and I will give you back your woman, Skywalker. That's a fair trade. One woman for the other woman, and we'll be gone and leave you alone and not come back."

"How many men did you come here with? You are down to eight men standing there behind you, and I know you came with about nineteen more. They are all dead. Why do you think that you can do any good now? We've got you. You don't have us. We don't need the fort anymore. We can attack you right now and your men would be dead in a second. Now turn her over and we will let you leave in peace."

"I know you are sweet on this woman. I'm fixing to put a bullet in her brain if I don't see Savanah walking forward. And you other men stop inching up closer. Just hold it right where you are. If you come any closer, I am going to turn my men loose on you all."

As Mondo was speaking, he was slowly moving closer to Split Face, and the four men on his left and the two on his right were keeping up with him as they slowly eased forward nearer to Skywalker and Split Face.

"I said stop. I mean it. I'll make another deal. I've got a thousand dollars in gold in my saddle bags right now. I'll send somebody and get that thousand dollars and I'll trade Skywalker for Savanah and I'll let you have a thousand dollars in gold. Now how does that sound?"

"We don't want your gold. We've got fifty men coming from Wildhorse Creek, and we've got the soldiers from the new fort coming. They will be here within the hour. Now you turn Skywalker loose and get the hell out of here so we won't have to kill you all. If you wait around, there will be enough people chasing you that you won't make Red River. Now forget about the gold. Do you want to live, or do you want to die?"

Split Face turned back to his men. "Go get the gold out of my saddle bag. Bring it here. I'll show the gold to Mondo. He probably doesn't believe I have it. He's not going to turn down the money, nobody would."

None of the men moved and Split Face looked back at them again and shouted. "Get a move on it. Get the gold."

"That's our gold," said one of the ex-rebs. "We are not going to give it up. We don't give a damn whether we get that Savanah or not. That's your problem. Enough of us have died already. We are not messing with this bunch any more. We're just going to split up the gold and leave."

The rest of Split Face's men started to turn away and walked back toward the horses. While Split Face was looking back at his men, Mondo and his people kept advancing in a careful steady walk toward Split Face and Skywalker.

Split Face turned back to the approaching group from the fort. Skywalker came out of a daze and saw Mondo and the men coming toward her and at the same time realized that Split Face's people were starting to turn and move back toward their horses. Skywalker stomped on the top of Split Face's boot, drew the knife from under her skirt, and drove the blade just under Split Face's right rib cage. Split Face loosened his grip on Skywalker, and Skywalker dropped to the ground, and yelled, "Kill him! Kill him!"

Mondo's people open-fired and charged forward at full speed.

Split Face fell to his knees, twisted around, and fired a bullet into Skywalker then hit the ground as bullets flew over him, and some of his men returned the fire as they ran toward their horses.

Split Face turned the gun on the charging Mondo and fired as Mondo rolled to his right and came back on his feet and continued charging toward Split Face. Split Face aimed carefully and fired again, and Mondo dove to his left and flattened himself on the ground. All this time, Maboola, who had emptied his shotgun, was charging as hard and as fast as he could move. Split Face turned the gun on Maboola and shot him between the eyes, which did not stop the black giant from taking one last step, raising his machete and cutting off Split Face's head before Maboola fell across the decapitated Split Face.

Mondo got there and rolled Maboola over and saw the hole in his head and a smile across his lips. Mondo turned to Skywalker, who opened her eyes and gave him a weak smile.

Bear Chaser and three men from Wildhorse Creek had run down to the west bank of the creek and were firing at the eight ex-rebs that were riding away from Little Beaver Valley leading Split Face's horse that carried the thousand dollars in gold. Mondo picked Skywalker up and carried her back to the cabin, and Savanah started doctoring the wound that didn't look too bad.

The battle of Fort Mondo was over, and the ex-rebs were racing for the Red River with the gold and their lives, but two of Mondo's friends were no longer alive.

CHAPTER 60

THE DAY SPLIT Face was killed, Mick had ridden north to find Red Granger and his men coming back from Abilene, Kansas, after the sale of their cattle. He found them about thirty-five miles north crossing the Washita River.

"Been looking for you all," said Mick as he took off his hat and wiped his head with his red bandana.

"Been coming back as fast as we could," said Red Granger. "Me and Delaware got wind from the drovers moving up the trail that a gang of KKK cowards were attacking Mondo's fort. Is it still standing?"

"Yes. I rode by yesterday, and the best I could tell, their cannon is wiped out but there's still about twenty or so ex-reb killers circling in for the kill. I was hoping you would let me borrow a few of your people to give them sorry bastards something to worry about from their backside."

"I'll do better than that. I'll go with you. Let's rest our mounts a few breaths and then take off in a quick trot for Mondo's place. How does that sound?" said Red as he turned to Delaware and his men for approval.

"Were they attacking yesterday?" asked Delaware.

"Not that I could tell, but I did hear shots after I rode off," answered Mick.

"Then let's ride fast right now," said Delaware. "We've got about twelve good rifles and we can all get fresh mounts. I think all of our men have been talking about it and they want some of that action."

Red Granger turned his horse and faced the black cow hands that awaited his orders. "Now, men, you didn't sign in for no war duty. But I think you know what's going down over at Mondo's fort. There's a bunch of KKK black haters paid by that rich maniac Purify Jones to kill all in the fort and take back his light yellow woman who doesn't want to go back to him. Now there's this so-called Black Death man called Maboola that is supposed to be in there, and he's killed a bunch of white people. So almost everyone that ain't colored is after him. But I think that he needs to be tried legally and not murdered or lynched. Anyway, I want to help those people because if those crazy killers are allowed to run free and kill ex-slaves, then we're going to have many years of lynching instead of law and order. There won't be real freedom for ex-slaves for a long time. So what do you say? Each man can go or stay, and I'll not hold it against him. You will all still have a job no matter what you decide."

Delaware Hunter raised his hand, and Red Granger stopped. "We've all talked it over already, Mr. Granger. We are all going. We know those crazy haters have to be stopped, both black and white. So let's get after those white maniacs."

Mick and Red Granger got to Mondo's fort right after the attackers had grabbed the gold and headed south. Mondo, Bear Chaser, and Hudson Greer had just taken Skywalker in the cabin, and she was being treated by Savanah. They walked back outside where Maboola lay dead next to the canvas-wrapped body of Storm.

When Red Granger and Mick rode up with the twelve cowhands, they all stopped and stared at the dead Maboola. Then one at a time, the black cow hands dismounted, walked over to the black giant, took off their hat, bowed their heads, and shed some tears. The great symbol of resistance to the white terror lay dead on the ground, and all those there knew that even though he had committed murder, he was someone who stood up to the white terror. Delaware Hunter finally looked over at Mondo. "Did any of them get away? I didn't see very many bodies."

"There was about eight that grabbed the gold that Split Face had brought and took off. I guess you saw the body of that ugly bastard that everybody calls Split Face. We got him and his men deserted with the gold."

"Yeah. I saw the body of Split Face lying out there on the field. You ought to leave him and let the buzzards pick him apart. But I haven't seen enough dead white men. As I understand it, there was about twenty-seven that came. How many do you think headed back for Texas?"

"I believe there were eight," said Bear Chaser. "I got a good look at them, and they were riding south as fast as they could go."

"How long ago did they leave? What kind of start do they got on us?" asked Red Granger.

"They've been gone almost an hour," said Hudson Greer. "I don't know whether you will be able to catch them before they hit Red River or not."

Delaware Hunter mounted up as did Red Granger and the rest of the men. "We'll catch them. If we don't get them before they cross the Red River, we'll get them in Texas if we have to chase them all the way to Purify Jones's doorstep," said Red Granger.

With that, Red Granger and his men along with Mick O'Ryan rode out from Mondo's fort and kicked dust going south as fast as their horses could carry them.

They hadn't caught up to them by the time they hit Red River Station and swam their horses across the river. As Red Granger, Mick, and the twelve black cowboys rode out from the Red River and into the little town called Red River Station, there was nothing but silent stares as the whites knew who they were and knew who they were after. Red Granger rode up to the ferry owner.

"When did those KKK raiders cross the river?"

The owner shook his head and shrugged his shoulders like he didn't know. Red Granger drew his gun and put it right up close to his face. "I'll give you five seconds to answer my question, or they'll bury your ass right here by your own damn ferry."

The ferry owner immediately answered. "They've got about an hour start on you. They were riding hard and riding fast, and they gave me some gold to keep my mouth shut. Now that they are in Texas, you better be careful who you pull that gun on. Most people think that they done some good. They are claiming they killed Black Death. You know the one that hung white Texans upside down after he cut their heads off. If that's so, the men you are after are the most popular men in North Texas right now."

"They may be popular, but I'm damn sure telling you one thing, they are dead sons-of-bitches."

"Are you trying to tell me that you are going to lead these darkies across North Texas to hunt down the men that killed that murdering Black Death? Are you crazy? Every white man in North Texas will be after you, Red Granger."

"Well, they can come and try me on for size because I'm tired of that Purify Jones spending money on those crazy ex-rebs and paying them killers to commit murder and nobody doing anything about it. It's about time somebody in Texas stood up for what is right. Now get out of my way."

With that, Red Granger jerked his horse around and knocked the ferryman off his feet. The black cowboys, Red Granger, and Mick O'Ryan spurred their horses on south, looking for the raiders.

They almost ran their horses into the ground chasing the KKK killers but caught up with them about ten miles north of Purify Jones's plantation. Since they had crossed the Red River, the raiders felt safe and were just taking their time returning to Purify Jones to report on what had transpired in Indian Territory. They all agreed to divide the gold and tell Mr. Jones that they had paid Mondo Hobbs the money, and Mondo Hobbs welched on the deal and had not returned Savanah. They also were going to tell him that they killed Maboola, the Black Death, and felt like with that news, Jones would probably let them get by with not bringing back his sweet light-colored darky to be his wife, and Split Face was really not liked by anyone.

Red Granger took half the men and Delaware Hunter took the other half and they circled the attackers who were just loafing along and not looking out for any danger. The attack was swift and quick, and death was immediate and to all. They came in on both sides, firing away, and most of the attackers received more than one bullet and either one would have brought death. It was over almost before it started, and all the attackers were dead.

Red Granger got the one thousand dollars in gold and led his men toward Purify Jones's plantation. As the group rode up, the armed guards of the plantation ran out with rifles to put a stop to them entering the plantation.

Red Granger raised his hand and shouted. "I want to talk to Mr. Purify Jones. We've got his thousand dollars in gold, and I'm returning it to him. His death money did not work. He doesn't have his sweet Savanah, and he'll never get her. In addition, even though Black Death is gone and killed, there's plenty of people across the Red River and there's some of us here in North Texas that don't like what he's doing. I want to talk to that son-of-a-bitch and I want to talk to him now. Get him out at once, or we are going to attack this place and burn it to the ground."

The guards hurried back to the plantation, and Purify Jones rode out to talk to Red Granger. The men got off their horses and met at the gate of the plantation. Red Granger flung the thousand dollars in gold at Purify Jones's feet.

"Here's your damn blood money. Take it and stick it up your ass. You've been causing nothing but trouble ever since you decided you had to keep that female slave that you were raping. How many people are going to die because you want somebody just for her body that doesn't want you? I know you are a big rich man and you've got a lot of power, but there's a lot of us in Texas that don't like what you are doing. You are an embarrassment to the whole state. Your greedy and vicious actions are going to start a war that we don't need. We've done lost one, and hardly nobody accepts defeat in Texas. By God, I'm here to say that if you send anybody else across the Red River or if you spend any more money on those crazy ex-reb killers, then I'm going to burn your place down, and if I need help, I can get the Cattlemen's Association to back my plan. You can raise an army, and I can too, and we better get this matter settled or we'll have problems for the next hundred years trying to adjust and live with the kidnapped slaves that we bought and controlled for years."

"What's your problem, Mr. Granger? I don't understand you. You want to just turn over the state to these carpetbaggers and their black friends? Don't you realize that if we don't intimidate them and keep them under control that they are going to run rampant and rape our white women and take over everything in the state? These people that you want to protect are not people. These people that you think are human are not human but are animals. They are savage animals that have to be controlled like you would your horse or your dog. And you want to turn them loose and make them equal. They can't read and write and they can hardly talk English. They don't know how to act or make a decision or anything and you are trying to advocate we treat them equal. That's ridiculous. You are one ignorant voice in Texas. I've never heard any good Texans speak up and try to force these savages down our throats. Your life is in danger and not from me but from everybody that's anybody in North Texas. Every white man is going to be gunning for you now. You, sir, are a traitor. You have ridden down some KKK members who represent the pure Texans who believe in a just God. That whole KKK is going to declare war on you. You're as good as dead. Don't you understand that? Now thank you for bringing back my gold, but I think you better get out and find a real good hiding place because your life ain't worth a penny."

"Well, I'll tell you one thing, my life may be in danger and I'm not sure about that but if it is, I'm going to come back and finish you before I die. If you don't stop providing money to the KKK and sending killers across the Red River to try to get back that

Savanah, then I'll come back, and by God, I don't need an army of crazy haters. I might die trying, but I'm going to put an end to you. You are bad for Texas, and it looks like you, sir, have got to die."

The little man puffed out his chest and produced a fake laugh. "You're big talk, and you're a big man, but you are not big enough to mess with me. You are as good as dead right now. I've got enough guns trained on you from the plantation fences around here to wipe you and all your darkies out right this minute. I always give a white man an honest break. I'd rather not have a battle right in my front yard and dirty up my fine lawn. But let me tell you something, you think you are going to kill me. Well, you're not. I'm going to get you. Now get out." With that, little Purify Jones spun on his heel, raised his head high, and marched back toward his plantation house.

Red Granger glared at him and looked at the number of rifles that were pointed at them from the plantation fence. Jones had more men than he had. He turned to his people. "Well, we better go now. We've got the bastards that rode across the Red River. I'm going to go back to the Cattlemen's Association and try to get some help. This guy is a sorry excuse for a human being, and he shouldn't be walking around. We've done all we can do now. Let us go and come back another day when we have the numbers."

With that, the men mounted up and left Purify Jones's plantation.

CHAPTER 61

ONDO LAID STORM over the Comanche's horse
and started the trip back to Storm's band in the Texas
Panhandle. As he rode west, Comanches picked up the news of
the death of the famous warrior and joined in the trip back to the
Palo Duro Canyon. The procession camped near the North Fork
of the Red River, and some Cheyenne and Kiowas rode in and
the group sang songs of praise to Storm late into the night.

The next day, an Antelope band delegation met Mondo at the
Texas border and five hundred warriors of various Plains tribes
followed Mondo to the Palo Duro Canyon. Storm's three wives
had cut their hair and slashed their arms and legs in their grief for
the famous Comanche whose medicine caused him to fight alone
during bad weather. When they all had gathered for the final ceremony, Mondo stood up at the request of Bull Bear and recounted
the last battle and the bravery of Storm during his final moments
and answered questions about why and how Storm died.

Bull Bear took the opportunity to make a statement concerning the need to stay with the Great Spirit's instructions and to
avoid getting mixed up in the crazy battles of the white men who
did not understand or care for the Antelope Comanches or their
customs and religion.

Bull Bear continued. "It is true that Storm was very loyal to
his friend Mondo. But his medicine was clearly known to all.
Storm's death was beyond bravery because he put his loyalty to
his friend above his protected medicine. The Great Spirit gave
Storm much power taken from the fury of bad weather condi-

tions. The Great Spirit had told Storm he must not fight and do battle or go on dangerous hunts unless the gods made the climate angry. The more ferocious the storm, the more power the Great Spirit gave this great warrior."

The gathered Indians all grunted or nodded in agreement because the unusual power of this warrior was well known by all tribes. The stronger the medicine or direction from the Great Spirit, the more an Indian had to obey the demands revealed to the warrior by the Indian gods.

"Storm fought when the weather was good, and Storm died. Storm got mixed up in the crazy hate of the whites for people of different color. The whites of Texas have always been killers for reasons not understood by us. First, it was for our land, and they stayed on the land forever and ruined it by destroying the ground with sharp plows and digging holes to store their body waste. They killed other whites for the right to own a black person. Now, these Texans kill all nonwhites that don't even live on their land. We, the Antelope band, learned many years ago to stay away from the whites that live in Texas. They kill all, either by many men with guns of all sizes and power or by unclean filth that they deliver to Comanches so that whole bands died of a new and unfamiliar sickness. Storm elected to get involved with the problems of the evil white men from Texas who liked to kill men who are not white. This has been their way forever, first with the Mexicans then the Indians and now with the blacks. We must not let our great warriors ride off and fight the battle of survival alone and away from the protection and power of our own band. So far, the whites have not decided to take our hunting grounds. I've been told that it's too dry for farming and too dry for raising cattle, and they will leave it to us and the buffalo. We are lucky that we live in an area that does not have enough rain for the whites to steal it from us. But I've been told that more whites come, and they want all the land and that they are killing all the buffalo so that we cannot exist on the land that we've lived on for ever and ever. I envision that the whites will substitute the longhorn cattle for the buffalo. If the buffalo can live on our land, so may their own cattle. Our grass will feed the longhorn and not our buffalo, and the whites will make their last big push on our band. We need all the warriors here to have any chance at all to keep them from killing us all. We cannot allow our great warriors to go off and get killed in any other white men battles. We need all to survive. So remember, stay together as one great undefeated band of Comanches and live your religion at all times and the Great Spirit will assist us, and we may survive for at least our lifetime."

Mondo stood up and answered, "What you say is true, Bull Bear. Storm did die for me. Storm did deny his medicine for my sake. Without Storm and my other friends, I would be dead now. He told me that he didn't want to live and see the day when your great band is attacked by many white soldiers and your band removed from your hunting grounds. The spreading death dealt by the white man goes on and on, and someday, you will have to fight the last battle. Men of color, whether Indian or black, must get together and demand fair treatment because I believe the whites will take control of everything and trample on all who get in their way. The whites have no honor among themselves. They kill each other like in the Great War where a half a million whites were slaughtered. They are a killing machine who cut all down without honor. Nobody can stand in their way. I pledge to do all I can to help Storm's people, like Storm did for me. So Storm, a great warrior, will not have died without a reason. All of us left on the land not controlled by the whites must get together to fight for every inch of our property being taken over by the white man's creeping greed. All of us must pledge to go down fighting for the right to live our lives as we want to live them and not like the whites want us to live. Until we join the battle as one, we will be divided and conquered as small problems to the whites who take over all our property and will destroy our way of living."

There was nothing but sad silence after Mondo's talk that ended Storm's funeral.

Mondo borrowed five horses and switched mounts as he rode back hard for Wildhorse Creek for the burial of his friend Maboola. The big African man had been taken to Wildhorse Creek for burial. Word spread of his death!

After Red Granger left Purify Jones's plantation, Jones reported a different version of what happened at Mondo's fort to the local newspapers. The headlines for all of the North Texas papers and eventually all the Texas newspapers carried the story of the killing of the vicious Negro who killed all whites and then raped white women. Black Death was finally dead and Jones put a stop to any reports of the defeat of the white men by the blacks in Indian Territory. Any newspaper that heard the rumors of the death of twenty-seven ex-rebs by the blacks and Indians were told not to publish the story. Jones convinced the newspaper owners that the ex-slaves would rise up and kill all white people aided by the Yankee troops and the Freedmen's Bureau if there was even a hint that a rebellion of ex-slaves could be successful. All black leaders and all acts of disobedience to the ex-white masters must be dealt with by the killing of those Negroes that resist control. Any news of success would encourage rebellion and most of all the black leaders had to be eliminated.

There was only one white voice, other than the Yankee carpetbaggers that no Southern person listened to, who spoke the truth about what happened in Mondo's fort. Red Granger, who was put down by most Texans as a darkie lover, told of the attack financed by Purify Jones because Purify Jones wanted to sleep with his ex-slave. "Sex was the motive for the attack," hollered Red Granger to anybody who would listen. "All Texans were killed by a combination of ex-slaves, a few Indians and a double half-breed called Mondo Hobbs who was half-Chickasaw and one-half African." The KKK backed by Jones kept calling Red Granger a liar and so far had managed to keep Granger's stories of the battle from being printed in any newspapers. But the rumors of the death of Maboola spread like a wild prairie fire throughout Indian Territory and down into Texas just like the word of freedom had spread up from Galveston on June 19, 1865, when the Yankee general arrived to take charge of Texas. When the rumor of Maboola's death reached the ex-slaves, many blacks slipped away to attend Maboola's funeral.

Mondo Hobbs made it to the Wildhorse Creek community before the burial of Maboola. Hudson Greer estimated that at least three thousand Negroes, mostly ex-slaves, had secretly traveled miles to view the remains of the man who never took anything off whites without a fierce fight. An African man who the masters could not master. From the time of his capture as a boy and during his time as a slave, Maboola had resisted the lack of freedom with all his might. Every human being no matter their color knew of the Black Death.

The poor ex-slaves who could not afford a horse walked hundreds of miles to view his body. Every time the date was set for the final burial, some ex-slave who owned a horse would ride in and tell Hudson Greer that there were hundreds of ex-slaves slipping through the Cross Timbers at night just to view the remains of the great man. So Mondo made it to Wildhorse Creek the day of the final resting, and three thousand gathered on the hill overlooking the Washita River to pay tribute to the man the whites called Black Death. The Chickasaw Lighthorse Police had given up trying to stop the Negroes' pilgrimage to Wildhorse Creek, but at least a hundred police had gathered on the outskirts of the funeral to make sure the services didn't turn into a mob of killing blacks who would attack the Chickasaw tribe and any white men that stood in its way.

The well-known Right Reverend Billy "Horseshoe" Johnson, who came all the way from Greenville, Texas, led off for the speakers who had gathered to pay tribute to the man from Africa called Maboola.

"Murder is a sin! We all know that. But is all killing a murder? God is supposed to forgive killing in a war. Our freedom came from killing. I am told a half a million men died and at least that many were left deformed or useless in the battle for our freedom being called the Civil War even though there was nothing civil about it. Now most whites say the man we bury today was a murderer, a cold-blooded killer of the whites. I've talked to the people who knew Maboola. He did enjoy killing whites at first. He did hate with a just and proper hate for the beatings he received, and he lived with a valley of scars on his back that drove him to do evil toward his oppressors. Most of his killings were in self-defense or in the line of duty protecting those helpless people who were being unjustly attacked by evil white men like the KKK and the white haters that loved to do harm to the people of color. But at last toward the end of his days and for the great joy from heaven, Maboola saw the light from God. He wanted to go back to his homeland in Africa. He stopped his thirst for the bloody killing of the people with white skin. He repented for his sins and wiped away his hate. He died a glorious death in pure self-defense and will ascend into heaven while the man called Split Face that Maboola killed as his final act will thankfully burn in the fires of hell for all eternity."

With that, a roar came up from the crowd as they rose to their feet and without any direction began singing the "Battle Hymn of the Republic." At the end of the song, there was total silence from all and then the Right Reverend Billy "Horseshoe" Johnson, with his booming voice, lowered his head for a final prayer. "Dear Lord. Look down upon our people and help us in our quest for freedom. Lead us on your way and let us keep on the right track so that we will receive justice and equality on earth as we will in heaven. Don't make us killers like the night riders who disobey your word. Let us live with Jesus and gain our place in society without any more hangings. Let us not follow the evil ways of the white men who ride and kill at night hidden behind white robes.

Let us live a life of peace and love so that we will never again have to gather to honor the death of a man of color who had to kill in his lifetime. Give us help so we can overcome the hatred poured down on our heads by the sick, evil devil worshipers that attack us without fear of punishment. Do not make us live in fear for the rest of our lives. Let us be able to look up into your eyes and feel free and peaceful before we pass on to the holy land. Maboola was not a crazy man, just a man, and he stood up and faced those who rode against him and did not hide as a coward behind white robes. He was a different killer from Split Face and the KKK and he was a killer who learned his lesson and wanted to kill no more. I know you will make a place in heaven for this great black warrior."

The ceremony and burial lasted a whole day as many spoke for Maboola and celebrated his life. At midnight, the man called Black Death was buried in a secret unmarked grave for fear the KKK would dig him up and display him as a trophy.

That night, a great rainstorm seemed to clean away the hate and bitterness of those gathered. Mondo looked over at Bear Chaser and smiled. "One great warrior is saying goodbye to another great warrior." Bear Chaser looked up into the dark clouds appearing between lighting strikes. "Yes. They are getting together to talk about old times and great battles of the past."

Chapter 62

R ED GRANGER WAS shot in the back and killed as he rode
away from Gainesville, Texas, where he had threatened the
editor of the local paper to publish the truth about the attack on
Mondo's fort or Red Granger would expose him as a cowardly
liar. The newspaper had printed the story that was being accepted
all across Texas that a bunch of ex-slaves led by the Black Death
had attacked and killed twenty-six innocent cowboys peacefully
herding cattle to Kansas and that's when Maboola was killed.

Mondo and his friends met Delaware Hunter at Fitzpatrick's
store in October of 1869, a meeting called by Delaware Hunter
to plan the attack on Purify Jones. Word had reached Mondo and
Bear Chaser from Hudson Greer who got the message from an
ex-slave walking up from Texas. The message was Red Granger
was murdered and it was time to cross the Red River and deal
with Purify Jones, the one who had hired killers to murder
Red Granger.

Fitzpatrick turned the store over to Mick and left the area.
The owner didn't want to know what he suspected was the reason
for the gathering of some tough, hard men who had the look in
their eyes that killing was to be discussed.

Delaware led off with his reason for calling the meeting. "You
all know that Red got back shot in the night after demanding
that the Gainesville paper print the truth about the attack on
Mondo's fort. He rode alone because he feared nothing, and he
always treated a man as a man, no matter where he came from or
the color of his skin. When a man proved he was a sneaky cow-

ard, Red dealt with him harshly no matter whether he was white or not. I never met a man who lived a straighter life. He never went along with popular view if it didn't seem right to him. You all knew him well. When some of the white ex-rebs complained about working under me because I was black, he fired them on the spot. He alone among the ex-Southern officers stood for truth and justice even after defeat. Since he was such a strong leader, he had to be killed by the crazy haters of the people of color. The question I want to find out from you, the people that Red Granger supported is, can we kill Jones, and is it worth it? I know for a fact that Jones paid for the killing. Do we want to become a murderer like him? Will it help or hurt our own people if we ride in and do away with that crazy man who wants to kill us?"

No one spoke and a silence held for a while as the other men pondered the questions. Finally, they all looked at Hudson Greer, who seemed to possess a steady, thoughtful approach to the issues of racial hatred and mistreatment of ex-slaves. Greer shook his head as if he wasn't sure of the answer.

"I don't know. We still remain a very outnumbered minority like the American Indian. Resistance appears impossible. The whites never stop and always answer violence with greater violence. The real question that we can't answer right now is, will the good Christian white people of the South continue to allow assault on minorities like ex-slaves, Indians and even Mexicans after the Freedmen's Bureau returns to Washington, D.C. and the Yankee army leaves the South. Will the South ever treat minorities as equals without being forced to do so by bullets and armed resistance? I'm thinking that the loss these proud Southerners are suffering at this time will be remembered by them for a long time. The so-called good white Southern Christians will not try to stop the mistreatment of black people whether we remain acting like slaves or whether we form an organization like their KKK and fight violence with violence. I don't want to belong to a group that kills at night behind hoods and sheets like the bloody white cowards of the KKK. Remember, the numbers that we keep hearing about from the Freedmen's Bureau in Texas. Every time a white person thinks a black has not shown the proper respect, violence is waged against that person of color. The haters have got the numbers, the weapons, and the experience in killing. If we kill one white, twenty blacks will hang. I don't think any good will come from the killing of Purify Jones. Violence by us will only strengthen their resolve to control us by fear. Their views of us as animals will only be increased if we ride into Texas and kill Jones. The whole state will come across the Red River after us."

Mick stood up with a deep frown on his face. "I know I'm white, but I'm also Irish, and we're considered a lowlife by most whites in this country, but they don't come for us at night or lynch us. And do you know why? Because the Irishmen stick together, and we can kill too. They may not treat us with respect and they may talk about how ignorant and uncivilized we 'Pope-loving' Irish are, but they damn sure don't dress up in robes and surround our house and try to string us up to the nearest tree because we looked at one of their daughters with lust in our eyes. That's because we'd find out whom they were and come for them. We've fought the prejudice from the English for centuries, and we don't allow it over here. If we don't scare those white haters, they will never stop. Most of the KKK is made up of very ignorant fools who love to hurt people or torture animals. They probably don't amount to ten to fifteen percent of the white Southern male, but the other eighty-five percent is letting them get by with these horrible crimes against people of color. If the noncrazy whites that know better think that they or their children will be hit in some crossfire, they'll stop the KKK fools that like to inflict pain and suffering on the less fortunate. A stand has to be made. We've got to make all whites see the problem and do something about it. The white American, or most of them by far, understand deep down one thing and that's power and fear. The majority will stop the minority of crazy haters who love to see pain on other human beings when the people of color, whether Indian, black, or Mexican show some power and put some fear in all whites. This is where we start the lesson the normal whites must learn. We ride in and hang Purify Jones from the tallest oak tree, and we will see change for sure. Americans don't respect anything but money and power."

Mondo leaned back in his chair and looked Mick straight into his eyes. "You're a hater, Mick. Ever since Purify Jones hired Split Face and those men to beat you to a pulp in Fort Worth, you've never been the same happy, caring man you once were. You're all white and you seem to be the one who wants to kill Jones more than the rest of us. Is that a white-born condition? Are all white Americans born to be natural killers who fight to the death if they think they are wronged by anyone? Is the white Bible and Christianity for forgiveness so that white killers can be saved and not burned in hell for murder? It seems to me that most good religions whether practiced by Indians, black people or whites should try to prevent murdering each other. I don't think it's natural for men to kill. It does something not good to men when he kills another man, no matter the reason. I want Purify Jones dead because the son-of-a -bitch brought about the death of two of my best friends, Maboola and Storm. I don't think it's a national issue. I don't think we will help or hurt the minority cause for equality. What we do will make no difference on how the blacks are treated in the future. To me it's real simple. Purify Jones should die because he killed three good people and because he continues to threaten my wife and child-to-be. Let's just get off the high talk of race issues and what's good for white or colored humans. Purify Jones is a complete asshole and we should kill him. If we don't, we'll be harassed by him forever. We've got reason alone without the color of our skin. Let us ride out together. If Mick and I and Delaware are the only ones, we still can get it done. Delaware says he's got a person who works for Jones that will help us. If we make it to his place, we can get in and maybe get out. That's the only question we should be talking about. Can we kill the bastard and figure how to get back alive? If we kidnap him and use him to keep the KKK off our backs, we may make it across the Red River alive before we kill the son-of-a-bitch."

Delaware Hunter smiled and stood up. "He's got it in a nutshell. It's simple. Jones should die. He's taken enough people from us. He's killed too many good men. I can get us inside his mansion. The rest will be easy. We get rid of a few guards, grab Jones and then ride like hell out of Texas. This won't start a war because there's still a lot of Yankee troops in Texas. The killing of Jones won't change Southern hate because that's here to stay for a long time for more reasons than we'll ever know or figure out. Who's going to ride with me?"

Bear Chaser stood and shook Delaware's hand. "I can't seem to outgrow this old Indian warrior blood. I've got a good woman and a good farm over on Cow Creek. If I had really grown up or become half smart, I'd let you young warriors go off and do the killing and probably get killed, but this, time I'm going off to war with you. You're not going to leave me here. I've run before when I was chased from Mississippi. Jones represents all the evil that the white man brings to this land. We're not going to solve any problems, nor are we going to stop any killings, but it is a way to live and maybe die with pride. I've hated the greedy takers in the white race all my life. I'm not running this time. I think I'll enjoy this trip no matter what happens. It's a way an old man may regain a little self respect."

Five men rode out to Texas to visit the home of one Purify Jones. The men were armed and ready to pay back the man who had sent killers to their doorsteps for two years. They all felt it was time to take the battle to the man who was behind most of the killing involving nonwhites.

CHAPTER 63

THE FIVE MEN became the night riders of mixed color.
Two Blacks, one white, one Indian and a half-Indian, half-black mix rode across the Red River at night and camped in the
Cross Timbers during the day like Comanche raiders. Not much
was said between the men as each kept his own thoughts to himself. They all thought they would be lucky to ever cross back over
the Red River. It was as if there was a silent agreement to die for
the death of one Purify Jones, the rich Texan who was above any
law. Mr. Jones was praised by most ex-rebs as the keeper of the
white power and Purify Jones used the Pinkerton Agency to buy
off or intimidate the local Freedmen's Bureau people who were
supposed to protect the ex-slaves. Also, money exchanged hands
in Washington, D.C., to keep the Yankee army from interfering
with Jones and his hired guns, the KKK. The Freedmen's Bureau
made some poor efforts to control the KKK, but nobody would
testify against the night riders for fear of death, and certainly no
one would openly accuse Purify Jones of financing the lynching of the black people, but most whites knew who was behind
the murders.

Delaware Hunter had spoken to most of the Yankee officers and bureaucrats that were supposed to protect the freedman and was told there was no evidence against Jones, and they
couldn't find anyone who would testify against the night raiders
in white robes.

So Delaware Hunter, who originally believed in law, lost his
belief in the law as it affects people of color. There was one law for

whites and another law for blacks. Even when the Yankees occupied Texas, the Federal troops, and the Northern civil servants who were supposed to prevent killing and intimidation of the Negroes were not effective. The Federal troops did supervise the 1869 Texas election for a new Texas Constitutional Convention ordered by the US Congress which did not allow ex-rebs to vote even if they took the pledge to support the US Constitution. And the new Constitution of Texas guaranteed equal protection of all men, but the whites who violated the new Constitution were never prosecuted. Life went on like before the Civil War.

If an ex-slave wanted to work, he or she signed a labor contract that paid them in shares of the crop which never seemed to cover the loan from the white land owner for food, shelter and clothing. So the old system went on as most ex-slaves could not read their share crop contract and could not even count money so that even if their contract was approved by the Freedmen's Bureau it was never fairly interpreted. The Negro workers were cheated and became more and more indebted to the owner of the land for the borrowed money to buy necessities. If a black broke the contract, he was arrested and forced to return to the field to work off his fine. The system was returning to the same inequality as before the war. The whites controlled the blacks even more after their freedom.

The South and Texas didn't give free education to the poor whites so the Freedmen's Bureau during reconstruction could never get Texas or any other Southern state to pay for the education of ex-slaves. Some Northern charities paid for the basic education of black children so that right after the war, more blacks were getting educated than poor whites. The poverty and the total control by whites continued even with the Yankees occupying the South. Ex-slaves were beggars, rapists, killers, and lazy workers in the eyes of the majority of whites in the South. The whites treated the ex-slaves as foreign invaders who were not civilized let alone advanced enough from their animal stage to be human. Also, the white Texans who had never lost a war blamed their loss and their extreme poverty on the Negro. Every time a Southern white saw an ex-slave, he was reminded of his destruction and poverty and blamed the color of a man's skin for all of the South's problems. Delaware Hunter spoke to the men of his belief that a man of color would not be able to live around Southern whites and feel like a man. Delaware did not want to live like he was still a slave and would rather die killing Purify Jones, whom Hunter thought represented the most deadly enemy of the blacks. Therefore, Delaware Hunter led the men to Jones's plantation.

The old black house servant that had hated Purify Jones all his life opened the secret door located in the high wall that surrounded the Jones's plantation and led the raiders through the darkness of the apple orchard and up to the locked back entrance of the large plantation mansion. Now the tricky part began as they tried to get into the house and to Jones before his bodyguards and armed protectors heard them. The men with Mondo were told that at least twenty well-armed bodyguards lived on the premises and at least six stayed inside the big house. This was going to be an almost impossible mission. The house servant had no keys, so a quiet break-in was needed to get safely to Jones. As soon as the servant touched the locked door, a voice demanded the identity of the person at the door. The five men backed up against the side of the house and the servant risked his life for the death of the main financial support of the KKK in North Texas.

"It's me, Sam. I lost my cane and needed it to visit my grandson over across the road. I'm sure it's in the house somewhere. Can you please open up for a minute and let me check and see if I left it inside?"

The guard mumbled something about "dumb darkies always losing stuff" and flung open the door. Mondo's left hand grabbed the guard's throat and lifted him outside without a sound except for the crack of the neck bone when Mondo snapped his head backward. As Mondo was laying the dead guard aside, Delaware Hunter dashed through the door followed by Bear Chaser, Mick and Hudson Greer.

Two armed guards sitting at the bottom of the stairway raised their rifles but never fired because bullets from four pistols tore through their bodies and knocked them dead to the floor.

"You two stay here and keep any guards from coming upstairs," shouted Delaware as he raised his handgun and shot a guard who appeared at the top of the stairs. Bear Chaser and Greer pulled large tables from the living room and took cover, looking both ways to protect the entrance to the stairway from the front and back door and from the interior of the house.

Mondo and Mick ran up the stairs behind Delaware Hunter as Bear Chaser dropped two guards charging through the front door. At the top of the stairs, bullets peppered the walls and Delaware dove for cover behind a love seat in the upstairs hallway. Mondo peeked over the top step and emptied his pistol into two men guarding a large closed door. Before the two hit the floor, Delaware, Mondo, and Mick were at the thick door the servant had told them was the main bedroom of Purify Jones. The door didn't bust open until all three drove into it at the same time and they went falling through and onto the floor, which saved their lives because little Purify Jones was firing a pistol at the doorway when the three hit the floor. The three attackers rolled away before the terrified little man could direct his shooting downward at them on the floor.

A lady screamed and ran to the corner of the room. Before either Mick or Mondo or Delaware could direct their bullets toward Purify Jones, his pistol started making the clicking sound of an empty gun. Jones dropped his pistol and began to cry. Mondo got to him first and threw Jones against the wall.

"Please. Don't hurt me. You can have anything you want. Just don't kill me. I'll give you all the gold that you can carry. And look at that girl, you can have her too."

The three men glanced over at a naked girl who huddled in the corner. She looked a lot like Savanah but not quite as light. Mondo lifted Jones to his feet.

"You're coming with us," said Mondo in a soft, controlled voice that scared Purify Jones even more.

"You can't make it out of here without my say-so. I've got at least ten men outside and a bunch more in reserve that will be coming here at the sound of the gunfire. If you let me go, I'll let you go. You can't get me out of here."

"I think we can. We know how many men you have. You're riding out with us as a hostage. If somebody shoots at us, we're going to blow your brains out. You better keep your guards off us. We're going to take you back to Indian Territory and try you for Maboola's death."

With that, Mondo grabbed the little man around the neck and pulled him along like he was a doll. The three men left the bedroom with Purify Jones without a word to the terrified naked woman who had been with the master of the house. Mondo put the pistol between Jones's eyes and whispered, "If you want to live one more second, you'd better call off your dogs loud and clear and do it right now!"

For a little man who was scared to death, Jones came up with a booming voice of command. "Hold up! This is Jones! Stop firing. We're coming out. Pass the word that I'm riding with these men back to Indian Territory. Allow us to leave my place without injury. Do you understand me? Obey my order! Now!"

The shooting stopped, and the five men came out of the mansion and carefully proceeded through the hidden door in the wall, mounted up, and started to ride the eighty miles toward Red River and the Chickasaw Nation.

Word of the kidnapping raced across the countryside, and within two hours, the twenty-five armed men who worked for Jones were joined by at least twenty-five more, most of them KKK members. The Texans didn't bother to tell the Yankee troops that were occupying Texas at the time. This was a Texas matter, and since when did Texas ever need Yankee help. No one ever invaded Texas and lived to make it back home. Even the great Yankee army never marched into Texas until the Civil War was over. An angry mob was riding hard to cut off the six men heading out of Texas and into Indian Territory.

CHAPTER 64

T HE FLEEING INDIAN Territory attackers were five miles from the Spanish Fort crossing at the Red River when the first batch of KKK caught up with them. The rays of the morning sun spread a dim light across the sky and lit up the riders so that the Texans could see their targets. Mondo tugged harder on the reins of the horse carrying the bound-up Jones but couldn't get any more speed out of Jones's horse. Mondo was dropping back as they neared the river crossing. The other four men were at least thirty yards ahead and riding low and fast as the bullets streaked around them from the guns of the charging Texans. It sounded like a regiment of US Cavalry as the KKK had the new repeating rifles that cocked a shell into the barrel with the flash of the right hand of the shooter. The noise of the rifle firing alerted the small Negro gathering known as the river rats that lived on the river. The rumor of the attack on Purify Jones had spread across the countryside, and every African-American knew that someone had gone after the leader of the KKK in Texas.

The first assistance that the fleeing Indian Territory men received was from the twenty-five armed African-Americans that lived along the Red River. The blacks gathered with all sorts of rifles, pistols, and shotguns and lined up on the south side of the Red River. The river rats also sent riders north to warn the Chickasaw police and to alert Wildhorse Creek African-Americans who wanted to assist the men coming out of Texas.

The first four reached the Texas side of the Red River without anybody being hit, but when Mondo finally entered the water behind the other four men, a bullet tore through his left shoulder and took him off his horse. Bear Chaser turned his horse back to help Mondo, who was struggling to hold on to his saddle horn and keep hold of the reins of Jones's mount. Jones's hands were tied to his saddle horn, and he had a real look of fear in his eyes since there was no way to swim if he fell off his horse. The Red River was running deep and fast and was at least a hundred yards across at the Spanish Fort crossing.

As the first group of KKK riders reached the south bank, they immediately spotted all the African-Americans on the other side, and instead of entering the water, they dismounted and knelt down for a carefully aimed shot at Mondo, who was still struggling to pull Purify Jones's horse to the north side of the river. Bear Chaser reached them and took hold of Jones's horse and also made sure Mondo stayed on his swimming mount.

Mick, Delaware, and Hudson Greer came out on the north bank and open-fired on the men on the south bank, and their gunfire was followed by the river rats on the north side of the river. The barrage of bullets sent the KKK men running for cover and gave Bear Chaser a chance to pull Mondo and Purify Jones toward the Indian Territory side.

Purify Jones kept yelling at the KKK not to fire for fear that he would get hit. His crying plea caused the pursuers on the south side to let up on the rifle fire and allowed Mondo and Bear Chaser to climb up the north bank of the Red River. By the time Mondo's people were out of the water and surrounded by the blacks who were trying to protect them, a large number of riders had arrived at the south bank so that there were around seventy to eighty KKK men wanting to cross and get back the captured Purify Jones. The KKK started to swim their animals across the river, holding on to the saddle to keep out of the way of the bullets coming from the river rats. When they got close to the north bank, the Texans opened up and drove the river rats and Mondo's people back from the north bank and into the brush along the river.

The river rats scattered, and Mondo and his men rode north, pulling Jones along with them. The river rat defenders disappeared into thick brush along the river for they had no horses and had built hideouts so that they could not be seen by any large group of black haters that rode across the river. The heavy tangle of trees, brush, and vines that grew along the river could hide anything.

The KKK men didn't bother to hunt down the river rats but rode full speed ahead after the five men who dared to raid Texas and kidnap one of their leading citizens.

The sun popped out and produced a clear day, and Mondo's bunch could see the hordes of KKK about five miles back and coming fast. Mondo knew that their horses were tired and that some of the fresher mounts ridden by their pursuers were moving into the lead and gaining ground. Mondo only hoped their horses would hold out one more hour until they reached the Arbuckle Mountains where they could find cover and hopefully some help from the Wildhorse Creek settlement. But the fleeing men knew that something to hide behind wouldn't be enough to stop the rampaging hoard of mad riders moving north with resolve to kill no matter what stood in their way.

Hudson Greer knew the fastest way to get to some kind of cover. He led them across Mud Creek and Clear Creek at the easiest crossings and rode into the cross timbers near Brushy Mountain. The riding was hard and dangerous through the short thick trees covered with vines that could rip a rider off his mount, but Greer had used this trail to slip ex-slaves into Indian Territory without being caught by Hurbert Dixon and the Chickasaw Lighthorse Police. So the fleeing men gained ground on the mob who didn't know the trail, which was only wide enough for three riders side by side in some places. The charge of the eighty KKK went from men spread out going fast to a group of three men in the lead followed in a line by the others moving half as fast.

The small trail ended after five miles, and Greer's lead group broke out of the cross-timbers and came into an opening where a man could see for five miles. The lead that Mondo's people got in the rough country kept them ahead. Within a half hour, the KKK was again within rifle range and started to take potshots at Mondo. Jones hollered for the Texans to stop shooting since he was the closest to the rifle fire.

It was about mid-morning when the exhausted riders and the more exhausted horses spotted the first rocky outcrop and a hilltop of the small Arbuckle Mountains. By then, the KKK had stopped shooting because they knew they were about to catch the kidnappers. As the Texans neared the exhausted horses of Mondo's group, a sudden barrage of rifle fire from over a small ridge met them head-on and took at least a dozen KKK men off their horses.

On top of the last ridge right before the Caddo Creek Valley, eighty men had open-fired. They were led by Hurbert Dixon the Chickasaw Lighthorse captain and Tan Bishop, the leader of the wild side at Wildhorse Creek. Word of the Texas invaders had spread through the Chickasaw Nation. The Wildhorse Creek settlement turned out in full force with all the weapons they owned, and instead of stopping them, Hurbert Dixon and his Lighthorse Police joined them. The Chickasaw Nation was tired of white men renegades from across the Red River riding out of Texas and doing what they pleased without any law or police authority to stop them. If the Chickasaw Lighthorse Police arrested a white Texan, they had to take that prisoner to Fort Smith for a trial, which usually resulted in dismissal for the lack of witnesses. This time, the Chickasaws were going to make a point, and there was not going to be any arrests. With Tan Bishop and his gang and the church side of Wildhorse Creek along with the Lighthorse Police, a very large lethal force met the outnumbered Texans. The hale of bullets ended the pursuit, and the KKK turned back at once for the cowards who wore robes at night wouldn't fight anyone when the sun was out unless they had at least ten-to-one odds.

CHAPTER 65

THE TRIAL OF Purify Jones occurred within three days. The freedmen wanted to do the right thing the American way, which called for a trial before hanging. The hearing was held outdoors at Wildhorse Creek since there was no building big enough to hold the large crowd of African-Americans who gathered to witness the trial.

Hudson Greer realized they didn't have any witnesses tying Jones to the KKK or the attacks into the Indian Territory. All the men involved in the attacks were dead.

The Chickasaw Lighthorse Police were aware of the trial but would not intervene because they felt if they took a rich Texan to Fort Smith for a federal trial, that he would get off by buying his way out or just get a slap on the wrist for what he had done. Also, no one would be brave enough to testify against such a powerful man. So the Wildhorse Creek people set up a trial to hear testimony before they hung Purify Jones over Maboola's grave.

A very important witness showed up a day before the trial, which made it easy for them to prosecute Purify Jones. The same house servant who let the kidnapers into Jones's house had escaped to Indian Territory and came to testify against his ex-master. The servant had seen and heard most everything that Jones had done. Mr. Jones had treated the witness as not being present, even when he was standing next to Jones. The servant had left Texas on the run for fear that he would be hung by the KKK if they ever found out he let the Indian Territory people into Jones's mansion. Also,

Savanah came and was willing to testify as to Jones's actions prior to her escape.

Hudson Greer prosecuted the case for the Wildhorse Creek community and all blacks living and dead. He called as his first witness, Tall Jackson, Purify Jones's body servant. The very tall servant was neatly dressed and spoke educated English like a college man.

"What is your name, sir?" asked Greer.

"I am called Tall Jackson by the white world, but my mother gave me the name that I prefer, John Jackson. The name Tall was given to me by Purify Jones because of my height."

"All right, John. How old are you?"

"I'm forty-nine years old."

"Where do you live?"

"Until I arrived here in Indian Territory yesterday, I never left North Texas."

"What were your duties on the Jones's plantation before and after the Civil War?"

"I was the body servant for Purify Jones. I went with him everywhere he went and witnessed everything he witnessed. I also bathed and dressed the little fart." This caused a roar of laughter from the crowd. Hudson Greer kept a straight face.

"Did your job change after the war ended and slaves were freed?"

"Jones didn't free anyone. Nothing changed after news of the Yankee victory came to us. I did whatever he told me to do just as I had done before. I fixed his bath, put out his clothes, helped him dress, and was supposed to protect him with my own life."

"So you were with him at all times and got to know him real well."

"I knew him better than he knew himself and better than I knew myself for I had no decisions to make about me on my own."

"What kind of man was he?"

"He was a preacher who married into wealth and poisoned his wife. He did as he pleased at all times. He satisfied his own wants no matter how it affected anyone else. If he didn't have so much money and power, he would have been killed years ago. Nobody really liked the evil little runt."

"Did he pay ex-rebs money to ride into Indian Territory and try to take back Savanah and kill Maboola?"

"Yes. Several times I overheard him bragging about the money he spent to get Savanah back and kill Maboola."

"Why did he want her back?"

"He fancied her. I don't think the man could love anyone, but he'd bought Savanah as a slave and taught her to act as he thought the perfect wife should act. She was supposed to be a beautiful Southern bell who did exactly as she was told." As he testified, Jackson glared with hatred at Purify Jones.

"How did Maboola get involved with Savanah?"

"He freed her. Took care of her two bodyguards who really was supposed to keep her from running away, and Maboola and Savanah ran off together across the Red River into Indian Territory where we are right now."

Throughout the testimony, Purify Jones sat straight in his chair like a disinterested straitlaced gentleman.

"Did this man order the killing of Negroes?"

"Yes, indeed. Jones had me listen in on all his meetings behind a hidden door. I was supposed to jump out and help him if anyone threatened him. So I was always by Jones himself to keep up with all his doings. He never went one on one with anybody. He always had a witness present, and I was always the witness hidden away ready to back him if anyone gave him trouble or got mad at him. I was big but never as brave as Maboola."

"Tell us about his involvement with the KKK and what is that organization anyway?"

"Someone in Tennessee started the night riders with faces hidden behind hoods. They wore white robes and attacked any Negro who acted free. Jones brought in several men to organize the KKK in Texas. An ugly, scarred man people called Split Face was a natural racist since he always liked to torture people. And after he got chopped by an ax down the middle of his face by a runaway slave, he especially liked to hurt Negroes more than anything. Jones financed the KKK in North Texas, gave orders on whom to attack and gave Split Face money to hire ex-rebs to raid and strike fear in all Negroes."

"Did you ever try to do anything to try to stop this man from his unlawful activities against Negroes?"

"Like I said, I wasn't brave like Maboola, so I told myself I never could do anything except help kill the evil runt, but that wouldn't necessarily save blacks. I always believed, and still do, that there will be several white men to take Jones's place. He partnered with other rich men to support the KKK. So by killing Mr. Jones, you might bring more death down on our people and cause equality to be much longer coming to us, if ever. What we think or do means nothing to most whites. Each time a Negro kills one white man, the whites say, 'See there, those black people are animals that need to be controlled like dogs.' Each time the KKK kills one of us, they say, 'See there, there's another bad Negro that got out of line.' If a lot of whites could, they probably would kill us all except the rich need cheap labor for the fields."

"But you finally contacted Delaware Hunter and helped him to get to Jones?"

"Yes. I was encouraged by the stand made by Red Granger when he confronted Jones. I saw that maybe Negroes could get together with a few good whites and solve this lynching. I hoped that fear sent back to the KKK might stop these killings and maybe the white Yankee troops and the Freedmen's Bureau might step in and enforce the law and control the KKK. After Red Granger was murdered, I helped Delaware, Mondo, Mick, and Bear Chaser and you to kidnap Jones just like he was trying to do to Savanah. I felt good for once in my life, but I was too afraid to stay in Texas."

"So your testimony today is that this person called Purify Jones ordered and paid for the killing of Negroes?"

"Yes, indeed. Many times."

"Did he ever tell you why he committed such horrible crimes against blacks?"

"Sure. It was simple to him. He needed Savanah in his bed and cheap labor in his fields, but deep down, he was afraid his past deeds would get him killed by an ex-salve. He really had a fear of being killed by Negroes if he ever admitted that blacks were human. He knew that ex-slaves would kill him if they were really human because that is what Jones would do if he was ever denied his freedom and beaten with a whip. He wasn't worried about dying and going to hell because he thought that all men, black and white, were evil, selfish creatures who only lived to satisfy their lust and hunger for money. He thought he was just like everyone else, just stronger and richer. Someone had to rule and control what he considered the ignorant, uneducated animals, and he thought he was just the man for the job."

"So Jones thought that the freed ex-slaves had to be controlled or they would rise up and kill whites?"

"Yes, and he could have been right. Maboola did rise up and kill some whites and you went into Texas and kidnapped Jones. Do you really think that the majority of whites will ever think that the raid in Texas to kidnap Jones was ever justified? The most liberal abolitionists in Boston, Massachusetts, will condemn our actions. This trial will never be accepted as justified or legal in the white world. Yankee troops might come after all of us here to make sure there are no more raids by Blacks. The whites will call our actions illegal riots and a revolution against the US government. That's what the whites will call any effort to stop the KKK from killing Negroes."

There was silence as the words of Jackson sunk into the gathered crowd and spread fear because everyone there believed the witness might be telling the truth about white action against Negroes for many years to come.

Hudson Greer continued. "Do you think we should turn this evil creature over to the whites for punishment? Surely, you know that with his influence, he will go free and continue his assault on all blacks with more vengeance?"

"Of course. But we're not going to change the Southern mind overnight no matter what we do. And the majority of people in the North will not step up and try to help us. For the next hundred years, for every white we bother and I'm not saying attack, I'm saying *bother* there will be ten dead blacks. It really doesn't matter what we do to Jones. We're going to suffer for many generations. There's just not enough of African-Americans. Fear and guilt will govern our treatment. It will take a long time before we are treated like whites, if ever. Do you think that whites would let their dogs and horses have the same rights as white men? That's what we've got to change. The white thought that we are animals and not humans."

Again, there was silence as Tall Jackson left the stand. The gathered crowd at Wildhorse Creek had images running through their heads as new ideas and new problems appeared that they had never thought about before as a slave and an ex-slave. The little defendant, Purify Jones, rose out of his chair in the open air court and proceeded to the witness chair.

"I've got some more witnesses," said Greer, but Jones sat down in the chair anyway.

"I'm going to speak before this gets out of hand. This is illegal anyway. There's no judge or jury and this is no court. I suppose you're going to have this uneducated mob vote on my guilt or innocence. We both know how that's going to end. You people are prejudiced against me. You don't understand anything. You have never had any education or even been taught to think, so you can't make a good decision. And I'm going to get my say and I'm not going to cry and beg for mercy because what I did was for all people, black and white, but you have to be educated and know history to understand why I did what I did and why it was right. This gathered mob will never and cannot ever understand. It will take Negroes a hundred years to realize that keeping ex-slaves in their place as underdeveloped people and savages will eventually save thousand of Negroes lives and give those ex-slaves time to learn how to be civilized and real humans like white people."

Hudson Greer nodded his head and spoke. "Go ahead. Convince us that the KKK and your treatment of blacks are doing us a favor."

"The whites and blacks were cave people at one time. Nobody could read or write. They'd kill animals for meat to eat and when there was a shortage of animals, they killed each other to stay alive. All men are born to be natural hunters, to kill for survival. That's history. Then some whites came out of the jungle and learned to read and write and learned to act civilized. They started to improve themselves. Less killing and more beneficial development. Less stupid and ignorant acts and more education. But whites slowly rose above the dog-eat-dog world of warriors and hunters and of savages without law and order. The male human naturally lives to control the animal instinct in all men. The white men joined in communities and taught responsibility and education. Books were made and printed so each generation could learn about living together and the obligation to make decisions for the betterment of the group and not just for the lust of the individual. It took those white people a thousand years to reach civilized behavior that the whites brought to America from Europe. The African natives never advanced with education or learned responsibility to the whole of mankind. They lived like the animals. It will take the Negroes a hundred years to catch up to the white world. If we didn't watch out for you like you were children, you'd rape and kill each other and run amok through society and set us back a hundred years. The majority of whites would kill all of you off because we are smarter and we know how to use weapons and we organize our killing in a good army manner and do not go about chopping off heads like ignorant savages. So by controlling you and your animal instincts, we are saving your life. You are like children compared to whites who have grown and improved in their ability to live together while limiting rape and violence against each other. You have to grow as the white world grew and become civilized persons with laws and responsibility. And you can't gain responsibility until you've learned to make the right decisions on your own. You are unable to do that now. A slave can't grow because he hasn't learned to decide anything. You people will learn from whites who took ten thousand years to jump ahead of the rest of mankind. You will learn to become a powerful force together and you will learn to work for the betterment of the community and not just individual desires and protection. No old tribe people can stand up to a civilized white community. That's why the Indians are being eliminated here and the world taken over by all the whites. If you black people want to stay alive and not be eliminated and gotten rid of because you have not kept up with the civilized world, then you have got to learn to become civilized. Learn to read and write and learn to be responsible so that you do the right thing without being told or forced or ordered or whipped and you do the right thing because you know by experience and knowledge and learning that it is the right thing. I'm sure you're too stupid to understand what I'm trying to tell you, but someday you'll see that I'm right. Now hang me and sentence yourself to die. Because when you hang me, the white world will hear of this and destroy this whole community. When the chips are down, the non-Negroes will lynch all black people who kill white people. That's a done deal. That's an accepted fact. That's the only way the civilized world will keep control of the animals and savages that run around in a frenzy raping and killing just like wolves or lions or any other animal in the wild. Don't you understand that the whites can kill and kill as a group and they outnumber you ten to one? Whites are trained, organized perfected killers. Don't you know that by hanging me, you're really hanging yourself? And will that be a good thing for you or all of mankind?"

There was a dead silence as the crowd felt hatred and a little fear as the words soaked into their brain. Hudson Greer stepped up to cross-examine Jones. "So what you are saying is that you're doing us a favor by killing us to save us from dying by the hands of civilized white men?"

"Yes. If you are allowed the same rights and respect as a white person, you will be killed off by the whites. You haven't earned the right to live unmolested in a civilized world. They will leave you alone when you learn to live white."

"You mention that we won't be civilized for a hundred years. Are we to do nothing to protect ourselves until we are educated and hold responsible jobs that the white men won't give us? For now are we supposed to stand back and watch the white men run around and hang us if we don't bow and scrape and acknowledge their so-called superiority? And the whites say we have to say, 'Yes, sir,' and 'No, sir' as if we are inferior to them. Is that how you gain confidence, education and a so-called civilized mind?"

"That's about it. If you act white before you are civilized, you'll die black. It's what all whites want deep down. They are afraid of uncivilized animals running loose and not on a chain. You have to learn to act like the whites secretly and among yourselves before you can act like whites in front of whites."

Hudson Greer shook his head in disagreement. "Any black who tries to buck your system of fear and control will be killed off because the white people like you can't stand for a leader to appear that challenges your beliefs. Civilization has more to do with being a good neighbor than education. Doing the right thing to others no matter their color, is the real civilized way. Anybody with any common sense sees how man interacts with man and knows that they need to live by the Golden Rule. But you're using the advantages of money, education, and power to keep the black race from doing good for anyone and everyone. It's wrong and since fear is the only thing you understand, I believe that by hanging you, we will make others like you think twice before attacking a black person."

"You're wrong and you're outnumbered. The whites fear the difference and will always stick together to fight against what they fear."

"You were once a Christian preacher. How does this theory fit into your Bible?"

"Christianity is a white-only religion. We allow the blacks to play like they are Christians because the Negroes are easy to believe in superstition things and as long as they believe in Jesus, they are less likely to follow their basic instinct to rape and kill. We try to tell Blacks to act like a Christian and their life will finally be good when they die and go to heaven."

Hudson Greer reared up and stuck out his chest. "I've heard enough from you. Step down, and I'm going to see what your hand made ex-wife has to say about you. I call Savanah to testify."

Savanah promised to tell the truth and took the seat provided the witness. Jones still stared at her with a yearning lust. A low murmur drifted through the crowd as the beautiful light-skinned woman sat down. Those who had not seen her before were stunned by her natural beauty.

"Please give me your name," asked Hudson Greer.

"Savanah, with no last name. That man listed me as a Jones in his slave records, but I refused to go by Jones."

"Were you owned by Mr. Jones until you were set free?"

"I was never set free. Maboola took care of the two men who were supposed to watch me so that I couldn't get away. I was supposed to make myself available to Mr. Jones whenever he wanted me. I ran here with Maboola to get away from Mr. Jones."

"Did you ever entertain the idea of going back to Texas?"

"Not at all. He raised me to be his wife and obey all his orders and used me whenever he felt like it. That never changed after the end of the Civil War."

"Did you know that the slaves were set free after the end of the War?"

"I had heard the rumors after the Yankees sailed into Galveston on June 19, 1865. The word came north pretty fast. Jones shot and killed two ex-slaves when they started shouting with joy at the news. Nobody dared talk about freedom ever in Jones' presence. You could hardly discuss it with another ex-slave because you didn't know who to trust. Jones kept everyone doubting who might be your trusted friend. Things didn't change one little bit after the Yankee troops moved into North Texas. The Northern army and the Freedmen's Bureau were both afraid to mess with Purify Jones."

"Did you witness Jones killing any of his ex-slaves after the war was over?"

"I sure did. Two slaves came running up to the big house shouting, 'We are free' over and over when the news reached the Jones plantation. Jones just stepped out on the big porch and shot both of them dead. The celebration was over. And Jones raped me in his bed that night. By then, I couldn't stand his touch. The man is pure evil through and through."

"After you escaped, did Jones send people to try to get you back?"

"Many times. He hired this ugly ex-slave catcher called Split Face and a bunch of other ex-rebel soldiers who attacked this settlement twice before Maboola, and I took off and ended up at Mondo's place west of here."

"Did he come after you there and how did you know the bounty hunters were after you and not just after Maboola?"

"Jones sent a lawyer from Gainesville, Texas, who offered money to Mondo to make me leave with the lawyer. The lawyer said Split Face had been hired to come into Indian Territory and get me back and would continue to come back until he had succeeded."

"What happened the first time Split Face attacked Mondo's fort?"

"We killed six of them and the rest ran off. They wouldn't take on any people of color who had guns and could use them. They were KKK cowards. If they couldn't get an unarmed black person by himself in the dead of night, they didn't mess with blacks."

"What happened the last time Jones hired ex-rebs to attack Mondo's place?"

"They brought a cannon and blew up the stockade gate, but Omar Culberson and six other black soldiers took out Split Face's cannon. Maboola died killing Split Face, and Storm, a great Comanche warrior and friend, died keeping them out of the fort. Finally, they were chased back to Texas by a white cattleman named Red Granger who was later shot in the back for helping us. His main man, Delaware Hunter, went with Mondo, you, sir, Bear Chaser, and another white friend called Mick O'Ryan and they brought Jones back here for this trial."

"Should Jones be hung over Maboola's grave like a lot of people want?"

"No. The killing must stop. Turn him loose and let him grow old alone and let him suffer from his guilt if that ever occurs in his old age. The evil in him will eat him alive whether he realizes it or not. We must be better than this ignorant white. We must be civilized and act in a way that the Bible tells us to. We can't sink to the level of the night riders who act as cowards and murder poor black people in the middle of the night."

A surprised moan drifted up from the gathered crowd as shocked expressions appeared on their faces. Some stood up and yelled no as Savanah's testimony sunk in.

Hudson Greer was taken by surprise. He stood silently stunned for a few seconds as if he didn't know what to ask next. Some shouted, "Hang the bastard," and others grabbed a rope and pushed their way forward as the hate spread toward Jones like the fury of an uncontrolled mob.

Greer felt the anger and turned, raised his hands to stop the people with lynching on their minds, "We must do this right. We must act in a civilized manner. We cannot let him live, but we cannot act like a lynch mob either. We will finish this trial and vote on this man's fate like the US Constitution calls for. We must learn to live under the papers that freed us. The Constitution is now set right for black people. We must behave under it or we will be thought of as uncivilized animals and savages that Jones says we are."

The mob held up. Mondo and Delaware Hunter then faced the angry crowd with their hands resting on their pistols. The angry cries died down.

Delaware Hunter stepped forward. "Enough talk. Let's vote now and get it over with. This here trial is over. We've been civilized long enough. Jones never gave any of us a chance to speak for ourselves. We've done a hell of a lot more for him than this man ever did for us and it's time for Jones to die."

Greer looked around and saw no objections except Savanah, who was shaking her head no. Greer turned back to the mob. "All in favor of hanging, say aye." And a roar came up from the crowd. "All opposed say no," and a weak no came from Savanah.

"Ayes have it. Let's string him up," hollered Hudson Greer, and the crowd went wild.

Savanah yelled a protest and attracted a few blacks who didn't want to hang Purify Jones. Most looked at her like she was still in love with the man with money and power and the man that had raised her for his own personal benefit. Since she didn't suffer like most of the ex-slaves, she was excluded as a voice of reason. Hatred rose up from the gathered ex-slaves as their past life was relived in fear and lack of independence. All had tasted freedom and now knew how evil slavery was to the inner person who was not allowed to develop his or her own personal beliefs or allowed to do what they did best or make themselves reasonably happy as a productive human being.

Purify Jones's eyes spread wide in fear, and he turned white as he finally realized from the feel and mood of the crowd that he was going to be hung. The rage spilled forth into a lynch mob no different than a white lynch mob where hate, fear of the difference of people, and lust for blood fueled by anger prevailed over any type of reasonable thought. Jones was dragged screaming and crying and begging for mercy to a tall oak tree. A rope was thrown over a large branch and wrapped around his neck. Black hands lifted the little man up into the air and his feet kicked for life when they let go. Jones's hands were not tied, so he grabbed the noose and lifted his weight off his neck. His struggles to keep air going to his lungs left him kicking and swinging in circles as he fought for a foothold to relieve the pressure closing off his windpipe.

The crowd danced around under the swinging body and shouted curses at the evil man. He didn't die at once, and so rocks were picked up and thrown at him as he swung back and forth, a terrified and squealing target. Each direct hit brought a roar of victory as if they were at a sporting contest. Jones could not scream at his own pain because of the tightening noose around his neck, but even if he could have yelled out in pain, it would not have been heard over the shouting of the people who jumped around below him yelling curses and cries for his painful demise.

After twenty minutes of loud demonstrations, the crowd went quiet as Jones's hands dropped from the noose, and his body seemed to relax in a final droop of a merciful death. The evil look on his twisted face made him appear to look like the devil himself. The crowd looked at Jones and then looked around and slowly cast their eyes down as they all seemed embarrassed at the evil demonstration of enjoyment of someone's very painful death. Silence lingered, and then a very deep voice started to sing "Amazing Grace," which was joined by a beautiful high soprano. Soon the religious song spread across the crowd and tears streamed down from the eyes of most of the people for reasons that they did not know.

Savanah was crying as if it were her real husband that had just been hung. Hudson Greer looked at her in confusion. "Didn't he do enough to you to deserve to die?"

She shook her head no and Bear Chaser put his arm around her and looked over at Hudson Greer. "She's crying because her people did not act any better than this most evil white man. She knows that people of color, which includes us Indians, are going to have to do a lot better than the worst white people before we are accepted as equals."

Savanah continued, "He knows me well. And everybody here knows deep down, whether they admit it or not, that what we did today sets us back. It may make some feel better and ease some hate and anger, but we've got to overcome our hate and anger without killing or we will always be looked at as uncivilized animals. Jones was evil, but until the majority of the whites do something about people like Jones, our problems will remain with us. I don't know how we'll ever be able to get the majority of the whites to side against the mistreatment of black people and Indians if we fight back with violence."

Hudson Greer was silent in thought, and Delaware Hunter stepped up and answered. "You're right of course, but by God I feel good about killing Jones as if I owed that to the best man I ever knew in Red Granger. Maybe I'm just too selfish to think about black problems as a group because I've had to pull myself up with my own bare hands from the day I was born. I didn't have the time or energy to fight for the whole black race. I only had time to do my best to stay alive and finally I had time to kill the man that killed my best friend."

Mondo raised his hand. "It's over. We've all got to think about staying alive. Let's bury Jones in a hidden grave and get out of here. I thought I was through killing at the end of the War, but I was wrong. It's got to be over now. Those who attacked us are dead and gone. I want to settle down with Skywalker and raise our child. I'm headed back to my place."

CHAPTER 66

Mondo and Skywalker rode back toward Mondo's place with Bear Chaser, Savanah, and Mick. It was quiet for several miles as most were thinking about the hanging of Purify Jones. What now? Most of them didn't know whether Jones's death helped end violence or only increased the future attacks from the KKK south of the Red River. About halfway to Cow Creek where Bear Chaser's place and Mick's new property were located, Mick decided he had thought enough about the hanging of Purify Jones and wanted to change the subject to more pleasant thoughts in his mind.

"Lucy and I are going to have a baby," Mick said.

Skywalker smiled. "That's wonderful. When's the baby due?"

"January the twentieth of next year," answered Mick.

"That's good," said Mondo and Bear Chaser answered yes and Savanah backed him up with a positive nod.

"Good," said Bear Chaser. "We'll help you raise the baby. Savanah is going to stay at my place. So we'll see a lot of each others."

Mondo was happy for Mick but deep down, he was still nagged by a negative irritation. The hanging of Purify Jones could not leave his mind. Mondo had come to Indian Territory to be away from the white man's need to kill. The Civil War had turned Mondo away from building up his ego by coming out on top of another man in a struggle of death. And now he was right back into the "attack, capture, and kill" mode that symbolized his participation in the big kill and forever battle called the Civil War.

And after the hanging of Purify Jones, Mondo did not feel any satisfaction or success for stringing up an evil person.

Did Mondo believe that there was any real benefit to mankind or even to minorities by the death of one like Jones who was a powerful, rich and influential person who could pay for killings and sponsor the KKK? Jones's protection of and financial support for those ignorant poor haters of people of color perpetuated the lynchings that went on in the South, but would the hanging of the leader of all North Texas hangings slow down the stringing up of minorities?

There was no place to run and hide from the evil of intolerance. Mondo had tried to dig a hole and cover up life and live alone from the bad deeds of mankind, but it didn't work. If you lived in and around any people at all, you could not avoid contact with people who liked to hurt people. The plan that Mondo had to live alone forever until he died in one particular place had failed. No more running away to hide. He had to settle down and do his best to protect his wife and future child. He could not always do battle with the bad people of the world. Live and let live. Survive by staying away from trouble. Don't look for trouble and do your best to avoid trouble when it comes calling. Mondo knew he wasn't going to change the world. His fort was a magnet for trouble. His stubbornness to stay at the place he built was suicide for himself and his family. If he lived near Bear Chaser on land legally leased to Mondo by his full-blood Chickasaw father, Mondo would have a place to raise a family. He did not want to teach his unborn son or daughter to be a coward, but people with Negro blood had to learn to walk softly and not carry a big stick. Fighting with the white majority who allowed the evil haters of color to get their jollies off the harassment and torture of minorities was going to go on for a long time. The balance between the feeling of worth and the hiding from bigots in a cowardly world would be difficult to teach his children. He would have to talk to Skywalker and find a happy medium between teaching feelings of equality and protecting their children from actions that could get a person with color killed. He looked over at Skywalker and smiled like he did every time he looked into her eyes as if it was the first time.

"Do you want to move over near Dad?"

"Might be a little safer," she replied.

"After what happened to Purify Jones, I'm really afraid that half of Texas will pour across the Red River looking to burn down my place on Little Beaver Creek. I think our family might be better off moving near Cow Creek which is on Chickasaw land for sure. You won't think less of me if I cut and run, will you?"

"No." Skywalker laughed. "Typical male worry. I've never been concerned about your bravery except when you were too brave or too stubborn to get out of harm's way by your 'here to stay' attitude. I think that you may be taking a big step in growth and maturity to think of your family first over your pride of never retreating. I've been ready to leave your little fort for a long time. I just didn't want to leave without you."

"That's great. I don't think I could live without you. I really feared you might go back to the rich life of a high-society, upper-class lady in Mexico. I can't offer to buy you near what you could have if you returned to your own country."

"I was never big on high society stuff. I guess I will also think that your place is my country. I like to ride through the countryside much more than participating in the stuffy polite parties where everyone puts on a show for each other. That's not a real life. I will be happy living out here in the open and free where a person is measured by his or her own deeds and not whether they were born with a silver spoon in their mouth. I'm here to stay with you no matter where you go or what you do. I just didn't want you to know that. I don't want to be taken for granted or not consulted on important family decisions, but I want to live with you and raise our children together."

Mondo guided his horse over next to Skywalker's and took hold of her horse's reins. He then leaned over and kissed her.

"Cut that out," said Bear Chaser. "We're not home yet."

Mondo smiled and turned to his father. "We've decided to take your advice finally and move over to Cow Creek and let go of my fort on Little Beaver Creek. How does that grab you?"

Bear Chaser reined up and studied Mondo then Skywalker and turned to Savanah. "They'll be living close to us. We'll be real close. Don't you think that's a good idea?"

Savanah nodded her head in agreement. "Sure do. The Bear and I have been doing some planning too. I've decided to stay with this old man as long as he lasts. I really don't want to go anywhere and try to see the world. I like it here and I like living with Bear. We both think it's good that you all will be close by. I kind of got used to us four as a real family that I never had."

Before Mondo could reply, the sound of a fast-moving horse reached the five riders. A US trooper came over the hill riding hard toward them. As he came closer, Mondo recognized Sergeant Omar Culberson, the buffalo soldier out of Fort Sill.

"It's Omar from the new fort they are building in the Wichita Mountains," spoke Mondo.

"He must have some big news or he wouldn't be wearing out that horse like he's doing," said Bear Chaser.

Dust flew as Omar skidded into a stop. "I've got bad news Mondo. The US Army just burned down your fort and tore up your rock house."

Mondo looked at Skywalker, and they both laughed. Then Mondo looked at a perplexed Omar. "We just decided to move out of there. Did they destroy our things and how about the horses? Are they still around?"

"We got all your stuff out before the army demolished the rock house and the captain let us hold your horses for you. I was told you were at the Wildhorse Creek settlement and I got permission to ride over and tell you what was going on. I'm sorry that we were ordered to tear your place down, but I'm a little confused at your reaction to the news."

"I'm moving over to Cow Creek near Bear Chaser, and I and Skywalker are going to try to live a peaceful life raising our family. Why did the army get ordered to destroy my place? What was the final blow that brought about such orders?"

"I'm not sure. Apparently, some Texans wired D.C. about a war that was about to break out between Texas and Indian Territory over the taking of that character that funded Split Face. So the Federals thought that destroying your place was like getting rid of a symbol of war to those folks in Texas."

"Well, I hope that settles that. Maybe they will leave us be and we'll not cross the Red River again. I've sworn off killing. I hope that those night riders in Texas think we're even. They've killed Maboola and Storm and we got Split Face and Purify Jones. The fighting has got to stop. But I'm not sure those KKK ever think about evening things out. They want to kill all blacks and lose no whites. That would be the only thing that would really satisfy those haters. All blacks dead."

Omar agreed. "Well, I hope it settles down. We've still got the Comanche and Kiowas to worry about and I'm glad we don't have to go against our own kind anymore. I'm going to ride on to Wild Horse and see my girlfriend. Let me know if I can help you get settled in your new home."

Mondo thanked Omar for his help with the destruction of the KKK cannon and Omar rode out toward Wildhorse Creek. The five riders continued west toward Mondo's place to gather up their things and horses and move back to where Mick and Bear Chaser had property on Cow Creek. Bear Chaser and Savanah dropped back from the three and began to talk about the death of Maboola for the first time.

Savanah spoke first. "I guess I loved him very much, but I don't know for sure. He was more of a guardian or protector from the outside world than someone that I really knew and cared about a great deal. I didn't know who I was or what I wanted to do except not be afraid to be myself, whoever that turned out to be. I always felt safe with Maboola, and he treated me real gentle-like and not tough or mean at all. I know that I wasn't afraid when I was with him, but I'm not sure I knew that I loved him. I really didn't know myself enough to know what I wanted or who I wanted or where I wanted to be. Now I think I know the answer."

"I understand," answered Bear Chaser. "He protected you when you struck out on your own to find yourself. He was a fierce man, but gentle with you. I was really kind of surprised when he found out about us and didn't take me out. He really was about what the Southern whites think a gentleman should be, at least to those he cared about. I want you to stay with me and give me another family to raise. I think I'll do a better job the second time around. I really don't feel I have to prove myself to anyone, and I think raising children with you would give me my greatest happiness. Will you stay with me and allow me to father your children?"

"Yes. I have no desire to go anywhere or try to be white. I've seen enough to know that there's a lot less evil around here and Wildhorse Creek and the Chickasaw Nation than if I tried to pass and live like a white person. I think I would be happier right here with you and near Mondo and Skywalker. Let's help them move and get settled and see what the future brings. Maybe with Purify Jones and Split Face gone, things will settle down and people will let us live free in your tribe's country."

As they continued to ride toward Mondo's place, the four people noticed that Mick was finally back to his old self. He was joking and talking a lot. Most likely the death of Purify Jones and the men he had hired relieved the anger of being beaten almost to death and left in an alley in Fort Worth. The anger and hatred that seemed to consume him and govern his decisions were slipping away the farther they rode away from the hanging of Purify Jones. Mick's personality was back to the time before he almost lost his life at the hands of Split Face and the KKK.

By the time the five riders came over the hill and looked down at the demolished rock house and the smoking embers of the fence around the little wooden fort, all five were fairly peaceful and calm about what they were doing now and what they were going to do in the future.

They rode down and gathered their things and horses and started back toward the Chickasaw Nation and their property on Cow Creek. As they topped the last hill, which was still in sight of the fort, Mondo looked back, smiled, shook his head, and waved good-bye to the place he thought he would stay forever. *Times do change when you get mixed up with people,* he thought. Mondo looked over at the pregnant Skywalker and smiled. "I thought I'd stay here or die trying. Things change don't they? Maybe we will find peace in the Chickasaw Nation and hopefully we will stay there forever."

The End